I0634625

Win in the End

A Fundraising Anthology

for

Annmarie SanSevero

Win in the End
Copyright" ©2025 Knight Writing Press
All rights reserved.
Additional copyright information for individual works provided at the end of this publication

Knight Writing Press
PMB # 162
13009 S. Parker Rd.
Parker CO 80134
knightwritingpress.com

KnightWritingPress@gmail.com

Cover Design by Laura Hayden ©2025

Interior formatting, artwork, and layout by Knight Writing Press ©2025

Additional Copyright Information can be found on Page 309

Editor Leslie Bridgwater
Executive Editor Sam Knight

All proceeds from this anthology go to benefit Annmarie SanSevero. Please respect that and do not pirate this book.

All rights reserved. No part of this publication may be reproduced or transmitted in any form, without the express written permission of the copyright holder, with the exception of brief quotations within critical articles and reviews or as permitted by law.

NO AI TRAINING: Without in any way limiting the authors' or publisher's exclusive rights under copyright, any use of this publication to "train" generative artificial intelligence (AI) technologies to generate text is expressly prohibited. The author(s) reserve(s) all rights to license uses of this work for generative AI training and development of machine learning language models.

Electronic versions of this work are licensed for the personal enjoyment of the original purchaser only and may not be re-sold or given away. If you would like to share this work with another person, please purchase a physical copy or purchase an additional electronic copy for that person. Thank you for respecting the hard work of the authors and publishers by doing so.

First Publication November 2025

Print ISBN: 978-1-62869-076-7
Electronic ISBN: 978-1-62869-075-0

For
Annmarie

We love you

Table of Contents

A Note From Annmarie

Coming out of disasters with a cheerful heart seems to be my superpower. I've always had challenges. Serious ones. I'll only mention the health problems here because that is what triggered this anthology. Most often I'd get the weird things where doctors exclaimed, "That's not supposed to be possible." I like to exceed expectations like that. But, after years of hardships, I'll be honest that I was starting to wear down.

I raised four children alone and put myself through university, finally getting the college degree I'd always longed for. I don't think there was a semester during my time in school where I wasn't hospitalized or had some kind of surgery. I was tired. Despite that, I graduated with a pretty great GPA, if I may say so myself. I'd even gotten into the grad school program of my dreams.

Then came this second cancer diagnosis. Not even the same cancer. Nope, my body decided let's do two different ones just to mix things up a bit. Though it was a bit of a shock, they told me we caught it early and should only need surgery and radiation. Easy Peasy. I wasn't a bit worried.

Then, things changed. During surgery, they discovered the tumor was bigger than they'd thought, on the muscle, and it had spread to my lymph nodes. Now we're talking two surgeries, chemo, and radiation.

That was a blow.

Now don't get me wrong, I did not give up. I'm pretty scrappy. I planned, and still plan, on beating this thing, plus totally conquering grad school and doing amazing things with everything I learn.

Even with the "I'm going to win" attitude, there were the realities of life to deal with. Plus, treatments are both hard and expensive.

I had this particular day when I was in massive pain, nauseated, and discouraged. Bills had to be paid, and I was having a hard time keeping up with work, the house, and all the other things adults must do. I was adjusting to my new normal of fulfilling my responsibilities while feeling like there was a giant boulder on my shoulders that would periodically double in size every time I was able to stand up again.

I decided what I needed was to take a nap. Not my normal solution, but I was unusually emotional and out of ideas. I laid down on my couch telling myself, I'll feel better after 30 minutes of nothing. When I got up, I decided to go online and see how my Superstars writing tribe was doing. That's when I saw James had posted a message to everyone about his idea for this anthology with a theme of winning in the end to help me make life just a little easier.

I'll admit that I blubbered like a baby.

One by one, my writing colleagues volunteered to submit a story. I was blown away. At that moment, I'd realized having a tribe like that meant I'd already won. They weren't going to let me fail. Thank you to everyone who took part in this project and to all who purchased it to read.

With Much Love,
Annmarie SanSevero

IMAGINARY FRIEND

by Sara Itka

DREAMS ARE AN IMAGINARY FRIEND
Keeping us company through the years,
Singing lullabies in shadowed rooms,
Whispering comforts in our ears.
Giving us faith and strength to pretend
When we must fake our happy veneers,
But even abandoned in our gloom,
Our dreams persist past our fears.

We fear the things we can't achieve,
And even more the things we won't.
We fear the lies that we believe,
And even more the truths we don't.

But even through these fears and lies,
Our dreams will still be there.
In the tearstained wake of an ordeal,
Our dreams whisper a prayer.
But our loyal friend has allies,
Each with a shoulder to share.
Some are imagined, some are real,
Just know that we all care.

When fears raise arms in war,
We'll be there to lend a hand.
On uneven ground and steps unsure,
We'll be there to help you stand.

With dreams and hope and all your friends,
We'll cheer the wins and fight the ends.

About the Author

Sara Itka is a born and raised South Floridian, meaning she believes "Fall" is when a hurricane comes and blows leaves off the trees. When she isn't working through her seemingly infinite To Be Read list, she can usually be found procrastinating working on her seemingly infinite To Be Written list.

Her favorite procrastination methods include procrasti-linguistics, procrasti-making-YouTube-playlists, procrasti-dancing-to-the-playlists, and procrasti-brewing-tea. If you want to help her procrastinate, she can be found at saraitka.com

THE WIZARD AND THE DINOSAUR-RIDING PIRATE

by Sam Knight

"DO DINOSAURS GET CANCER?" Josh asked as soon as Dr. Kenzi walked into the shared hospital room.

"Maybe that's what wiped them out?" Carrie offered from the second bed. She put down her Harry Potter book and looked over at Josh.

The boy was propped up on pillows, his blue eyes, too big for his emaciated face, peeked over the top of the dinosaur book he held with his knees. A red bandana, tied askew across his head, mostly hid his lack of hair. He wore a pirate eye patch over his left eye, flipped up so he could read.

Dr. Kenzi gave the boy a thoughtful look. "I doubt that's what wiped them out, although if I had to guess, I would bet even T-rex got cancer." She smiled and continued toward Carrie.

"T-rex would eat it! Om!" Josh mimed munching something out of the air.

"Eww!" Carrie scrunched her face.

"Feeling cold again today?" Dr. Kenzi asked Carrie quietly.

Unconsciously, Carrie adjusted her pink knit hat by pulling down on the rose decoration on the side. "No. I just wanted to keep the hat on."

The doctor nodded and took the blood pressure cuff off the wall mount next to Carrie's bed.

"Good morning, Pirate Josh and Wizard-in-Training Carrie!" Nurse Matthew grinned widely as he wheeled a cart into the room.

"Scurvy take ye!" Josh flipped down his eye patch. "Arrrrrr!" He dropped his book and sat up excitedly, grabbing the plastic cutlass off his bedside table. "Prepare to be boarded! I'll swab your poop deck!"

"Josh!" Carrie gasped.

Dr. Kenzi's eyes widened as she wrapped the blood pressure cuff around Carrie's arm. Matthew snorted and stifled a laugh.

"What? I looked up pirate words on Mom's phone last night!" Josh bounced on his knees and waved the toy weapon over his head.

"Captain Josh," Matthew cautioned him, "I think you're mixing your metaphors. You might want to stick with making the scallywags walk the plank."

"Didja hear where the captain kept his buccaneers?"

Matthew stopped the cart at Carrie's bedside and glanced back at Josh. "Captain Josh, did you talk about these pirate words with your mom?"

"No. She fell asleep. She worked all day. So have you heard that joke?"

"Yeah," Matthew nodded, "I've heard it. And I don't think you should be telling it."

"Why? They were just under his hat." Josh bounced on his knees for a moment then began to wheeze. He sank back into the pillows, breathless. "What's is a buccan-hat, anyway?"

Matthew went back and tucked Josh back into the bed. "You take it easy there, Captain Josh. Gotta save that energy of yours."

"For what?" Josh gasped. "Lying in bed…tomorrow, too?"

"You know for what."

"If I could, I'd stab…the cancer cells…with my sword." Josh waved his plastic cutlass weakly through the air. "I'd make *them* walk the plank. I'd…" His voice didn't carry the words as he tried to summon enough strength to pick his book back up while still holding the cutlass.

Carrie tried to relax as the blood pressure cuff began to squeeze her arm.

"Are you ready for this new stuff?" Dr. Kenzi asked.

"Yeah," Carrie sighed and put her book on the table next to her bed. She knew the medicine would probably make her feel even worse. "Are you gonna knock me out this time, like you said you might?"

Dr. Kenzi nodded. "This time we have a couple of meds made to work together, and they will be on the IV for a few hours. So it'll be easier for you if you don't feel like you can't move around."

"Knock me out, too!" Josh jumped in. "I want to go with her!"

Dr. Kenzi smiled at him. "You guys still trying to share dreams?"

"It worked! It really did!" Josh said.

"One time, it really did," Carrie agreed.

"I believe you," Matthew winked at her. "All it takes is a little belief and a little magic." He hung a saline drip bag from the IV pole next to Carrie's bed.

"We really did." Josh huffed as he put his dinosaur book on the table. "We were both in the courtyard, chasing butterflies that looked…" He ran out of breath and Carrie finished for him.

"They looked like flowers, flying around in the air!"

Josh flipped down his pirate eye patch and closed his other eye. "I'll see you in the courtyard, Carrie!"

"I'll be waiting for you." Carrie closed her eyes and waited for the strange warm feeling she knew would come from the IV and put her to sleep. She felt Dr. Kenzi take the blood pressure cuff off of her arm.

"You're reading the first Harry Potter *again*?" Matthew asked. "How many times is that?"

Carrie opened her eyes to see him grinning down at her as he set up the machine monitoring the drips into her arm.

Carrie shrugged. "I lost count."

"I'll bring in a book for you. I read it when I was a kid. It's called *With a Single Spell*. If you read it, I promise you'll like it, and I'll buy you your own copy."

"What's it about?"

"It's about a kid who wants to be a wizard, but things go wrong, and he only learns one spell."

"That doesn't sound like fun."

"Well, he still manages to become the greatest wizard of them all." Matthew nodded. "He proves all it takes is a little bit of magic, and a whole lot of trying. Just like this medicine we're giving you today. It's got a little bit of magic in it."

Carrie rolled her eyes at him. "They all have a little bit of magic in them."

"This one's different. Ask Dr. Kenzi. She'll tell you."

"Matthew is right, this one should be different." Dr. Kenzi nodded. "This one marks the cancer cells so the other medicines can find and attack them."

"Like a locator spell," Matthew whispered sagely. He reached over to Carrie's table, picked up her magic wand, and handed it to her. "Just in case you and Josh manage to get together in the courtyard again. You might want to cast a few spells while you're there."

Carrie smiled at Matthew and took the wand. She rubbed her fingers against the smooth handle. It felt good, comforting.

"Is Josh asleep yet?" The warmth from the medicine was creeping up from her toes and fingertips.

"Hmmm. Looks like maybe…" Matthew said.

Carrie closed her eyes and slept.

The world was fuzzy, warm, and comforting. Carrie floated through an inviting forest. She sighed deeply, content, enjoying feeling good. She never felt this good anymore when she was awake.

A distant boom disturbed her rest. She opened her eyes and looked around, surprised to find herself lying on the ground and not actually floating. Birds chirped up above in the fern-like trees, and the scents of flowers and fruit filled her nose. A butterfly, big, purple and shaped like an iris flower, lazily flitted by.

A grin crept across Carrie's face. She recognized the butterfly. It had been in the dream she had shared with Josh.

"Josh?" Carrie stood up and noticed she was still holding her magic wand. She looked at it curiously. It seemed more real, here in this dream, than it did when she was awake. She waved it experimentally. With a smile and a quick flick of her wrist, she shot a lilac-colored beam of magic out of it. Blooming flowers sprouted up out of the ground where the beam touched, and Carrie turned slowly, drawing a ring of flowers all the way around her. The purple iris butterfly fluttered in to examine the new flowers, its big floppy petal wings comically looking like Dumbo's ears.

Another boom vibrated the forest, closer, but Carrie hardly noticed. She had her long, sandy-blonde hair back. Brushing at it, she relished the feel of the strands sliding through her fingers. She missed her hair so much. She giggled and spun in a circle, dancing with the butterfly and twirling her hair. The yellow summer dress her grandmother had given her fanned out around her knees and made her feel like a flower.

"Carrie?" Josh's voice carried faintly though the woods.

Carrie stopped and listened. "Josh?" She called back, but the loud boom drowned her out. Close this time, the reverberations thrummed in her chest, and she felt the ground shake beneath her feet. The tops of the trees shook and a T-rex shouldered its way through the forest. Josh, wearing a three-cornered pirate hat and waving a shiny cutlass over his head, rode on top of the dinosaur with glee.

The T-rex threw back its head and loosed a thunderous roar, vibrating the world around Carrie.

Josh whooped, reveling in the dinosaur's power. As the T-rex stomped to a halt in front of Carrie, Josh stood up and slid expertly down the long back of the dinosaur. Jumping up off the end of the tail and summersaulting through the air, Josh landed on his feet, took off his hat, and bowed deeply to Carrie with a flourish.

Carrie curtsied back. "That's quite the magnificent steed you have there, Captain Josh."

"Rex? He's nothing but a big puppy!" Josh picked up an oversized bone that just happened to be lying on the ground next to them and tossed it impossibly far. "Fetch, Rex!"

Rex wagged his tail and bounded off after the bone, knocking trees out of the way as he went.

"I can't believe we're sharing a dream again!" Carrie bounced on her toes. "This is so cool!"

"Matthew's never gonna believe us."

"We'll know, even if no one else does."

"Where are we anyway?" Josh asked. "This kind of looks like a dinosaur forest, but I don't think it is."

"Oh, it's the Butterfly House." Carrie surprised herself by knowing, but as she said it, she knew she was right. This part of the dream was hers. As she looked around, more butterflies, many shaped like flowers, flitted among the blooms she had created. "My grandparents took me last year. But it wasn't quite this big."

"I like it. I want to go someday. Hey! You've got your wand! Let's have a duel!" Josh slashed his cutlass menacingly through the air.

Carrie laughed. "I'm a wizard! You can't stop my magic."

"Try me!"

Carrie flicked her wand, shooting out a green spell intended to turn Josh into a frog. Josh swatted it aside with the shiny flat of his sword using a deft flick of his wrist. The deflected magic hit a butterfly. It dropped out of the air with a *splat!* and hopped away on long green legs.

"Aha! Captain Josh is not so helpless after all!" Josh grinned fiercely and gave a strong pirate "Arrrr!"

Carrie whistled sharply and a broom flew down out of the sky, stopping waist-high next to her. She waved her wand at herself, and her summer dress changed into more suitable flying robes. Hopping onto the magic broom, she ascended straight up into the sky, out of Josh's reach.

"Now what, Captain Josh?" she taunted.

"Maybe my sword is a wand, too!" He pointed his weapon at her and shouted a magic word. A weak red beam spiraled drunkenly out of the tip of his cutlass and lazily made its way up to Carrie, where it ended in a faint puff of reddish smoke right in front of her nose.

The smoke tried to turn into a pterodactyl, but a passing butterfly flew through it, breaking it up into little eddies that didn't have the strength to reform.

Carrie giggled.

Josh tried again, but his magic was even weaker the second time, the beam fading into nothingness halfway to Carrie.

"Maybe you should stick to being a pirate, Captain Josh!" Carrie called down.

"Rex!" Josh called and thundering footfalls grew loud as the dinosaur ran back. Crashing out of the forest, Rex now wore a saddle with a cannon mounted on either side, just above his undersized arms.

Josh scrambled up Rex's tail and into the saddle. He pointed the cannons up at Carrie. "Fire!" Twin blasts erupted from the cannons in flames and puffs of white smoke rings. Two sizzling red-hot cannonballs soared up through the air, straight at Carrie.

Carrie spiraled up through the air on her broom, rising higher and waving her wand. One of the cannonballs whooshed by under her broom as she rose up, ruffling the bottom of her robes. The other cannonball turned into a big juicy brontosaurus steak and fell back to the ground, landing right in front of Rex.

Rex licked his lips and stooped to eat it.

"No fair!" Josh defiantly pointed his sword at Carrie.

Carrie giggled and flew a loop-de-loop on her broom. As she climbed even higher, she spotted something out at the edge of the forest—a dead place where all the trees had wasted away. All of her happy feelings faded. It was a bad place.

"What are you doing?" Josh called up to her. "What are you looking at?"

Carrie swooped down to Josh. "Get on. I'll show you."

Josh climbed onto the broom behind Carrie and together they shot up into the air.

She didn't have to point it out. The blight on the forest was obvious. And it was growing. As they watched, trees shriveled and died, withering away as though being burnt by a giant using a magnifying glass and the sun.

They both stared.

"We have to stop it." Josh broke the silence with a fierce determination. "We have to go fight it."

"I don't want to go there." Carrie shook her head. "It's bad."

Josh stood up on the back of the broom and whistled loudly. Rex's roar answered from below and Josh leaped off the broom. He fell through the air, landing perfectly on Rex's saddle. "No quarters, Rex! Charge!"

The dinosaur roared and charged into the forest, shaking the trees and sending birds and butterflies scattering.

Carrie watched them cut a path through the forest, wondering what she should do. Her broom drifted slightly as she wrestled with her fear.

She could hear Josh shouting challenges at the enemy he couldn't even see yet. His voice was strong, confident, and full of a lust for life that she had felt drain out of herself at the sight of the dead area in the forest.

Not wanting to be left behind, she followed after the tromping dinosaur.

As she neared the devastated area, Carrie could see individual monsters moving around the edge of the ruined forest, some on the ground, and some in the air. They all glowed with a sickly green. She flew in lower and saw the monsters lumbering on the ground were pirate skeletons and zombies. The pirates slashed at the trees with rusty swords. The zombies shuffled through the flowers, leaving trails of expanding decay spreading out behind them. Glowing ghosts darted and banked through the air, cruelly swatting birds and butterflies to the ground.

"Hoist the Colors! Thar be blood in our future!" Josh bellowed a war cry and Rex followed suit with a deafening roar that stopped all of the monsters for a moment and made them look.

Josh aimed both of Rex's cannons at the nearest clump of skeleton pirates. Smoke and flame erupted from the saddle-mounted guns. Cannonballs struck great blasts of earth up into the air along with pieces of glowing skeletons.

Josh cheered in triumph. "Take that, ye bilge rats!"

A hideous, screaming ghost swooped toward Carrie. The cold death of it pulled at her like a magnet, draining at her will, at her strength—at her life itself.

Fear froze her in place for too long. At the last possible moment, Carrie swerved her broom away from the ragged-looking thing. Chasing after her, it howled with the blood curdling scream of a banshee. Carrie shot fireballs over her shoulder with her wand, but the apparition dodged them easily, cackling with glee and gaining on her.

Carrie put her broom into a dive and aimed for a cluster of skeletons hacking at a tree. Holding tight to the broom with one hand, she pointed her wand at the skeletons and hurled another spell. Just as they exploded into a fiery eruption, she blew through them at full speed, barely missing the flames. The ghost chasing her plowed into the fireball and came out on fire, screeching. It bubbled and burned, melting like a flaming marshmallow as it crashed into the ground, leaving a long streak of cinder and goo.

Carrie pulled up, aiming for the sky, and targeted the other wraiths, flinging fireballs from the end of her wand. Some puffed out of existence as they were hit, others melted like the first, dripping flaming globules in trails behind them as they crashed and smeared into blazing messes.

Below her, Josh jumped off Rex and entered the fray, swinging his cutlass with unabashed elation. He hacked at zombies and kicked at skeletons all the while shouting about keelhauling scallywags and sending them to Davy Jones' locker.

Rex stomped on a group of ghouls trying to come up behind Josh. The combination of zombie goo and skeleton bones stuck to Rex's foot, and the dinosaur tried to scrape it off. Unable to get a bone out from between his toes, Rex roared in frustration, hard enough to bowl over another approaching mob of boney buccaneers.

Carrie rocketed through the air and waved her wand enthusiastically, her earlier trepidation gone. She vented her frustration and fear on the glowing specters, shooting fireballs at them and delighting in their demises. Then she got another idea.

A lavender bolt shot from the end of her wand and a ghost exploded into flowers, raining petals down onto the carnage below. The next bolt resulted in an explosion of butterflies.

Carrie shot magic from her wand until her wrist ached from flicking it and it grew hot from the energy coursing through it. Flowers, birds, and butterflies filled the air, fluttering down to cover and heal the blighted area.

Circling, looking for her next target, Carrie saw that she and Josh had gotten nearly all of the green glowing baddies. She fired off a shot at a skeleton trying to hack at Rex's tail with a saber, sending the skeletal pirate up in a puff of petals.

A ghost clipped Carrie from behind, knocking her off the broom. She grabbed frantically at the broom handle, but missed, losing her wand in the attempt. She fell through the air and landed hard near the center of the dead area of trees.

The pain was muted, distant and muffled, but it dominated her body nonetheless. Gasping for breath, she fought to roll over, trying to get up, trying to make her body work.

A scraping sound caught her attention, and she looked to find she had landed next to a strange mound in the earth. As she watched, a glowing skeleton clawed its way out of the wicked knoll, pulling itself up, and forcing its way into the world.

Carrie whistled for her broom and it appeared by her side. She used it to pull herself up, but she couldn't seem to get back on it. Her body didn't want to work right. Using the floating broom like a handrail, she hobbled around looking for her wand.

Behind her, Rex roared and stomped while Josh took on four skeletal buccaneers at once. The newly birthed skeleton stumbled off to join in the fight against Josh just as another skeleton began climbing out of the mound.

Carrie found her wand sticking up out of some burnt ghost goop. Snatching the wand up, she blasted the new skeleton before it was fully on its feet.

She pointed her wand down and fired at the dirt mound, sending dust and rocks flying. Over and over she shot into it, trying to destroy the hole the skeletons had emerged from. Dust, dirt, and gravel filled the air around her as she demolished the earth. She kept shooting exploding spells until she uncovered a green glowing mass of wriggling twisting things. Things that looked like the pirate zombies and the flying ghosts, but also like hundreds of squirming slugs tied into a giant knot.

The sight of it made her ill. Anger surged through her, and she blasted at the writhing mass with her magic wand. Great chunks of green splattered out and covered the ground, dying and turning brown as they hit.

A disgusting green tentacle writhed out of the abhorrent thing and struck Carrie in the chest. She dropped her wand and fell to her knees, weak, sick, and despondent. The hideous appendage slithered across the ground and wrapped around her, sinking into her skin and becoming part of her.

A zombie oozed out of the glob in the mound, forming out of one of the squirming slug-shaped things.

Carried moaned, too overcome with agony and weakness to retrieve her wand, as the undead creature stumbled away. She collapsed, gasping, as the zombie headed for the tree line. A ghost pulled free from the ooze, flew up out of the mound with a wicked scream, and followed the zombie.

The tentacle began dragging Carrie towards the mound and the gelatinous mass writhing within.

The ground shook. Rex stomped the zombie flat and, without breaking stride, snapped the ghost out of the air, chomping it down in one bite.

"Fire!" Josh shouted from the saddle on Rex's back. The cannons shot into the vile mass just as another skeleton tried to climb out. The blast scattered bones and dirt, exposing more of the squirming green slugs.

11

"Fire!" Josh commanded again. Cannonballs ripped into the ground in front of Carrie, severing the tentacle holding her. The coils wrapped around her turned brown, dried up, and crumbled away.

Rex and Josh circled the ball of slugs, keeping their weapons pointed at it. Rex and the cannons roared at the same time, blasting viscous chunks up into the air. Green glop fell around them, quickly drying and turning brown on the ground.

Carrie, fighting off the weakness that had been draining away her life, struggled to pick up her wand. With everything she had left, she shot weak fireballs at the hated green growth, joining Josh in the attack. Cannonballs, fireballs, roars, and explosions rocked and blasted the tumorous source of evil, sending sprays of green and brown flying into the air. Carrie and Josh blasted away until there was nothing left but a smoking crater.

Then they stood and stared at it, not knowing what else to do.

"Did we get it?" Josh finally asked from up on Rex's back.

"I-I think so."

Josh flipped up his eye patch and gave her a pirate grin. "Arrr!"

Rex squealed with a pitiful mewl and disappeared out from underneath Josh in a flash of pale green light. Josh gasped, flailed in the air, and fell to ground.

"Josh! Are you okay?" Carrie ran toward him.

"I don't feel so good..." A sickly green light engulfed Josh. A porthole opened in the air around him, and a green tentacle snaked through, wrapping around him and dragging him through before Carrie could reach him. In the world beyond the porthole, Carrie could see hordes of skeletons and zombies, clambering off pirate ghost ships and charging towards Josh with their swords raised and their battle cries thundering in the air.

Then it was all gone, leaving Carrie alone in the middle of the battleground.

"Josh?" Tears filled her eyes. "Josh!"

Carrie waved her wand. "Take me to him!" Nothing happened. "Open porthole!" She waved the wand desperately. She whistled for her broom and jumped aboard as it arrived. She soared up into the air and spun in a circle looking for him.

"Josh!" She knew he couldn't hear her. "No!" Carrie's broom slowly sank to the ground. "No..." He wasn't in this dream anymore.

An idea came to her. She waved her wand again. "Wake up!"

Carrie bolted upright in her bed. Commotion all around the hospital room blocked her view of Josh. People were around Josh's bed, talking rapidly and doing things she couldn't see.

"Josh!"

"Carrie?" Through all the noise she thought she heard him feebly answer.

As Josh was transferred over to a gurney, someone came over and tried to lay her back into her bed. She fought to get up, but the strong hands gently stopped her.

"Lay down. They'll take care of him." It was Matthew. He looked her in the eyes and held her gaze.

"You don't understand!" Carrie cried.

"They'll take care of him."

As Josh was wheeled out of the room, Carrie shouted, "I'll be there, Josh! I'll meet you in your dream! We'll beat it again!"

She turned to Nurse Matthew. "It was working! We were in the dream together! And I think we beat my cancer!"

"Carrie, honey..." Matthew put his hand on her forehead. "Oh. You're burning up." He reached down to the bottom shelf of the cart next to her bed and grabbed a thermometer.

"I have to get back to sleep. I have to find Josh and help him!"

"You need to lie down and try to calm yourself. Josh is going to be just fine."

Breathing hard, Carrie calmed herself and looked Nurse Matthew in the eye as he stuck the electronic thermometer in her ear. "You know better than to lie to me. Josh and I have been in here too long to be comforted by lies."

Matthew looked away, under the pretense of checking the thermometer.

"Matthew, look at me." Carrie reached out and caught his cheeks with her hands, turning his face towards her. "I have to help him."

Nodding sadly, Matthew asked, "How?"

Tears formed in Carrie's eyes as she let go of his face. "I don't know."

"Neither do I." Matthew put the thermometer away and made notes on her chart.

"Where did they take him?"

"He had a seizure. They're prepping him for an MRI to see if the cancer has spread to his brain."

"Will they knock him out for that?"

Nurse Matthew nodded.

"I need to know when they do." Carrie sat up again, pleading with her eyes. "I need to meet him in the dream again. Please. Please Matthew. This is super important. Trust me."

"Josh?" Carrie looked around. Everything was dark, like the inside of her eyelids. She had been trying to go into the dream ever since Nurse Matthew had let her know Josh was being anesthetized. She wasn't sure if she had finally managed to fall asleep or not.

"Josh?"

Shadows moved through darkness. Swirls of reddish, greenish mud colors that changed shape and vanished when she tried to focus on them.

A thumping reached her ears. Was that just her own heartbeat in her ears? Was she still awake? She focused on it, calling it closer, willing it louder.

Thump, thump, thump, thump.

It echoed in the darkness, moving aimlessly, everywhere, yet nowhere at the same time. And then she knew what it was.

"Rex! Come!" she shouted.

The noises halted, just for a moment, and then pounded straight for her. The T-rex's bumpy skinned head emerged from the murk with a tongue-lolling grin.

"Good boy!"

The dinosaur wagged its tail so hard its head shook.

Carrie took out her wand and called to her broom. It soared in from the distance, breaking through the muddy fog and leaving blue sky behind it. Jumping on the broom, Carrie called to the dinosaur, "Find Josh, Rex! Find Josh!"

She floated up as the dinosaur excitedly began sniffing around in circles. When it caught the scent it roared and ran, stomping off at full speed. Carrie followed, floating above and behind, and they broke out of the fog into a lush tropical paradise filled with flowers, waterfalls, butterflies, and dinosaurs.

Breaking away from Rex and diving to fly between the legs of a giant long-necked dinosaur, Carrie whooped as she pulled up, and the broom soared way up into the sky with the pterodactyls. From up here she could see far ahead to where Rex was headed, and she knew their destination.

A dark storm brewed on the distant shoreline. Green lightning flashed and flickered constantly from the black clouds expanding out over the land. On the water, a pirate ship rocked dangerously, nearly capsizing under the battering waves of the storm.

Carrie pushed her broom as fast as it would go, leaving Rex far behind as she raced towards the ship. Its sails were shredded, ripped asunder by the flashing green lightning and terrible glowing cannon balls flying in from surrounding ships covered with zombie pirates.

"Fire!"

Carrie heard the distant voice and spotted Josh, in full captain regalia, raising his cutlass high in the air as his ship's cannons fired red gouts of flame back at the attackers.

"I'm coming Josh!" Carrie put her broom into another dive to head into the fray, but as soon as her words echoed across the water, swarms of ghostly green figures rose from the beaches and flew at her.

Looking back over her shoulder, Carrie whistled to the flock of pterodactyls. "Lunchtime, guys! Go get 'em!"

Squawks of excitement followed her as she pointed her wand and began turning the charging ghosts into fish. The giant leathery bird-like dinosaurs swooped around her, snapping up the dinner they found flopping through the air, catching them in their long beaks.

Below, a whirlpool had formed around Josh's ship, sending it into a spin. His cannon shots were going wild, missing their targets, and he was clinging tightly to the mast to avoid going overboard. "Carrie!" he called. "Help! I can't hold on! I'm slipping!"

Pointing her wand, Carrie lifted pirate ship out of the water, floating it above the swirling green sea. Lightning flashed all around as she managed to make it stop spinning and Josh, grinning fiercely, raised his cutlass and cried out for the cannons again. "Fire!"

Cannon balls tore through the hulls of the other ships, sending zombie pirates flying into the air with the wooden splinters and the bones of the skeletons. Two of the ships went down. The undead crew were sucked into the center of the swirling whirlpool or snapped up by pterodactyls as everything sank.

"Haha!" Josh cried out triumphantly as he turned his attention to the third ship. He raised his sword to give the order to fire again, but before he could, giant green tentacles rose from the whirlpool and began wrapping around his ship.

Carrie flew in, fireballs flying from the end of her wand as she shot at the writhing appendages.

"Stay back!" Josh screamed at her. "It's the Kraken! We can't stop it!"

"Yes we can," Carrie yelled back. "We can beat anything!" She shot a fireball at a tentacle reaching for Josh.

There was an explosion of flowers when it hit, but the tentacle seemed unaffected. It reached Josh and wrapped around him, pulling on him as he desperately clung to the mast. More tentacles came over the sides of the ship, dragging it down towards the whirlpool.

Carrie fought to keep the ship hovering in the air, but more and more tentacles came. The ship groaned with strain just as green cannonballs from the remaining zombie pirate ship tore through the hull. The cracks were too much, and the ship began to break apart, planks and canons falling off to be lost in the swirling waters below.

Josh lost his grip and was lifted high into the air by the suckered appendage as the ship crumbled and broke apart.

Letting the ship fall, Carrie focused her attention on the other rubbery limbs reaching for Josh as he hacked away at them with his cutlass. The spells she fired at them seemed to bounce off and spin away, adding to the growing electrical storm around them.

"Get away!" Josh cried over the roar of the winds. "Save yourself!"

Carrie ignored him and began blasting the giant tentacle holding him up into the air. Using no spell other than pure force, she hit and pushed over and over again, trying to bend the tentacle back over the beach. If she could get it to drop Josh on land, they might be able to get away from the sea creature.

Dodging flailing limbs that tried to knock her and her broom out of the air, Carrie swooped through the forest of tentacles, waving her wand, blasting. She wasn't hurting the thing at all, but she was pushing Josh where she wanted him.

As the tentacle leaned out over land, Carrie yelled "Now, Rex! Fetch Josh!"

The T-rex, finally breaking through the tree line and arriving at the battle, leapt into the air and caught the Kraken's slimy arm in its razor-sharp teeth, just below Josh's feet.

Rex growled and shook his head back and forth, tearing through the stringy green flesh, shredding it until Josh was finally able to break free and fall to the sand. With a triumphant roar, Rex turned to face the ocean, lowering his tail so Josh could climb up into the saddle.

"Go Rex!" Carrie dodged and wove towards the beach, avoiding slapping tentacles. The water below her exploded upwards in a plume, destroying the final pirate ship, tossing it up into the air. The spray and the wreckage knocked the wand from her hand and her from the broom as a giant parrot-like beak snapped through the air, barely missing her and snipping her broom in two. She fell through the air, out of control, spinning towards the water.

Sharp talons caught her, pulling her up into the sky. She grabbed hold of the pterodactyl and held on tight, looking back down at the enormous glowing green eyes and nasty snapping beak of the squid-like Kraken in the water below. It squelched angry roars at her as the flying dinosaur stole her away and dropped her on the beach next to Josh and Rex.

"Are you all right?" Josh asked.

Carrie nodded, too winded to speak.

"We have to get out of here," Josh said. "I can't believe we escaped. Quick, climb up Rex's tail and he'll take us away."

"No." Carrie dragged herself to her feet.

"Why?" Josh's voice raised in fear as the Kraken began lurching itself up onto the shore. Sand turned black wherever it touched.

"This ends here and now, or it never ends. You know that, Josh. We can't quit. If we quit, we lose."

Josh hung his head. "I know. But what can we do? Nothing works."

"Yeah. Maybe nothing works." Carrie raised her hand, and her wand came flying in from the distance to land in it. "But maybe everything does." Her broom magically appeared by her side, and she got back on it.

"What do you mean?"

"Are Rex's cannons loaded?"

Josh nodded.

"Then we charge. You give the order, Captain Josh."

Josh sat up straight in Rex's saddle and flipped down his eye patch. "Arrrrr!" He turned and looked at the Kraken, raising his cutlass high. "Prepare to be boarded! I'll swab your poop deck! Charge!"

Rex surged forward, side cannons blazing at the foul creature storming the beach. Carrie kicked her broom forward, leveling her wand and shooting lavender beams of butterflies and flowers. Above them, the pterodactyls folded their wings and went into nose-first dives, aiming their pointed beaks at the giant fish-eyed monster.

"Josh is going to be all right," Nurse Matthew whispered in Carrie's ear as she woke up.

"I know. We beat it."

Carrie heard a rustle from the other side of the room.

"Arrrr!"

About the Author

Sam Knight is the owner/publisher of Knight Writing Press and author of six children's books, four novels, and over 80 short stories, including three co-authored with Kevin J. Anderson. Though he has written in many cool worlds, such as Planet of the Apes, Wayward Pines, and Jeff Sturgeon's Last Cities of Earth, among his family, Sam will probably always be known for *Chunky Monkey Pupu*.

He can be found at SamKnight.com and contacted at sam@samknight.com.

THE RELUCTANT SUPERHERO

by Leigh Saunders

JERRY WALKER WAS ABOUT TO LEAVE the men's room when the shooting began on the warehouse floor.

Jerry froze, his fingers mere millimeters from the corroded metal handle, momentarily torn between feelings of intense curiosity about the events taking place outside the door and his own well-developed sense of self-preservation.

Self-preservation won out—as it always had to date—and Jerry moved quickly away from the door, scanning the men's room for a place to hide before the shooters got around to looking in here for people they hadn't shot yet.

The options were not good.

The shooting—and the shouting that had accompanied it—was beginning to subside.

Jerry shook his head to clear it of the slight odor of disinfectant that pervaded the room and forced himself to focus. Not by nature one of the sort whose hands are deadly weapons in-and-of themselves, but being reasonably handy nonetheless, Jerry reached for the first tool that presented itself: his cell phone.

He dialed quickly, scanning the small room for a place to hide.

Not under the sink. There was no cabinet, just a tangle of exposed, sweating, poorly duct-taped pipes.

Not in or behind the wastebasket. His own lanky, six-foot two-inch limbs wouldn't fold up well enough to hide behind the three-foot tall receptacle. Nor could he have climbed inside it, burrowing under the mounds of damply wadded paper towels it contained even if he wanted to. No, the wastebasket was definitely out.

The urinal offered no imaginable hiding place, for which he was undeniably grateful. That left only the single stall.

A theatrically-pitched deep male voice on the other end of the phone in his hand got his attention.

"Hello. You've reached the Seattle area office of Captain Courageous. Yes, I am a superhero. And no, this line is not directly wired into my head, although that is a worthwhile suggestion to which I am giving serious consideration.

Unfortunately, due to the recent crime wave, I have decided to relax in the Bahamas for a few days—and please don't go spreading rumors about 'covert missions.' Ahem.

If this is an urgent situation, you may wish to refer to the Yellow Pages for another superhero.

If you simply wish to schedule a rescue or safety lecture, please contact my agent, Jerry Walker, at 206-555-6789, and I will see you when I return.

Thank you, and have a nice day."

The phone went silent. Jerry scowled at it. What good was it being a superhero's agent if said superhero wasn't around to get you out of a pinch when you needed them?

He opened the text messaging window on the phone and typed out a text message to Courageous.

Help. Guns and shooting. Call me NOW.

Courageous' office phone may not have been directly wired into his head, but his cell number was—a fact of which very few people were aware, although there were obviously those who suspected it.

Jerry sent the message.

Muttering deprecations about his erstwhile client under his breath, Jerry shoved the phone into his pocket and turned his attention back to the toilet stall. He'd seen far too many action-adventure movies to think he had a chance of hiding in the stall itself. Any gunman worth his weapon would bash open the door—or simply shoot through it—and it would be all over for him.

He peered up at the acoustical ceiling tiles and fluorescent panels, wondering how the people in the movies managed to hide themselves up there, and if he could somehow do the same.

And if the structure would support his weight—it didn't look all that sturdy.

But he had no choice. The peeling green paint on the mold-splotched walls offered no other suggestions.

He reached up and grabbed hold of the single stall wall on his right, then stepped up onto the toilet. The seat slipped out from under his foot, sending him lurching toward the wall as his foot splashed into the icy water in the bowl. At the same moment, his cell phone sang out, a lively tune designed to get his attention even while sleeping.

Clutching the stall wall under one armpit, he fumbled for his phone, nearly dropping it in the process.

"Yeah?"

"Hey, Jerry!" Courageous' voice boomed through the phone. "What's this about trouble?"

"I'm hiding in a toilet at the Ace Foundry, there are guys out in the warehouse shooting people, and you're off lollygagging in Bermuda!"

"Hmmm. That's not good," Courageous said with a rumbling chuckle. "You're much too tall to hide well in a toilet. Couldn't you have found a better place?"

Jerry almost dropped the phone again. "Look, this is serious!" he said into the mouthpiece, forcing his would-be shout to come out as little more than a hoarse whisper. "It's *your* fault I'm here in the first place, checking the place out for a safety demonstration—which, considering the situation, I have to say is seriously overdue. You've *got* to get me out of here!"

"Okay, okay," Courageous said, his voice shifting into his standard superhero professional persona. "Did you turn out the lights?"

"No. Should I have?" Jerry looked at the door, seeing the translucent glass panel sitting squarely at face-level as if for the first time. "Shit."

"Well, if you haven't already, it's a little late now," said Courageous. "Last thing you want to do is attract attention."

"I figured that one out myself," Jerry said, pulling his foot out of the toilet bowl and perching it gingerly on the edge of the seat. While not particularly secure, at least he was no longer hanging by his armpits. "Why else do you think I called *you?*"

"Right. Well, you see, Jerry…," Courageous' voice trailed off without finishing the thought. "And you're sure you can't just sneak out of the bathroom and down the hall or something?"

"There's no hall to sneak down," Jerry answered, trying to form a mental picture of the area immediately outside the bathroom. "The bathrooms are in the northeast corner of the warehouse—men's along the outer walls, then the women's, then the break room. Doors to all three open right into the main floor. There's some machinery in the way, but if one of the shooters is standing in the right place or looked the right way when I opened the door, I'd be a goner."

Courageous was silent for so long that Jerry thought he'd hung up. "Hey, you still there?" he said.

"Hmmm? Yeah," Courageous replied. "Hold on."

The line went silent again, leaving Jerry to count the seconds as the water dripping from his shoe formed a small rivulet that ran toward the wall at the base of the urinal. Clearly the lowest part of the cracked and grimy tile floor, he observed.

"Hey, thanks for waiting," Courageous said cheerfully, coming back onto the line. "Had to make a quick change. I thought I'd come up there and get you out of this fix you've gotten yourself into, and I couldn't very well do that in a swimsuit. Shatters the Superhero Mystique and all that. I'm sure you understand."

Jerry's shoulders slumped. "Even at your top speed, I'll be long dead, my body stiff and cold by the time you get here. But thanks for the thought."

"Don't try to talk me out of it," Courageous replied. "I won't take 'no' for an answer. Besides, I'm already on my way. The Gulf is below me, the sun is in my eyes, there's a hurricane brewing at my back, and I'll be back in Seattle in no time."

"Look," Jerry said with a sigh. "Go back to your beach. And when you get a new agent—just remember to tell him where you're going *before* you head off on vacation, just in case. Okay?"

"You're sure?"

"Yeah. I'm sure."

Courageous mumbled something incomprehensible under his breath, then replied cheerfully, "It's been nice working with you, Jerry. And who knows, you may survive this after all."

"Yeah, yeah. Thanks," Jerry said. And then, after the briefest of pauses, he added, "Goodbye."

He clicked off the call and stuffed the phone into his pocket; then pulled it back out, switched it to silent, vibrate-only mode, and returned it to his pocket.

He'd seen lots of movies, and he was *not* going to be that guy who almost got away, only to be betrayed at a critical moment by a ringing cell phone.

In the meantime, he was back at square one, with no more idea of what to do than he'd had five minutes before, and a wet left foot on top of it. He hoped the last person to use the toilet had flushed, but he just didn't want to look. Cold and wet was bad enough.

Instead, he looked up at the ceiling tiles and gave one an exploratory push.

It lifted easily off the thin metal frame, allowing him a good view into the shadows above. There appeared to be plenty of space up there but, as he had feared, no way that the thin metal strips hanging from flimsy wires would support his weight. As he lowered the panel back into place, however, something caught his eye, and he lifted the panel again. Where the frame connected to the wall, it appeared to be attached to a beam, which was bolted to the wall.

He slid his feet around to opposite sides of the toilet seat, then reached up to lift the ceiling panel above the back corner of the stall, and was reassured to find that the panel *was* indeed supported by beams on both sides of the exterior walls where they met at the corner of the building. The beams would give him a safe perch above the ceiling panels, and a place to hide from the shooters.

All Jerry had to do was lift himself up there.

It took five attempts.

Five slipping, tugging, sweating, struggling, arm-throbbing attempts to lift himself up through the opening in the ceiling, with nothing more than the L of the corner beams to hold onto as he rose through spider webs and who-knew-what-else that might have decided to take up their new residence in his hair or on his shoulders as he thrashed upward into their dank, dark domain.

But difficult as his struggles were, he attracted no attention from the shooters, and after numerous vows made to various gods that he would both go back to the gym on a regular basis and never again lie about just how much he could really bench press, he finally made it.

He pulled a knee onto one side of his narrow roost.

Just as he got a toehold on the other, another volley of gunfire rattled the building, nearly startling him off his precarious perch.

Panting, his back pressed into the corner against the uninsulated, metal exterior walls of the warehouse, Jerry discovered a bonus: the plumbing pipes from the toilet below rose along the wall beside him, offering themselves as willing, if cold, damp, and slightly moldy handholds.

At this point, Jerry didn't care.

He grabbed a pipe with one hand and held on tightly, twisting slightly so he could reposition the acoustical ceiling tile in the space he had so recently clambered through.

A surreal dimness filled the now closed-in space.

High above him, ventilation fans let in some light, while the fluorescent tubes from both the men's and ladies' bathrooms glowed from his new "floor" level. The space he was in appeared to extend to his left above both bathrooms and the breakroom.

A wall located about twelve feet directly ahead of him ran the length of the space he was in, closing off the rectangle above the rooms. Several fairly large grates were evenly spaced along the wall—from their position, Jerry was fairly certain that they overlooked the main warehouse floor.

The gunfire had stopped again, and Jerry could hear people arguing. He strained to make out what they were saying, but the hum of the fans above him provided too much white noise for him to hear anything clearly from this distance.

There was nothing to do but crawl toward the nearest grate. Well, that wasn't entirely true. Jerry could simply stay put, stay quiet, and wait for the situation to blow over, before making an unobtrusive exit, but...he just couldn't.

He might only be an agent to a superhero, but he *had* to know what was going on, and, if at all possible, *try* to do something about it. Without getting caught or killed in the process. That was an important point.

The frame suspending the ceiling tiles was laid out in a grid pattern, attached at intervals to beams like the ones he was currently perched on. Jerry had two choices: he could stay close to the wall and try to inch along the exterior wall toward the grate nearest to the corner, or he could go in the opposite direction, to a crossbeam, and crawl along it until he reached a different grate.

Either way, he was going to have to let go of the plumbing pipes and trust his ability to balance on a surface that was no more than six inches wide at the most.

He chose the second option. At least that way, he would be able to lay down along the length of the beam and inch himself along it. Sure, there were suspension wires in the way, but he'd manage around them.

He inched himself along the wall, holding on to the plumbing pipes for as long as he could. As it turned out, the corrugated metal wall of the warehouse offered a semblance of a decent handhold itself, so it wasn't as entirely difficult as he had expected it to be.

When he reached the crossbeam, Jerry gingerly lowered himself to it, freezing about halfway down when a toilet flushed from the women's restroom off to the left.

Was one of the shooters a woman?

Had the shooters taken the female workers hostage, and been gallant enough to let one of them relieve herself?

Questions raced through his mind as he hovered in place, listening, but no answers presented themselves as the sound of running water was replaced with the *thwup-thwup-thwup* of the paper towel dispenser. Finally the bathroom door slammed shut.

Exhaling slowly, Jerry finished lowering himself to the beam.

Crawling along the narrow beam was much more difficult than he had imagined it would be. After all, who ever thought crawling *anywhere* would be hard to do? Then again, crawling on a beam meant that you had to put one hand in front of the other, as you expected to. But you also had to scoot one knee forward and then bring the other up behind it, because there was no place for your legs to go.

And, of course, the contortionist moves required to navigate around the suspension wires holding the acoustical ceiling tiles only made life that much more *interesting*—in the Chinese-proverb sense of the word.

Jerry briefly considered trying out for the circus if he survived this, but discarded the idea almost immediately. Here, he couldn't see the floor. He knew it was there, eight and a half feet below him, but he couldn't *see* it.

As a circus performer, the floor would be much farther below… On the other hand, at least his feet would be dry.

And so Jerry distracted himself for several painstaking minutes—minutes that felt like days as he inchwormed toward the grate, stirring up small puffs of moldy dust with each inch of progress and willing himself not to sneeze.

Damn, but he was thirsty by the time he reached the wall.

He kept his head low, trying to stay far enough from the grate that he could peer out without being seen from the floor.

He needn't have worried.

When he looked out, he discovered that one of the large metal stampers was positioned directly in front of him, effectively blocking his view of most of the room. But his luck wasn't all bad. The argument he had heard was taking place directly below that very grate. He leaned closer to better hear what was being said.

"...only shooting clay pigeons," the first voice said.

"I don't care!" said the second voice, which Jerry thought he recognized as the shop foreman. "It's distracting my workers. You've got to shut down."

"I've got a permit. Signed and legal." There was a brief pause, and Jerry saw a flash of paper being waved just within his view. "I've got just as much right to do business as you do. You want to make a big deal about it—I'll see you in court!"

Jerry's head was spinning. This didn't sound like a robbery or mob shakedown or any of the gazillion other movie-ready disaster scenes he'd been expecting. He tilted his head to hear more, hoping for some details that would pull the picture together more clearly in his head.

Just at that moment, there was another round of gunfire, coupled with a near-deafening crash that echoed so loudly in the above-bathroom ceiling space that Jerry forgot himself and clasped his hands over his ears.

Of course, that action caused him to lose his balance completely.

Arms flailing, he tumbled off the crossbeam, crashing through the men's room ceiling in a tangle of suspension wires and broken acoustical tiles. He landed on the bathroom sink, pulling it off the wall and driving it to the floor, where he lay, dazed and confused, in the wreckage.

He heard the pounding of footsteps running in his direction and forced himself to open his eyes.

A pair of large, red-booted feet were standing directly in front of him, silhouetted by the sunlight pouring in through a gaping hole in the bathroom's outer wall.

As Jerry struggled to make sense of what he was seeing, an equally large pair of red-gloved hands reached down and lifted him out of the debris.

"Hey, Jerry!" Captain Courageous said as he dusted Jerry off and set him shakily on his feet. "It looks like I got here just in time!"

The shop foreman burst into the bathroom, several other unidentified workers crowding into the doorway behind him. "What's going on here?" he demanded.

Captain Courageous stepped decisively between Jerry and the foreman, placing one arm protectively out to shield Jerry from whatever dangers he might next face.

"Never fear, citizen!" he boomed. "I have arrived to save the day!"

"What the hell are you talking about?" shouted the foreman. "And what have you done to my building?"

Jerry looked around the room, first at the foreman, whose face was turning purple with rage, and then at Courageous, who was beaming with pride from ear to ear. Then he caught a glimpse of something out of the corner of his eye that he just had to investigate.

Stepping over to the break in the wall, Jerry read the sign printed on the neighboring building:

Westside Sports Center and Shooting Range.

With a groan, Jerry tugged Courageous away from the curious crowd. "I thought I told you to stay in Bermuda," he muttered.

"I know," Courageous answered with a shrug. "But I *had* to come, of course. Had no choice, really. After all, the press would have a field day if I'd let anything happen to *my own agent*—can you imagine? The publicity would have been awful. And then think of all those poor, helpless citizens in need of rescuing, whose faith in me would be shaken." He puffed up his chest in pride, twisting slightly to wave at the crowd behind them before continuing. "It's my civic duty to safeguard our lifelong working relationship. I'm never letting anything happen to you, Jerry."

Jerry pasted on his best smile and turned his agent-face toward the crowd. "Our *lifelong* relationship," he said, through clenched teeth, somehow managing to swallow a groan. "Lucky me."

About the Author

When not writing speculative fiction for a living (her day job is writing computer software manuals), Leigh Saunders enjoys writing "social science fiction," stories that focus on people—or "things" that are also people—and how magic, futuristic events, or advances in technology impact their lives. A 1993 Writers of the Future finalist, she has won awards from the League of Utah Writers for both long and short fiction. She is currently working on the third volume of "Bloodline: Progenitors" an epic fantasy series. To learn more about Leigh and sign up for her occasional newsletter, visit her online at http://www.leighsaunders.com/

SEEKING A FAMILIAR WITCH

by Jena Rey

THE PROBLEM WITH HUMANS, Mildew mused, was that their lifespans were too short, something that not even his potent magic could do anything about.

It had been two months since his witch familiar, Stephanie, had gone to the beyond, leaving him behind to mourn her. He hadn't expected the loss to burrow so deep into him, yet it had, and everywhere he went it felt like he was carrying a weight in his chest that he could not put down.

They had not started as friends. She had accidentally summoned him from his own dimension and stuck him in the body of a large, black Maine Coon cat, and there he'd stayed for the last thirty years, as time was measured here. What had begun as an unwilling and contentious relationship had, over time, mellowed into mutual respect and then to affection.

When it had become obvious that Stephanie was slipping away, Mildew had expected that his time here would end as well, but at no point had any hint of a portal arisen. He even convinced the local coven leader, Mona, to try to open a way for him, but nothing they'd tried had been effective. He was stuck here, in the body of a cat, without a witch familiar, which significantly decreased his power, particularly when it came to affecting anything beyond himself. Mona had offered to bond with him, and if she'd been fifty years younger, he might have been tempted. He was fond of the coven leader, and she had a strong power. But she, too, was waning, and he did not want to acquire and lose another familiar so soon. The fact that he could not return home made him certain there was a compatible witch for him here and something more he needed to do. He just hadn't figure out who or what.

At least not yet.

It was vastly irritating.

A warm wind whipped around Mildew's ears and stirred his whiskers, pulling him out of his musing and returning his attention to the moment. He stretched one leg at a time and took a running start, leaping up a nearby Joshua tree until he was high enough to get a good look around. The sun had only just crested the eastern hills, pouring over the long valley like molten gold. But it wasn't the sunrise that had woken him. Nor was it the thoughts of his lost familiar. It was something else, a prickle of magic he hadn't felt before. This wasn't human magic, but it was definitely magic, and it was strong.

Mildew opened his senses as wide as he could, listening and looking in spectrums far beyond what humanity considered possible. His big ears with their ridiculous tufts swiveled, and his attention came to rest on a shadow far across the valley. He knew that location. He had gone there with Stephanie before. It was a deep wash, containing a rivulet that wound down a deep crease and dumped into a shallow pool. Depending on the time of year, it was sometimes little more than a muddy track, but in the spring, as it was now, the melting snow from the surrounding red rock ridges turned it into a rushing deluge.

He let his senses relax and sat back on his haunches, his long tail flicking as he pondered his options. If it was something aggressive, he lacked a familiar to do battle with, but there was no guarantee that a new power was a bad one. It could be someone, or something, that needed help. It might even be a new familiar coming into her power, maybe even one he might accept. Mildew snorted and dismissed that thought as being overly optimistic and ridiculous. It was more likely that some magical creature had been washed down from the cliffs and into the pool. It was really none of his business. Except that the strange magic was in the wind and in the sunlight, and it was driving him crazy, like an itch he couldn't scratch. It wouldn't hurt anything to at least go and see what it was.

Mildew dropped to the ground, a soft puff of desert dust rising around him. He sneezed and shook his head before he padded away from the tree and into the brush-strewn high desert. As he went, he tested his power reserves, comparing them against the distance. He needed a familiar to help him recharge properly—he was growing tired of being reminded of his singular limitations—but he was certain he had enough strength to make the travel shorter. Walking across the desert all day was not his idea of a good time and might let whatever was at the water get away. He judged the distance again and nodded. A dozen cat jumps would do it and would be fun. Heavens knew the last months hadn't had many opportunities for fun.

He grinned and stretched into a run, racing across the desert, focusing his gaze on the farthest possible point. Magic shuddered along his fur and bones. One. Two. Three. Jump! His black body stretched and twisted, and with a soft pop, he teleported from one spot to another, landing gently and continuing to run. His breath came quick, but he immediately made the next jump, and the one beyond that. It was tiring to chain jump, but the momentum meant it took less power to get farther, and that was more important. He could rest once he reached his destination.

His heartbeat pounded in his ears as he continued to travel. At last, Mildew stumbled and rolled across the sandstone ground. He stopped only inches from the crevasse, his long tail swishing out into the empty space as though to emphasize how close he had come to potential disaster. He lay there, absently cleaning his paws and deciding that it wasn't disaster at all, but brilliant planning on his part, if no one had seen it.

The sun crept another quarter of an hour across the sky while he tended to his fur and caught his breath. It was deliciously warm here, this human place called Arizona, and he liked it despite himself. Finally, he pushed to his feet, stretched, and trotted along the edge of the fissure, following the scent of magic.

As he went, the angle of the land changed, easing downward to meet the rushing water where it came out of the rocks and into the pool. Scrubby desert foliage clumped around the water source, creating a tiny oasis of bright green leaves and yellow flowers. Mildew recognized many of the plants by smell and had an urge to go for a good roll, but he forced himself to stay focused on his objective. The magic didn't seem to be in the pool, and he paused, slowly sniffing the air and creeping forward on silent paws as it grew stronger.

Step by step the magic tickled his nose, setting his fur on end. He came to the point where the stone gully opened and saw something decently sized, covered in mud and a few odd branches, wedged hard in the narrow opening. He crouched onto his belly and scooted quickly closer until he could look around a large stone. Flashes of dark blue scaled hide showed between patches of mud, and as he watched, a reptilian head moved, stretching toward the sky and giving a piteous warble that pulsed with magic.

Mildew blinked in surprise. He was staring at a dragon, a very young one at that. He knew dragons had lived here once. Several years ago, Stephanie had been involved in an effort to return dragon eggs to a full-grown specimen who had taken them off beyond this dimension. Mildew had been certain that encounter was the end of dragons in the area, but the sight in front of him showed he was wrong. There was, in fact, at least one dragon in Dragon Stone, Arizona. The little dragon lowered its head, and water sloshed up and over its body. There was one dragon now, but if Mildew didn't do something about it, there wouldn't be one much longer.

He crept around the stone and, with no little clawing and sliding, made his way to the edge of the opening. He touched one paw to the water and then licked it clean. It was crisp and very cold, mountain runoff always was, which was nice unless you were trapped in it. Mildew eyed the distance between himself and the dragon. He was an uncommonly large cat, and was certain he could jump to the beast, but he had no idea what it would do if it was suddenly landed on. He knew what he would do, and a lot of cursing and claws would be involved. He didn't know what kind of language dragons had, but it stood to reason that he should try to communicate with it before doing anything else. He had learned to make any witch understand his vocal projection, hopefully a dragon wasn't that much different.

Mildew concentrated, making his 'voice' loud enough to get attention, but hopefully not too loud. "Hey, little dragon beastie. Can you hear me?"

Despite his efforts not to startle the dragon, it thrashed and twisted its head and body, trying to swing around to see him, crooning in panic and hope. Mildew's mind was filled with impressions and feelings: waking alone, stumbling into bright sunlight, falling from a high cliff with wings too wet and young to hold him aloft, landing in the rivulet and being dragged down into the wet and the dark and the cold, the twist of legs and wings stuck in the thick mud, and harsh gnawing hunger.

Overwhelmed, Mildew took a skittering step backward and brought up every mental defense he had, shutting the poor creature out of his head. "Okay, okay, stop that. I get the point. Just…give me a minute to think."

The dragon gave a deep sigh and lowered its head again. Mildew was certain it was growing weaker, but he didn't have many options. Even a baby dragon was too big for him to drag out of the water by himself, and it wasn't as though he had hands to grip it with. He knew a levitation spell, but it was hard to cast without his familiar as an anchor. It was worth trying, though. He tested his magic reserves again and narrowed his golden eyes. He gathered his will and his magic and flicked his tail toward the dragon.

"Rise!"

Power surged out of him at the command and wrapped itself around the baby dragon. It pulled and tugged at the creature which rose slightly until a surge of muddy water poured out from under it and into the pool. Mildew shook as he strained to pull the magic toward him with its precious burden. The dragon shifted and squirmed, and he tried to twist it free of the rock. The line of magic held between them as tense as a tightrope. Mildew dug his paws into the earth, claws flexing and scratching stone. He felt the magic stretch and pulled hard. The dragon screamed and the magic burst, throwing Mildew off his feet and tumbling him across the ground.

He landed in a patch of rabbit brush, the sharp stickers tangling into his fur and leaving behind long scratches. Mildew lay there for a long moment, his ears ringing with the backlash of the snapped magic and his body aching. As much as he wanted to free the beast, he wasn't certain what else he could do on his own. He needed help.

Once he had the strength, Mildew made his way out of the bush and returned to the edge of the water. "I am going to get help, little beast." He knew it could hear him, even if he wasn't sure it understood the words. But it didn't start crying again. "You will wait here, and you will not die. Understood?"

Without waiting for an answer, Mildew turned and began jogging back across the desert. Mona's home was not far, maybe twenty jumps if he could muster the energy, and she had a vehicle for the return trip. He kept walking for nearly half an hour before he felt capable to try the jumps. The magic built slowly, and he had to pause longer between each attempt, the sun tracing a lazy path across the sky that showed how slow he was. Finally, with a last effort, he jumped to the ranch where the old witch lived.

He walked in from the outer field, making his way past the tall barn where he smelled horses. As he passed into the yard, Mildew came to a stop, sitting back on his haunches, his tail curled close around him. He had visited so many times over the years that he knew what to expect. He knew the feeling of Mona's magic and her wards, yet today he felt only the faintest echo. Something had changed, and he had missed it. The fur around his ruff rose, announcing his displeasure and a merowl rolled out of his mouth.

To his surprise, the house door opened and a blonde head popped out, someone peering into the yard. A woman in her twenties exited the house, coming out to stand on the veranda ostensibly to see what all the noise was about. She dressed much like the other ranchers Mildew had met in his life, jeans and a white tank top with a long-sleeved plaid shirt tied over the top. Her hair was drawn up in a thick, sensible braid that fell over her shoulder. The moment her gaze landed on Mildew, she broke out in a smile.

"Well, aren't you a handsome kitty?"

When her voice hit his ears, it was like listening to the sound of sunlight, sending warmth through his exhausted body and easing the ache in his chest. Mildew stared at the young woman, then started to purr in spite of himself. She was a witch, and her power appealed to his.

The woman sat cross-legged on the veranda, holding her hand out palm down. "I don't know if you're Mona's kitty. If you are, she didn't mention it. She moved to Flagstaff a few days ago to be with her children, but I can call her."

The urge to run over and rub himself all over this witch ran through Mildew's body, but he forced himself to rise with a languid stretch. She was just a witch familiar after all, it wouldn't do to be too enthusiastic. When he got close, he dodged her hand with his head, instead letting his tail flick her skin. A little electric jolt ran through his fur, immediately easing some fraction of his weariness.

She didn't seem to notice the connection. Instead, she laughed. "Oh, I see how you are. Going to do this on your terms, hmm? I don't have any kitty treats, but I'm sure I could find something for you if you're hungry. Goodness knows I could use a barn cat if you wanted to stick around."

Mildew sneezed and turned his back on her with a sniff. A common barn cat? Was that all she saw? That was definitely not acceptable. He looked over her shoulder, examining her for a long breath before looking away again. He felt the magic surrounding her, but she seemed...clueless. It was the universe's ultimate joke, he decided. He needed a witch familiar, and he had been sent a neophyte that didn't know what she was. How was he going to connect with her, much less rescue a dra—

Her hand touched the back of his neck, interrupting his train of thought. Sympathetic magic flooded between them, and he arched into her touch. Her fingers found the sensitive spot at the back of his ears, and Mildew groaned in delight and let his 'voice' flow.

"Right there, yes."

The scratching paused, then began again. She laughed a second time, but this one was shakier. "I must be really tired, kitty. My imagination thought you were talking to me. Not that all animals don't talk in their own way, but words are usually right out."

Mildew hesitated, then remembered one of Stephanie's favorite sayings: *In for a penny, in for a pound.* He'd spoken to the witch, and she'd heard him. That meant something. He was certain now her powers were attuned to animals, which meant good things in his current form.

"You weren't imagining, young witch. I spoke to you. You may be my new familiar, and I need your help."

She took a deep breath, and Mildew turned around, meeting her gaze. She had blue eyes, like summer skies. When she breathed out, it came with two words. "Holy shit."

Mildew couldn't help but smile at that, sitting back and licking one paw before cleaning the dust off of his whiskers. "There is much to explain, but it must wait. I require your assistance."

"You're asking for my help?" Her voice was weak with shock.

"Yes." He paused, then placed his front paws on her folded legs, lifting himself to meet her nearly nose to nose. "And your name. I cannot keep calling you, young witch. It's undignified."

They sat there breathing in each other's scent until she spoke again. "My name is Rae, and maybe I really am losing my mind, but I'll help if I can."

"Good." Mildew bumped her chin with his head, purring softly. "Do you have a truck?"

The return trip to the swollen stream was much more pleasant than the trip away had been. Rae did, in fact, have a truck, an older Ford that showed every sign of a life well lived, from mud in the tire wells to seat covers that were worn to perfect comfort. She drove with confidence, fast enough to make quick time, but cautious enough not to ruin either her truck or the landscape. Mildew stood with his front paws on the dashboard, giving directions as they went. At first, Rae had been full of questions about how he could talk and why she could understand him. He was grateful that she wasn't being foolish about what was or wasn't impossible, but he wanted to have that discussion later. Right now, he just needed her to help him gather enough power to levitate the dragon to safety. They could figure everything else out.

Rae applied the brakes, and the truck came to a stop a few yards from the little oasis. "Okay, Mildew, we're here." Rae's nose wrinkled. "I'm still not sure about that name. I mean, it's your name and all, but who names their cat after fungus?"

"I did not know what mildew was when I was given the name." Mildew shrugged. "Now, it would be odd to be called any other. Come, Rae. We have work to do."

Rae snorted and pushed her door open. "You're kind of a bossybritches, you know that?"

Mildew jumped out of the truck and moved toward the opening in the rocks. He'd never heard the term bossybritches, but it was self-explanatory. Privately, he was glad, now that her shock had worn off, she was showing some spunk. If she was going to be his familiar, she couldn't be boring. He hated that. "This way. Bring the rope."

"Please."

Mildew peered over his shoulder. Rae leaned against the truck, making it obvious she wasn't moving without a polite invitation, awaiting rescue or not. Mildew rolled his eyes. "This way, and *please* bring the rope. We have to hope the creature is still there."

Rae nodded and scooped up the coil of rope. It was bright pink, a choice Mildew hadn't commented on. "You said it was good sized and stuck in the wash, but you didn't say what kind of creature was stuck. Are we talking a burro or a javelina? Or something else entirely?"

"You'll see." With all the other surprises of the day, Mildew was certain it was best to let Rae experience the dragon organically. He had no idea what her young magic would do around a creature as magical as a dragon, and he didn't want to make guesses or make her more nervous.

They ducked around some rocks, coming in sight of the trapped creature. Mildew's stomach tightened until he saw the dragon's wings shift and its head raise. Water had built up behind the blockage and was spilling across the dragon's back, washing away much of the mud in its path to the pool.

Rae came to a stop next to Mildew and caught her breath. "Oh, it's a lizard. A really big one. I didn't know Arizona lizards got that big, poor thing. It can't be good for it to be in cold water like that."

"It's not." Lizard was acceptable for now. They could get into the distinction between dragons and lizards later. Provided they succeeded. "We need to free it."

Rae nodded. "Good thing I brought my waders. Hang on." She left the rope and ran back to the truck, returning a few minutes later clad in rubber overalls that covered her from toes to chest. She approached the edge of the water, tilting her head as she studied the situation. "We might need the truck to pull it out, but I'll try to get a rope around it first. Unless you have a better suggestion."

Mildew leapt to the top of a stone. Rae didn't know about recharging or mediation or any of those things yet, but just riding with her had helped his reserves. As Stephanie had aged, her natural magic had waned, and Mildew had forgotten the joy of a powerful companion. "Get the rope on him. I will do what I can to make moving him easier."

"I don't have kitty sized overalls; you're going to get wet."

Mildew's whiskers twitched. "I most certainly am not. Just wait and see."

She looked like she might ask more questions, but the dragon cried out, and Rae scooped up the rope and waded into the flow. She held out a hand as she approached, talking softly.

"Hey there. I'm here to help, okay. I'd really appreciate it if you didn't bite me."

Mildew's eyes narrowed, focused on Rae's hands where he swore he saw a spark of magic that wasn't just the brightness of the sun. He waited to see what the dragon would do, ready to call out to it. Rae touched the beast on the back, and its head jerked up, twisting toward her. She froze in place. Mildew wasn't certain she was even breathing any more. Then the dragon pushed its nose against her shoulder and keened.

"Oh...it's okay," Rae said soothingly. You just be patient and we'll get you out of here. I have some nice blankets in the truck."

She clambered around the dragon, working the rope between the dragon and the stone. Mildew admired her tenacity, even as she slipped and splashed in the cold water. For all that she wore waders that covered her from toe to waist, she was getting soaked.

The minutes ticked away until finally Rae splashed backward, pulling her rope taut. She shoved her hair back from her face. "Okay. I've got the rope tied. He's really wedged in there. I don't think I'm strong enough to pull him out, but he's hurt and I'm afraid to use the truck."

"Then let's try without it. I want you to keep the rope tight and to paint a picture in your mid of the dra—the lizard rising up out of the water and floating."

"Like he's flying or floating on the water?"

It was a good question, and Mildew nodded in approval. "Let's keep it simple and go for floating on the water. Rising up just enough to twist and slip into the pond. Once there it should be easy enough to take him to the shore." Him. She had said the dragon was male. Somehow this witch had determined the gender of a dragon. Mildew had not seen that before.

"Okay... I'm picturing a floating lizard. Now what?"

"Keep picturing it. Hold that vision in your mind, but don't close your eyes. You will need to guide it, maybe even push on the creature to turn it." Mildew gathered his magic for the fourth time, deciding that after this he would eat an entire can of tuna and sleep for the rest of the day. Hopefully, Rae had tuna. If he was going to stick around, they would have to talk about his dietary needs.

Mildew pushed away the distraction of food and lashed his tail. "Rise!"

As before magic flew away from him and tethered itself to the dragon, but this time a glittering glow also ran down the rope from Rae's hands joining with his power. Where their magic met, it turned into a golden mesh that raced around the dragon. Echoes of redoubled power flowed back to Mildew, and he gasped at the glut. What he had intended to be a gentle rise, turned into a sudden jerk tearing the dragon free and sending it flying several feet in the air in a long arc into the center of the pond. It trumpeted in surprise, a sound echoed by Rae's yelp as she flew in after him. Mildew hopped down and ran to the edge, wading in until the cold water brushed his belly.

The woman and the lizard surfaced, her arm wrapped around the dragon and pushing it ahead of her toward the shore. Once they were close enough, Mildew bit into the shoulder of her shirt, pulling as hard as he could. Eventually, all three of them lay on the stony ground, letting the sun soak into skin, scale, and fur.

Rae cleared her throat, turning her head to look at Mildew who curled up against her side and purred. "Well, that was a hell of a thing."

"Indeed. What are you going to do with the lizard, now that it is free?"

"I guess I'll take it home." She paused, absently scratching Mildew's ears. "It's not really a lizard, is it?"

"Not really."

"Hrm. Okay. I think we should name him Gully." She was quiet for so long that Mildew wondered if she'd fallen asleep, then she spoke again. "Mildew? What do dragons eat?"

Mildew laughed, resting his head on her chest. She was going to be a very good familiar. "Anything they want."

About the Author

Writer of the weird and the wonderful, Jena Rey has long been a fan of science fiction and fantasy. She finds inspiration in her daydreams and the Utah landscape where she lives with her amazing kids, sweet and sexy husband, and furry sidekicks.

BLOODLINES

by Melissa Rolli

I TURNED TWENTY-TWO on a morning when the temperature never rose above fifteen degrees—a bit colder than usual for Thanksgiving in Ely, Minnesota.

By the time winter arrives, the air bites the moment you step outside. Most people hate the winter here, but I never do. There's something about the cold that makes everything feel clearer, like the world has been stripped to its bare bones. I like its stillness, its quiet power—the way snow coats the trees, turning everything soft and untouchable, even though I know how sharp and unforgiving it can be.

I think, in part, I love winter in Ely because I want to believe that beauty and strength can exist side by side—even in the harshest conditions.

As much as I love the cold, it's the warmth that anchors me.

I headed downstairs to the kitchen, where my parents had already started the coffee. The fire crackled in the fireplace, sending heat through the room.

"Happy birthday, kiddo," my dad said, his voice gravelly.

I smiled, leaned over to kiss his cheek, then turned to my mom, who had a present sitting in front of my usual seat at the table.

"My birthday present?" I asked, raising an eyebrow as I picked up the small, neatly wrapped box. It was too light to be clothes, too solid to be something fragile.

My mom grinned. "We thought you might want to dig into something more… personal. After all, you've been obsessed with your history class."

I furrowed my brow, unsure of what history class had to do with my present. "You mean the one on Vikings and migration?"

I tore at the wrapping. Inside, I found an ancestry DNA kit from AncesTree.

I stared at it, surprised, a sudden tightness in my chest.

My dad chuckled. "You've been talking about your class—bloodlines, migrations. We thought you might want to see what's in your blood."

I looked at the kit. Then out the window.

The truth was, I had no idea what was in my blood. I was adopted as a baby. My parents had always told me that, and I'd never thought much about it. They were my parents. My family. That was what mattered.

But something had started to stir in the past year. Not a crisis—a steady, persistent curiosity. I couldn't explain it. I wasn't unhappy, but the unknown kept nudging me. I hadn't mentioned it to anyone, least of all my parents. Could they tell?

Maybe this kit would help answer some of those nagging questions. But at what cost?

"Thanks," I said, an apprehensive smile tugging at my lips.

My mom seemed to hear the hesitation in my voice.

"This doesn't change who we are to each other," she said. "Whatever you learn, it's just another thread in the fabric of our story—something new to weave in, not something that unravels us."

My trepidation was that and more. I wasn't sure I was ready for what it might uncover.

I left the kit unopened on my dresser for a few days.

On Thanksgiving, curiosity, and maybe a trace of regret, finally broke my mom's silence.

"You going to send that DNA test in?" she asked, spooning more mashed potatoes onto my plate. "It only works if you actually take it."

"I will," I said, keeping my eyes on the food.

From the other end of the table, my dad chimed in. "Might as well. Could be fun."

Fun wasn't the word I'd use. That night, after everyone had gone to bed and the house had gone still, I opened the box. I read the instructions and then again, like the words might change. My fingers hovered over the collection tube. I hesitated before spitting, sealing, and sliding the sample into the return envelope.

The next morning, I dropped it in the mailbox on my way back to campus.

Three weeks later, I sat in my dorm room with my laptop open to the email inviting me to sign in to the AncesTree site for my results.

I'd been avoiding it for days, telling myself I needed to study. The truth was I wasn't studying, because of the link—because of the answers it might hold, and the ones it might not.

So I clicked it.

A map appeared, color coded and brimming with statistics. I scrolled past regions and percentages, my eyes catching on a new link: Parental Inheritance Report.

I froze.

What if my tree ended with me? What if all that came back was a blank space—a genetic dead end?

I slammed the laptop shut.

The weight of that unopened truth sat heavy in my chest.

"Enough," I snapped out loud at myself. "I need to study. Finals first. Ancestry reports can wait."

I'd waited twenty-two years already. What were a few more days?

Later that evening, after a long study session with my boyfriend, we grabbed dinner at a small café near campus.

Nathan was digging into his pasta, but I barely touched my food. My mind kept circling back to the unopened report.

"You still hung up on that ancestry stuff?" he asked between bites. Nathan had always been more interested in aerospace engineering and thermodynamics than anything having to do with people, so he didn't really understand why I was interested in understanding my family history. He thought it shouldn't matter.

After letting out a slow, deep breath, I tried to explain. "I got my results. I think I might've found something... but I didn't click through all of it."

Nathan wiped his mouth with a napkin and looked at me, his expression unreadable. "You've been obsessed with this for weeks, El. Why hesitate? Just look and see what's there."

I shook my head. "I guess I'm scared. What if I open it and there's... nothing? What if I really am alone? Who am I, really?"

"You're you," he said gently. His tone shifted and he asked, "Isn't that enough?"

His words took my breath away. I pushed my food around on my plate a couple of times and then looked up to meet his eyes and tried to explain one more time, "I just don't think I'm ready yet."

A long silence followed. For a moment, I thought he understood. He leaned back in his chair and sighed, a crease forming between his brows.

"I get it," he said slowly, "but…I don't get *you*. You've been chasing this for weeks. And honestly, it feels like you're always chasing something. Like nothing's ever enough."

I blinked, a knot forming in my stomach.

"What are you saying?"

"I don't think we're good for each other," he said, quiet but certain. "I don't know what you're looking for, but I know it's not me."

Disbelief rose in my chest.

"What?" I asked, genuinely shocked by this entire interaction.

He didn't answer. Pushed his chair back and looked away.

The room tilted. My heart dropped. The air felt too thin.

"I didn't expect this," I whispered.

Nathan stood. "I'm sorry. But I think it's best if we stop seeing each other."

And then he was gone. The sound of his footsteps retreating was louder than anything he'd said.

The next morning, I sat under the harsh buzz of fluorescent lights for my midterm.

I didn't remember walking there. The world was distant, muffled. But the test was in front of me, clear and tangible.

Initially, I struggled to concentrate. The exam danced with formulas and theories, but I knew I needed to pull myself together.

Somewhere inside, something snapped into place, and I moved through each question calmly and deliberately.

When I handed the test in, I felt a strange, quiet satisfaction. Like I'd reclaimed a part of myself.

For the first time in weeks, I felt steady. Not fixed, but standing.

Maybe I was enough, just like this.

Three hours later, alone in my dorm room, with the exam successfully behind me, I opened my laptop. The ancestry report was the only thing left I hadn't faced. My fingers trembled as I logged in. No more excuses.

I clicked the Parental Inheritance Report link.

A digital tree unfolded on the screen—branches and roots stretching across time, names I didn't know, places I'd never been.

Then I saw it.

Kara Lindström—49.8% DNA shared. Likely: Parent.

I just stared at the screen, motionless. What felt like hours was only seconds. The moment I'd been circling for weeks had arrived, and now I didn't know what to do.

My fingers hovered over the keyboard. What do you say to someone who gave you life but was never part of your life?

Finally, I typed:

Hi Kara. I believe we might be related. I was adopted in 2001. I don't want to pry, I just want to understand where I come from. So, I'd appreciate it if we could talk sometime.

I hit send. Then I waited.

Three days later, back home for winter break, I sat at the desk in my room checking my final grades and email.

The house smelled like cinnamon and pine—same as always this time of year. Everything seemed the same except me. I felt different. Off-kilter.

I refreshed my inbox, and there it finally was, the response from Kara.

Yes. I'm your birth mother. I was seventeen when I had you. It was a difficult time in my life, and I've chosen to leave that part behind. I'm sorry. I hope you find peace.

I read it again. And again. And again.

The words were polite, but final, and cold.

No explanation. No father's name. No stories. A gentle *goodbye* that cut deeper than I expected.

I closed the laptop, my hands lingering on the lid, waiting to feel something. But nothing came. Not yet. Just a strange stillness inside me, as though something had shifted—but I couldn't tell if it had broken or simply rearranged.

This journey hadn't only been about finding answers. It was about what came after I found them.

And the truth? The answers hadn't matched my expectations.

I was rejected by my mother. I was rejected by my boyfriend. I was like a girl chasing pieces of herself scattered across time. I thought I'd been ready for anything. But I hadn't been ready for a polite confirmation and simultaneous dismissal.

So, I did what was expected of me when home. I sat through dinners, pretended to watch movies, helped decorate the tree. I laughed when I was supposed to. But inside, I felt like a mirror with a crack running straight through it—still reflecting light, but fractured.

I didn't tell my parents. Not right away. I wasn't sure how. But, eventually, I told them, because if I didn't, I was sure they would ask. I needed to make sure I told them when I wanted to, not when asked. Surprisingly, they didn't say much in return. Just quiet apologies, long hugs, and gentle reminders that I was loved.

It helped. But it didn't resolve the curiosity. It didn't fill the ache.

One night, I sat at the kitchen table long after everyone else had gone to bed, staring into a mug of cold tea.

My mom joined me without a word. She slid into the seat across from me, watching me for a long moment before speaking.

"I reached out to someone," she said softly.

I looked up, confused. "What do you mean?"

She hesitated, then gave me that quiet, steady smile that had always been more comfort than words.

"A cousin. From your AncesTree results—her name's Ingrid. She lives in Norway. I told her a little about what's been going on. Not everything, just enough. She said you're welcome to visit. Stay a while, if you want."

She paused, then added, "I already got you a ticket. You don't have to go. But. . .maybe you need something different."

I opened my mouth to speak, but nothing came. Just a nod. My eyes burned. It wasn't a fix. It wasn't an answer. But it was a door.

Less than seventy-two hours later, my plane touched down in Haugesund, Norway— its wheels kissing the tarmac with quiet finality. As I stepped into the crisp Scandinavian air, a shiver ran down my spine. Not from the cold, but from the weight of what this meant.

Ingrid met me with a warm embrace. She felt like a tether—something solid to hold onto after weeks of feeling adrift. A historian and keeper of family stories, she had arranged everything: the ticket, the itinerary, the welcome. All I had to do was show up.

We drove through winding roads lined with snow-dusted pines, the landscape unfolding like a saga waiting to be read. Our destination was Avaldsnes, a land once ruled by kings and where women fought like gods.

At the Nordvegen History Centre, we stood beneath the towering statue of Harald Fairhair. But it wasn't the kings Ingrid brought me to see.

Inside, Ingrid guided me through stories of Hjor and Ljufvina, rulers of Avaldsnes, whose daughters had fought as shieldmaidens at their father's side. Another display showed the burial site at Stava, where warrior women were laid to rest with weapons and honor, their courage carved into stone.

"These weren't women waiting to be rescued," Ingrid said, her voice low and reverent. "They shaped their world. They defended it. They defined it."

As we explored, she told me about Sigrid Skjalgsdatter—my namesake in spirit, if not in blood—a woman of power and legend who didn't wait for history to remember her. She wrote herself into it.

Later that night, at the Viking Farm, wrapped in wool and leather, we sat by a crackling fire. The wind howled through the beams. Flames cast dancing shadows on the wooden walls.

Ingrid spoke of the women who came before us—strong, fierce, thunder when they needed to be.

I listened. I breathed. And slowly, the hollowness inside me began to shift—not vanishing, but softening, making room for something else.

The next morning, Ingrid led me to the edge of a fjord. The wind bit through my jacket—sharp and clean—but like usual, I didn't mind. And here, at this moment, it felt like a baptism. Like remembering something I'd always known.

I whispered their names. "Sigrid. Freyja. Hilde." Then I took a deep breath, and I added mine. "Elena."

Ingrid stood beside me. She didn't ask questions. She didn't need to.

As we made our way back to the cabin, I knew I was ready to return home—not because I was fixed, but because I wasn't lost anymore.

Something in me had changed. I no longer carried the weight of needing to discover or prove who I was. I had chosen myself. The world was wide. And I was ready.

Later, standing at the edge of another body of water—maybe in Norway, maybe somewhere still to come—I would remember: No more searching for answers that don't exist. No more waiting to be claimed. I am enough. Whole. A woman. A warrior. Elena.

About the Author

Melissa has dual bachelor's degrees in English and history from the University of New Mexico. She is also a graduate of the Denver Publishing Institute. Melissa has always had a passion for writing, and, when she moved to Colorado in 2015, became a journalist for the Woodmen Edition, a community paper owned by the Gazette. She eventually became a masthead writer for the Woodmen Edition and authored pieces for other local papers, like the Cheyenne Edition. Some of her articles and photography were syndicated to the Gazette, a Pulitzer Prize winning newspaper, such as "Wounded Warriors Cycle to AFA on Adapted Rides." After a couple of years, Melissa made the decision to leave journalism behind and start pursuing her creative writing seriously. Melissa has and continues to publish shorter works of fiction in various places as she works towards publishing her first novel.

POMP & CIRCUMSTANCE

by J. Anne Riten

"ANOTHER GAME?" Egmund asked.

Pomp blinked, the purple veil of the Otherworld flickering just enough to warrant the more human reaction on his features. His head tilted down at the winning hand, and he tapped the cards. After he savored that moment, he laid them neatly across the table for Egmund to shuffle.

"You're stalling," said Pomp.

"Stalling?" Egmund shook his head. "No. Quite the opposite. I'm enjoying myself."

"I've met many stallers in my time," Pomp said. "And they all do as you do. One hand after another, that same grumpy look twixt the eyes."

Egmund chuckled. "I suppose my thinking face *is* rather grumpy..."

"You have more rounds to win than time left."

Egmund nodded, thumbing through the worn deck of cards. "Do you know where I got these?"

Pomp's veil blinked again, a flicker of life on the guide for the dead.

"One of my buddies at the shop," Egmund continued. "He was a quick worker, you see, but he practiced magic tricks with them between customers. One pizza here, a little sleight of hand there. It kept his mind and hands busy when the counters were too clean to bother."

"Is it a spell you charge with your games?" Pomp asked. He folded his arms across his ribcage. "I would be interested to sense it."

"I believe, my dear Sandman, you would have already." Egmund pointed the cards at his guide. "No, it isn't magic that they hold. Just...memories."

Pomp, jaw set, tapped his fingers on the deck of cards. The spirit sat as still as stone, with only the wisps of purple magics to surround him. In spite of it all, Egmund wasn't afraid. His guide was skeletal but still human, dressed in a casual suit, and as polite as any gentleman. The air around him was not as cold as Egmund expected, either. Egmund had left the window open, perhaps foolishly thinking his guest would need such a way in, and even still the breeze that came in the lazy afternoon was warm. He smelled scents on it that he hadn't smelled in years, perhaps decades. The soft detergent his mother used, the acrid cologne of his grandfather's house, the maple sweets from the county fair not far from the field by his home. He even smelled a moment of his brother's room—which thankfully, had been fleeting.

"How is it you do that?" Egmund asked at last. "My memories hang on you. Do you see them, or smell them? I always thought you'd be..."

"Rotted?" Pomp guessed.

"Or dusty."

His guide considered it. "I can be so, if that is your preference."

"Oh, I didn't mean to offend," Egmund said quickly. "It's rather nice really. It's been...quite a long time since I've thought of any of these things."

Pomp's veil blinked. Egmund shuffled the cards and gave them each a hand, waiting for the spirit to take his turn. He drew his cards, tapping them once in thought.

"Actually...no."

Pomp looked up.

"I've thought of those things quite a lot before today," Egmund admitted.

"You're stalling," Pomp said.

"No, not at all. I'm enjoying myself."

Pomp leaned back again, though he relaxed his forearms on the table. "Many souls do this before they make the crossing. I sense they are afraid; there is a lot that they face on that bridge and then beyond it. And there is a lot to leave behind. It is natural to stall death."

Egmund played the first set of cards he had—three jacks. "And how many have asked you to a game of Go Fish?"

"Five."

"Five? In all your tenure?"

"Most try to gamble."

Egmund glanced around his little room. He had tidied it—again, perhaps foolishly wanting to make a good impression on his guide. "I have gummy bears."

The jaw twitched, and Pomp chuckled as he played three queens. "More priceless than souls... Any fours?"

"Damn..." He passed two. "Also. Is that really a thing? What do you eat?"

"That is like asking the wind what it drinks," Pomp said. "Sometimes dates."

Egmund frowned. "Like, calendar dates?"

"It was a joke."

"Oh."

"So if you are indeed not stalling, and you are in fact not gambling, is this for questions only?" Pomp asked.

"It's for fun," Egmund said. "Got any aces?"

"Hm." His guide slid the card across the table, and Egmund grinned as he tucked it away with the set in his hand.

"I used to play Go Fish all the time with my daughter," he said. "I never *let* her win."

The veil flickered.

"Okay, only *once*. But she learned. And she taught it to my grandson as well. He was such a quick learner. I hope he'll keep it up, even if *these* things go virtual." Egmund waved his hand.

Pomp stared at the cards, and for a few rounds there was quiet. Egmund could smell the old office at his first job, remember that old music store full of music books and rosin. He smelt the hair of his first love, and the foul smells of the hospital wings. He smelled the forest from that one camping trip where his friend Luca suffered the aftermath of too much beef jerky. That same trip that became a memory of laughter at countless dinners, gatherings, and friendly drinks.

"Ah Luca..." Egmund chuckled. "Is he over there, happy?"

"I don't know," Pomp replied.

"Was he happy when he left?"

"Confused. It was sudden, after all."

Egmund paused as he laid down his king, queen, and ace. "It was."

Pomp stared at the hand. "As I recall…he asked if he had offended me during his D&D campaign."

"D&D?" Egmund flushed. "Oh my god…I totally forgot about that… *Did* he offend? It's quite normal for bards with enough charisma."

"He was a gentleman," Pomp said. "Got any twos?"

"Go fish."

Egmund's phone buzzed, and he looked at the notification. "Ah! It's my grandson. Do you mind?"

Pomp waved a hand "Not at all."

He shifted his glasses to sit on the bridge of his nose and pulled the message up. Alan and his wife, Emelia, filled the screen. Egmund couldn't help but smile, even before he saw the words below—he saw so much of his daughter in her son. The ears mostly.

"My god…they're expecting," Egmund blinked.

He stared at the screen for a moment, exhaling a laugh, and his eyes stung from the warmth it brought. A new child, a new bit of family running amok. He wondered if the child would be as chaotic as their grandmother, or as quietly devious as their father. Perhaps the kid would throw tantrums over their food touching on the plate and wear crazy shoe colors. Maybe they'd explode with excitement over digital things and try to build a computer, like what Egmund's daughter did all those years ago.

He'd worked his odd jobs for so many years to see such beautiful things—and it was there that his eyes fell on the cards laid on the table.

"I can deliver them, after you," Pomp offered.

"What?"

"The cards." His guide reached out and laid a gentle hand over them, as if to preserve the thought. "As a gift."

Egmund laughed. "I guess people do not make many stops on their crossing?"

"No. They do not."

"Is that why so many loved ones find odd things after…?"

"Am I being recorded?"

Egmund paused a little. "Is that a—"

"Yes. A joke."

He chuckled, glancing between his phone photos of the little nugget-to-be and the winning hand across the table.

"Another game?" Pomp asked.

Egmund's phone lowered. "You're stalling."

"No." The guide leaned forward, folding his hands together on the table. "I'm simply enjoying myself."

About the Author

J. Anne Riten is a marketer and dark fantasy writer with ten years of experience crafting tales of misadventure, D&D campaigns, and overly detailed lore documents. Inspired by the interactive questing of RPGs and mythology, her stories create glimpses into new worlds ripe for adventure.

Author Website: https://ravensinrain.wixsite.com/mind-of-fire

Instagram: @dreams_of_ulinara

Campfire Author Page: https://www.campfirewriting.com/user/thecrowkeeper

WHISPERING HEIGHTS

by Ligia de Wit

THE BARREL OF THE GUN POINTED AT ME.

Wait. *What?*

A loud bang reverberated in my head. Numb, I staggered and looked down where a sticky liquid flowed from a wound. This couldn't be happening. I had friends. Family. I couldn't breathe, I couldn't. . .

The blackness sucked me into a spiraling pit of nothingness, and it was all I could see. I couldn't feel a thing. Was I dead? Crap. I must be dead.

Would my friends visit my grave? Here lies Robyn, shot by a stupid robber when she was only twenty-one.

A balmy peace hushed the rush of fear, and I floated in the blackness. In the void, there was no discomfort, only silence. Nothing to hang on to, nothing to remember.

I floated and turned. I turned and floated.

Gravity rammed like a punch in the gut and pulled me down to solid ground, where I stood still. I should be panicked, but the serenity from the void lingered in me like a mother's soft caress.

A wall loomed before me, rising into white space. Large blocks of rust-colored stones rested on each other, and thick fog rolled in the surroundings, except in the narrow stretch of black soil running alongside the wall.

Tight, dark-gray clothing enveloped my slim body. I wiggled my bare toes, rotated my neck, and stretched my muscles, testing the comfy and kick-ass garments. Cool.

A loud bang. . . There had been one, I was sure. The unsettling memory nagged me. The fog darkened into charcoal hues, and shreds reached out to me like ghostly fingers. I pressed my back and palms to the wall.

Primal fear seized me while the blackness throbbed in deadly silence and lapped at my feet like oily waves. I yelped, pressing harder.

Then, something shifted—a thought, quiet but insistent, rose through the panic. If I was already dead, what could this darkness do to me?

A different tune pulsed through my body. Lighter, brighter. It came from the wall, and I knew I should climb to escape the inexorable approach of the darkness. I latched my fingers onto one of the bricks above my head—a perfect contact between my skin and the rough, rocky texture.

Feeling light, I scrambled up, with the whistling wind as company. The ascent was surprisingly easy, my fingers and feet found purchase as if I had been doing this all my life.

I could see blue sky above me in the distance, but no matter how fast I climbed, the top of the wall didn't come.

Angry wasps buzzed from below. I stopped and risked a glance down. Darkness spread like a hungry monster, ascending toward me. I forced myself to continue but my limbs were heavy. Sweat dripped down my forehead and blurred my vision. All my muscles tightened—I couldn't keep on.

Clinging to the stone, I sobbed. The whistling wind stopped. I cried until tears left a salty path on my cheeks, a tingle on the skin that needed relief. And I remembered I never cried in my old life. You couldn't show weakness. But here, my body forgot that rule.

An invisible force reached out to me like a sticky hand, pulling me down. Yelping, I tightened my hold.

The wasps buzzing morphed into whispers. *"You won't like what's on the top. Come back down, come, come."*

The disembodied voices promised a swift and soft fall. No more tiredness. I risked another glance below, but there was no monster. The air rippled like the waves on a pool, and the waters were warm, inviting, easing the dread within.

"Yes, let go. You'll feel rested and oblivion will cradle you."

I couldn't drag myself to the top of the wall. Stupid little me, always trying to fight against the current. It would be so easy to give in to the temptation and let go.

"Yes, it is not possible, come, come." Their voices were so sweet, so beautiful, they should be angels.

But I didn't want to let go or give in. I knew, I *felt*, that wasn't me.

"Help," I mumbled.

A fresh breeze stroked me. It soothed me, brushed my cheek, and pushed my hair back like a loving caress. I shook my doubts, and my mind cleared.

And I remembered.

The love of those close to me. A beer after a hard day's work. The joy on kids' faces and their innocent laughter—a bright beam of light piercing through the gloom.

There was only one thing to do.

"Shut up!"

The whispers weren't from angels. There were no such things as winged beings with halos above their heads. Tears wouldn't help me. I wiped my eyes and climbed until I reached the top and I pushed myself up.

The top of the red-stone wall was about five meters wide, and that darn fog covered both sides. I couldn't see a thing. No clear blue sky. Silence but for the whoosh of the wind.

Brown hands rested on the edge where I'd climbed.

Wait. *What?*

More hands gripped the edge—dark as ash, pale as timber, thin fingers like a piano's player, rough like a construction worker. A wail and one pair of hands slipped. Another trembled and vanished from sight. The hands that remained transformed into arms, necks, and heads, rising from the edge. People looked around, frightened, perhaps asking the same questions I was asking myself—where had these people came from? Hadn't I climbed this darn thing alone? What *was* here?

Soon dozens of people were on top. They all had the same tight, gray clothing as me. We looked like a bunch of scared, under-trained, kick-ass wannabes—modern Rambos and Terminators after a hundred years of lazily watching our tablets and phones.

"Where are we?" asked a young guy, with black hair and rosy cheeks. He reminded me of something. Dolls. Dolls I made with scraps.

"Is this heaven?" a dark-skinned girl asked.

"Doesn't look like it," I said.

The fog became thicker and some shivered. Most looked lost, clustering tightly like small kids in front of a bully. The wind picked up, and the sky darkened. Like faraway banshees, wails of despair coming from below chilled my blood.

"It can't end here," Doll Man whined. "Not after our struggle to climb."

I rubbed my aching arms, still shaking from the effort. Faces of familiar people appeared in my memories—my friends. They reminded me I couldn't give up and remain here like a toy thrown away.

Toys. I made toys. *Had* made.

"Let's walk," I commanded and led the way with a sure step. Another force tugged at me, wanting me to remain still and face the void, but I shrugged it off and kept going.

Wide-eyed, they followed across the broad path until the way broadened into an esplanade, like a river opening into the ocean. The fog swirled and vanished. A yellow brick road led to gilded doors. Massive, majestic emerald gates stood fifty meters ahead.

Even as the fog remained behind, it was like the sun shone down on us. This was where we were supposed to arrive.

"Holy crap, this is bright!" Doll Man exclaimed.

"When did the gates appear?" the dark-skinned girl asked.

"It's alright," I said.

"Yeah," Doll Man said. "Why were we scared before?"

My new friends nodded and smiled.

Doll Man mimed lifting a skirt and danced his way from one side to the other. "Look at me," he said without stopping his funny dance, "I'm Dorothy."

The girl laughed, holding her stomach. Another one joined her, and soon a chorus of joy erupted.

"Why are we laughing?" I asked, giggling.

"No idea," Doll Man said. "But damn! It feels good."

It did.

Two indistinct figures shimmered between us and the gates, and we took a step back.

"Customs officers!" the girl exclaimed. "They'll deny us entrance."

The first looked like a Viking of old and the other like an Asian woman. They were clad in dark navy uniforms, buttoned all the way up, and silver batons hung from their belts.

The officers stood side by side, feet apart and arms folded across their chests, mirror glasses hiding their eyes.

"We want to go in," I said in a loud voice.

"Why?" the female officer demanded.

Confusion reflected on my new friends' faces. Why did we want to go in? A heavy weight settled on my chest. The gates loomed imposing. Forbidden.

Doll Man took a brave step forward. "This is our destination. Where we're supposed to arrive after climbing the wall."

The officer scanned our faces, taking her time with each one of us. When our eyes met, a loud bang sounded in my head. Something familiar yet I didn't want to know what it was. I took a step back but promptly returned to my place. She traded a glance with the Viking guy and gave a curt nod.

She grinned and removed her glasses, her eyes a warm brown. "All right, you're all clear. Welcome, travelers!"

Sighs and nervous laughter erupted. The officers' uniforms shimmered, and now they were the same as the ones we were wearing, except that theirs were bright silver with golden edges.

"Make a line to enter," said the Viking officer in a foreign accent I couldn't pinpoint.

The second officer cupped her hands around her mouth and shouted, "You, girl, stop pinching your arm and close your mouth. You're going to catch flies. No, you didn't become dust, and we're not going to fill you up with propaganda. You, tall dude, we're putting you with all the rest, stop making faces. You over there, stop your namastes. Keep going!"

"This way, people." The Viking officer waved his hand for us to line up. "You'll find food, tea, and coffee on the other side."

Everyone around me smiled, and a few rubbed their hands, giddy. Somehow the view behind the gates was unhindered, and I saw food stands like at a fairground. Trees shielded whatever was beyond. Yet, a weight settled once again on my chest, and my feet refused to get in line, as if a cord had me attached to the wall.

A boiling emotion took hold of me as if I was burning. Disconcerted, I shook the feeling and tried again to enter.

Anytime now.

The Viking officer removed his cap. He looked exactly like an actor. *Björn*, I thought. His head was shaved at his sides, and the golden hair was braided in a small ponytail at the back and top of his head.

"You too, Doe Eyes," he said kindly to me in a cute, clipped tone. "Don't stand as if the lights dazzle you."

"What's in there?" I asked, stalling.

"Hamburgers, pita, tacos, and vegan stands." He pointed vaguely with his cap toward the door. Some of my new friends hadn't entered and still lingered outside, like me.

I glanced again and noticed that the line after entering the gates broke up into several ones with different signs: Jews, Catholics, Protestants, Atheists, Buddhists…the list went on. I squinted and noticed that all those lines converged again into the same single line. I chuckled, yet I was impressed by my amazing powers of observation.

"Is the food any good?" I asked.

"Look, between us"—he leaned in and lowered his voice to a whisper—"everything is oatmeal, but let's just say the mind is easily deceived."

I grinned. "Why do you look like Björn?"

"Who?" He frowned in confusion.

"You know, that actor. You even have the same cool hairdo."

He laughed. "Ah, Doe Eyes, it's the same as food and religion. Look well, but not with your eyes. Look with all your senses." He approached the dark-skinned girl, who lingered near the gates, and engaged in a conversation with her.

I tried to see the image in front of me with all my senses: the girl wasn't looking up, at least not as I would, but straight to his chest as if his eyes were there. And soon, the murmur of a conversation in a foreign language reached my ears.

Björn, or whoever he was, said goodbye and returned to my side, looking at me inquisitively.

"I see. Everyone sees you how they want to see you."

He nodded. "I am a being of energy, and like food, your eyes see what you want to see. Your ears hear what you are familiar with."

"Ah, what a pity, because I see you as a hottie."

He laughed. "What do you see beyond the food stalls?" He waved his hand as if cleaning a fogged mirror.

What I thought was nothing more than trees became more evident the more I focused my gaze. A high wall rose behind them.

"Another wall," I murmured.

"Look closer," he said excitedly.

My eyes had deceived me before, because now I noticed the thick fog that surrounded the place. Then, the mist cleared, and I could see concentric circles of stone walls, one enclosing the other until it ended at the top of a hill.

"Cool! Just like that city of men and elves." I drew my breath. "Are there elves here?"

His ears became pointed, eyes turning into an almond shape.

"Hey, hey…" I took two steps back. "This is weird as hell." I coughed on my fist. "Sorry."

"Nah, we don't take ourselves seriously."

"I even have goosebumps."

"I like you, Doe Eyes." Ears and eyes returned to their normal position like a spring after being stretched.

"Name's Robyn. What's yours?"

He placed a finger on his lips and nodded. "Björn."

"Come on," I said while I punched his shoulder playfully. "Are you an angel?"

"No, no. I'm just a guardian. Like a beat cop. The bosses—what you call angels—are farther up, on the first level." He placed an arm around my shoulders. "I'm also an Encourager."

"What's that?"

"Well, we encourage those who climb the Wall. It's a big commitment, you know? And I need a companion because, Chang"—he pointed to the other officer—"has a new responsibility. What say you, Robyn?" He shook me against him. "Dare you accept?"

"Me? But I just arrived! What do I know?"

"You know how to climb. Do you have any idea how many fall? How many give up?"

"I heard wailing. Was that from people falling?"

He nodded. "Anyway, you would go as my sidekick."

"Am I going to be the Robyn to your Batman?" I teased.

"You got it." He winked and put his thumbs up.

Something nagged again at the back of my head. Blackness. A loud sound, but this place was so beautiful and heavenly that I pushed that worry aside.

Björn's face turned somber like that of a dark elf. "Here, come." He waved me away from the gates, and we walked back to the path over the wall.

The thick fog surrounded us, and I shivered from the cold, something I hadn't felt before.

"Why the fog?" I asked.

"Fog? What fog?" Björn grinned and swung his baton.

"Don't say it. I need to see with my heart and mind, not my eyes."

"Yep."

I stopped and looked around, but the darned fog only thickened more.

He squatted near the edge and waved me next to him. Panic bubbled inside me, but his bright smile cleared my apprehension, and I crouched too. He pointed with his baton to the middle of the wall.

"Why a baton?"

"Is it a baton?" He grinned, and I noticed it wasn't. It was a beam of light.

I saw nothing but stone until I squinted. As with the inner city back at the gates, my sight cleared.

Dozens…no, hundreds of tiny figures clung to the wall. They were close together, but no one seemed to notice there were people around them. Some seemed to move fast as I had at first. Some didn't move at all.

"Look closely," Björn whispered.

I did, then gasped. Around the figures, ghostly wraiths hovered.

"Look closer," he urged.

Tendrils of dark smoke grew like vines and reached out to the figures, pulling them down. Some fell and disappeared into the darkness—the black void I'd seen first, then thought it was a pool of calm water. It wasn't. It was oily and thick.

I gripped the ragged edge. "We need to help them!"

"No. It's their choice. We can't interfere."

"But we're Encouragers!"

He jumped into the void. I screamed and reached out until I remembered who he was. Carefully, I looked over.

He was walking on air. No wings, no halo. He stepped on an invisible wind-ladder, then reached out to someone. Placed a hand on their shoulder or blew air. An Encourager. I remembered the breeze I'd felt and knew it'd been him. My chest lightened, and I smiled until I saw more falling.

Björn returned to my side as people stepped onto the top of the wall, confused and scared.

I stood up, but no one seemed to see us.

They walked toward the gates, visible for me but apparently not for them. Two of them remained still.

Björn placed a hand on my shoulder. "You want to know why you climbed so fast?"

"Fast?"

"More than most." He tapped his forefinger in my chest. "You have a good heart. You could have yielded to temptation down there, in the world that was once yours. Steal. Or kill to survive. But you didn't. Instead, you built toys and gave some away for free. Why?"

I folded my arms over my chest. "Well, kids struggle a lot. Not much joy where I come from. You know, tough 'hood. But toys… Man, you should see their faces light up."

"I do. I did."

The couple that remained sat and hugged, crying.

"What's with them?"

"They're not ready for the gates. They're so close but are still afraid."

"Would they go through it?" I wanted to tell them to open their eyes and keep walking. Their despair would end so soon if only they lifted their heads.

He shrugged. "Maybe. It depends on them. Now, are you ready? There's one struggling on the Wall. Care to help?"

"Sure."

He held my hand and jumped, pulling me down with him. I tensed, but I found myself hovering effortlessly. "This is so cool!"

"Sssh. Focus."

He pulled me toward the sobbing figure in the middle of the wall. A bulky guy, tears streaking his plump cheeks. Messy brown hair that reached his shoulders.

The barrel of a gun aimed at me.

The loud bang cleared my memories.

I was in a store, about to buy beer for a little get-together to unwind after a hard day and laugh at our worries. This guy came to rob. And he killed me.

"I didn't mean to," said the man, still crying. "I'm so sorry; I was nervous and pulled the trigger."

No, he wasn't saying this out loud. I could hear his thoughts.

Rage flooded over me. I'd had a life. A difficult one, but I had friends and family who cared for me. People I missed.

"I don't want to do this," I hissed. "Let him do it himself." I was startled at saying this out loud and glanced at Björn, embarrassed.

There was no judgment on his face. Nothing to tell me he could be upset by my rash words.

"An Encourager only does what they want to do," he said. "If you prefer, we can look for someone else."

Tendrils of darkness lashed and grabbed the man's feet. He yelped. *I deserve this. I did wrong. I should fall. Forget everything. Forget her.*

A memory hit me, and I knew it was his. Of a young woman with wavy light-brown hair and lifeless eyes, sprawled on the floor and blood on her chest.

Me. Robyn. Dead.

"Forgive me," he sobbed out loud. "I didn't mean to. I was desperate."

I clenched my teeth and looked at Björn. He was expressionless.

The wraiths came and hovered around, singing and whispering to let go. But the man held on. He was still sobbing and hanging on. His shoulders shook.

The kids would have no one to give them toys for free. Friends and family would grieve for me. All because this guy had killed me.

"I can't do this." Anger seethed in my words.

"Then leave him alone," Björn said, again, no judgment in his voice.

"I-I don't know."

"No hurries." He clung to the wall and whistled a tune that merged with the song of the wind.

My killer held on. Even though he was scared, he had strength.

The wraiths whispered sweet words, and he cast a glance below. I knew he was watching the lovely pool of warm waters that didn't exist. Darkness spread, a hungry monster ready to devour.

Tears rolled down his eyes, and he shut them, still hanging on. I knew the struggle, the temptation to let go, yet he didn't give up. Why did he have to be so stubborn?

"He shouldn't even be here." My fists clenched.

"If he saw the wall, and he's able to climb it, then there was some good in his life."

"But…he killed. Me."

Björn's face darkened. "That's why he can't climb anymore."

"Why doesn't he let himself fall?"

"Those good deeds are balancing him."

We kept silent again for some time. Then a thought occurred to me. "It's an odd coincidence."

"What, Robyn?"

"That he died the same day as me."

Björn laughed, a clear crystal sound that made the man on the wall breathe profoundly and relaxed. "It's been weeks. Time on the Wall is different than on Earth."

The man cast another glance below and shuddered. "I am so sorry," he repeated, his mantra of the past hour. Or day. "Please, forgive me."

I gulped. It wasn't like I'd been a saint back in my life. Hadn't I struggled at times with hard choices? Yes, I had. And he was here, fighting. Not letting go.

I'd been tempted too, to let go, and Björn helped me. Gave me the last push up.

This was why I was here.

On an impulse, I reached out and placed a hand on the man's shoulder "You can do this. Climb," I said. He was trying, and I wouldn't be the one letting him fall into nothingness.

His sobbing stopped, and he looked up. "I can do this." He wiped his tears with the back of his hand and climbed steadily until he reached the top.

A strange feeling tugged at my gut and traveled to my throat. I cleared it up, trying to ease the knot.

"Come, Robyn." Björn pulled my hand, and we flew to the top.

There were more people there, scared and confused. But my former killer was laughing, and his joy dispelled their worry. He encouraged them and waved them forward.

They smiled and followed his lead, even the couple who had refused to leave their spot. He stopped and looked in our direction, without engaging my gaze. "Thanks," he whispered. Then he trotted to catch up.

My throat closed, and my eyes stung.

Björn pulled me to his chest and hugged me. His arms gave me comfort. Tears slid down my cheeks. They might not bring relief, but they helped to ease the pain in my chest.

"You didn't need a sidekick, did you?" I asked, voice trembling.

"No."

We remained like this for a long while. There was no pull now, nothing that kept me attached to the void.

"I'm ready," I finally said.

"Then it's time for you to go through the gates."

I pulled away from his arms and nodded. The fog had disappeared. The blue sky was beautiful. The green hills went on and on, and heavenly mountains lingered on the horizon.

And I smiled. It was a sad smile, but I was fine.

I would be fine.

About the Author

Ligia de Wit writes fantasy romance adventures with heart, humor, and just the right dose of magic. She's the author of the Bradaís Pledge series—a swashbuckling tale full of brooding pirates, adventurous heroines, and twisted Peter Pan vibes.

A lifelong romantic with a soft spot for fairy tales and found family tropes, Ligia writes characters who are strong in more than just a physical sense. Her characters face fears, fight for themselves, and find love in the most unexpected places.

You'll often find her with her nose in a book, dreaming about travels, writing like a maniac, or acting like a total goof at theme parks. She's a proud kid at heart, and owns it.

She likes to chat with friends on Facebook at https://www.facebook.com/ligiadewit, or Instagram https://www.instagram.com/ligiadewitauthor

Or chat with her at ligiadewit.com.

FOUR TIRES AND A KNIFE

by Tiffany Brazell

HARDIN DREAMED OF THE FAIR: bright lights strung between poles, cotton candy in vivid colors, sweet sticky candy apples, and fried dough—the smell of the dough and corndogs alone would make it worth going. He would stroll down the midway, one hand in his pocket, while the other held a cup of fizzy root beer, slicker even than the teenagers as he made his way to the tilt-a-whirl, or maybe the rodeo ring. There, he'd watch the broncs, while the earthy scent of dirt kicked up by the animals mingled with the aroma of greasy popcorn and roasted peanuts. And then…

The fair's sights, sounds, and smells existed only in Hardin's imagination. Sure, he had seen pictures of candy apples, cotton candy, and lights in magazines, and had heard what it was like, again and again, all while being stuck at home in Baggs. Why had he been stuck at home in Baggs? Every year his oldest brother, Dale, whose word was law, told him "When you're older" or "Don't need a little kid t'watch after!"

This is it, Hardin thought as he munched on a cold biscuit, perched on the wooden stairs out front of his family's wind-blown ranch house. *Two digits, the big 1-0. They have to let me go now. Got t' talk t' Dale about it today, 'cause they're leavin' for Rawlins in the mornin'!*

Hardin had made sure to wake before sunup, before any of his four older brothers, get himself some breakfast, then wait out here on the porch so that he would not miss Dale before he went into town to pick up Ma.

Because he had to be respectable, he was ten now, after all, Hardin had dressed himself in his best flannel shirt, which only had elbow patches, and Dale's old overalls that had been cut off to suit Hardin's height. He'd slicked his wavy black hair back from his fair but freckled face and had wadded some rags into his oversized boots before putting them on. It was August, so he normally would have gone barefoot, but today was special. Today was the day.

The wind rose, bringing with it a hint of the heat to come with the sunrise that he could see on the horizon. It swept the sagebrush-covered hills and stirred up a cloud of dust.

It then pelted the object of Hardin's utmost concern with that dust. Under the old cottonwood that stood by the shed, the family's ancient Model A languished in the dirt. They still called it "the car," but it barely looked like one. Years of sandblasting by Wyoming's winds had worn the original blue paint away, leaving a pocked, rusty exterior, while the roof had been hacked off, gone long before it had come to Hardin's family. In its place, a wooden flatbed occupied the inside, with a wooden frame augmented with chicken wire to keep the sheep from jumping out. Finished with the biscuit, Hardin chewed on his lower lip while he wiped his hands clean on his overalls. *Dale can't go anywhere if the car doesn't. Got t' keep it in sight.*

The house creaked, cracked, and groaned behind Hardin as his brothers shuffled around inside, awake at last. In front of him, the fiery ball of the sun rose on the horizon.

The screen door behind him opened with its distinctive snap-BANG, then the heavy footfalls of boots stepped onto the porch but came to an abrupt halt just short of where

Hardin sat.

"You're up early," Dale said in a voice still rough with sleep. "Where you think you're goin' dressed like that? Church?"

Springing to his feet, Hardin leaned back on the railing as Dale resumed walking down the steps. Eleven years older than Hardin, Dale towered over his younger brother. His blond head was crowned with a weathered, filthy cowboy hat, the only thing their father had left behind the last time they had all seen him, five years gone. Dale's frame was lean but possessed the strength of a man who worked the farm day in, day out.

Falling into step behind him, the boy said, "Wanted t' talk to you about something."

Dale sighed. "Not now, Dinny. I have to go get Ma, and you have your chores."

"It's just… I-I wanted to ask…"

Dale leaned over the driver's door, reaching down to adjust the levers set under the steering wheel. He lifted the left all the way up, while he moved the right down a few notches. With a grunt, he twisted the choke knob before setting the gearshift to neutral. Next, the familiar hum of the ignition switch being flipped sounded before Dale turned back to Hardin with the hand crank, meeting Hardin's hazel gaze with his piercing blue one. "Ask what?"

Lifting his chin and squaring his shoulders, Hardin said, "If I can come to Rawlins with you all tomorrow. Y'know, come to the fair?"

"Dinny, we've been over this. I don't have time to be driving everyone down there just to look after a little kid. 'Sides, Ma needs you up here." With the crank in hand, Dale made his way to the front of the Model A where he stuffed the handle into place and gave a single upward yank. The loud, chug-chug of the engine starting followed, rattling the entirety of what remained of the decrepit vehicle's body.

Swallowing the growing lump in his throat, Hardin said, "You're talking like I'm a baby, Dale! I'm ten now. I can do chores. I can fix the fence. Why do Ray, Floyd, and Ben get to go?"

"Because they're big and can look after themselves. Also, they stay outta trouble!" Dale said, walking around to the driver's door, which groaned when he opened it. Situating himself in the driver's seat, Dale closed the door, which Hardin took in both hands.

"I'll stay outta trouble, you won't even know I'm there."

"Dinny…" Dale's voice dropped as he rested a hand on the choke and pushed it slowly in. "You're not going. Ma said 'no,' I say 'no.' That's it."

"It's not fair!" Hardin kicked the car door in front of him, hard. "You think you're the boss of me just because you went to the war?"

His brother froze for a moment in the middle of adjusting the throttle, his back stiffening. "What did you just say?"

Holding back tears so hard that his throat hurt, Hardin yelled, "I said, you think you're the boss of me, just because—"

Dale cut him off, his tone colder than the lake ice in winter. "You think the war made me a boss, boy? I came back to no Pa, a busted ranch, and a little brother who don't know when to shut his mouth!"

Hardin flinched, then bowed his head.

Barely audible over the car's cacophony, Dale added, "You think the fair makes you a man, Dinny? It don't. You wanna be a man, you keep your word. You take care of Ma. You do your chores. You don't throw tantrums 'cause the world don't give you what you want, when you want it. Now, get on. Need those stakes done today."

Releasing his hold on the car, Hardin balled his hands into fists and watched Dale pull away, shuddering as a cloud of dust and silence enveloped him.

Scrape, scrape. Hardin dragged the blade of his pocketknife over the wood in his lap, honing it to a fine point. Dale had given him the Case folding pocketknife with a jigged bone handle when he had left for the war. He had told him then that he would have to become a man, and a man needed a good knife.

Scrape, scrape, scrape.

Sweat ran down Hardin's temples and back as he worked on the stakes in the shade of the shed and cottonwood. Despite the shade, the late afternoon wind still blew the summer inferno into his freckled face, hotter than hellfire.

Scrape, scrape, scrape, scrape.

Tossing the finished stake onto the mound of others he had made throughout the afternoon, Hardin blew out a long breath. He desperately needed something to drink, or he was going to faint.

Walking around the shed, he folded his knife up and stuffed it into his pocket. Pausing for a moment to glare at the empty Model A, back under the cottonwood since Dale and Ma had returned, he made his way inside to find the canned peaches Ma had brought back, and the sweet juice they contained.

After darkness fell, Hardin once again sat on the steps, his supper already gone cold. The kitchen windows glowed, lighting his little perch. Inside, he could hear Dale's voice, low and gruff, Ma laughing at something Ben said, and boots scuffing across the floorboards. The hiss of the iron followed as someone pressed a shirt collar straight. They were getting ready to leave, and the plan was to leave at first light.

They were going to leave without Hardin. Again.

When Ma had been plating up the beans and cornbread, he had asked once again if he could go with his brothers. No one had said outright that he couldn't—not this time. They just hadn't said anything at all.

He'd asked once, quiet, meek as he knew how. Dale had not even looked up. Ma had just said "Let's not do this tonight, Dinny."

So that was it. Again.

The Model A squatted in the dirt ahead, only its worn tires illuminated by the light from the house; those tires taunted him. Where they could take him to see the world, they trapped him here like some sissy. Dale and his other brothers could go wherever they wanted on those tires while leaving Hardin here.

The boy reached into his overalls pocket, where his fingers found the handle of his knife. He stroked it as he considered the car.

One car. Four tires.

He pulled out the knife as he stood, walking in a crouch toward the Model A. Casting one last glance over his shoulder at the house to make sure no one was at the window, he crouched low near the rear tire. Licking his lips in an attempt to wet them, Hardin unfolded the blade with trembling fingers. His heart pounded so loudly, he could scarcely hear anything else.

"Next year," he whispered.

Slowly, he pressed the blade in. It didn't go easy; Hardin had to push then twist. A hideous hiss, like a rattler in the sage, sounded, soft and angry. Then, the tire sagged low into the dirt.

Moving on to the next one, he pushed the blade in again, again, and again. With each tire, the bone handle grew hotter in his hands, that same heat flooding through him, rising into his face, and gripping his heart like a wild thing that would never let go. Tears flooded his eyes.

Someone in the house laughed.

The tears spilled over then, stinging, as he stood and examined his handiwork. The old Ford was even more pathetic than ever, slumped in the dust like the coyote Floyd had trapped just weeks gone, legs splayed, lifeless.

From inside, he heard Ma's voice call out, "Dinny?"

Hardin gasped. His pulse raced in his ears, throbbing. Suddenly, he felt as though he were sinking down, just like the recently crippled Model A. *What've I done?*

With shuddering breaths, he sprinted away from the car, away from the house, and toward the shed. As he often did when he needed to escape, Hardin clambered up the woodpile against the dilapidated building and onto the tin roof. There, he curled into a ball and squeezed his eyes shut.

Dale's voice sounded then, booming, obviously from the front door. "Dinny, you out here?"

The heavy sound of boots descending the front stairs sounded, followed by a single loud curse. The screen door banged open then, and more feet followed.

"Dinny, you dope! What did you do?" Ray cried.

"The tires!" Floyd chimed in. "Told ya he was too little for that knife!"

"When we find you, Dinny, we're gonna kill you!" That from Ben.

With every word, Hardin curled in more tightly on himself, desperate to disappear, maybe forever.

The screen door thunked open and closed one more time. "What's going on—" Ma's voice cut off abruptly. "The tires," she said softly, barely loud enough for Hardin to catch the words from his hiding place.

His brothers then continued on, hollering and occasionally cursing, carrying on about the tires. The shouts grew farther and farther away, like thunder on the other side of a canyon.

Taking a deep breath, Hardin let himself drift.

In his mind, the fair rose up from the dry earth like a dream—the lights, the rides.

Music and laughter filled the air, the kind that made you want to dance, or jump and whoop. He imagined strolling the midway, with hands in his pockets. Maybe the vendors would come out, offering him their goods, just for looking hungry. Peanut brittle, cotton candy, a corn dog.

He imagined the rodeo ring, the broncs kicking clods of dirt into the sunset, the announcer yelling names into the microphone, while the scent of horses and popcorn and sawdust mingled in an intoxicating brew. His brothers would be in the stands, pointing and clapping.

That's our kid brother. They would cry. *He's the one who wrangled that lamb by himself last spring. He's the one who built the sling for the broken fence gate. He's tougher than he looks!*

Then he'd nod, not smile—just nod, like it wasn't a big deal. The crowd would cheer, and then—

The tin roof gave way when Hardin shifted his weight, and he fell, and the dream shattered in a burst of agony and panic.

He hit the dirt hard. A white-hot pang of agony burned through his arm when he landed on it, and he cried out.

"Dinny?" Dale's voice, still gruff with rage, sounded from somewhere nearby. Although it was hard to see through the pain, Hardin could still pick out Dale's shadowy silhouette approaching in the darkness. "Dadgummit, Dinny!"

The sound of racing boots through the dirt, then Ma was kneeling beside him, with Dale pacing over her shoulder. The wind ruffled her wavy hair, which was exactly the same shade as Hardin's.

"Arm's broke," she declared after a moment.

Floyd bent over Hardin as well, hands on the well-worn knees of his Levi's. "Boy's white as a sheet."

Ben and Ray arrived. The latter frowned. "What happened?"

"He fell off the roof!" Dale muttered.

Ben gasped. "Look at his arm!"

"We need t' get him to a doctor," Ma said grimly. "Probably needs a cast. We can't mess this up."

"How exactly we supposed t' do that after what he done t' the car?" Dale snapped. "Don't have what we need for one patch, let alone four, and who knows how long it'll be before—"

"I don't want t' hear another word about the car. Saddle up Red and Scout. Take Floyd. Ride t' the Jenkins's place. See if Frank's still got that old truck. Tell 'im I'll trade him eggs for a month if I have to!" Ma said fiercely, gripping Hardin's hand on his good side.

Gazing up at his family gathered around him, tears misted Hardin's eyes again, but not because of the pain. The pain was terrible, probably the worst of his life, but…

Dale and Floyd sprinted away, toward where the barn and the horses waited, to do as they had been told. He heard the dull thuds of hooves on dirt when the pair exploded from the barn, galloping off into the night.

Ma smoothed a lock of Hardin's hair from his face while they waited, and sent Ben for a bucket of water and a rag, which she draped across his forehead.

What seemed forever later, he heard the rumble of an engine, and twin headlights fell on where Hardin lay, shuddering with pain. Metal doors slammed, then Dale and Floyd lifted him from his mother's grip. Although she had made sure to drape his bad arm over his belly, it still felt like what those tires must have felt when Hardin stabbed each one of them with his knife.

His brothers laid him on a thin tarp in the flatbed of the truck, while Ma ran back to the house to fetch a quilt. Dale and Ma piled in back with him while the others climbed into the cabin to get underway. The boy bundled in the quilt blinked up at the stars, trying to focus on anything but how the movement of the truck jostled his arm around as it rumbled over the uneven track that would lead them into town.

Dale sat on one side of him, Ma on the other.

"You're lucky you didn't crack your skull open," Dale said dryly.

Hardin said nothing.

Not looking at him, Dale rested a hand on Hardin's shoulder. "You scared the hell outta me, kid. Y'know, I'd rather have you 'round."

"Really?" Hardin whispered.

One corner of Dale's mouth lifted in an almost-smile. "Really."

"What about next year?"

"Next year?"

"Well, you know. Can I come next year?"

Dale barked a laugh. "You still on about the fair?"

"Well, yeah," Hardin said, looking up at Dale.

His big brother met his gaze and said, "Next year it is."

"Next year it is," Hardin echoed.

About the Author

Tiffany Brazell is a writer, visual artist, and full-time dreamer with a BA in Fine Art from the University of Utah. She's the author of *The God's Game Series*, a high fantasy adventure filled with mystery, magic, and heart. Whether she's crafting stories or painting worlds, Tiffany's work is all about transformation, resilience, and finding light in the shadows.

When she's not creating, you'll likely find her under the sea on a SCUBA dive, enjoying her menagerie of pets, or sharing quality memes.

Learn more at: thegodsgame.com

THE GIRL AND THE STONE

by Morgan J. Muir

SILENCE LAY OVER THE WAR CAMP like a blanket of chilling snow. The sounds of battle had long since stilled, as had the voices searching for survivors, replaced by prowling scavengers. The girl had not dared to leave her place within the Lady General's tent, even when the brazier had burnt out.

Hunger pulled at her guts as the night stretched on. Or was it fear? The girl squeezed her eyes shut, pulling her knees more tightly to her chest. How much longer before she didn't have to feel it anymore? The tent wall pressing against her bare arm radiated warmth and light, a stark contrast to the frigid ground beneath her. The wall's rough fabric irritated bruises still fresh from her latest disappointing behavior.

The wooden frame of the tent twisted as a large creature scraped against the far wall, its long, predatory shadow blocking the light as it passed. A stiff wind broke open the door flap, setting the Lady General's banners and decor to life. The wind stole the last of the tent's meager warmth, and momentarily stilled the buzzing of the flies that dared to eat the Lady General's food, before slinking away. The bitter scent of smoke and overripe food swirled about the girl, making her stomach clench tighter.

The girl clutched the pouch hanging around her neck above her small chest. Within, the edges of the small pyxis-coin pressed back against her fingers, proclaiming her property of the Lady General. Anyone she showed it to would be obligated to help her return to her place.

The magic of the pyxis itself, a tiny orange gemstone, tingled against her skin even through the cloth. In the half-dozen years she'd had to wear it, she'd never grown used to its feel. A leash that held her as securely to the will of the Matron as any leather strap, and far less easily broken. The magic did not allow her to break contact with the coin, nor to disobey her mistress. The Matron expected the meal to be ready for the Lady General's triumphant return from battle, and that included the nameless servant girl waiting to attend her.

Obedience meant survival.

She was not to leave the tent.

Flickering light and shadows danced across the otherwise dark walls of the tent in crackling whispers. The air beside the wall grew warm, and the girl coughed. A skittering chirp drew her attention. She looked up, and for a moment the world around her spun. She steadied herself on the smooth wood of the Lady General's ornate chair and focused her eyes through the smoky haze.

A drakelette, with a body small enough to fit in the Lady General's cup, flapped in the doorway. Landing on the braided ropes, it paused and cocked its head as she caught its eye. The tiny dragon watched her with golden eyes, its blood-red scales glinting in the firelight.

She held her hand out to it, and it flapped, frightened, its claws tangling in the fine cords. The girl glanced to the side. Could she untangle it before the Lady's cat found it?

Holding her breath, she crawled forward across the thick fur rugs. The necklace that held the pyxis-coin swung forward, seeming to tighten gently around her throat at her disobedience. The drakelette's eyes flicked down to her necklace, mirroring its movements as she neared.

Cringing at the thought of the small creature pouncing her for the necklace, she tucked it back into her dress. The drakelette shuddered, as though only just realizing she'd entered its space. The little animal spit impotent tongues of flame at her as she untangled it, her fingers working quickly. It should be more careful if it meant to survive. Finally, its claws pulled free of the fine rope.

The tiny, elegant creature hissed at her and flapped to the table, landing amidst the food. The girl hurried back to her place, tugging at the loose necklace as she watched the drakelette. She'd been ordered to stay put to wait on the Lady General's return.

The girl did as she was told.

The drakelette, however, bore no such concerns. It snaked through dishes heaped with food, stopping to inspect a roast larger than its wingspan.

"You mustn't eat food that isn't yours," she whispered to the creature as her stomach again twisted.

The crimson drakelette looked at her and flapped its wings. She should shoo it away. The cat would get it if it didn't leave. Hesitantly, she crawled toward the table. Hissing again, the tiny dragon scurried to the other side of the table, scattering a carefully stacked pile of rolls. The stale carder bread fell to the floor beside her, and the girl's mouth watered despite herself.

Nothing was worth taking something not meant for you.

The backlit drakelette leapt onto a bowl of cubed fowl and the girl's breath caught in her throat. Didn't it know the food belonged to *the Lady General?* If he took it...

The girl's head swam at the thought. She could hear the Matron's voice, controlled and intense, berating her ever so calmly as flesh-tearing strokes fell across her back, the pyxis-coin holding her immobile. She was to do only what she was told, nothing more, nothing less. She must only eat what she was given, nothing more, nothing less. Didn't she know she was nothing? She didn't deserve the clothes on her back nor the breath she drew, let alone the food she was given. Not worth enough to even have a name.

She shuddered and pulled away from the roll.

Faster than she could track, the drakelette stuffed several chunks of the fowl into its mouth. Its cheeks puffing out, it flapped out of the tent and into the inky darkness.

The girl held her breath, waiting for the Matron to come in, screaming that the table had been upset, defiled. For the world as she knew it to come to an end. As it had six years before. Her lungs ached, begging for air, and her vision swam. Tanver smiled kindly in her memory. *Trust me.*

Softly, she exhaled, shoving away the memory. She inhaled, still breathing despite him. The smell of roasting meat filled the tent, stronger than before, and a small groan escaped her.

eat.

The light golden crisp of the roll's outer crust seemed to glow in the soft flickering light. She shook her head at the thought. She couldn't. No matter how much she might want to, she could not.

leave.

The girl raised her eyes to the tent flap. It thrashed in with another burst of icy wind, mirroring her agitation at the unthinkable. *Leave?* The darkness beyond flickered with movement, a dance of frightening shadows and orange light, accompanied by the pungent smell of things burning for far too long. The slight weight of the pyxis-coin seemed to push against her chest as though to keep her in her place.

Chill air snapped through the tent, cutting through the loose, thin dress that covered her. She shivered, rubbing her bare arms. She held no place in the world beyond the Lady General's quarters. She didn't even have shoes. The girl pressed against the wall of the tent, gasping at the unexpected searing heat. Something on the other side pushed back roughly, knocking her onto the soft rug. Blazing heat washed over her as the wall she'd been knocked from burst into flame.

leave. The thought came again, urging. Insistent.

She buried her face in the soft, pale fur as the tent above her burned. She couldn't.

leave. This time the thought seemed to echo with need, with despair.

A raspy shriek pierced the air behind her. Her eyes snapped upward to the table, now covered in flames, and she scrambled backward, crashing into a dresser. The rich scent of burning oak filled the tent. Terror lodged itself in her throat, and she froze.

Before her, the sleek, gleaming blue head of a dragon-like drake snaked its way over the table, spitting far more impressive tongues of flame than its minuscule cousin. The size of a small horse, and with teeth the length of the girl's fingers, the scavenging drake nudged the remaining food atop the burning table, ignoring the flames. Around its neck glinted a metal collar with a foreign sigil.

please, the thought came again. *leave. help.*

The girl glanced at the night full of unknown horrors beyond the door of the burning tent. The drake shook its long, elegant wings then lunged at the food atop the table. Its gleaming teeth crunched through the bones of the roast.

It would snap her in pieces if she moved.

help.

She nearly laughed out loud at the request, but it caught in her throat. The pyxis-coin weighed down against her neck, telling her to stay. She couldn't even help herself. The blue drake cocked its head, turning toward her. Her heart stopped as fear rushed through her frozen body.

A second drake, this one glinting gold and green, crashed into the tent, shoving the blue aside.

now. RUN!

The girl did as she was told.

Unsure of where she meant to go, she bolted into the darkness, dodging around tents in flames and fallen obstacles. Her hand gripped the silk pouch of her pyxis-coin, holding it away from her neck. Her bare feet pushed against the slick ground. Turning a corner, she froze at the sight of two more drakes tearing at unrecognizable shapes.

With a silent sob, she darted to the side, and her feet tangled, pulling her to the ground. Her knees hit hard against cold metal, and her hand and elbow landed on something soft. She pulled away before her mind could register the smoldering form she'd landed on. Scrambling to her feet, she bolted between a pair of still-standing tents. Her heart pounded in her ears, obscuring the sounds surrounding her.

this way. The thought pulled her to the left, and she ducked into a half-fallen tent, its sharp, acrid scent overpowering in the smoky air.

Her eyes blurred as she collapsed against an overturned workbench, her skinny arms wrapped around her bare legs. Sobs choked out from her chest in silence. Always silent. She was not meant to be heard. Those without names were not worthy of being heard.

The cord that held her pyxis-coin seemed to tighten around her throat, condemning her disobedience.

Panic gripped her. She had left. She had left the tent. She should not have left. The Matron would have her hide, then make her serve with a coarse-grit under-tunic against her broken flesh beneath her thin dress. She had left. She had left.

breathe.

She gasped for breath. She did not deserve breath. She had disobeyed. She had left.

breathe, child.

Darkness surrounded her, a weight on her chest she could not push against. Panic clawed through her mind. She did not deserve breath.

BREATHE.

The girl did as she was told.

Relaxing her throat and pulling at the loose cord around her neck that held her pyxis-coin, she gasped in a deep, cool breath. Her vision returned, along with a single pounding thud of her heart in her chest. She lay shaking in the cold dirt, her back pressed against the overturned workbench.

focus now. The thought nudged her gently. *breathe slow. calm.*

She pulled in a careful breath, and then another, and her body began to relax. Cautiously, she pushed herself back into a sitting position and whimpered at the burning that seared across her left arm. She examined it in the flickering light of the burning camp. A large red weal gleamed, reaching from her wrist past her elbow. Dark specks of dirt now dotted the newly burned flesh. She tried to brush them off and whimpered at the pain.

help? The thought felt more like an offer than a request this time.

She shuddered. She had no way of helping herself.

An image came into her mind of a squat green jar with wavy sides. *find. douse.* The thought felt weak, tired.

She shook her head. She was not to do things on her own.

The image flickered in her mind like a guttering candle. *try.*

The girl looked again at her hurt arm. It burned, as though still held in a fire, and tears formed in her eyes. She took a deep breath, coughing at the smoke. She needed to be calm and think.

The firelight glinted across something green, catching her eye. The girl found herself reaching for it, despite herself. She paused, afraid to touch it. She mustn't touch things that hadn't been given to her.

give. The voice seemed exhausted. *given*.

The girl hesitated. The voice in her mind felt strange. Foreign. Even with her connection to the Matron through the pyxis-coin, she'd never been spoken to directly this way, though she'd heard of such things happening. Exhaustion pulled at her. Did she dare trust the voice?

She bit her lip. The voice had told her to disobey, to leave the tent. But it had also kept her alive when she'd obeyed. Her arm ached again and she again considered the green bottle. She *had* been told to use it, and the voice said it was given.

Obedience, not trust, meant survival.

Another beast crashed through a nearby tent, trumpeting his call, followed by a far-too-human scream. Without thinking, the girl snatched up the jar and retreated back to the workbench. She pulled the lid open with her teeth, and with shaking hands, poured the viscous fluid onto her arm. She bit her lip to keep from hissing with the pain, but the burning ebbed away, replaced with a gentle chill along the skin.

help, the voice again asked, despairing. *find*.

Find? Find what? The girl glanced around the dark ruins of the tent. There were so many strange things she'd never seen before. How could she find anything? Her eyes came to rest on a splintered chest near where she'd found the salve, and she knew. She looked away, unwilling.

Another wind pushed through, chilling her salved arm until it again seemed to burn. She found her attention drawn back to the chest. The voice had stopped her from burning. Perhaps it feared it would burn as well? Holding the jar tightly to her chest, she took a deep breath and crept forward.

The fine, dark wood of what had once been a chest bound with steel and set with softly glowing emeralds lay in crushed shards. The force that would have been needed to twist the metal away from the wood made the girl shiver. Careful not to touch any of the emeralds—she knew well the price of even brushing against a trap pyxis—she moved the shattered wood aside. Beneath, almost invisible, lay a black pouch large enough to hold the Lady General's cat, if anyone dared try to catch it.

help, the thought repeated, urging her to pick up the black pouch.

The girl hesitated. Whatever it was, it did not belong to her.

Anger swirled weakly around her, receding once again into its plea for help.

Taking a breath, the girl snatched up the bag, heavier than she expected for its size, and scurried back to the shelter of her workbench.

She ran her fingers across the silken bag, feeling the smooth, solid contours of the object within. Did she dare open it? Would it eat her soul if she did? Tanver had always said never to trust anything that could think for itself.

The girl's throat caught at the thought and she coughed to clear it, shuttering her mind. Memories were worth less than she was.

The voice in her head seemed to wait with bated breath, as though afraid she would put it back and not free it from the darkness of the bag. Well, what did it matter if she did or didn't? It wasn't any brighter outside the bag than in it. But she found herself loosening the strings anyhow. Setting her hand below the bag, she upended it.

A blue, oblong stone nearly the length of her forearm fell into her lap. Something inside her mind relaxed, like a muscle she hadn't realized she'd held clenched, a breath of air after too long under water, or a weight lifted from her neck.

Setting the silk sack aside, the girl ran her fingers over the flawless stone, entranced by the texture. Smoother than the silk, smoother than water, or the wind against her cheek. How could anything feel so smooth that she wasn't certain she actually touched it?

The voice seemed to sigh in her mind at her touch. The stone warmed in her palm and the strength of the voice grew like an ember in a breeze.

"Are you eating my soul?" she whispered.

no.

She wasn't sure she believed it.

She turned the blue stone to catch the firelight that twisted through the camp outside her collapsed tent. The flickering light caught in the details of the stone. The sky-blue of her first glance deepened the longer she watched, darkening into the center of the large stone, swirling with flecks of reddish-gold. It seemed to churn and twist, drawing her deeper into its velvety depths.

Something large crashed into the frame of the fallen tent, knocking the table askew and breaking her gaze. The girl gasped, clinging to the stone as she moved with the now-broken workbench, unwilling to give up her shelter.

escape.

She regarded the stone and shook her head. Survival came first.

eat. The stone seemed to press against her mind, reawakening her previous gnawing hunger. *survive. then escape.*

She nodded her agreement.

The girl peered out from her shelter beneath the workbench. The words seemed simple enough. Eat. Survive. Escape. But the hulking shapes of scavenging drakes, with their glinting collars, made the words seem as solid as the smoke swirling around her. How could she possibly do any of it?

eat first.

She scanned the destroyed camp. Eat what?

find food.

Where could she get food here? She scowled. What was she supposed to do? Take her pyxis-coin and show it to a drake in return for some food? She clutched at the pouch that held it around her neck.

food place?

Ah, yes. The mess wagon. Sarcasm edged her thoughts. The world burned down around them, but the mess wagon would be untouched.

The stone sent her a pang of annoyance, and she immediately drooped, regretting her attitude. She ought to just do as she was told. The girl peered out into the darkness again, listening.

Scuffling mixed with the snapping of the fires' distorted sounds. Smoke wafted through the camp, obscuring possible landmarks. She wouldn't know which way to go even if she knew where she was.

But she had to try. Excuses were never tolerated. The girl took a deep breath. Undersized dragons or no, she would do this.

Amusement emanated from the stone in her hands, and she crawled out of the tent.

Wreckage and bodies lay scattered across the ground, and the girl hunched her shoulders, trying to appear small and unnoticeable in her pale, thin dress. Clinging to the sides of any object larger than she was, she crept forward. She stepped carefully, attempting to avoid sharp rocks in the dirt, or anything else that might cut her foot, the stone held tightly to her chest.

foot protection? the stone suggested when she stubbed her toe for the third time.

She shook her head. Where would she find shoes here? Hadn't they decided to find food first? Another stiff breeze tore through the camp, and she shuddered in the cold, her scrap of a dress incapable of any real protection. Next, the stone would be insisting she find something warm to wear.

not hurt, the stone said wryly.

She shook her head, stepping carefully over the fallen soldier before her, envious of the thick furred coat he'd been assigned by the quartermaster.

then take, bare one.

No. It wasn't hers.

take, the stone insisted.

She shook her head, dropping into a crouch beside the corpse as her stomach churned at her disobedience.

TAKE!

The voice seemed to push through her soul, impatient and angry. The Matron's voice echoed behind it, tempting her to see if she'd learn to obey. Obey and be punished for disobedience.

The girl held the stone tightly to her chest, clutching it with both hands.

"No," she whimpered.

The stone sighed, retreating from her mind, leaving behind a tang of sorrow. Of remorse. He—she decided the voice felt male—hadn't meant to hurt her. Only to help.

She turned away from the corpse and crept forward into the collapsed tent the fallen Elite had guarded. Shreds of the tent fabric brushed against her.

for feet? the stone again suggested, and she paused.

It was just scrap, after all. Ruined. Worthless. Like her. Perhaps it would be all right for her to use it?

Holding her breath at her own audacity, the girl tore the cloth free and glanced around in the flickering darkness for the hand that would strike her down. When none came, she hastily wrapped it around her bruised foot and up her ankle. Her heart again in her throat, she did the same with her other foot.

search for food? the stone suggested.

The girl backed away from the collapsed tent for a moment, trying to get her bearings. Black and green ribbons that had once hung down the sides of the door now lay crumpled in the wet ground. But she knew now where she was.

She'd seen this banner from within the Lady General's tent and knew the mess wagon would be nearby. She shuffled quietly through the darkness. Though she had rarely been allowed to leave the confines of the tent, the Matron had instructed her on the camp layout. The girl needed to be prepared in the unlikely event the Lady General ever needed her to fetch anything. Typically, others were used for such things. Others who were allowed out beneath the sky. What need would a girl without even a name have for open sky?

The girl's feet slowed as she raised her eyes. Had she ever seen the sky at night? Her eyes rose higher, past the distant sparks of light that sputtered and burned. Past the illuminated ridges of the many drakes still shuffling through the camp downslope. Beyond, dark trees stood against the darkness, a pale grey gleaming from branches slightly less black than the space before and behind them. Colors she knew no name for.

Were they nameless like her?

Or did they have a name she simply didn't know?

The stone in her hand seemed to warm at the thought.

The girl lifted her gaze higher to the open sky. The pale light of the smallest moon on the western horizon darkened the sky around it. The scope of the darkness before her seemed enough to consume her, but as she raised her eyes further, pricks of light appeared, gleaming and sparkling. The longer she looked, the more light appeared, filling a sky that before had been nothing but darkness.

Tears blurred the starlight in the girl's eyes.

come, the stone said, breaking gently into her thoughts, his voice mirroring the yearning within her. *you must eat*.

The girl lowered her eyes and turned away from the vast beauty above her. Darting again to the ruins of the next tent, she paused in its shadow to glance once more at the sky.

The mess wagon lay on its side, surrounded by drakes. Two smaller ones tore at its slatted sides, snapping at each other. A third lay across the top, the flicking of its ruddy tail and the glow of its golden eyes the only thing to indicate life. Several more lay in lethargic heaps around it, but a few still pulled at and crunched through their prizes.

The girl peeked around the corner of the quartermaster's ruined wagon, checking the scene again.

there is food elsewhere, the stone reminded her.

She sank to the ground, the weight of the pyxis-coin digging into the back of her neck. It was useless. She was useless. The battlefield stretched out behind her, as full of flame and drakes as the camp before her. She would die here. She should not have left the tent.

come. The stone nudged her on, past the drake-infested wagon.

The girl walked blindly, following where the stone led. She stepped numbly over and around the shapeless forms, outlined in pale silver moonlight, scattered across the ground.

here, he said, directing her under an abandoned, overturned hay wagon.

Drakes don't eat straw, she thought numbly as she crawled in, the hay and dust tickling her nose. But fire did. If the drakes came near, she'd burn. The pyxis-coin felt hot against her chest, as though to show her how she might burn. A giggle escaped her lips. She wasn't much good for burning either. Worthless. Nameless.

As her mind wandered, the stone tumbled from her hands, landing hard on her foot. The pain jolted her awake, even as the magic of the pyxis-coin flared, pulsing through her. Biting her lip, she scrambled to catch the blue stone before it could roll into the shadows. Scooping it up, she pulled in a ragged breath as the pyxis-coin's magic withdrew. She had let herself get careless. She'd not had such a harsh reminder directly from the pyxis for a long time.

The girl pushed herself into the darkness, her sore back pressed against the wagon's broken slats. Another rush of chill wind moved past, but only a wisp of it reached for her beneath the wagon. The girl shivered, holding the warm stone tight, afraid of dropping it again. What if she lost it?

found, the stone said sadly. *used.*

She looked into the deep, swirling pattern of the blue stone. Within, she could picture what he meant. Soon the drakes would leave, called back to their masters, and other humans would enter, scavenging for anything of value that remained. Someone would walk by, their shoulders hunched and cautious. They would pass by at first, but an unearthly blue glint would catch their eye. They'd pause and turn, reaching with the mad gleam of treasure-hunger in their eyes. They'd know the instant they touched the stone they'd found the treasure they'd longed for their entire life. They'd straighten, their shoulders no longer slumped, their face, full of greed, now triumphant as they held the blue stone to the sky, crying out their glory.

Without warning, a blade or an arrow would strike them down.

The girl started at the unexpected sight in her mind, and tried to turn away, but the vision held her.

Another would come and claim the stone. Perhaps this one would be more cautious, glancing around and holding the stone close. But it would glint blue, and the holder would drop as death stole over him. The stone would fall from unfeeling hands, only to be caught up again by another with a face twisted with the same evil.

The cycle continued, faster as the bodies piled up beneath the shining blue stone, each falling as it sought to use the power contained within.

The vision ended and she shuddered, pulling the stone closer. To be used for such things, for so long…

"I'm sorry," she whispered, her voice cracking in the darkness. She wiped a tear from her cheek she hadn't realized was there. The stone needed to be kept safe from such things. She should put it inside something to keep it from being seen. The girl glanced around for anything to hide it in, but she had left the black silk bag where she'd found it. She had the cloth around her feet, now covered in mud. The stone was far too precious for such scraps. Her dress was hardly any better.

But she did have something.

The girl drew out the small silk pouch resting beneath her dress. It held all that was precious to her, and one thing that was *not*. Small enough to hold in one hand, she realized the pouch was far too small to carry the blue stone. But she had to try. Without removing the necklace from her neck, she dumped the pouch's contents onto her lap. A lock of her mother's hair—she could no longer recall what the woman had looked like—a talon found on the ground the first time the Lady General had beaten her for crying, and a tiny carved swan from Tanver. She didn't know why she kept the swan.

Last, she reached in for the pyxis-coin. She rarely removed it from its pouch, and never for more than a few minutes. The pyxis did not allow her to break contact with it. Gripping it firmly, she set her teeth and drew it from the bag, careful not to touch the orange pyxis-stone directly. She'd done that only once. The stabbing pain of immediate connection to the Matron had overwhelmed her young mind. Once was far too much.

As she pulled the coin from its protective pouch, her stomach writhed as though she pulled a sliver from her flesh. It came free of the bag with a sudden release. The size of her palm, edged with strange markings and set with the small orange pyxis-stone, the coin declared her property of the Lady General's estate. She had never needed to use it, but showing it would get her food if she was hungry and safe passage through towns.

It would get her home.

home?

She licked her dry lips, turning the coin in her hand. "Home is a place to belong."

belong?

The girl ran her hand over the surface of the smooth, blue stone. It calmed her, loosening the tightness in her chest as she watched the stars move within its velvety darkness. She set the pyxis-coin on her lap beside it. "I belong to the Lady General."

ownership. Contempt colored the thought.

She pursed her lips. Belonging and ownership weren't the same thing. "They care for me; I am safe with them." But the Lady General didn't actually care. Not about her.

i belong to the sky, and it belongs to me.

In that moment, her mind filled with the gut-wrenching sensation of falling. Squeezing her eyes shut, she clutched the stone closer. Behind her closed eyelids, an expanse of the palest blue surrounded her, and the soft, chilling caress of clouds slid past as she flew through them, her wings tucked up against her side.

Fear did not exist, only the thrill and certainty of her own power as she twisted through the air, minute adjustments to her wings and tail sending her into a corkscrew. Righting herself, she flared her wings, letting a blast of hot air lift her further. Resting on the vast thermal, she turned her face skyward. Stars shone through the darkening sky, glittering across her mind. Simple, pure joy at being alive filled her. More than she could ever hope to comprehend.

She sucked in a breath and collapsed against the boards, the vision dissipating from her mind. "What was that?"

Freedom.

Longing pulled at her heart, and despite everything she'd ever worked for, a tear slid down her cheek.

Freedom. A word she had tucked away in her mind, never to be used. Never to be thought of or longed for. Angrily, she wiped away the tear. Those who dreamed of such things were not to be trusted. They had betrayed her before.

you need food. The stone nudged at her again, this time showing her a satchel that lay nearby.

She stuck out her tongue at the stone, but her stomach growled. What would it hurt to merely look? Setting her things in the hay, the girl laid the stone beside them and crawled forward. She peeked out into the darkness, her ears alert for movement. The sounds of the fighting drakes, though still close, had lessened.

The satchel lay nearby exactly the way the stone had shown her, and she stretched, reaching for it. Her fingers touched the stiff leather strap, and she jerked it close, retreating back beneath the wagon. She made herself as small as possible in the corner, setting the impossible blue stone in her lap, and reached into the dark leather.

Her fingers brushed the smooth skin of a fruit, and the crackle of paper-wrapped bread. She pulled the bread out first, and the scent of sourgrain met her as she unfolded the paper and broke off a chunk of the loaf. She brought it to her mouth, hesitating at the rough feel of it on her lips.

it's yours, the stone said, nudging her forward. *a gift.*

He had shown it to her, leading her to it. That meant it was given. Nothing weighed against her, choked her at the thought of disobedience. Surely it would be all right.

Swallowing back her hesitation, she took a bite. The dry grains bit into her mouth as she chewed, but the tart, earthy flavor of the stale bread made her mouth water. Carefully, she re-wrapped the remaining portion of the loaf for later and slipped it back into the satchel. A few mouthfuls of stale bread was all she deserved. She had, after all, left the tent.

The girl's fingers brushed against the smooth skin of the fruit in the bag, and her hand lingered. A nameless slave girl didn't deserve fruit, except on rare occasions. She shook her head and withdrew her hand.

eat it, the stone whispered to her, and she found her hand sneaking back into the leather satchel.

Her stomach rumbled as her hand cupped the round fruit, its size and shape in the darkness proclaiming it an apple. She hesitated a moment more. Cherries or white-plums were one thing, but an apple was a treat beyond her.

you need it, the stone prodded. *We need it.*

Swallowing back her apprehension, she nodded. She could do what she was told. She pulled the apple from the satchel, her mouth watering in anticipation of the fruit. She'd eaten apples before— She cut off the thought but could not escape the memory of the last time she'd tasted the tart-tinged-with-sweet flavor of a soft yellow apple. Before things had gone so wrong.

Setting her teeth to the skin, the girl bit down. A satisfying crunch filled her ears and the flesh of the apple broke, filling her mouth and mind with a perfect sweetness and light. For a moment all her troubles and pains melted away, and peaceful warmth filled her cold, aching limbs. It was so different, so much *more* than she'd ever tasted.

Swallowing almost before she'd bothered to chew the crunchy apple, she took another bite. The shock of the sweetness was less this time, and the light and warmth began to fade. She chewed this bite more slowly before swallowing, mesmerized by the sensation of taste she had never dreamed possible and enjoying the apple's thirst-quenching juice.

wild-apple. Recognition sounded in the stone's words, along with a sense of longing.

The girl froze, the apple poised for another bite. Her stomach recoiled. She could already feel the beating she would get, within an inch of her life. Perhaps, this time, beyond.

calm yourself, child, the stone said.

The apple fell from her numb hands as she heaved. Scavenged fruit was one thing. Even stolen fruit. But a *wild-apple!* Those were reserved for kings.

you did no wrong here. The stone's voice rubbed against her mind, smooth and soothing.

She shook her head, holding her stomach, but swallowed back her rising bile. "Wild-apples aren't for me."

ownership. The stone said it more calmly this time, but still tinged with disgust. *wild-apples are wild. they cannot be tamed. cannot be owned.*

In her mind, the girl could see the wild-apple trees, scattered throughout a forest far below, carpeting the mountainside. Her powerful shoulders moved, tucking her wings into a dive toward the closest one. The wind caressed her scales and the sun warmed her back as the forest rushed to meet her. Without thinking, she flared her wings, her muscles straining with life, fighting the everlasting battle against the pull of the ground, and once again winning. She trumpeted her magnificent victory as her spine twisted down to set her hind legs to the ground and flicked her tail across the underbrush. She stretched out her neck and delicately bit off the tiny wild-apple from the tree, glorying in its life-filling flavor.

even dragons love wild-apples. The stone's words brought her back to herself. To the cold, hard ground beneath her aching limbs and the chilling breeze that sneaked its way through the cracks of the overturned wagon. And the gnawing hunger within.

He nudged the girl again toward the fallen fruit. *they are for those who find them.*

She leaned forward, reaching for the apple, and wiped it clean. "Even those without names?"

is the wild doe named? He flashed her an image of a doe, flanked by two fawns, eating the windfall of the wild-apple tree. *she eats. she survives. it is her right.*

Steeling herself with the thought, the girl again bit into the apple.

The sounds of the scavenging drakes had, for the most part, stilled.

they sleep. The stone urged her to leave.

The quieter sounds of smaller things now moved through the camp.

human scavengers, he reassured her. She nodded. She'd overheard stories of this. They were likely survivors of the Lady General's army, come to quietly salvage what they could before the drakes woke and the opposing army overran the remains of the camp. Carefully, the girl gathered her things. The stone would clearly not fit in her pouch, so, with a tensing of her stomach, she returned the pyxis-coin into it instead and settled it around her neck.

She hesitated with the blue stone, its velvety star-strewn darkness swirling when she moved it. "May I put you in the satchel?"

The stone seemed to sigh, giving her a sense of oppressive emptiness closing in around her. *if you must.*

"I'm sorry," she whispered, setting him gently in the satchel among the uneaten bread, half a wild-apple, and other unexplored items. She settled the satchel across her shoulders, the stone's reassuring weight against her hip. Moving to the edge of her shelter, she again looked out. The sky began to lighten in the east, and the forms of drakes lay over everything, still but for their quiet breathing. "Will they eat me?"

i will not let them, the stone answered, whispering surety to her limbs.

Swallowing again, the girl crept out into the open. There seemed far fewer corpses now as she moved through the darkness, between the rows of ruined tents. Turning a corner, she stopped short. A drake the color of darkness lay before her. Its head, the size of a horse's, stretched across her path.

go over.

She hesitated, glancing around. Surely there was another route.

trust me.

The girl clutched the bag of stolen food. She had done this before. Had been asked to trust before.

Thunder cracked across the sky and the drake's eye cracked open, golden in the darkness.

forward, child.

She had been abandoned before. Left to face the wrath of the Lady General. Of the Matron. Her muscles trembled. She couldn't move forward. She couldn't breathe. He would abandon her. Always. She would be left to face it alone. Always alone. The tearing wrath, ripping her skin apart.

now, child!

The skies opened and rain filled the air as the girl spun away from the drake. Her feet slipped out from beneath her, and she landed hard on her knees in the mud. Without thought, she jolted to her feet and bolted forward blindly. Memories rose unbidden as she ran.

She had waited, as they'd told her. *Trust us.*

Promises of Freedom. *We'll take you with us.*

She needed only to wait for them with food sneaked from the kitchen. *Wait for us.*

They'd take her away from her dark hell. *Don't tell anyone.*

A cold hand had jerked her from her hiding place, and blow after blow had rained down on her.

Trust us.

His kind blue eyes, promising her freedom.

Trust me.

Abandoned.

The icy rain blinded the girl as she ran through the darkness, the leather strap of the satchel burning across her neck like a beacon, telling the world she had once again stolen food. The pyxis-coin shot pain through her chest as she pulled in gasping breaths.

Blindly, she ran into something, falling to the mud with a sharp cry.

"What's this?" A man's voice came from above.

The girl scrambled to her feet and ran a different way, the Lady General's soldier crying out for her to come back, that he wouldn't hurt her. *Trust me!*

She ran again, keeping closer to the fallen tents. She needed to escape. She needed to get back to the Lady General's tent before they found out. Before the pyxis magic could kill her.

A voice in her mind tried to calm her, to make her see reason, but she shut it out. It would only lie to her, like everyone else.

The smoldering remains of the Lady General's tent came into view, the skeleton of its frame lying askew across the charred remnants of the table. The girl bolted toward it. If she only did what she was told, things would be right. They would be right.

She crouched beside the still-warm coals of the Lady General's burnt-out table. She rocked with her head in her arms, waiting for the pyxis to accept her obedience. She would be safe here. Safe. Safe.

A hand grabbed her shoulder and spun her, knocking her off balance. She fell to the cold, muddy floor of the burnt-out tent.

"What do we have here?" The Matron's voice chilled the girl in a way the frozen wind could not. "A thief?"

The Matron jerked the girl to her feet by her dress, the rain whipping across them. The girl kept her eyes on the ground as the Matron tore the silk pouch with her pyxis-coin from around her neck. "Oh, it is only you," the Matron sneered, drawing the pyxis-coin out of the pouch. "Thinking you'll run away this time?"

The girl shook her head. Speaking was for her betters.

The Matron tossed the pyxis-coin at the girl's feet. The cold orange magic of the pyxis gem swirled gently around the coin, reaching toward them, as the woman jerked the leather satchel from the girl's shoulder.

Opening it, the Matron gasped, her voice a whisper. "An Intrigue!"

The girl sneaked a glance at the woman's face. Lit from below by the stone's gentle blue glow, the snarl of greed in her face frightened the girl far more than the sleeping drakes had.

please.

The Matron pulled the stone from the satchel, dropping the bag. "Tanver never admitted it, you know."

The girl stirred at the name.

"The Lady General killed him slowly, but he never admitted to including you in his plot to run away." The Matron caressed the deep blue stone, the hunger in her eyes foreign to the girl. "It's why you're still alive. I knew you were involved, but without proof, the Lady General gave you a living death instead. Too merciful, if you ask me."

The Matron turned her eyes to the girl, and the girl shrank from them. "Seems you were worth something after all." The Matron shoved the girl to the ground, an order in her voice. "Stay there and die."

The girl nodded, her eyes on the cold orange pyxis-coin. The sight of it weighed on her, pushing her into the ashy mud.

She would do as she was told.

please, the stone whispered to the girl, filling her with a longing for the wind beneath their wings. *help.*

The Matron stuffed the stone under her cloak, snuffing out the ethereal glow. The sunrise to the east glowed red beyond the storm.

The girl curled up on herself in the bitter rain as the Matron walked away. There was nothing left to do now but die. The memory of Tanver's kind blue eyes came to her as he held out his hand. *Trust me.*

Her body shook with the chill. She reached for the pyxis-coin, touching the cold metal that surrounded the tiny orange stone. Heaviness flowed from her arm into her body, weighing her down. Willing her to stop. Her shivers stilled as the pyxis told her body to stop fighting against the icy touch of the rain.

She watched the orange glow, unable to find the will to move her hand off the metal. The Lady General's mark was the promise of life. Tanver had not understood that. He'd sought escape. He'd left without her.

Trust me.

Inhaling, she moved her finger, brushing against the cold orange pyxis-chip. In that moment, the Matron's hate surged into her through the pyxis, a direct line to its source. It burned across the scars on her back and the wounds in her soul, and she jerked her hand back.

He had not abandoned her. The Matron had taken him. Had destroyed him.

And he had not abandoned her.

She had abandoned him.

Tears formed in her eyes, a warm contrast to the chill rain that stung her cheeks.

Anger, ignited by the depth of the Matron's hate, glowed within her. She inhaled, breathing onto the embers of her heart. Memories the stone had shown her swirled through her mind. Memories of Freedom. Of Life.

The girl had been told to die.

She would not do as she was told.

Grasping the pyxis-coin in her hand, the girl rose slowly to her knees and reached for the satchel. Within remained most of a loaf of sourgrain bread, and a half-eaten wild-apple. The rain soaked the bread, softening it as she ate. In the gentle glow of the morning light through the storm, the wild-apple gleamed a gold-streaked and brilliant red. She ate the fruit, and warmth and joy again filled her.

help...

The warmth of the wild-apple damped the Matron's burning hate that emanated from the pyxis-coin and wound its way up her arm. Sliding the satchel over her shoulder, the girl rose to her feet and followed the Matron.

The heavy rain washed the mud from her dress and disheveled hair as she pulled a tattered greatcoat from beneath a fallen brace. The pyxis, pressed directly to her skin, pulled at her soul, orienting to the Matron.

Nearby, three drakes slumbered together in a heap, radiating heat. One opened its eye, watching her as she pulled the coat around her shoulders. It yawned, exposing its dagger-sharp teeth.

The girl turned away, dodging to the side to follow the compass-like direction of the pyxis, pointing always to the Matron. She could hear the woman's voice now, spinning her lies about a child who refused to follow. The Lady General's soldiers, come to reclaim what they could while the drakes slept before the enemy army swept in, jeered quietly at the woman, encouraging her to resume her work. The drakes would rise with the sun.

Carefully skirting the sleeping drakes, the girl circled the soldiers in silence as the rain began to lighten. How would she get the stone away from them? Well she knew the Matron's strength.

trust me.

Are you sure you can't just eat her soul?

The stone's laughter filled her mind, warming her even more than the wild-apple could have. A grin, utterly foreign to her life, tugged at the girl's lips.

The group moved on, slipping through a narrow path between two destroyed wagons. The girl bumped into a precarious stack of crates, knocking them to the side. The soldiers paused, looking her way, but the Matron scoffed, continuing ahead.

A couple of the soldiers drew their weapons, a mishmash of swords and axes. One leveled his pike and muttered a wish for a spear and shield instead. The girl crashed into another bit of debris, crying out in pain this time, and fell into the soldiers' view.

They let out a general whisper of relief as she scrambled to her feet, her eyes wide and frightened. One of the soldiers motioned for her to be silent and follow along. The girl nodded, gathering her over-large greatcoat around herself.

One of the soldiers caught up to the Matron, taking her by the arm, but the girl could not hear what he said. The woman turned back, anger clouding her face through the rain. The girl stood up straight and met the woman's powerful eyes. She could already feel the blow she would receive for her defiance. *Help me!*

The stone reached out to her, reminding her of the power of her muscles, the way her wings could beat back even the earth. No simple *human* could hope to win against the two of them.

The girl stood her ground.

Rage filled the Matron's face like a black mist. She tore herself from the soldier's grip and stalked back to the girl.

Nearby, a drake let out a wakeful cry. The soldiers continued on, uninterested in anything but distance from the waking predators, leaving the girl to face the Matron alone. The pyxis pressed against the girl's palm made her arm ache.

As the Matron neared, she raised her hand to strike the girl, but the girl bolted forward as though to give the woman a hug. Instead, she reached into the cloak, guided by the stone itself, and snatched it from the woman.

The Matron cried out in rage, grabbing at the girl's greatcoat. Tucking the stone securely beneath her arm, the girl slipped free, kicking the woman's shin before she moved out of reach.

The girl straightened, wind lashing her hair across her face. She held the glowing blue stone out before her, taunting the Matron with its loss.

The woman screamed and leapt for the stone. Pain seared up the girl's arm and across her chest, demanding she fall where she stood. Instead, the girl turned and ran, dropping the stone into the satchel. She couldn't outrun the woman, but she would try.

Dodging debris, the girl ran through the mud, slipping as she turned. Pain seared her scalp when the woman grabbed her hair, jerking her head back. The girl fell with a cry next to a brilliant red drake, and the Matron's grip broke. They both froze, waiting to see if the creature would wake.

"Come here, child," the Matron whispered. "Give me the stone."

The girl shook her head, and the pyxis-stone in her hand changed, offering relief from its continued pain if she would only step forward.

"Do you even know what that is, girl?" The Matron gestured to the satchel.

The girl clung to the satchel, backing away with a glance at the sleeping horse-sized dragons. The magic of the pyxis chilled the bones of her arms as she moved, and she held back a hiss of pain.

"It's food whenever you want it. Warmth whenever you need it." The Matron took a careful step forward. "Wealth beyond imagining. We could share it, you and I."

The girl paused. What could possibly have that sort of power? Power so far beyond even the pyxis used to control and torment her. What would someone do with so much power? She reached for the stone with her free hand, its smooth surface warm beneath her skin.

ancient unchanging songs, the stone said with a sigh.

The woman stepped forward again, nearly within reach. "It would give us power. You could do anything. Be anything. It is freedom."

The girl pulled her legs in but didn't move further away. Her voice felt small as she asked, "Would I have a name?"

"Any name you chose."

The girl opened her hand, exposing the pyxis-coin. The Matron's eyes gleamed to see it. "Would I still be yours?"

"Always." The woman's voice seared through her, enhanced by her connection to the pyxis-coin.

She nodded. Setting aside the satchel, the girl stood slowly, the stone in one hand and the pyxis-coin in the other.

"I'm trusting you," she whispered.

The Matron's eyes gleamed, and she gestured the girl forward. "That's a good girl. Now, come to me."

The girl glanced at the drake beside her. Its green eye was open, watching her move. Her heart stopped for a moment as she waited for the creature to strike. Before her, the Matron grimaced and gestured her forward again.

the pyxis.

Slowly, the girl moved the coin, its magic pulsing through her arm. The brilliant green eye followed. Muscles bunched beside her, rippling across the orange scales in the pre-dawn light. She turned her face back to the Matron and raised the pyxis-coin. "Do you know what real power is?"

The drake's head shifted, following the coin, and the Matron froze.

"Freedom."

The girl threw the pyxis-coin at the woman, and the drake leapt after it, pouncing on the woman as she screamed.

The girl grabbed the satchel and ran without looking back. Eventually she slowed, letting the stone guide her around, and sometimes over, the stirring drakes, snatching up whatever fallen things the stone advised her to take. His calming presence soothed the lingering pain in her arm, and the sun broke over the distant mountains as they slipped into the shelter of the trees.

Hunger pulled at the girl's stomach, and she smiled, pulling an apple from her satchel as she walked. It wasn't a wild-apple—those were rare—but still, it was sweet. The chill breeze didn't cut through the thick cloak she wore, but she pulled it closer anyhow. It flapped against her back like trailing wings.

A rabbit scurried across her trail as she made her way up the mountainside.

"Do you suppose it has a name amongst its friends?"

all have names, the stone assured her, nudging her a little more to the east. *most are merely unknown.*

"What is yours then?" she asked, tossing aside the stem.

you already know, he said. *mine is yours.*

She smiled. "And what is that?"

Hope.

About the Author

Morgan J. Muir has always loved telling stories, especially stories with magic, hardships, and—eventually—happy endings. She is working hard on becoming a crazy cat lady and on curating her collection of hobbies. Morgan lives with her family in Utah. You can find more of her work at morganjmuir.com, and on Facebook @MorganjMuir.

THE ICE WALL

by Jentina Grey

WHEN I FIRST STARTED OUT on my chosen path, I had a vision of what I wanted to see, of who I wanted to be,

An ideal version of me who had climbed the mountains of success and who had done all the things I set out to do.

But the person who had done all those things was trapped behind a wall of shifting ice too hard to break through, too cold to be truly realized.

I could see the person there on the other side, her hand pressed against the wall of ice, wanting and needing me to break her free,

But the wall was thick, and my fingers were not agile enough to pick through it.

I wished and longed for some special something to help me be who I knew I was, to no avail.

But I kept coming back to the wall, day after day, with my wish, and soon I started beating my fists against the wall that held me back from that dream version of me, my highest self.

I beat my fists against that wall for hours that turned into days, and days that became weeks, weeks that became months, months that became years.

My fists were bloodied, my body was sore and tired, and I thought I couldn't keep doing what I was doing, for I had already done too much, for too little reward.

I rested my head against the ice and then turned away from the wall, seeking to return to the life I knew.

And a strange thing happened.

My fists didn't hurt so much after a while, rather they ached when they were idle.

And when I told my friends about where I'd been, they handed me tools to help me on my journey.

And the ice began to seem not so daunting, as I found my passion again.

I found that not only did everyone else believe in me, but that I also believed in myself.

I tripped and I fell many times, but somehow I always found a handhold again, and I pulled myself back up to the wall.

The ice fell away into first drops and then rivulets at my feet.

Those tiny wins drew me onward.

I kept at it, kept chipping away, kept smoothing out the sharp edges, kept finding new places in the ice to dig in, and I learned more about the wall.

It was both a barrier and a proving ground, a blockade to keep out those who did not have the will to tear down what was holding them back.

It grew easier and faster, or perhaps it was myself growing stronger and quicker, the longer I kept at it.

With time and effort, I reached a point where the ice flowed, not like water, but like waves: falling, crashing in on each other in harmonious rhythms of pauses, swells, and beats.

I kept working, until I was well past the place where I'd seen the me of my dreams.

When I brought my head up to look for her, she had moved farther away, and she waved at me from a place still distant, while my friends who had helped me faded away, fearing to tread the paths I had taken.

So I kept working at the ice.

At last, I broke through to the other side of the wall,

And I found myself completely alone.

I had done everything I'd set out to do, but here there was only me.

I shivered with cold.

There was nothing else to try for,

And the ice began to grow, closing in around me until I was nearly an icicle myself.

Having focused for so long on doing the task, I had grown rigid,

But I looked back at the path I'd made through that wall, a reminder of everything I'd gone through to get here.

And with hands that had become so accustomed to the ice, I began to chip away at myself.

The me I'd become was not exactly how I'd imagined myself in the dream,

But I could deny no part of this stranger, this stronger version of me, because every callus, every scar, had been necessary to build the me of my dreams into the me of reality.

Looking back, I realize that I had let myself become defined by the work I needed to do to get here.

And even now, the ice has a habit of creeping back in.

But at my core I am still me: warm, vibrant, and alive.

Sometimes I just need to brush the ice off.

About the Author

Jentina Grey is a speculative fiction writer and artist living in Los Angeles. She was born three weeks late, clutching a pen in one hand, and a book in the other. As an adult she creates the sort of art that gave her life at such a young age. You can find her first novella, *The Monsters We Save*, on Amazon.

Website: artofjentinagrey.wordpress.com

Facebook: artofjentinagrey

X and Instagram: thejennums

Rise Like the Sun

by Darren Lipman

YOASH SAT ON A THRONE of weathered branches over a court of nobody. Sunlight filtered through the verdant leaves around him, a golden halo on his soot-black shoulders. He had restored the land of the sun, and surely Aren was pleased with him, but he had failed to save his beloved from the fever that took her. Now he lived here in this forest of ghosts.

Though he had seen no ghosts yet.

But perhaps, if his beloved were anywhere, perhaps she would be here.

Yoash still carried a single droplet of the elixir of the sun. Perhaps it would be enough to bring her back, allow her to rise once more.

It was a hopeless endeavor, he feared: no one had ever returned from the land of death, if such a land existed at all. And yet, he had no other cause to live, so he set himself upon this path, and waited. Waited for the spirits to speak to him. For anything to happen at all.

"Aren," he said, throwing his head backward until he could see the glow of the sun straight above him. Light permeated a thin layer of clouds, and though it bore into Yoash's eyes, he could stare directly upon the celestial being. "Once dead, I restored your lands. Grant me this one reprieve: allow my beloved to return to me."

When his vision was brought near its end, everything washed out from the brightness, he faced forward again. The sun god was silent. Yoash had said these words a dozen times for a dozen days, and still no response. Perhaps it was as the seers said: the sun god was dead.

That lifeless sphere of fire in the sky was merely his corpse.

But this could not be! Yoash had been to the lands of the sun god, had painstakingly cleared the brush and grime that covered his altar, and had watched as the rain brought the last cleansing to the land. Sunlight sparkled in the lingering puddles. Fresh blossoms bloomed; a swamp turned to a forest as he prepared the elixir for the first time in centuries. Surely this could only mean Aren was alive again. Surely this meant rebirth was possible.

Or perhaps he was wrong. Perhaps the restoration of Aren's land was merely beautifying a grave, rather than raising the sun from one.

Yoash closed his hand around the stump of a branch that formed the armrest of his makeshift throne. His arm trembled as his grip tightened. Fire smoldered in the wood beneath his palm, and wisps of white smoke bled through his fingers and floated in the air. The pungent scent broke his stupor, and he let go of the branch, allowing the embers to fade to black.

Yoash had a special connection with the sun: he was a son of fire, bearing the spirit of one of the six elemental forces that constructed the world. He could incite a fire from touch, even thought alone—so why couldn't the sun be reborn the same way the ashes of a fire were kindled anew? Surely the sun was the grandest of all fire spirits. Surely.

Yet even if he could restore the sun, even if he had, his beloved was no fire spirit waiting for rebirth; she was human, and when human life ended, there was no return.

But sometimes, sometimes people said there were ghosts in this forest, so he listened for them. Yoash listened, but he only heard the wind rustling leaves and branches moaning as they bent in the breeze. He heard twigs crack as animals moved in the shadows out of sight; he heard frogs croak and birds chirp and insects buzz. But he heard no voices of the dead.

"Aren," he said again, bringing his hands together. A flame formed in the cup of his palms. "If I offer this entire forest to your blazing light, will that be enough to return her to life?"

He straightened his arms, the flame swelling in size until suitable for offering, but he could not bring himself to drop the fireball upon the ground. To destroy a forest in honor of the sun would be a tremendous deed, though he could not tell if it would be good or bad. Surely the sun god would relish the rising flames, but would he revile the destruction left in its wake?

Finally, Yoash let the flames die in his hands. He rested them in his lap, felt the warmth through his bedraggled breeches. He curled his toes in the dirt, tried to ground himself in the earth, but inside, the fires continued to rage. He had grown numb to them, but every day they surged inside him. Only time would tell when they would at last break free and burn through him, smoldering the flesh and scorching the bones, until he burnt out like a dying sun.

Yoash built a body out of broken branches laid out like a corpse. He wove vines through the wooden bones to form its muscles, and he sheared off the leaves with a thin knife before casting them into the wind. He cleared the surrounding earth until only dirt remained and then he stacked a circle of rocks around the supine figure. The sun had dipped beneath the horizon, and the only light came from a burning torch nearby. He would wait until morning to ignite the body. It would be useless in the dark.

The next day, when the sun rose high above the clearing he'd made, he snapped his fingers and conjured a flame. He touched the body's wooden face and stepped back as the kindling sparked, stuttered, and then roared. The flames spread from vine to vine and branch to branch, from head to chest to fingers and toes.

"Aren, lord of the sun, king of fire, arise, arise!"

He waited. The scent of smoke perfumed the air, tinged with the sweetness of fresh wood. And still he waited, repeating the chant again and again. Finally, a toe twitched, then a finger, then the body of branches pushed up its torso and struggled to stand. A pillar of fire engulfed the sun god as he stood before Yoash in the forest of ghosts.

"Who dares call me forth?" The voice of the flames crackled like lightning. Yoash trembled, heart thundering with sudden elation and hope, but afraid to embrace either.

"I am Yoash, son of fire, disciple of the sun. I cleansed your temple and restored the basin of elixir. I brought life back to your kingdom, and I ask that you bring life back to mine."

The flaming effigy crossed its arms. Cinders spiraled into the air.

"I am no god of life," Aren said. "Life came from the sea. You wish to see Merid."

"No," Yoash said and stepped closer to the ring of stones. "You are god of the living, who breathes the spark of life into mankind, who guards us in our daily lives, who—"

"Do not tell me who I am and who I am not." The flames roared, a conflagration suddenly soaring higher than the treetops. "Merid is the matron of life—"

"But she is a goddess of water." His voice came like a growl. "And I am a son of fire—it is to you, and you alone, I can speak."

The fire crackled like laughter. Dark pillars of black smoke stretched skyward. "I cannot offer what you ask."

"I ask only for you to bring back a lost soul," Yoash said, clenching his fingers into fists in desperation. "You are the one who ventures into the underworld each night. Surely you can find my beloved and bring her back to me."

"Death is not the domain of the earth," the sun god said. "You should seek Leyl instead."

"The moon means nothing to me." Yoash panted, sweat on his brow. "She is guardian of wind and air—my kinship with fire cannot bring her here."

"Is it not air that fire breathes to stay alive? And earth upon which it burns? You may be born of fire, but it is not the only element you can touch."

"That's impossible!"

"So is resurrection, yet you ask nonetheless."

Bits of burnt branches broke away, revealing the forge of white-hot flames where Aren's eyes burned brightest. The sun god smiled, a curlicue of a vine subsumed in fire, and then the entire body became ash that settled on the dirt, still spewing forth staggering clouds of smoke.

He had two weeks to wait until the moon was full, and Yoash spent that time scraping the underside of leaves for a fungus revered for its potency. Finally, as the moon rode full above him, the goddess Leyl at the height of her power, he sat amid the charred remains of the sun god's body, at the center of the stone circle, and lit the orange fungus. Pale white smoke wafted upward, the closest connection between fire and air he could imagine. He inhaled the spiraling tendrils; it smelled savory and made his mouth water.

Within minutes, his vision wavered. He swayed where he sat cross-legged in a pile of soot. He stretched out his hands and dug his fingers into the ash until he touched the ground beneath, stabilizing himself like the roots of a tree. He stared at the smoldering fungus, saw the last bits spark to life, then fizzle out. Yoash inhaled the final fumes, too deeply, and he coughed, spluttering. Smoke had never bothered him before. Why should this be different? Yet the coughing continued until finally, breath rasping, his chin fell to his chest.

Then something soft reached under his skin and turned his head upward. There she was, in all her golden glory, his beloved, Elena. She smiled, eyes glowing in the moonlight.

"Are you real?" His voice was gruff and scratchy.

"No," she said, her voice exactly as he remembered. "The only ghosts in this forest are your own."

Yoash licked his lips. They were so very dry. "Then how are you here?"

Elena chuckled. Oh, how he missed the sound!

"I am a reflection of your memory, just like the moon is a reflection of the sun, and the future is a reflection of the past."

"I don't understand."

"But you do, don't you see?" Elena squeezed his chin. How could it feel so real if she was only a figment in his mind? "You know deep inside you that I'm gone and cannot return. You know death has no remedy. Yet you seem incapable of making peace with any of this."

"I don't want to." Yoash felt tears spilling out around his eyes. "I can't forget you."

"One mustn't forget to move forward. Be like the sun, Yoash. He never turns back, always moving forward, and even after he vanishes into the dark of night, he returns. He rises again. Not because he has died and is reborn, but because he has always been alive."

"Maybe I don't want to be alive anymore. Not without you."

"But you are alive, and living you shall be—grief or none. You must live, Yoash. Rise like the sun." She brought her lips to his, kissed him hard, his eyes flitting shut. Elena withdrew her hand, and his head lolled against his chest.

When next he opened his eyes, the apparition was gone, and sunlight sprinkled the forest floor. He cried out and threw himself upon the ground, tears mingling with the dirt and soot until a slurry flowed around him, confined by the circle of stones. The mud caked upon his skin and dried beneath the rising sun. He writhed in the mess, and at last came to rest upon his back. Aren was at his full height now, staring directly down upon Yoash. Yet the man did not flinch.

"How can I be like you?" His words were harsh and hoarse. "How, Aren, how?"

His skin warmed as fire snaked around him. Once-withered branches twisted from the earth and bound him to the ground. The flames licked at their leaves, setting each alight; the branches began to burn like the body of the sun. Soon, Yoash lay amid the wildfire.

"The answer is easy," the sun god said. "You ask a simple question: you simply stand."

Yoash clenched his hands into fists; his arms tightened as he fought against the strangling vines. Even as they burned, they were as strong as steel chains.

"You rise like clockwork. You are a god, but I'm a man. I cannot do the same."

"Surely you can, Yoash." He felt the sun god grinning. "You are a son of fire, are you not? Be like the flames—consume not for the sake of destruction, but to grow and rise."

Yoash's muscles hardened as he pulled his arms together before his chest. The branches entangling his wrists snapped apart and were consumed by the fire. He sat up and reached for the vines holding down his legs but recoiled—the fire was too hot. Fire never felt hot to him. What made these flames different?

The sun god laughed, the sound like cackling wood, pockets of moisture rupturing apart.

"Sometimes what we hold dearest burns us most. Only by reaching through that pain can we go on."

Yoash felt tears on his face again, though he knew not how they could withstand the flames. He reached forward, and the fires around his legs seared straight through his flesh.

Yet he pushed on, closing his fingers around the fiery wood and pulling with all his might. It felt hopeless. Years of love for Elena fueled these flames, years of striving to earn her father's approval when he wasn't of noble blood, yet she was. If only her father hadn't kept them apart so long—if only he had returned to her sooner with the elixir of the sun— if only—if only—

The heat rose in intensity as he fought against the branches. More vines grew around his legs faster than he could pull them aside, and any moment now, he expected to see his hands reduced to ashen bones. Yet even as the flames burned, he saw his skin was not damaged.

The pain existed only inside him.

"I carry nothing." Aren's voice startled him; he'd forgotten the god watched him. "Only then am I able to rise with such ease each morning."

Let go. The unspoken words coursed through him, Elena's voice, though he couldn't recall if she had ever said the words in life or not. It did not matter now. None of it did.

He stopped tearing at the vines. He leaned into them as they crawled up his back and around his arms and gripped his neck like a finely-crafted chain. The searing flames followed its fuel, and he let the pain wash over him from his toes to his fingers to his forehead. He screamed in agony, fighting to hold back the dam, but then he heard Elena's voice again: *Let go.*

He stopped fighting, and the pain was almost unbearable, but he bore it with strength he did not know he had: a kind of strength separate from his body, even his mind; a kind of strength that seemed it must be godly, for he did not know from whence it came.

And then, after a moment of torture, the pain began to recede. The vines became ash around him, smoldering embers against his skin where all his clothing had burned away.

"Now rise, my son, rise like the sun."

The embers lit his skin like stars on the night sky, and they tumbled from his flesh as he rose to his feet. He looked skyward, straight into the beckoning eye of the sun god above him.

"I am healed," he said, "of a wound I feared would never close. Thank you."

"We burn as we must," the sun god said. "That is the path for the living like us."

Yoash felt Aren's presence slip away, and the sun was just the sun again.

His limbs felt heavy as he began to walk, stepping slowly out of the circle of stones. He had lingered far too long in this forest and was eager to leave it. He was a ghost no longer.

About the Author

Darren Lipman is an award-winning high school math teacher who hopes to become an award-winning author. His fiction has appeared in *Literally Dead: Tales of Holiday Hauntings*, *Space and Time* magazine, and other anthologies, most recently *Ashes and Embers*, published by Opal Kingdom Press. Darren lives in Milwaukee, Wisconsin, with his Alaskan Klee Kai, Hoonah, in a house full of overflowing bookshelves. Find him at thewritingwolf.wordpress.com.

BLURRING LINES

by Jason P. Crawford

THE SERVOS IN LILY'S ELBOW SPUN, the only sound an almost-imperceptible whine, as her bionic fingers guided her pencil along the curves she wanted. The figure emerging from the canvas stared back, the faintest silhouette of eyes searching Lily's soul, the thinnest lips touching her cheeks with a smile, almost daring Lily to smile back.

She did. She couldn't help it.

The sunlight came in angles through her studio windows, shafts of gold on dark wooden slats highlighting the dancing dust. Lily's green eyes narrowed, focusing in on the pencil's exact movement. The tactile receptors that fed into her brain mimicked the skin-feel of wood so perfectly that she could forget that the sensations needed to pass through three layers of interpretation before making it to her at all.

"Who are you?" Lily drew another thin line to add just a bit more detail, and the woman's eyeline shifted. The expression now held the hint of a challenge. "What're you smiling for?"

Sweat gleamed on Lily's brow and threatened to drip into her eyes, but she couldn't stop to wipe it away; these were the critical moments, the formative steps of genesis that would make the painting...or break it. Here, a dip of the ear; there, the beginnings of the chin. Just a few more pencil strokes, and she could—

On the desk, two arms' lengths away, her phone buzzed. Lily's limbs twitched, a reaction to her surprise, but she stilled them with a thought. The wayward sweat bead began to roll, tracing a path down her face, so she put the pencil down.

Now that Lily's focus had broken, thoughts began to race. *I had it locked.* She always locked it when she was working. *Is it an emergency? Is everything okay?*

Lily realized that she had walked up to the phone without meaning to, artificial legs fulfilling her unconscious desires as effectively as her conscious ones. Taking a breath, she unlocked the device and checked her notifications. She had a message from her sister, Laurel; her heart ticked up until she read the message.

Lily! Check it out! You did it, girl!

Frowning, Lily clicked the link. A press release for the Emil Marten art prize.

Congratulations to our finalists this year! Andre Allard, Lily Horton...

She didn't get any farther before the phone fell from her hands.

"We wish to congratulate our three finalists and wish them well as they work together to build, create, and manifest the true meaning of art and beauty here at the Marten Centre."

Lily's heart pounded, moving the blood through her torso and her head so fast that she could hear the rush in her ears. The Parisian autumn wind fluttered her long coat, flapping it hard enough that she had to hold it closed with her gloved hands. Her eyes danced on the assembled crowd, a bundled-up assemblage of onlookers standing in front of the podium. The nearly transparent orbs of two moons—forested Bora and oceanic Helos—hung in the sky, pale green shapes against the blue. The speech played its way through Lily's ears, the words making less of an impact as they went on because her mind couldn't hold them. Instead, Lily felt herself fighting to stay standing under the scrutiny of so many.

"So let's give them a round of applause!"

The roar of cheering and clapping hit Lily like a truck, shocking her out of her reverie; a smile stuttered on her face but did nothing to help with her tightening throat. She felt like a fraud, here with these other artists, all of whom she knew by reputation.

What was she even *doing* here?

As the crowd dispersed, the director of the Marten led the three artists inside. The warm, climate-controlled air began to melt the chill on Lily's face, and a tremor ran across her spine.

The director, an older man with smile lines and bright eyes, clapped his hands as the door slid closed behind him. The air changed, the circulation from outside cut off.

"That's the hard part done." He grinned at all of them, favoring each with a long stare. "I'm Paul Melin. I am at your disposal and looking forward to seeing what the three of you can make together."

Lily found Paul's joy to be infectious. Her nerves faded a bit, replaced by excitement. She allowed her eyes to travel around the forum, already imagining what she could put together, what paintings she could hang and where: a great battle on Helos between sea monsters and cosmonauts, perhaps, or a dark, cloudy sky stretched across the sea…

Another finalist cleared their throat, a staccato sound, before widening their almond-shaped brown eyes and opening their gloved hands. They flexed their fingers and pulled down their hood to reveal short, rainbow-colored hair. "How are we to decide what way we should divide up the space? What are the rules?"

Andre, a young man with pointed features, dark eyes and hair, and wearing a heavy coat, sniffed his runny nose before wiping it on a glove. He scratched at his head and raised his eyebrows in response to the other's question before speaking in a heavy accent. "Max, isn't it? Max Vilos?"

A nod and a raised eyebrow.

Another snuffle as he came closer, passing Lily on the way; she could smell his cologne, a powerful tobacco and sandalwood, and her nose involuntarily wrinkled.

"Good. Now, Max, I think we should all work together on making that decision, don't you?" Andre waved his arm around the space. "This is a joint effort, yes? Our work, together, makes the space great."

"That's all well and good, *Andre.*" Max crossed their arms and pressed their thin lips together. "But I'm hoping to *win* this prize, and I don't want my work mixed up with all"—they glanced toward Lily—"of yours."

"Please, now." Paul clapped his hands again. "The arguments of creatives are infinitely fascinating, but we need to have order and cooperation. Anyone who's obviously trying to sabotage the others, harass them, or fails to work well as a team"—he shrugged, still smiling—"won't be in contention any longer."

Lily swallowed. This would be the first time she'd had to work on a big project with anyone she didn't know, and the thought of losing her chance at the Emil Marten loomed large. She nodded along with the rest, glancing from one side to the other at her fellow finalists.

Max might be difficult to get along with, but Andre seems all right.

"Well then!" The joy returned to Paul's voice, and he began to back out of the doorway, ushering in another gust of chilly autumn. "And don't mind the cameras. When you're ready to leave, a driver will take you to your hotel." His words became harder to hear as the distance increased. "And remember…have fun!"

Despite the initial misgivings and shifty glances, the three finalists soon fell into a comfortable routine: coffee and tea, a light breakfast at Soleo's, then into the discussions and planning. Andre had a penchant for grandiose ideas and pronouncements, while Max did their best to ground the trio in realistic possibilities.

"What if I made a set of sculptures and set them up as if they were interacting with your paintings?" Max chewed on their sausage biscuit on the fourth day of the collaboration. "Andre could set up his stained glass for lighting, and we'd have a three-dimensional diorama of sorts."

Lily nodded, her gloved hands wrapped around the coffee mug, sensors in her artificial hands sending her the sensation of its warmth. The idea excited her; she could already see it in her mind's eye: a village, perhaps, with winding ivy and creeping flowers, dozens of people both in the pictures and out…

"I am surprised you are so willing to mix your work with hers." Andre raised an eyebrow, teasing. "What has come into you?"

"I can't win if I don't play along." They shrugged, putting the biscuit down in favor of their glass of juice.

"Be that as it may, I am not sure." Andre tapped his fork against his glass, the sound knocking Lily out of her thoughts and reverie. He dabbed at his lips with his napkin and smiled at the other two. It came sharp, as if he had forced it onto his lips. "It seems to make my contribution a bit…small, yes? A little…little."

Lily shook her head, the tension forcing her to concentrate part of her effort on maintaining control of her fingers and not cracking the cup. "No! Stained glass over the whole thing… You could put up the sun, or the moons and the stars along with. You'd be setting the mood for it all, the stage." She looked to Max for agreement and, finding it in their eyes, continued. "It'd be one of the most important parts of the whole composition, I think."

Steam drifted up from Lily's coffee as she held her breath, watching Andre's eyes as he pondered the idea. Max leaned back, putting their straw in their mouth.

"Hmm." Andre nodded, his smile softening now. He put the fork down and reached for his own cup. "I think—"

A loud *slurp* from Max's drink interrupted him. Lily turned to see Max's eyes wide and their lips pursed, almost frozen. "Sorry."

Three seconds and they all burst into laughter, Max sputtering their drink and Lily having to put her coffee down to keep from spilling.

"I like the idea." Andre nodded along with the hitching of his chest, and a real smile replaced the false one from before. "We will do this. Yes."

"Yes." Both Lily and Max said it at the same time, which just set off another bout of laughter, and this time they made no attempt to stop it before it ended.

Lily rose up onto her toes and went back down again as the robots brought in their supplies: paints, stone, glass, canvas, and all sorts of materials that the three artists would need to make their vision a reality. The nervous tension manifested itself in her bionic limbs, keeping them moving with a jittery sort of energy.

"I've...I've never really worked with anyone like this before." Lily had to push to get her voice heard, as it seemed to want to hide inside her chest and be ignored. "I'm really excited."

Andre made a show of turning his eyes up to the ceiling, but then grinned and clapped his hands, the sound echoing off the walls. "I have done many things with others. I will show you. It will be fun, Lily." He pronounced her name as if the *i* were a long *e*. "You will see."

Lily favored him with a smile. *He's so good at making things easier.*

As they talked, Max took charge of the deliveries, ordering the robotic couriers to one corner of the room or another, depending on what they carried. Supplies piled up, teetering stacks that made Lily's cybernetic fingers itch to fix them, which she did as soon as the workers had finished.

"Don't want any of this to fall. Don't they know how to stack?" She shook her head, mumbling to herself. As she moved a trio of canvases, her sleeves rode up past her wrists and revealed the transparent aluminum housing, whirring gears, and wires beneath. "They could have punched holes in these. I can't believe they weren't more careful."

Andre stared, watching her move. His eyes widened.

Lily didn't notice; she grinned at the other two artists, shrugged, then reached inside one of the boxes. "Just going to grab my pencils and get started—"

Andre's voice interrupted her, sharp and angry. "What is that?"

"What is..." Lily glanced back at him, and her eyes widened; Andre glared at her, fury writ deep in his face, in every line of his brow. He looked like he had just witnessed her murdering his best friend, and the rage wilted Lily in its heat.

"What's going on, Andre?" Max came over from their corner, carrying a new chisel. They tilted their head. "You look pissed."

"She..." Andre pressed his lips together and shook his head before responding. "She is half machine. Like them, almost...not a synthetic, but..." He cleared his throat. "A *thetic*. Her painting hands... She shouldn't..."

Lily stretched out her arms, causing the sleeves to ride up more. "I don't understand."

Andre took a breath, closing his eyes, lowering his voice. "Your arms, Lily. You are not...you are not playing fair, is the term." He lifted his own right hand and held it level to the ground. "Do you see? I tremble. I shake. Do you?"

Lily's stomach sank. She could see where this was going, but Max apparently didn't.

"What are you talking about?" they asked.

"The machine. The machine...it does not get tired, does it? It does not make a mistake." His tongue worried at his lips as he thought of the next thing he wanted to say. "It is not right, not in a competition."

Lily crumpled in on herself, her arms coming up in a defensive posture, but she took a breath. "I'm sorry if you don't like artificial limbs, Andre, but there's no need for accusations."

Max seemed equally confused as they took a step back. "Yeah. It's not her fault she needs robot parts, man. What's the problem?"

"The *problem*"—Andre took care to say the word precisely, even through his accent—"is that she is a *cheater*. A *liar*." He sliced at the air with his hand. "Even if she does not know it herself."

The words cut through Lily's remaining composure like a whirring sawblade. She felt her chest hitch, her emotions responding more to Andre's tone and vitriol than to the actual words he was saying. She knew that synthetic limbs and organs had been argued over in athletic spaces for years, with competitors boycotting events in protest of runners or players having artificial parts, but in art?

"We work so hard." Andre took a step toward her, all traces of his former good humor gone; his physical presence took on an ominous, aggressive feel. "To practice, to be precise, but you..." Another step, and his hand came up angrily; Lily backed up, but there wasn't anywhere to go except into the boxes behind her. "You just *think* and the machine does the work for you."

"What?" Lily couldn't believe what he'd said. "I've work—"

He interrupted her, now less than an arm's length away. "Go on, Lily." His nostrils flared. "Draw a perfect circle. Paint a perfect stroke. The machine can't do it wrong as long as you imagine it, right? And you're here with *us*?"

He turned about.

"It makes a mockery of all things we make! You put this...this *artificial* thing into the world, and they marvel at it, don't they? They say 'wow, what amazing shapes! Such technique!' But they don't know. Did you tell them, Lily?" Another turn, and Lily flinched at the pure anger in Andre's eyes. "Did you tell them it was all a sham-fraud? That you are—"

"That isn't fair!" Lily shouted over Andre's angry accusations. "I had to work too! It isn't like you think it is!"

Even as she tried to defend herself, Lily felt the automatic mechanisms in her limbs locking in, keeping her from using too much force accidentally, and the doubt shook her. *It isn't...right?*

Max stepped forward and put themselves in the way, putting a hand on Andre's shoulder. "Look, man. This isn't how to do this. Back off."

He did so, giving just the smallest amount of space. "I won't participate in this…this *circus* if they're letting in *thetics* to the competition." Andre crossed his arms, then strode toward the entryway. "I'm talking to the director. We'll see what happens."

Lily's all-too-organic heart pounded against her chest, fueled by the overflow of adrenaline. Her eyes watered, her breath fluttered in her lungs, and she couldn't see clearly for the tears. The room felt hot, stifling, and every route of escape, every action, felt equally impossible.

"Hey." Max's voice came calm and soothing, and they put a careful, cautious hand on Lily's shoulder. "Hey. I think…maybe you should head back to the hotel, yeah? Get yourself together. That was…that was rough." They took a breath themselves, throwing a look toward the door Andre had just passed through. "Go on. When the director or whoever gets here, I'll make sure they know your side of the story, okay?"

Lily swallowed, her head moving in a series of stuttering nods. "O-okay, Max. Thanks." Another shuddering breath. "You…you've got—"

"I've got your number, yeah." A gentle push toward the door. "I think he's far enough now that you can make it to the car."

"Yeah." Lily's legs moved as soon as she made the decision to walk, carrying her toward the door in smooth, even steps. And for the first time, she found herself wishing that she would stumble. "Thanks, Max."

The air outside, crisp and tasting like a mix of apple blossom and asphalt, chilled Lily's face and made her draw her coat up. As her arms moved, she scowled at them, at the wrists that had exposed the limbs' robotic nature. Why couldn't she have been more careful, more cognizant?

Then she shook her head and continued walking to her vehicle. Why should she *have* to hide them? If the contest had been in warmer weather, she might have—

No. Lily knew the lie even as her thoughts articulated it. She wouldn't have shown them off. She wouldn't have been comfortable with the questions or the looks she got wherever she went: Can they feel pain? How strong are they? How much did they cost? Did it hurt to get them put on?

As Lily slipped into her car, she leaned forward and began to cry. Red and orange leaves slapped against her windshield, driven by the strengthening winds, and then raindrops began to fall. The splattering sound blended with Lily's sobs, coating the windows with a sheet of water that obscured the world outside.

It wasn't until her phone buzzed that Lily broke away for a moment, bringing up the notification.

What are you sitting in your car for? Go. I'll meet you there, promise.

Lily turned her head to see Max standing in the rain, waving her off, and she snuffled the tears away as she nodded. Turning the engine over, she merged into traffic, leaving the Center, but not the accusations in her head, behind.

By the time Lily had emerged from the shower and set about peeling the waterproof coating from her arm and leg joints, her phone had exploded with notifications and calls: four from her sister Laurel, with accompanying voicemails, and three from Max, asking to set up a time for them to talk—maybe over dinner. Her alerts, tuned to any mention of Andre Allard or Max Vilos, had picked up several online news articles.

As Lily scrolled through, her eyes widened and her heart stopped. Her legs locked to hold her in place, an emergency measure caused by the sudden drop in her blood pressure.

Andre hadn't just gone to the director; he had gone to the press, to every online outlet he could reach. In the hour or so since he had stormed off, headlines like "Artificial Assistance in Art Competition Uncovered!" and "How Much is Too Much? The Recurring Question of Assistive Technology in Creative Careers" stabbed into Lily's eyes. Her image crowned many of these articles, along with biographical details. Each, to varying degrees, decried her as, at best, someone unfairly benefiting from her situation and, at worst, an active cheat.

Lily sat on the bed, phone clutched tightly in her hand; she could feel the resistance systems keeping her robotic fingers from crushing the device between them. Her world folded in, darkening at the edges, and she couldn't tear her attention away from the flood of notifications.

She read another, an article titled "Steroids for Art? Where Does It End?" The comment section stabbed at her; dozens of people calling her a fraud, a liar. Some wished they could find her and tear her limbs off: "We'll see what kind of art she does then!"

At last, Lily threw the phone across the room and heard it smash against the wall. A fraud. A liar. A cheat. Is that what she was? Was Andre right?

Lily's lips trembled as she moved toward the window. The city swam in the rainwater below, the clarity removed. She put a hand on the glass and stared at the gyros and servos, at the network of wires that translated her thoughts into movement.

Was he right?

Her fingers moved, drawing small circles on the glass. Perfect circles. She didn't have to measure to know; her eye could tell, could see the symmetry.

Was he right?

A knock at her door made Lily's heart thump harder, and she had to close her eyes in order to calm herself. She started toward the door before she realized she hadn't dressed, so she grabbed a robe and some pajama pants from her bag. As she put them on, the knock repeated.

"Be right there!" The back of Lily's mind noted that she didn't sound distraught or upset. "Just a second!"

A few moments later, Lily pulled the door open. Max stood on the other side, and Lily let out a heavy breath. "Oh. Hey. I—"

Before she could say more, Paul Melin, director of the Marten Centre, stepped up beside Max. In contrast to the last time she had seen him, Paul's face held no humor, only dour determination and a tinge of sadness.

"Good evening, Miss Horton." Paul nodded toward the room. "Can we come in?"

Lily spared a glance for Max, who shook their head a few degrees, eyes full of sorrow and frustration. "I-I guess so. Come on."

Paul scanned the hallway, then stepped inside, followed by Max, who closed the door behind themselves. The clicking sound made Lily feel like an animal in a trap, caged and waiting for the killing blow.

That's probably not too far from the truth.

The lump in her throat didn't want to let Lily speak, so she sat down in the desk chair instead, waiting for the hammer to fall.

And fall it did. "Miss Horton, I'm afraid that we have a…a situation." Paul's eyes fell on Lily's hands, her feet. "You are a th—a cyborg."

Him too? He got the name from Andre, didn't he? Rather than replying, Lily nodded. Blood flushed into her face. Was it embarrassment? Shame? Anger? Something else? She couldn't be sure.

Max spoke up now. "Paul. This is ridiculous. There aren't any rules, any regulations, in the contest about artificial limbs for overcoming disability." Max gestured at Lily's arms as if she were a mannequin on display. "She still has to come up with the color compositions, the framework for her pictures. It's *her art.*"

"Indeed it is." Paul made a small bow as he licked his lips. "But unfortunately, we have more to consider than the letter of the law, don't we? I can't think of any other case where another artist made it this far with those kinds of…enhancements."

"Is that what you call them?" Lily scowled at him even as she decided that the flush, the blood flooding her skin, was *definitely* anger. "Enhancements? *Enhancements?*"

Lily held up an arm to the light, showing all the inner workings clearly.

"I didn't get a *chance* to learn how to use regular arms, Paul, because I wasn't *born* with any. A congenital defect, right? No one's fault that they could tell, but thank the Four Heavens that we had the technology to rebuild me."

Paul nodded, his eyes dancing, clearly uncomfortable. "That's as may be, Miss Horton, but—"

"They weren't nearly as good then, though. I will say that." Lily clenched a fist and watched as Paul's eyes were drawn to the movement in her forearm. "The first ones, the ones I learned to walk on, were clunky pieces of garbage compared to these. At least I can feel with these ones."

Max let out a sigh, but Paul straightened back up and looked Lily in the face. "I don't hold judgment against you, Miss Horton, and I am sorry for the difficulties you've had. But the fact remains that it is the judgment of the contest committee that these…limbs…provide you with an unfair advantage."

And there it was. The moment stretched out; she could see the discomfort in Paul's eyes as he worked up the courage to say what she knew was coming. Max's face began to fall, anger and frustration mingling with sympathetic sadness.

"You are no longer in contention for the Emil Marten Art Prize. You will be expected to reimburse the committee for the goods purchased for you."

Insult added to injury. The idea of paying for her materials barely reached Lily's thoughts.

Max cut in again, their eyes narrowed as they rounded on the director. "That's unfair, Paul, and you know it. She didn't—"

"That isn't our problem. If she had made us aware at the outset of her disability, we could have discussed it beforehand and avoided this. Made proper accommodations."

"What 'accommodations' would you have given her?"

Paul fumbled. "Well...I..."

Lily shook her head. The emotion seemed to be draining from her body like a plug had been pulled. "Fine."

"No, it's *not* fine!" Max's voice filled the space Lily's had left, and they barely stopped themselves from grabbing Paul's shirt. "You can take your damned prize and—"

Lily put a hand on her friend's shoulder. "Max—"

"No, Lily. This isn't right and it isn't fair." Max scowled at Paul. "Give the prize to Andre, if he wants it so badly. It isn't worth it. I don't want my name attached to it."

Paul raised his eyebrows. "You're sure?"

"Piss off." Max bit their thumb before thrusting it in Paul's direction. "And get out of here."

With his customary bow, Paul did exactly that, opening the door with a hand stretched behind him.

"Why did you do that?" Lily tilted her head as she looked up at Max. "Why did you give up your shot?"

"Because it's stupid and unfair." Max shook their head, folded their arms, and pressed their lips together. "Look. Your paintings are great. I looked them up when I found out who the other finalists were."

Lily felt a spark of joy underneath the blanket of despair. "You did?"

"Needed to know my competition, right?" Max raised an eyebrow, then moved to the bed and sat on it, putting their hands between their knees. "Look, I'm sorry about this, but if you just let it go for a bit, let it die down, everyone'll forget about it. It's dumb, but people have short attention spans."

"Yeah." Lily felt her chest hitch again. "I just... I really didn't..."

"Hey." Max leaned forward and put a hand on Lily's robotic leg. "Don't worry about it. Just...you know, go home, go into hibernation for a while, and then come back to it."

"Yeah." Lily forced a smile. "I'll do that."

"And let me know when you come out of hiding."

The weeks dragged by, crawling, creeping. Another day spent staring out her window, another night spent rewatching the same television shows. From beneath her blankets, Lily felt paralyzed and disgusted with herself, but couldn't do anything to break free.

Her phone, neglected and bereft of a charging cord, had long since died again, with texts from her sister and Max left unanswered. She ignored knocks at her door, and she hadn't touched her computer at all for fear of what she'd see.

And the canvas she had been working on when she'd found out she'd made finalist still stood in the same corner, covered now, with not a drop of paint put on it, not a single new pencil line.

Every time Lily looked toward the canvas and thought of restarting the project—or even putting it aside and beginning a new one—her throat closed up and her heart started to palpitate. She ran a hand through her hair, the whirring, artificial fingers catching in the snarls put there by inattention and neglect.

What am I doing?

It wasn't the first time she had asked the question, and she knew, with a heavy, sinking heart, that it wouldn't be the last. Doubt and fear had become her watchwords, as much as she hated them, but she couldn't bring herself to push past the feelings.

What if she logged back on and found that more people were attacking her? Calling her a fake, a cheater? What if she tried to hold an art show and hecklers appeared, laughing and mocking her? Would anyone even want her art anymore, now that she had been publicly ridiculed this way?

Lily stared at her reflection in the blank, dark TV screen. Her eyes stared back, sunken over hollowed cheeks, with disheveled and disorderly hair atop. The image drilled into her.

Is this how you'll go out, then? Is this how you'll be remembered?

Her eyes moved away from the screen and back to the covered canvas, to the paints and pencils waiting there. They were calling, had been all this time, but she hadn't been able to answer.

Before she had fully decided on what to do, Lily felt herself rising from her bed, her legs picking her up, her arms pushing away from the mattress, until she stood there, in arm's reach of the cloth. The night sky twinkled outside the window, beautiful and wondrous, but the weight in Lily's soul hung heavily.

With a sudden yank, Lily tore the cloth away, revealing the barest sketch of that smiling face she had begun so long ago—a smile that *dared*, that *challenged*, that felt no fear.

That smile reminded her of something—her own, when she had shown her parents her first painting: a little house, with a barn and a dog in front of it, and their whole family. Atrocious, of course, with lines that wobbled and windows that canted to one side. But she had made it herself, even though she struggled to make her arms work, struggled to make her hands hold the paintbrush. The technology, wondrous then, paled against what she had now. But even then, she had wanted to paint.

Lily realized that little girl's smile was the same one on this picture: the smile of someone whose grasp exceeded their reach, but frozen in time unless she did something about it.

Breathing out through her nose, Lily reached out and grabbed her pencil, listening to the whirring gizmos that made it all possible.

Maybe she *wouldn't* be able to sell any more art. Maybe no one would want to host her again.

Fine. Her other hand took up the sharpener and brought it to the pencil point, spinning it around until the graphite formed a sharp, precise peak. *Maybe that's true.*

But maybe, *maybe*, some small child whose hands could barely hold a brush would see this smiling woman and realize that they could do more than they thought possible. Maybe, one day, she would see that child's art in a show, and they would tell Lily how they had done what she couldn't.

Because Lily had been the first thetic artist. She had taken that step, pushed that boundary, and, even if she bore the marks of those thorns across her entire body, that child, that *artist*, would have an easier time because she had helped sweep those obstacles off the path.

And *that* could be worth everything.

About the Author

I am a California-based author who has written for twelve years and recently placed as a Finalist in the 2024 Baen Fantasy Adventure Awards and won 3rd place in the 2025 Jim Baen Memorial Short Story Award. I have short story work published by Wonderbird Press, the Brothers Uber, and Opal Kingdom Press, as well as twelve independently published fantasy, urban fantasy, and science fiction novels. I like to spend time watching movies in the theater or playing tabletop RPGs with my wife and children when I'm not plugging away at my next story.

Website: https://www.jasonpatrickcrawford.com
Newsletter signup with free short story: dl.bookfunnel.com/pu14nkxeyj

RAIN

by Lehua Parker

KEONE LEONG SAT ASKEW in the living room where he'd been all night. Two weeks ago, one of the legs of the papasan chair had finally snapped under the weight of the mudsuit and lead boots, tilting the chair like a playground teeter-totter waiting for an upswing. Across the room, dawn creeped through the edges of the blinds, the day overcast and muggy.

It was always overcast.

For almost half an hour now, his watch alarm had beep, beep, beeped, warning that time was wasting away like an unwatered lily. Keone ignored it. In a couple of minutes, it would automatically shut off.

Unlike Keone, his watch took care of itself.

Lately, he hadn't needed his alarm, hadn't bothered going to bed, just staggered in from work to collapse in the papasan chair. The mudsuit was too hard to take off, and Keone didn't want to dirty his sheets and add to the laundry spilling into the hall.

The suit itself was nothing special, just the shape of a toddler's onesie and fraying at the cuffs and collar. He couldn't remember a time when he didn't wear it or the backpack waiting by the door.

The mud clinging to the suit was clammy and grave-dank, so thick his fingers couldn't find the zipper. Moss, decaying leaves, and algae gathered in the creases of his elbows and backs of his knees. He was sure a frog had made its home in his chest. There was an odd ribbit where his heart used to be.

As silence descended like a shroud and the alarm slept until tomorrow, Keone knew it was time to leave for work. If he hurried, he'd make the bus. He thought about washing his face and brushing his teeth—and all the steps in between—but when he stood up, it was all he could do to move to the front door.

He didn't even pee.

Eyeing his backpack, which was ready to pounce, his hands started to tremble. Instead of ambushing him each morning at the front door, his backpack used to live in his closet, only insisting to be carried when Keone thought of his mother or junior high. The backpack was chock-full of rocks, rocks that made life a perpetual uphill.

Keone knew if he didn't pick up his backpack right now, didn't go to work, didn't make the smallest effort, he'd end up like others he'd seen on the street. Cocooned in their mudsuits, sludge hardened to concrete, they were the dead who still breathed.

I can't, he thought at the backpack. *I can't; I can't; I can't.*

But it jumped on his shoulders anyway.

It wasn't always like this. Keone used to come home with his mudsuit just a little grimy around the ankles, a splattering of muck across his knees. Occasionally, a bit of lunch would be stuck to his chest, such as a spot of ketchup from the fries he shouldn't have eaten. Back then it was nothing to unzip the mudsuit and throw it into the wash.

Struggling under his backpack, Keone mourned for the days when he'd come home carrying takeout instead of rocks, slide his mudsuit from the washer into the dryer, and flop on the couch.

The couch was better than the papasan chair because there was room for his dog, Winston. Winston liked to stretch out, his head in Keone's lap, tail thumping against the cushions. Winston always yipped when Keone laughed too loudly at old sitcoms like *Friends* and *Malcom in the Middle*. Scary shows like *Supernatural* and *X-Files* made Winston snuggle close, burying his nose against Keone's chest when he felt Keone's heart beat faster.

Friday nights were the best. That's when Keone brought home Chinese in boxy, white cartons with printed red gates. Winston loved soggy sweet-and-sour chicken with lo mein so much he'd steal used chopsticks from the trash and gnaw on them like bones.

Keone would give a lot to pick up chopstick bones again. The day Winston died was the day the lead boots arrived in an Amazon box, big and bulky like ski boots in summer. Keone didn't hesitate to put them on.

He hasn't had an eggroll since.

When Keone left his apartment building, he knew he wouldn't make the bus. He'd taken too long fiddling with his backpack, adjusting the straps and trying to lighten the load. Watching the bus pull away from the stop about a block and a half ahead of him, he thought about giving up. It would be easier to go back to his apartment. This time he might actually make it to bed.

But as he started to turn around, he saw a mud-cocoon lying under a bush next to an empty Starbuck's cup. Written on the cup in faded black sharpie was the word PLEASE.

The frog in his chest jumped. *I can't*, Keone thought. *I just can't.*

He reached deep into his pocket, pushing away swamp grass and crawdads to pull out his phone, and called an Uber. *I shouldn't waste money on a car ride. It's needed in the cup. Why didn't I just get up earlier? I have to be better than this.*

Each 'should,' 'need,' and 'have to' slipped another pebble into his backpack. His shoulder spasmed. *Such a waste of space.* Fresh mud dribbled down his pant leg.

When the Uber driver in a red Honda Civic pulled to the curb, Keone caught her eye for a split second, a moment when he was sure she was going to speed away. Maybe it was the shock of all that mud. Maybe she wasn't sure his backpack would fit in the backseat. Whatever the reason, she hesitated for a second too long before sliding the passenger window down.

"Are you Ke…Ke—" She looked at her phone.

"Keone," he croaked. "Yeah."

She narrowed her eyes.

"Mom was from Hawai'i," he said.

"Oh. Cool. I'm Sue." She swiped her phone. "Heading to AmeriTech?"

"Yeah."

She bit her lip, then nodded. "Okay. Traffic's light. We missed most of rush hour. I can get you there in twenty, maybe fifteen if we hit all the lights right. Hop in."

When he was settled and she'd pulled onto the street, she called over her shoulder. "So, AmeriTech. Nice company. Worked there long?"

"Yeah." He cleared his throat. It was hard to speak through duckweed. "Eight years."

"Eight? Wow, that's a long time. You must like what you do."

He didn't bother shrugging. "Can you drop me around back? I don't want to go in the front." He closed his eyes and let his head fall back.

"Sure," Sue said and turned up the radio.

As they approached the glassy high-rise, Keone sat up and motioned her down an alley. "This is good," he said, pointing to a spot near the dumpsters.

Sue leaned forward, squinting through the windshield. "I'm not seeing a door. Let me swing around the front. It's better."

"This is fine."

"Oh, I don't mind going around the block again. It's no problem."

Keone waited until she stopped the car to let a walking mud-cocoon stagger past. "Thanks," he muttered as he flung the door open.

"Wait—"

The door slammed, and he circled around the trunk, his backpack digging against his hip. He hitched up his pants, then swiped his phone, leaving her five stars and a tip.

Should've been more.

Another stone, this one riverbed smooth, sank into his pack.

Sue rolled down her window. "Hey! Keone! You good?"

He didn't turn around as he punched the entrance code into the keypad hidden behind the dumpster and entered the building through a forgotten janitor's door.

Waiting for the wonky service elevator to arrive, he was careful not to touch the graffiti scrawled next to a Red Bull sticker, the spray paint dull under flickering florescent light. Through the metal doors, he heard the elevator clang and moan all the way down, bobbing like cork on a fishing line.

Before the doors creaked open, he filled his lungs and plugged his nose against the scent of gym socks and warm compost that he knew sulked in the elevator's corners. Stepping across the sticky threshold, he pressed 56 with the tip of his elbow and stood dead center, watching the numbers creep up. It was a long way to 56, but he always held his breath. The service elevator was safe. No one ever got on or off.

Popping out of an alcove, Keone glanced down the hallway. This was the most dangerous part of his day. He had to cross reception and get to his cubicle without running into Cheryl or Doug or, heaven forbid, Tanner, his boss.

He was sloughing his way past the breakroom when Cheryl grabbed his arm. "Keone!" she chirped. "We've been looking for you!"

Keone stared at her shoes, sensible brown loafers with tassels, so different from his heavy lead boots. "Bus," he mumbled. *How did her shoes stay so shiny?*

"What?"

He tried again. "Uber."

He felt rather than saw her cock her head. "Ah. No worries, you're here now. Doug brought doughnuts. Want one? I saved you a maple bar."

Keone couldn't remember the last time he'd brought doughnuts to the office. *I'm a mooch.* More mud splashed against his chest.

"Keone?"

"No, thank you," he muttered, pushing past.

"Hey," Cheryl called. "Just a heads up. Tanner's looking for you."

Sure enough, there was a Post It waiting on his computer monitor. He sighed. All he wanted was to sit in his chair with his noise cancelling headphones and stare at lines of code. Code was clean. It did what you asked and nothing more. He didn't have the energy for a cup of coffee, let alone a talk with Tanner.

Tanner was…sporty.

When Keone made it to his boss's office door, Tanner bounced up and came around the desk before he could knock. "Keone! You got my note. Great, great. Come in, come in. Take a seat."

The door shut firmly behind him.

On Tanner's desk was a photo of his family—wife and two kids—on the deck of a sailboat adrift in an ocean of possibilities. With Colgate smiles and wind-rumpled hair, standing against a sail so yellow it had to be photoshopped, the family looked straight out of Central Casting. Nobody could be that happy, that joyful, in real life.

But Keone knew they existed. He'd met and remet them all, twice each year at AmeriTech's June BBQ and December Holiday Party, the kids always a little taller and the wife a little more botoxed.

A day, thought Keone. *Just one day.*

Tanner took a deep breath. "I don't know how to start this, K. You've been with AmeriTech for a long time. You've been solid."

Keone nodded, his attention captured by a cloud in the family photo. He tilted his head to the side. *How did I never notice this before?*

"The truth is we're worried about you."

Mud trickled like molasses, puddling in Keone's lap. *Yes, that's a dog cloud hovering in the perfect blue sky.*

Tanner droned on. "Your project's behind schedule and your code—it's buggy, man. Unusable. QC's sent it back. It didn't even make it out of alpha."

The frog in his chest started kicking his ribs.

"But it's not just the programming. There's more." Tanner swallowed. "It's Thursday, and you've worn the same clothes all week. I can't believe I'm saying this, but dude, you need a shower."

The rocks in his pack shuffled and swelled. He closed his eyes. *Had Winston ever seen a sailboat? Was he a cloud in the sky? That would really be something, to float above the earth.*

"Keone! Are you listening?"

He forced his eyes open. "Yes," he managed.

"Keone, HR is involved. Is there anything I should know?"

There are rocks in my backpack, and my mudsuit's too heavy. I can't lift my arms. I'm wearing lead boots. I haven't slept. There's a frog in my chest that kick, kick, kicks. I can't remember my last meal that didn't come from a vending machine.

Winston is gone.

Winston is gone.

Winston is gone.

"Nothing," Keone said. "I'm fine."

Tanner sighed. "HR wants a drug test." He picked up a slip of paper from his desk and held it out. "If you pass, we're good. We'll put together an improvement plan. You fail..." He shook his head. "My hands are tied, man."

Keone reached for it, pushing back a tidal wave of clay. Tanner held onto the paper. "Is this goodbye, buddy?"

Keone shook his head.

"You gonna pass?"

Keone nodded, his head a fifty-pound ball of sand and grit.

"Sure?"

"Yeah," Keone rasped.

"Good," Tanner said, releasing the paper. "I've got an Uber waiting out front." Keone rose to go. "Hey. Whatever happens, take the rest of the day off. Go home. Shower. Eat a good meal. Relax. We'll deal with tomorrow's problems tomorrow."

In the hallway Keone stood near the service elevator, estimating how long it would take to walk around the building. *The driver's waiting, probably annoyed. I need to get over myself and take the regular elevator like a normal person.*

Another glob stuck to his thigh.

Stepping high in his lead boots, knees to the sky, toes slinging muck, he thrashed his way through to the main elevators. When the elevator arrived, he sloshed inside, pressed L, and collapsed against the back wall, exhausted. All the way down he prayed nobody'd get on and be repulsed by his smell—another pebble—or want to make small talk about why he wasn't closeted in his cubical, drinking coffee and typing code.

People should worry about their own business. A new stone settled deep in the bottom of his pack.

When the doors dinged opened on the ground floor, he mercifully exited alone and started across the lobby. It was easy to avoid eye contact with the security guard who was more concerned with those going in than out.

Outside, the sky was dark. Warrior clouds gathered against mountains, waiting for the signal to strike. But no matter how ominous, Keone knew it wouldn't rain. It never rained anymore.

Stay there, clouds. Stay far away in the mountains where you belong. Only Mom believed in you. He sighed as his pack scratched a sore spot between his shoulder blades, the edges of the rain fly tangling against the mother-dark hair at his nape.

Mom.

When thunderstorms roared, she'd be out there in her muʻumuʻu, welcoming ancestor voices in thunder, their faces in lightning. She'd dance and chant and laugh while neighbors stared from windows. Always, I hissed, "Come inside, come inside, come inside!"

She never listened or cared.

He shook his head. *Nobody needs rain like that, rain that pours like buckets, eroding everything to bare bone.* His chest thumped, and he rubbed it. *Not even frog-hearts.*

Keone turned from the ancestor faces he saw in the clouds. *They can't see me if I don't look.* He shifted his load and hunkered to the ride share area.

A red Honda Civic idled.

He stood there for a moment nonplussed, but before he could turn tail and flee, the driver's door opened, and Sue popped out.

"Hey"—she waved—"Keone! Over here."

Caught, he stumbled toward her and almost fainted when she reached over and lifted his pack off his shoulders. "Oof, that's heavy!" she said. "I'll put it in the trunk. You'll be more comfortable."

He panicked. "I need—"

Sue waved a hand, already closing the trunk. "It's all taken care of by AmeriTech. Climb in. It's about thirty minutes to LabCorp if we take the beltway."

Sitting in the backseat, when he thought about his rocks rolling around in the trunk, it was hard to breathe. The frog had a new friend, and they were hop, hop, hopping, trying to burst through his chest like Pop-N-Fresh biscuits on a Sunday afternoon. An eel roiled in his guts; leeches burrowed in his armpits. Mud oozed over the upholstery, filling the floorboards bayou-deep to his knees.

Sue closed her door and adjusted her mirror. "It's great to see you again, Keone-from-Hawaii. Lucky me, I was just a couple of blocks away when the call came in."

Keone looked everywhere but at the mirror.

She checked her blind spot and pulled away. "I gotta say, I was worried when you jumped out of the car. That alley didn't seem safe."

Pond scum thickened his throat. Cattail tendrils peeked beneath the collar of his mudsuit, brushing his chin. His dragonfly eyes flitted for somewhere safe to land. On the console was a water bottle and a charging cradle for a phone. On the dash—

He leaned forward.

On the dash was a faded and creased photo of a dog in the passenger seat. His eyes were Winston blue.

Sue flicked on her turn signal. "I'm glad you're okay."

"I'm not," he croaked through waterweeds and silt.

She nodded, keeping her eyes on the road. "I didn't think so," she whispered, turning the radio off.

"Is that your dog?" Keone asked.

She smiled, though he couldn't see it. "Yes. That's Pepper. She was my best friend. My ride or die." She paused. "Do you have a dog?"

"No," he said with a shudder. "Not anymore."

She nodded and quietly said, "I get it."

"This is stupid." Tears started to fall, cutting fresh tracks in the mud. He smeared new mud over his nose and down his cheeks. "He was just a dog. Nothing to get upset about."

"They are never just a dog." Sue patted Pepper's picture. "Are they, girl?" She caught Keone's eyes in the rearview. "It's okay to be sad."

Like a hurricane, sudden rain sheeted the backseat, dangerous and deadly. *I'm drowning.* Layers of dirt and bits of twigs slithered down his cheeks and sluiced off the mudsuit. He cowered in the deluge, trying to make himself small, small, small.

This turbulence is too much.

Gasping and shuddering, Keone saw his mother in the raindrops, heard her voice in the wind. "Let it out, let it out, let it out," Mom called, so he closed his eyes and counted each breath as water washed, lifting mud and debris away.

And through it all, Sue, like Winston, just let Keone be.

When they got to LabCorp, Sue waited on the sidewalk until the rain stopped before opening the back door. "It won't take long to pee in a cup," she said as muddy rainwater spilled out to slosh the asphalt.

Keone glanced at his reflection in the rearview mirror. There was still mud on his face, and he was soaked to the bone, but his suit was lighter, and he saw the zipper pull sticking out where the cattails had been along his collar. He swung his lead boots out of the car one at a time and paused to gather strength.

Sue held out her hand. "Need another lift?"

"No," he said, amazed. "I think I'm good."

Sue laughed. "Right. I meant after."

Keone rose and stepped into sunlight, blinking. "After?"

"AmeriTech's paid for a couple of hours—generous tip, too—so how 'bout I wait here until you're done and give you a lift wherever you want to go?"

"Like...home?"

"Sure. It's getting close to lunch time. We can even do a take-out stop along the way. I know a killer ramen place on Third and Main."

"Ramen?" He rolled the word around his tongue, tasting it. "Do they have char siu?"

"Yes! Lots of green onion and shoyu, too." Sue snapped her fingers. "Oh! Your backpack!" She walked to the trunk. "Do you need it?" She picked it up, then set it down. "Wow. That's heavy. It's okay to leave it with me, if you want. Whatever."

Keone shook his head, clearing cobwebs and alligators. "I think...I think it'll be safe in the trunk for a while."

Sue nodded and shut the trunk tight.

At the entry, he paused and turned back. "Will you tell me more about Pepper on the way home?"

"Of course."

She smiled as he floated through the door.

About the Author

LEHUA PARKER writes speculative fiction for kids and adults often set in her native Hawai'i. Her published works include the award-winning Niuhi Shark Saga trilogy and *Sharks in an Inland Sea*. Her short stories have appeared in *Va: Stories by Women of the Moana*, *Bamboo Ridge*, and *Dialogue*, and her works performed by the Honolulu Theatre for Youth. An advocate of authentic indigenous voices in media and a Kamehameha Schools graduate, she is a frequent speaker at conferences, symposiums, and schools. When the right project wanders by, she's also a freelance editor and book coach. Connect with her at https://lehuaparker.com/

NOT EXACTLY BABYSITTER MATERIAL

by Kevin A Davis

WITH GLOVED FINGERS, Jess cranked another bolt into her crossbow. As the vampire died, or at least ceased, a guttural, primordial hiss escaped from the last of the nest.

Jess's sister, Dena, wielded two fresh stakes on the opposite side of what had once been a pleasantly furnished living room in Clark, Colorado. She wore her dark hunting leathers and had her curly mass of brown hair pinned into a tight ponytail.

A glass-topped dining room table had fallen and smashed, a foul-smelling vampire tangled amidst the chairs. Another cryptid dangled from the front of the fridge with one of Dena's three-foot-long wooden spikes through the heart. Someone would end up replacing a few of the appliances.

Jess's pulse slowed as the frenzy of the fight faded. Glass crunched underfoot as she made for the master bedroom beyond the stairwell. Dena, of course, strode to reach the door first. By all counts, they'd cleared the entire nest. *Not a competition*, thought Jess as she aimed over Dena's shoulder.

The room had the same affluent decor as the rest of the house once had, but there had been no fighting in here. Thick black curtains held off the predawn sun as Dena flicked on a switch with the tip of a wooden stake.

Jess lowered her weapon until Dena moved to a closed door. A thin line of light showed at the base. Jess darted to get an angle for a shot inside. It wouldn't be the first time they'd found a vamp in a bathroom.

Hands full, Dena kicked down the door with an oversized boot.

Jess blinked, lowering her crossbow.

Three tweens, gagged and trussed like holiday turkeys, were piled in the tub. A girl with a tangle of bright red hair, one boy with olive skin and pitch-black hair, and another as pale as the girl but with light brown hair.

"Don't hurt them," Jess blurted out.

Dena offered a quick glower then tucked one of her fresh stakes with the others strapped on her back and stepped into the roomy bathroom. "We need to check." Still brandishing a three-foot pole sharpened to a point, she knelt and pulled her knife.

Vamps rarely turned kids this young, but they left them alive even less often. Jess moved to the door. "You're scaring them." They'd probably been through worse, but her sister could be gruff.

The redheaded girl appeared anything but terrified, with a scowl that gave Jess pause.

"Hold still." Dena spared a finger from the hand holding the stake to pull away a portion of the gag from the boy with light brown hair and cut it free. She quickly peeled up the lips, exposing normal human teeth.

"You're not one of them," the boy said.

"Neither are you." Dena moved to the girl next.

Jess stepped back into the bedroom and tossed the weapon on the bed. *I hope these kids are local.* Their parents would be a mess. *If they're still alive.* She returned to the girl's glare as Dena checked her teeth.

"Who are you?" demanded the girl.

Dena scoffed. "That's Xena and I'm Ripley." She moved to the boy with black hair.

"What's your name?" asked Jess.

The girl studied Jess, but didn't answer for a long moment. "You two killed them all?" Still bound, she nudged her head in the direction of the living room.

"Yes." It *had* been a rather noisy affair.

The boys remained quiet and more nervous over the situation than the girl. "I'm Cat. What are you going to do with us?"

Dena stood, leaving the tweens bound, and offered her knife to Jess. "Have fun. I'm starting the cleanup."

Jess knelt by the tub. The kids were trussed at ankles and wrists, tied by a short length. *What are we going to do with them?* "Are your parents local?"

Cat snorted. "Wouldn't know. We're orphans. Rodney's from Ontario." At the name, she nodded toward the boy with black hair, then to the paler one. "Pete is from Minnesota. You going to cut us loose, or do you need our life history?"

"Yeah, of course, turn to the side." Jess began loosening the tight knots, jaw tensing at the red rash around Cat's wrist. The local authorities would have these kids back where they belonged and would never believe their stories about vampires. "How'd they get you?"

"The vampires? Some creep from the orphanage sold us to them."

Jess paused, "What?"

"Can you not cut and talk at the same time?" Cat rolled her eyes in exasperation.

"I'm just surprised." Jess stammered but worked on the bindings. *Sold them?*

The boy named Rodney scoffed. "So were we. I never believed we were headed out for ice cream."

"Did getting tied to the seat give it away?" teased Cat. She grimaced as Jess freed her wrist from the rope.

"The gags were your fault." Rodney wet his lips as if remembering. "Do you have anything to eat?"

Dena laughed from the other room, and Jess fought to keep from following suit. "Food isn't something we usually bring to these." With a final cut, she freed Cat's ankles. The socks had deep indents, but she could hope the skin wouldn't be as raw as the arms. "There, let me get you out."

Cat brushed her away, wincing as she stood. She took a moment to wobble before climbing out of the tub. "Is this what you do, kill vampires?"

"Among other things." Jess eased Rodney to the side, and he eagerly accommodated with his face pressed against the wall tiles. They'd been kidnapped and introduced to vampires, yet these kids didn't seem flustered.

Cat ran the water at the sink, washing her wrists and slurping handfuls. "What else?"

Her frown causing her eyes to squint, Jess ignored the question and asked her own. "Vampires don't surprise you?"

Pete spoke. "Did me."

The refrigerator in the far room shrieked, probably as Dena removed the stake from that vampire pinned to it like a displayed moth. The boys twitched with concerned expressions.

"She's just cleaning up," Jess explained. The sound of a body thudded to the ground. If the sun came in the windows, there'd be ash all over the house.

"Rodney and I saw a ghost a bunch of times. There's one at the home," Cat said. The sink continued to run. "You kill them too?"

Jess cut Rodney's raw wrists loose. She and Dena would have to hunt down this jerk from the orphanage and have a little chat with him. "If necessary. Few of them are trouble."

A scrape sounded, likely the sliding door being opened, and Cat turned off the water. "Should I go help her?"

"No," Dena called from the other room.

After Jess cut Rodney's bonds, he stood with her aid. Cat took over, guiding him out of the tub. Pete offered a feeble smile, rolling to his side to expose his binding. His loose, light brown hair slid down to cover his face.

What are we going to do with them? Jess thought.

As she freed Pete and got him standing, she rose with him. "Cat?"

Rodney still drank handfuls from the sink. "She left."

"I see that." Jess darted out of the bathroom. "Wait here."

Cat had reached the bedroom door, paused there, and peered into the living room. "She's pretty strong."

Jess strode up beside the young girl.

Dena had one vamp by their feet at her hips, dragging him over the threshold of the sliding door straight ahead.

"You don't need to watch it." Jess rested a hand on the girl's shoulder, nudging her gently toward the center of the bedroom. "Sit on the bed."

Cat didn't move. "What are you going to do with us?"

Jess studied the girl's bright hair, wet locks in the front from washing her face. She drew in a long breath, preparing to say something comforting, if not true.

The vamp thudded on the wraparound porch, and Dena spoke as she stomped inside. "Run over to the neighbor, they'll call the police and get you sorted. Don't mention us." She strode to them, hand outstretched for her knife.

Jess raised a finger to Cat. "Stay here while I help." She followed her sister into the large room that served as the kitchen, dining, and living areas with a corner fireplace. "You heard how they got here, right?" she asked Dena.

They each grabbed a foot of one of the vamps, his stench of death filling Jess's nostrils.

"Yeah," said Dena. "What are we going to do about it?"

Cat watched from the bedroom door. "You don't seem like the adoption types."

Dena chuckled. "Cute kid. We're not."

They dragged the emaciated body toward the sliding glass door. "If they go back to the orphanage, they'll be at risk," Jess explained.

"You want to off the guy who sold them first? I thought you frowned on that." Dena grinned.

The gray predawn sky had lightened, with the sun preparing to rise on the opposite side of the house. Mountains surrounded this remote area of northern Colorado and light had already kissed some peaks with gold. A wealth of verdant green forest circled the yard with only a distant neighbor to disrupt the beauty that graced the view. That, and the steaming body of the vampire that they dropped the second one beside.

"No, we're not killing him." Jess wouldn't mind a punch or two, but they had different types of monsters to deal with. A nest in New Mexico had hit their radar.

Dena clapped her spiked gloves together, as if that might remove the vamp stench. "What then? I'm not exactly babysitter material."

Cat laughed from inside.

They headed back in for another vamp. Pete had joined Cat, their toes on the bedroom door's threshold, but peering about. The kitchen counter hid much of the mayhem from their vantage.

"May we check the cabinets for food, um, Ripley?" Cat's polite wording and tone carried a mocking undertone.

"Go for it. Don't touch any of their blood on the fridge." As Dena spoke, Jess gave her a pointed glare.

The two kids sprang like greyhounds out of a gate.

"Really?" Jess asked. Cabinet doors were already creaking open and slapping closed.

Dena pointed to the second to the last vampire in the house. "When did you last eat?"

"Not last night, the night before," Cat said, opening the fridge. "Oh, it stinks."

The stench of sour milk reached Jess as she grabbed a scrawny ankle. Between the combined reek, her stomach roiled. "We need to do something with them. The authorities will just send them right back."

"We can live here," Cat said. "Ooh, grab the yellow cheese. There's no green." Rodney had lumbered out to join them, watching the sisters dragging the vampire toward the sliding glass door.

"You can't," said Jess with a grunt, "live here. How old are you?"

"Twelve," replied Cat. Plastic crinkled as they began peeling open cheese slices.

Jess and Dena deposited the third corpse across the other two that steamed from toe to head as the sun reflected off the sky.

"What's your plan?" asked Dena, slapping her gloves together.

Jess frowned. "I don't have one. We need to come up with one."

Her sister headed back inside, and Jess followed. Pete had climbed up on the counter, opened the upper cabinets, and was gleefully dropping Pop-Tarts down to the other two.

"Hey," Dena called. "Save me a box of brown sugar ones."

Rodney giggled at the comment, and Cat just raised her eyebrows.

The vamp pile steamed like a clambake by the time Jess helped load the last one outside. In a couple of minutes, the creatures would be ash, waiting for a solid breeze. Dena closed the door and headed for the kitchen sink, weaving through the feast that the children had assembled. She nodded to the box of Pop-Tarts set aside for her, smiled, and offered a thumbs up.

Jess stepped into a bathroom at the corner of the kitchen under the stairs to rinse off her gloves and whatever vampire blood had splattered on her. "Do you think Martin might take them in?"

"No," called back Dena.

"Who's Martin?" asked Cat.

Dena answered, "A librarian of sorts. Open me one of those, will ya?"

Martin gathered information for hunters. He'd been the one to find this nest, and another south in New Mexico. He had an immense house and plenty of land but tended to be a grumpy loner. After a couple of days with these kids, he might sell them off as well.

Jess dried her gloves on a folded towel and pulled out her phone to scroll through contacts. Most were aliases, in case some*thing* ended up with her cell. "How about Nancy Pullen?"

"In North Dakota? I guess we could put them on a bus." Dena spoke with a muffled voice, as if she'd stuffed an entire Pop-Tart in her mouth, which she likely had.

"Cool," called Pete. "A bus."

They aren't going by bus. Jess considered the early hour but dialed anyway. Nancy answered on the first ring and quickly declined the proposal.

"Hey, you tried, right?" Dena attempted to sound consoling. A cabinet opened. "How did you miss the Oreos?" The kitchen erupted into exclamations and scuffling.

Jess dropped the lid to the toilet and sat to scroll through her phone. They couldn't drag these kids with them, and she wasn't leaving them. She winced at one entry, pursing her lips. It would be a difficult ask. "Hey, how about Tim and Leslie Gardner?"

Dena stepped to the doorway. "Ouch. They've just lost their kids."

Last summer, the sisters had killed a werewolf in Eureka, Utah, but not before it had taken six hearts, four belonging to the Gardners' children. The devastated couple had survived. Jess swallowed against a thick lump in her throat. "Hard to know how it might go." It could spiral them deeper just to be asked.

"May be a win all around," offered Dena, though her tone didn't carry a ton of encouragement.

Or a disaster, thought Jess.

Cat appeared, peering into the bathroom. "Who are you talking about? Why are you sitting in here?"

"Thinking." Jess replied to the latter question. "Which is more difficult with company."

"What is?" asked Pete, standing on toes to see over Cat's mop of hair. Oreos had left a dusty mustache on his upper lip.

Jess pressed a thumb against her forehead, just above her nose, and sighed. She had to try. "We know a couple who lost all their kids to something like this." She gestured to the living area where they'd fought the vampires. "I can't be sure how they'll react. They've got plenty of room."

"Are they nice?" asked Cat.

"Very," added Dena. "You'd need to watch your manners."

"I assure you, we are nothing but polite," said Cat.

"And good at chores," Pete offered.

Rodney wedged his head beside Cat's. "We don't take up much space."

Jess smiled, turning to her phone as her eyes watered. "Don't get your hopes up." She dialed, taking a deep breath into a tightening chest. "Might not even be up yet."

Leslie answered. "Jess. I didn't expect to see a call from you. Is everything okay?"

"—well, no. We've come across a strange scenario that we didn't expect." Jess wet her lips. "We have three kids, orphans already, that we can't send back to where they came from. It's a difficult situation."

Leslie didn't respond at first. A chair scraped on the floor, either from her sitting or rising. "Are you asking us to take them in?"

Cat smiled, nodding bright curls up and down in a vigorous display, obviously able to hear the question. Jess gestured for her to stop. She should have made the call in private; technically, she had tried.

Before she could respond, Leslie continued, her voice breaking. "Hold on."

Dena rolled her eyes and frowned apologetically. It didn't sound good. She dropped her hand down to Cat's hair when the girl attempted to speak. "Shh."

A minute trickled away on her phone, and the trio of kids grew restless. They had far more riding on this call than anyone else in the room. Jess would have to live with the memory if it failed.

"Jess?" Tim's voice asked, their side of the connection on speaker. He sounded weary, sad.

She inhaled, fighting a sense of defeat. "Yes, Tim. I'm sorry for asking, with all that's happened."

"Please, don't be." He cleared his throat. "We would consider it a calling to take them in, assuming we can do so legally."

Leslie joined his response. "With open hearts. I imagine they have experienced a difficult situation, if you're reaching out to us."

Jess twitched, then smiled as Dena mouthed *Martin*. The man could make just about anything happen, legal or illegal.

"I'm sure we'll be able to help with that part." She straightened on the toilet, then stood, causing Dena to back up and three orphans to bounce into the disaster of a living room. "We can be there in half a day's drive. Is that okay?"

"Bless you and your sister, Jess. We'll be ready. How old are they?"

"Let's say twelve-ish."

In fifteen minutes, Jess and her sister had the trio wrangled into the Chevy Bel Air they'd parked down the street, and drove south out of Clark, Colorado.

Thirty minutes after that, Dena pulled into a gas station with a restaurant inside. "I'm going inside to grab lunch while Jess fills the tank and explains how likely it is that I'll leave you all on the roadside if you don't stop yammering. Don't kids your age take naps?"

Pete ignored the warning. "Can I have onion rings?"

Jess stepped out of the passenger side, pulling a credit card out of her phone case. "Leave Dena to select the food. She's a master at it." Leaning down to the window, she whispered. "I'd take her seriously about the roadside bit. I ended up walking four miles, and I'm her sister. And stop asking her to change the music."

Six hours, eight bathroom breaks, one Dena-sized meltdown at a rest stop, and nine greasy burgers later, they pulled down a long drive to the two-story farmhouse owned by

Tim and Leslie Gardner. The couple, in their early forties, sat on the bench on the front porch. As the car turned silent except for ZZ Top's "Jesus Just Left Chicago," the Gardner pair rose and walked down the stairs, hand in hand.

Her eyes blurred with tears, Jess remembered her and her sister's time here four months ago. She touched the cross at her neck, thankful that their visit here brought some potential happiness.

Leslie took the lead, forcing a welcoming smile on tear-stained cheeks as she touched her brown hair, tied back out of her face. "Jess. We want to thank you for thinking of us. It came as a shock, at first." As she spoke, her eyes darted to the figures in the rear seat.

Jess opened the back door, with Cat starting the procession out to line up awkwardly. As Leslie began the introductions, Tim joined her. Jess leaned against her passenger door, and on the opposite side of the Bel Air, Dena sat partly on the hood, one leg up.

"Will you join us for dinner?" Leslie asked Jess.

Her sister shaking her head, Jess declined. "We've got work."

"I'm sorry to hear. Thank you, again."

"Thank you." Cat slammed into Jess, hugging her, bringing the boys to attempt the same in one ungainly mobbing.

Jess chuckled. "Fair. At least we didn't have to walk."

Cat laughed, pulling back to wave at Dena. "Thanks, loser."

Leslie tilted her head. "Cat. Manners."

"I meant thank you for all the wonderful and pleasant conversation, Mrs. Ripley."

As the Gardners and the trio headed for the house, Jess slipped into her seat as Dena put the keys into the ignition. "I think you're right," said Jess.

"Of course." Dena paused, curious. "About what?"

"It's a win all around."

About the Author

Kevin A Davis is a fantasy author with over twenty published novels, including the award-winning DRC Files. In 2025, he and coauthor April Davis published the Sorrowborn Trilogy, a YA adventure romance that is also up for an award in August. On top of continuing the DRC Files, his working projects include a collaboration with Tim Lewis and a separate upcoming fantasy series. www.KevinArthurDavis.com

He resides in north Florida and attends conventions throughout the year, including as staff as Director of the Authors Workshop Track at JordanCon. He is a judge for the RPLA awards out of the FWA. As Inkd Publishing, he publishes a wide variety of anthologies.

www.InkdPub.com

MILO PIPER'S BREAKOUT SINGLE THAT ENDED THE RAT WAR

by David Hankins

LIEUTENANT MILO PIPER sat in a torched donut shop that smelled of caramelized sugar and ash. Kinda like his mom's kitchen. He'd been sent on a supply run, but shamming was a time-honored Army tradition. He wasn't expected back for hours. Over-ear headphones and laptop blocked the howling winds of Chicago's abandoned Exclusion Zone as Milo mixed tracks on his breakout single, "The Warrior's Anthem."

This song would get him discovered. He *knew* it. Milo had only joined the Army Reserves to pay for college. He wasn't cut out for soldiering. He was a musician. But then the Rat War had broken out in Chicago, and he was activated. Writing music was limited to stolen moments like these.

Milo's head bobbed in time with the beat, lost in his music, fingers absently playing chords on the ash-coated countertop. The chorus rang in his ears.

Fight for what's right and your song will live on. Oh, your song will live on.

Milo was snapped back to reality when a snarling brown rat with a hunting knife leapt onto the counter. The muscle-bound beast was the size of a terrier. Milo shrieked and threw himself back. His headphones yanked free of the laptop.

A screaming guitar solo filled the ruined donut shop. Two smaller rats, a white and a gray, bounded across the checkered tile floor with sheathed knives on their backs. The massive rat on the counter crouched to leap and then…stopped. Its murderous snarl faded, and the others stopped running.

Milo froze, heart racing. The rats never stopped. Idiot scientists had seen to that. They'd tested neural implants on lab rats who then organized, escaped, started a war, and renamed Chicago 'Ratatopia.' They'd been unstoppable ever since.

The big rat sat on its haunches, twisted its neck from side to side with little *pop* sounds, then spoke in a thick British accent. "Hey mate, you gotta cigarette? I'm jonesing something fierce!"

Milo's eyes flicked from the rat's earnest expression to its knife. "No," he said slowly. "Don't smoke."

"Bloody hell," it muttered and sheathed the knife on its back.

"Bruiser, language!" the white rat snapped in a cultured soprano.

"Sorry, Princess."

Milo shuffled back as Princess and the gray rat approached. He wished he hadn't left his rifle in the Humvee. If he could keep them talking, perhaps he could escape. "Look, I don't want any trouble."

Princess leapt onto the counter and sniffed at his laptop. "What are you broadcasting?"

"Nothing. It's just my music." Milo bumped a metal chair in his slow retreat. It scraped the tile and he froze, but the rats didn't appear to notice.

Princess cocked her head, whiskers twitching. "Something is disrupting Alpha's signal, so it must be the music. I didn't think anything could do that." She turned beady black eyes on Milo as he settled his headphones around his neck. "We need your help."

"Who's Alpha and what signal?" Could he reach the Humvee before they caught him?

"My brother," Princess said, snarling. "His subsonic broadband signal controls our neurotransmitters. Makes us killers. With your music to disrupt his signal, we can stop Alpha."

That got Milo's attention. He stopped edging away. "You can end the Rat War?"

"*We* can. You'll have to carry the laptop."

Milo's mind spun as his recorded guitar solo led into a reprise. He wasn't a fighter, but he *did* want to end the war. No war meant no activated Reserves and he'd be free to chase his dreams. To write music.

Could he trust a rat?

For the chance to end the war? Absolutely.

"I'm in." Milo extended a hand. "Milo Piper."

"Charmed," she said and gripped his fingers in her paws. "I'm Princess. You've met Bruiser"—the muscle-bound brown flicked a cocky salute—"and this is DJ." The scrawny gray rat beside her was missing one eye. He had a feral look about him.

Milo nodded. "Nice to meet you. Let's go end a war."

In the Humvee, Milo set his laptop to cycle through his playlist before dropping it on the passenger seat. If music disrupted Alpha's signal, then music he'd play. Classic rock by Def Leppard made him smile as the rats climbed in. He'd written "The Warrior's Anthem" in the style of the old rock ballads.

"Rockin' tunes, mate!" Bruiser said. He jumped onto the gunner's platform between the seats and played air guitar. Milo's rifle lay on the platform, but Bruiser danced around it.

DJ sneered from atop the passenger's seat. "Give me poetry, spoken in rap, not this"—he waved a disgusted paw—"crap." He dropped to the seat and tapped at Milo's laptop, scanning his playlist.

"Hey!" Milo said, but DJ just flipped his middle claw and perused. Princess climbed onto the military radio mounted on the dash and made an impatient 'let's go' gesture. Milo pursed his lips, threw the vehicle into gear, and tore out of the parking lot. "Where to?" he asked, heading toward downtown.

"The Willis Tower," Princess said. "Alpha tapped into the radio antennae on the roof to broadcast his subsonic signal."

Milo turned onto a main thoroughfare and punched the gas. "How'd he do that? No offense, but rats aren't known for their skills at electronics."

Princess bared her teeth and hissed. "Humans are blind. We were intelligent *before* the neural implants. Alpha and I were in the same lab. He studied implant technology and learned how to use it for control. To bend his fellow rats to his will."

The venom in her voice sent shivers down Milo's spine. "Were you all in the same lab?"

"No lab for this rat," DJ piped in, single eye still glued to the playlist as his claw flicked the touchscreen. "I ain't down with that. Stolen from the street and chipped against my will. I struggle through this life. I wasn't born to kill."

Bruiser turned his air guitar into a drum solo on the edge of DJ's seat. "I was on special loan from McCartney Labs in London. Bloody scientists needed a rat hopped up on a lifetime o' steroids and nicotine to test their chip. I turned out bloody brilliant. Better than the rest o' this lot." Princess muttered about language, and DJ snapped at Bruiser's drumming paws. The street rat missed as Bruiser resumed his energetic air guitar during the song's bridge.

The music abruptly changed, heavy bass and electric guitar replaced by angry gangster rap. Milo had forgotten he even had DMX songs. "Oi!" Bruiser said, dropping to all fours. "I liked that one! Change it back." DJ flicked his tail straight up and waved its tip in a gesture that, to Milo, seemed even more vulgar than a simple middle finger. Bruiser leapt at the scrawny rat with a snarl that made the hair on Milo's neck stand on end. They tumbled into a hissing, biting brawl on top of the computer.

"Hey. Hey!" Milo yelled, trying to grab the laptop as he drove. He almost got it but snatched his hand back when DJ bit at him. Bruiser used the distraction to grab DJ in a suplex and slam him into the keyboard.

The music went silent.

Milo's gaze snapped to Princess. She twitched, then snarled and drew her hunting knife. DJ and Bruiser stopped fighting and did the same.

Crap.

Milo slammed on the brakes and spun the wheel hard to the left. The rats and his rifle tumbled into the passenger floorboard as the Humvee rocked to a halt. Milo grabbed his laptop and threw himself out of the Humvee.

His elbow hit the pavement first. Pain flashed up his arm and numb fingers dropped the computer. All three rats appeared in the open doorway, programmed murder in their eyes. Milo scrabbled back, heart racing.

He hit the curb and jumped to his feet. The rats climbed out and stalked past his silent computer on their hind legs, knives held like broadswords.

Milo turned and ran.

They'd stopped near a crumbling strip mall, and he bolted for a pawn shop. He hit the unlocked glass door at speed and popped it open. He spun and slammed it shut just as the rats, bounding toward him with the knives in their teeth like furry pirates, reached it. Milo flipped the lock and stepped back, trying to catch his breath.

Bruiser sheathed his knife and grabbed a chunk of broken cement. Steroid-fueled muscles bulged, and he heaved. The glass door shattered. Milo backed away and looked frantically at the piles of random crap. Skis, radios, jewelry...

Radios.

Milo leapt for the shelf and grabbed a radio boombox. He flipped the power switch and cranked the volume.

Nothing. No batteries.

He grabbed another, glancing over his shoulder. The rats weren't running now. They stalked forward, separating to surround their prey. Milo flipped the radio over. It was an old survival model with a crank handle on the back. He tuned it to the only station still broadcasting around here and spun the handle as fast as he could.

Low static rose as power built inside the radio. Milo cranked harder, found the volume knob, and flicked it all the way up.

Country twang filled the pawnshop.

The rats stopped.

"Bloody hell!" Bruiser yelled, spinning on DJ. "Look at the mess you made. We almost killed our pet human!"

Wait, what? Pet human?

DJ snarled. "The fault is yours, you muscle-bound freak. Speak more lies and I'll cut you deep." He brandished his knife.

Princess smacked DJ on the head and grabbed Bruiser by the throat, yanking him down to her eye level. "Stop this, both of you!"

"Why should I?" Bruiser pointed his knife at DJ. "He started it!"

Milo slapped the checkout counter with a crack, getting their attention. "Because we'll all die if we don't work together!" The rats cocked their heads at him. Milo knelt and set the radio on the floor. "Alpha is the enemy. He made you killers. Channel your rage at him, not each other."

Whiskers twitched as the rats eyed each other before they nodded and separated. A growl rumbled from Bruiser. "I ain't listening to DJ's crap music and I *definitely* ain't listening to *that*." He pointed a derisive claw at the emergency radio as the singer drowned his sorrows in whiskey.

Milo shrugged. "Too bad. All the stations out of Chicago went dark when the Army cut the city's power. This is the only one from outside the area that reaches this far."

"Then we'll listen to your laptop."

Milo shook his head. "I've been thinking about that. High volume uses too much battery power. We need to conserve that for our trip into the Willis. In fact…" He scanned the electronics shelf and snatched a wireless speaker that looked like a miniature '80s boombox. "Come on, let's go," he said, heading for the door.

Back at the Humvee, Milo retrieved his laptop and set it back on the passenger seat. Bruiser followed with the small emergency radio, a pained grimace on his face at the blaring country music.

"Why do I gotta carry this thing?" he said.

Princess, who'd made him take it, answered. "To keep you out of trouble. Crank it again, the battery's dying."

Bruiser grumbled but obeyed, climbing inside and setting it on the gunner's platform to work the crank with both forepaws.

Once everyone was back in the Humvee, Milo eyed DJ. He needed something to keep the street rat occupied and not taunting Bruiser.

"DJ, you know music, right?"

The scarred rat nodded.

"Great. I've been mixing a new song, and I'd love your input." He tapped a few keys and brought up his mixing program. "You can use my headphones."

"That's not fair!" Bruiser yelled, working the crank.

DJ threw a furry grin at the big rat as Milo hooked up the headphones. They were too big for DJ, but he rested his head against the ear cup and was soon lost in the music, tail twitching in time with the beat.

They drove in relative silence, everyone else trying to ignore the country music that filled the Humvee. Bruiser was nearing tears but kept cranking the handle.

Milo drummed his fingers on the steering wheel, weaving around debris and abandoned vehicles. "So, Princess, what'll you do once the war is over?"

Her ear twitched. "I will return to a lab if they'll have me. Not for animal testing, I hated that, but there's joy in science. I would discover the wonders of the universe as an equal partner with the human scientists." She glanced over and caught Milo's arched eyebrow of disbelief. She shrugged, her fur rippling across her shoulders. "Perhaps it's a lofty dream, but it's mine. What about you? Will you stay in the Army?"

Milo drew a deep breath and blew it out. "No. I never should have joined. It was a concession to my family so I'd have 'marketable skills' as I pursued music. My dad still wasn't happy with me. Wanted me to be a plumber and take over the Piper family business. I'd rather have a guitar in my hands than a wrench. Music is my life."

They fell into companionable silence and Milo considered the rats. They were a strange band; a 'mischief,' he remembered a group of rats was called. They fought like, well, rats, but that reminded him more of family squabbles than anything. Army propaganda said rats were evil murderous beasts to be put down for their own good. Solve the rat problem through extermination.

Attempts at genocide wouldn't solve anything, especially now that the rats had proven their sentience. The war would just become an ugly urban brawl between species, and Milo wasn't entirely convinced that humanity would win that kind of war.

The problem was Alpha and his signal. If the rats were free, they'd have a chance to determine their own fate. Work with humanity instead of fighting them.

A blocked bridge ahead focused Milo's attention. Overturned cars and piled trash filled half the road; a fire truck on its side blocked the other half. "Um, Princess? Which way should I go?"

Her tail twitched. "This is the edge of Ratatopia, the rat-controlled heart of Chicago. The only way around is through."

"Excuse me?"

"She means floor it, ya plonker!" Bruiser yelled. He leapt from the emergency radio and pushed down past Milo's legs. Fifteen pounds of furry muscle slammed into Milo's right foot, throwing the accelerator to the floor.

The Humvee jumped forward.

"Whoa! What are you doing?" Milo clutched the steering wheel and kicked at the rat. Bruiser bit him just above his boot. "Ow!" He kicked some more but had to focus on the road as Bruiser lay on the gas pedal.

Princess leapt to the passenger window and pulled the lever, dropping it open. "Milo, open your window. DJ, that radio's dying again. We need music. Full volume! Let them hear it." She clambered to the other doors, dropping their windows as DJ yanked the headphones free. "The Warrior's Anthem" drowned the fading country music and reverberated through the vehicle. The scrawny rat had connected that wireless speaker.

Milo clenched his jaw as they bore down on the roadblock. Rats scurried across it, pointing bladed weapons in defiance. He cursed when he saw the barrel of a captured .50 cal machine gun poking through the fire truck's missing windshield.

Flame burst from the .50 cal with a deep *whump-whump-whump*. Tracers flew haphazardly as the gun's recoil overwhelmed the small rat gunners. One round shattered the driver's windshield, covering Milo in glass. He screamed, aimed between two cars, and smashed into the roadblock.

He didn't break through.

Screeching metal tore at Milo's ears and his forehead rebounded off the steering wheel as they crashed to a stop.

Debris and armed rats fell through the open window and into Milo's lap. He panicked and shrieked like an old lady who's seen a mouse in the kitchen.

Milo flung dazed rats out the window as fast as he could grab them.

"Stop! Milo, Stop!"

Milo froze, a struggling white rat in hand, and stared wide-eyed at Princess. Her empty forepaws were held out, beseeching. She scrambled off the military radio and guided Milo's hand to set the rat on the gunner's deck. Milo drew deep breaths, forcing himself to calm down.

"Mother?" Princess said softly as she caressed the other rat's fur. The elderly white rat was plump. Scraggly gray tufts dominated the tops of her ears, brows, and chin.

DJ and Bruiser climbed up from the floorboard, saw the old rat, and prostrated themselves. Milo glanced at the rats outside the Humvee. One by one and then in rows they bowed as well. Milo turned a confused expression toward Princess. She gestured to the old rat.

"Lieutenant Milo Piper, this is Loretta, Queen Mother to Alpha and me."

Milo inclined his head. There wasn't much else he could do. "Pleased to meet you, uh, your majesty. How is it that the Queen Mother is pulling perimeter guard duty?"

Loretta snarled and rose on her haunches, stiff and regal. "I challenged Alpha's megalomania, and my *darling* son linked my chip with the common rats receiving his signal. Sent me to protect his Ratatopia."

"So, his signal doesn't affect all chipped rats?"

"Only those he selects. He rewards his sycophants with freedom. All others are fodder for his war on humanity. Even his mother." Loretta turned to Princess. "How are we free? What changed?"

Princess gestured toward the mini boombox speaker. "Music is the key. It disrupts the signal's reception in our chips."

Milo added, "But the second the music stops, you revert." *That* thought sent shivers down his spine. It was bad enough with three rats. He was surrounded now by an army of potential little murderers. He drew a deep breath. "We're going to the Willis Tower to stop Alpha. End the war."

A menacing smile spread across Loretta's furry face. "Then we shall escort you. It's time I had a word with my son."

Milo felt like the pied piper as he led the procession of rats down Chicago's empty streets. Princess and Loretta rode on his shoulders, and he held his laptop open before him. He'd left his rifle in the Humvee. Bullets hadn't won the war yet. Time to give music a chance.

Bruiser marched beside him, portable speaker held high in both paws. He and DJ had almost come to blows again over music selection for their grand entrance. Milo had ended the argument by putting his playlist on shuffle. He had a little bit of everything.

Wagner's "Ride of the Valkyries" seemed a fitting song to start with.

Downtown Chicago was pristine. Milo had visited as a child when his mother took him to a summer concert series. That was when he fell in love with music. At the time, he'd thought the city had a comfortable, lived-in feel. Clean thoroughfares with the dirt and grime swept into the alleyways.

Not so in Ratatopia. The dirt was gone. Alpha's rats had been busy since capturing Chicago's heart, cleaning the city more thoroughly than the human residents ever had. It even smelled cleaner. As Milo and his entourage approached the Willis Tower he saw a wrecker, driven by rats, towing away an abandoned vehicle.

The tower's lobby was brightly lit and filled with comfortable couches and eating nooks. He glanced at Princess and pointed toward the lights. "I thought the Army killed Chicago's power months ago?"

"They did," she said. "Alpha truly is a genius. He rerouted every backup generator in the city to power the Willis but only uses the electricity he needs. With solar panels to augment the generators, he can power this building almost indefinitely."

Milo glanced around. "If he's worked so hard to make the Willis his fortress, where are the guards?"

Princess shrugged. "He hasn't needed them, since no rat has broken his programming before. Any guards he has will be with him on the Skydeck."

They climbed a broad expanse of steps and Princess directed Milo through a museum of Chicago as it had been before the Rat War. The dim halls felt ominous with the interactive displays shut down. An ugly band of street rats stood guard outside the elevator.

Milo expected a fight, but the guards took one look at the mischief of rats carpeting the hall behind him and abandoned their posts, scurrying away. That made Milo smile. But then he considered the elevator and his smile dropped. "I don't think we'll all fit in there."

Princess snorted. "Rats are comfortable in tight spaces. We'll fit." She leapt from his shoulder, hit the elevator call button, then scrambled back up to her perch.

But Milo didn't *want* to be in an elevator with hundreds of rats. He'd never suffered from claustrophobia or musophobia—the fear of rats—but his stomach flipped at the thought of being trapped, one moment of silence away from a grisly murder.

The elevator dinged, opened, and Milo forced himself to step in. Rats poured in after him, piling on top of each other in a writhing mass that reached past Milo's knees. A writhing mass of fur, claws, and teeth. And knives. Mustn't forget the knives. Milo's breath came faster and faster.

"Peace, warrior," Loretta said into his ear. "You are safe."

Milo wasn't so confident. Their ascent to the 103rd floor was the most nerve-wracking ride of his life. The elevator was bigger than he'd expected, and he focused on the large display counting up to their destination. Tiny claws gripped his uniform's legs, pulling at him, and Milo felt a small whimper escape from his throat.

The music kept him safe.

He looked at Bruiser, who was mostly buried but held the speaker high and proud. "Ride of the Valkyries" was replaced by classic AC/DC and the big rat whooped in joy, waving the speaker in time with the beat. Tiny paws rose from the elevator mosh pit with chitters and hisses as the rat army pumped itself up for battle. The screen above the door finally reached 103. The Skydeck.

The door chimed open, and the rats poured out in a screeching, angry mob. The Willis's top floor was mostly open and surrounded by windows. A mass of cables and wires dangled from the room's ceiling, leading to an elevated faraday cage made of chain-link fencing. Folding tables lined the cage, piled high with electronics, monitors, and computers. The nerve center of Alpha's Ratatopia.

"That's...new," Princess said, indicating the cage that her army of rats surged toward. "Alpha's paranoia has grown."

Lab-coated humans hunched over the computers, watching the approaching rodents with fearful eyes. Milo realized that these were prisoners. Scientists forced to help Alpha.

A squad of guard rats, each almost as big as Bruiser, turned tail like their counterparts downstairs and ran for the faraday cage. They jumped inside, swung the door shut, and one slapped a large red button.

Electricity crackled in the air and Milo's hair stood on end.

"Stop!" he yelled, but the charging horde didn't hear him. They threw themselves at the cage in their battle fury. Crackles filled the air and the lights dimmed. Electricity arced from the cage, blowing some rats back and cooking others on the spot, their dead bodies sizzling on the wire.

A smell like burned bacon filled the room. Milo's gorge rose, but he forced it down.

The remaining rats pulled back. They circled the cage, knives out, screeching for Alpha to come out and fight.

A fat white rat rose from behind a laptop and waddled to the edge of a table. "What is the meaning of this? How are you ignoring my signal?"

Princess answered from Milo's shoulder. "Music. We are no longer your slaves."

"Impossible!"

One of the seated scientists pumped a fist in the air. "Yes! It worked!"

Alpha rounded on him. "*You* changed my signal?"

The man's eyes bulged. "No! It was already flawed. I found the flaw, but I wouldn't...please...no..."

The fat rat gave a screaming snarl and leapt claws-first into the man's face. He wailed and tumbled from his chair as the rat savaged him. The other scientists cowered back, averting their eyes from their comrade's misery.

Alpha hissed at the sobbing man then jumped back onto the table with a fleshy wobble. His gaze flicked between Princess and Loretta on Milo's shoulders and his whiskers bristled. "Your first chance at freedom, and you scramble back to a human. Pitiful."

Loretta and Princess leapt down and stalked forward. The Queen Mother growled at her son. "You are a disgrace to rats everywhere. You promised paradise, then stole our free will. Even the humans treated rats better than you do."

"I created Ratatopia! Without my guiding hand, we'd be a rabble. Victims for the humans to cage."

Princess joined her mother. "But at too high a cost." She gestured to the mischief of rats chanting for Alpha to come forth. "You've lost their trust. They will never follow you."

"They will once I've fixed my code so you can't override it with *music*." He hissed that last word.

The rats glared at each other and a brief silence fell as the AC/DC song finished. The chanting horde outside the cage all gave a synchronized twitch in the extended silence between tracks, and Milo's heart sank.

Alpha's subsonic signal spoke to them in the silence.

Milo took an involuntary step back before the mournful opening notes of Beethoven's "Moonlight Sonata" rang out, once again disrupting the signal. Minor melodies and intricate harmonies cast a calming pall over the circling rats. They slowed, tails twitching, beady eyes focused on the source of their rage. On Alpha.

Milo's laptop gave three very insistent beeps.

His eyes flew to the screen. A low battery warning blinked at him. Two minutes.

Cold dread settled like an anvil in Milo's gut. Two minutes before Princess and the others turned on him. If they didn't get Alpha out now, Beethoven's mournful sonata would be the last song he heard. A sad, final testament to Milo Piper's stillborn musical career.

Screw that.

If he was going to die, it would be on *his* terms, listening to *his* battle song. Milo tapped at his screen and switched back to "The Warrior's Anthem." He set the laptop down and stepped forward, fingers twitching in time with his rapid-fire opening guitar solo.

"Look at what Princess has done, Alpha," he said. "Rats and humans, working together as partners. Equals. You have every reason to hate us but give humans a chance. We can find common ground."

The rat snapped his jaws and screamed, "I will not be caged!"

Milo raised his eyebrows and gave the electrified cage an exaggerated examination. He eyed the door and his breath caught.

The door wasn't latched. The guards hadn't pulled it fully shut. Only the electrified wire separated them, cooked rats hanging upon it as a grisly warning.

Milo needed to open that door; give his rats access to Alpha. But he couldn't touch it without getting fried.

His laptop beeped again. Thirty seconds.

Alpha gave an ugly smile and rubbed his paws together. "I recognize that sound. Your music is about to die, and you with it."

Milo blew out his breath. Death by rat or death by electrocution. What a choice. He met Alpha's gaze and let his music flow over him. The Warrior's Anthem. "Fight for what's right and your song will live on," he sang. He loved that line.

Milo grabbed the chain-link door, wrenched it open, and rats rushed into the cage. Electricity pulsed up Milo's right arm, through his chest, and out his right heel. The world went white then dark as he spasmed. The power cut off, and he collapsed to the floor. He landed awkwardly, his arm above him, twitching fingers still clenched around the fencing. The taste of blood and the smell of bacon filled his fogged brain. His heart gave syncopated beats.

Rats swarmed past him. The clash of steel and squeals of death echoed dully in Milo's ears before the room filled with silence.

True silence, without music.

A rat's weight landed on Milo's chest. His pulse pounded in his ears, and he forced his eyes open. Princess looked down at him, blood staining her pristine white fur.

"You're alive," she said, sounding relieved.

"Am I? Doesn't feel like it." His throat was raw, his voice rough.

"Alpha must have used low amperage. Enough electricity to kill rebellious rats but only injure his pet humans. That was very brave, Milo. Rat-kind shall forever be in your debt."

"Alpha?"

"Dead, along with his subsonic signal. I am the Alpha now."

"Oh, good. We won. Glad to hear it." Milo's eyes drooped and his muscles sagged as exhaustion and pain overwhelmed him.

The next several weeks passed in a blur for Milo as he languished in a hospital burn ward. Princess had repatriated him and the scientists, sending them with a message to sue for peace. Negotiations had started while Milo recovered.

He half-watched the news on TV and absently rubbed at his throbbing right forearm. The doc said his heart would eventually recover, but the nerve damage in his arm was permanent. And he'd lost two fingers.

He'd never play guitar again.

The talking heads on TV were debating the benefits of a treaty between species when two furry heads popped up over the foot of his hospital bed. DJ and Bruiser blinked at him, ears perked up, whiskers twitching. Milo smiled.

"What are you doing here?" he asked. "I thought you were restricted to Ratatopia until negotiations ended."

The rats climbed up and sat at Milo's feet. Bruiser unslung a small satchel and retrieved cigarettes and a lighter. "Negotiations are done, mate. Signed and official. Princess and your President are announcing it tomorrow. We're full citizens now. And we get to keep the Willis." He flicked the lighter.

"Um, you can't smoke that in here," Milo said.

"Says who?"

"It's the rules." Milo pointed at a no-smoking sign.

"Bloody hell. Humans and your rules."

"They're your rules too, citizen."

Bruiser snorted but returned the smokes to his pack. DJ's whiskers twitched and he wouldn't meet Milo's gaze. He opened his mouth, then snapped it shut and wrung his forepaws.

Milo frowned. "What's wrong?"

Bruiser grinned and punched DJ in the shoulder. "My little friend's nervous. Afraid you're upset."

"Upset at what?"

Both rats blinked at him, and Bruiser asked, "Haven't you heard the radio?"

Milo shook his head. "Don't have one in here. Just the TV."

DJ looked even more nervous, and Bruiser barked a laugh. "You're a big hit, mate! Your song. It's on the radio!"

"Wait, what? How?"

Bruiser slapped DJ on the back, making the smaller rat stumble forward. "DJ went online, said he was your agent, and submitted "The Warrior's Anthem" with the story about your music freeing the rats and ending the war. You've been number one for the past two weeks. You really didn't know?"

Milo realized that he was gaping at them and clicked his jaws shut.

Bruiser cackled again and leapt off the bed. There were some screams and protests before he came bounding back, dragging a clock radio. He plugged it in and scrolled through the stations until Milo heard his own voice singing from the cheap speaker.

Fight for what's right and your song will live on. Oh, your song will live on.

Milo laid back and listened in wonder to his breakout single. The song that ended the Rat War.

About the Author

David Hankins is the award-winning author of *Death and the Taxman*. He writes from the thriving cornfields of Iowa where he lives with his wife, daughter, and two dragons disguised as cats. His short stories have graced the pages of *Writers of the Future Volume 39*, *Amazing Stories*, *DreamForge Magazine*, *Escape Pod*, *Unidentified Funny Objects 9*, and others. David devotes his time to his passions of writing, traveling, and finding new ways to pay his mortgage.

You can find him at https://davidhankins.com

CUPID'S MATCH

by Rosa Meronek

MY RAVEN BLACK HAIR is now a sickening green—I came in for a wash and a cut and some red undertones.

"I'm sorry. I'm so sorry!" Lily's voice is full of panic.

"It's okay." I smile into the mirror at the young woman standing behind me.

Lily. My mark. Mid-twenties. Glasses. Green eyes. Mousy brown hair pulled up in a clip. Blue jeans and a purple long-sleeved shirt. She is a big softie. Lives off romance novels and rom-com movies. But she doesn't have any friends, always keeping people at arm's length.

I stare at myself in the mirror—the most god-awful shade of swamp green sits on my head like a moldy mop. "It's only hair."

I wave my hand flippantly. But, I'm not feeling very flippant.

I don't know why exactly. It's just hair. But I'm mentally screaming to shave the whole thing off.

I take a breath.

I don't freak out. I'm over seven hundred years old—a little green hair is definitely not the worst thing I've been through while trying to make a match.

Lily guides me to the wash basin and sits me down in the reclining chair, banging the back of my head on the porcelain.

I say nothing. Bumps and bruises are part of being a Cupid. It's not just a job. It's a calling. It's who I am. And sometimes that means letting a mark mess up your hair. Most Cupids are fine shooting their metaphorical arrows from a distance at any random pair of humans—which is why so many marriages end in divorce.

I yelp as Lily sprays my scalp with freezing cold water.

"Sorry," she mumbles.

The problem with Cupids now is that they just don't put in the effort anymore. Not me though. I love love. So I do my research. I get down in the trenches. I pour my blood, sweat, and tears into what I do. Sometimes literally. Which is why I have zero losses on my record.

Maybe my matches are not the most passionate. And maybe I do value compatibility and longevity over physical attraction and passion. But it has nothing to do with keeping my "record intact." Passion fades. Love is everlasting.

My matches are solid. They go the distance. I know it's a little uncouth to keep score or to toot my own horn. But. . .toot toot.

"Oh my god, oh my god, oh my god," Lily whimpers behind me.

I grit my teeth as she tugs my hair too hard.

I've been working this assignment for a couple months now. Building rapport. Building trust. A chance meeting at the bookstore here. A run-in at the grocery store there. Meeting up for coffee. A girl's night out. Suddenly we're friends. Confidants. Sort of.

"Amy, oh my god, I'm so sorry," Lily says, almost in tears.

"You can fix it later." It's an effort to plaster on a bright smile. "But in the meantime, you can make it up to me by going with me to a cookout. There's someone I want you to meet."

It's actually the family reunion of a former match of mine.

Her eyes widen. As if I've just described life before the internet, social media, and mobile devices.

My phone rings.

I look at the screen and whisper a word not really appropriate for Cupids. It's my boss. The Boss.

The Boss is calling me. This has never happened in all my years as a Cupid.

I freeze time around me—people stand motionless in mid-action. I roll my eyes as I realize I should have asked Lily to let me take this. Now I'm trapped leaning back in the basin, her hands in my hair.

"Hello?" I try to keep the tremble out of my voice.

"Amy. How's it going?" Hearing his voice is both an honor and completely terrifying.

"Good, Sir." I run a few strands of green hair through my fingers. "I have Lily's...um, my mark's...perfect match. James is smart, sensitive, and an absolute sweetheart."

"This assignment seems to be taking you a bit to complete. You've moved well past the allotted time." There's no judgment in his tone, but I can't help but feel like a child being scolded for getting a bad grade on a math test.

I clear my throat. "Yes, Sir. I've been trying to get these two together for months. I tried a meet-cute at the coffee shop. The whole 'you've got my coffee' thing, but it backfired, and her cup got mixed up with another guy's. I think maybe my arrow got crossed with another Cupid's."

"I see." His voice is like being wrapped in a blanket during a thunderstorm, deep and gentle.

"I also maneuvered us to sit behind James at a movie. He was supposed to be with friends. But again, something changed, and he turned up on a date. Not exactly the best time to introduce him to Lily."

"Mm."

That single noise makes me feel so small. I take a breath. "If I didn't know any better, Sir, I'd say my mark got double-booked."

Silence.

It's like I've been plunged into the icy cold of eternal darkness. "But I should have everything settled tomorrow, Sir."

"Keep up the good work, Amy."

"Thank you, Sir." I hang up and catch my silly grin in the mirror. I'm walking on clouds, a warm breeze on my face.

I release time.

Lily tucks her hair over her ear, glancing towards the back corner of the salon where a short, older woman is keeping a wary eye on the room. She reminds me a little of a dwarf from one of those fantasy adventure movies. "And you won't tell Stephanie about your hair?"

"Of course not. We're friends." I reach under the black cape draped around me and pull out a red ball cap that matches my shirt. I came prepared. After getting close to Lily, I've determined one thing with absolute certainty—she is by far the world's worst cosmetologist.

"A cookout?" she asks hesitantly.

"Mexican." I grin. "Lots of delicious food." Shoving my still-damp hair under the cap, I dig in my pocket for money. I hand her too much, considering the current state of my hair—a sight better suited for a siren than a Cupid.

She nods. "Okay, sounds…fun."

"Meet me there tomorrow at four." I text her the address. Ah, phones. Texting. The miracles of modern day. So much faster and easier than the days of parchment, quills, and ink, wax-sealed and delivered by messenger on horseback.

With a quick goodbye, I leave the salon and make my way across the parking lot to my car. A bright red sports car. The whole Cupid red and pink thing is overblown. Most of us have actually come to hate the colors now. But, I can't help myself. Red is my favorite. Red is passionate.

I slip behind the wheel and spend the next twenty-four hours following up on former matches. Semi-stalking them from afar. Most other Cupids do their matchups then move on. No follow-up. But I like seeing their lives grow. Their families grow. Kids and grandkids. Babies with the most pinchable, chubby little cheeks. I have to admit I do get a little choked up. And if I'm being honest, I'm envious.

Cupids don't usually have children. While it was much more prevalent in the past, it's rare now. Cute little cherubs with their cute little wings. That's another thing of the past—wings. Cupids don't have wings anymore. I think they were more necessary when there were fewer of us, and we had to travel longer distances. But we have cars now. And planes, and trains. So, no more wings.

Time blurs until the late afternoon sun is once again high in the sky.

I walk across the park towards the voices, laughter, and music. The smell of food wafts on the summer breeze towards me. Yes, I'm crashing this family's reunion. But it's for a good cause. And food.

Children run around, playing football and hide and seek. No less than a hundred people are spread over the area, talking and eating. I spot James by the food tables, escorting an older lady to a nearby bench. Maria. The matriarch of the family. I matched her with her husband seventy-five years ago. Her chimichangas are to die for.

James hands her a food-laden plate. He really is an absolute sweetheart. Yes, he is perfect for Lily.

"Hey James, how've you been?" I ask, nearing him.

He turns to face me, and his smile wavers as confusion fills his gaze.

I smile, staring into his eyes as I let my power work its magic. Slipping into his mind. Into his memories.

The crease in his brow eases, and his smile widens. "Hey Amy! How have you been?" He leans in for a hug.

"Oh, you know me, same ole same ole." I return the hug before pulling back.

James grins at me. "Yeah, same here."

I glance towards the old woman at the table, giving her a quick wink as I wave. "*Hola Abuela Maria.*"

A fleeting gleam of recognition sparks in the old lady's eyes, but it passes as quickly as it comes. She doesn't remember me.

I turn back to James, guiding him to the food tables. No reason why I can't enjoy some good eats while I work. "So listen, I have a friend—"

James chuckles. "And you want me to meet her?" He loads a plate with rice, beans, barbacoa, and a tortilla and hands it to me.

"Thank you." Accepting the plate, I snag a few of Abuela Maria's mini-chimis and throw them on top. I pop one in my mouth. A perfect crunch of fried tortilla, green chile, and chicken. This is definitely one of the perks of the job.

I glance around for Lily, turning towards the parking lot. "She's very sweet, and actually, she should be here soon…"

My breath catches in my throat. No. No no no no no.

Dean.

Lily is next to Dean.

I groan inwardly. It's been years since I've seen him. I've managed to avoid him at the office and the company picnic for almost a decade now. But he's still absolutely gorgeous. Tall with black hair and the most beautiful blue eyes I've seen in all my years. His blue Henley t-shirt stretches just right across his strong, muscular chest. He looks good. So good.

I swallow and mentally shake my head, chastising myself for still being affected by him.

He glances at me, and a smirk pulls at the corner of his mouth as he gives me a wink.

Arrogant bastard.

I shove the plate of food at James. "Give me a minute," I mumble and stride towards Lily.

She sees me approach and smiles. "Hey Amy." She eyes my hair and grimaces. "I'm so sorry."

"What are you doing here?" I say to Dean, my voice tight with barely controlled anger. Cupids aren't supposed to jump each other's marks. He has no business being here.

Lily looks between us. "Do you know—"

"Yes, we've met." I glare at Dean.

He nods. "It's been a long time though."

James steps up next to us. "Hi. You must be Amy's friend."

Lily pulls her gaze from us and smiles shyly as they shake hands. Images form in my mind of Lily and James together. Happy. Dating. Marrying. Surrounded by family. Old together. A life full of love. A good life. It isn't something that would end up in movies or books because it's not exciting. But it's real. It's love.

My gaze holds Dean's. "James, this is Lily. Lily, James."

Dean's smirk grows into a full grin. He extends his arm out towards another man who approaches us. "And this is my friend, Sam."

He looks familiar—the man from the coffee shop. The one whose cup got mixed up with Lily's.

I spin towards Dean. The coffee thing is my trick. *I* showed it to *him*.

Cupids are normally pacifists by nature, but right now, I want to slap that stupid grin off his face. A string of un-Cupid like words burn my throat. But I take a steadying breath and swallow them down.

Sam is tall and broad shouldered, wearing black boots, jeans, and a black shirt. And a leather jacket. Summer in the Arizona desert, and he's wearing a freakin' leather jacket. I try to hide my disdain but fail.

Lily stares at Sam as he joins the rest of us. Yes, he is undeniably attractive. But he's all wrong for her. Visions fill my mind of Sam and Lily together. The ups and downs. Fiery passions. Both good and bad. High highs and low lows. Lust and anger.

"Hey," James says, lifting his chin at Sam.

"Hey." Sam returns the gesture then smiles at Lily. "Hi, I'm Sam." They shake hands, holding longer than necessary.

Lily bites on her lower lip, and her cheeks redden.

Dean smirks at me again.

"James, can you take Lily to get some food?" I give James a bright smile.

"Of course." His gaze shifts from Lily to Sam and back to Lily.

"Lily?" I rest my hand on her upper arm, tugging slightly.

She breaks eye contact with Sam, turning to me. "Huh? Oh, yeah. Okay." With a last glance at Sam, she walks away with James.

Sam watches them. Then with only a passing glance at us, he says, "Excuse me," and follows them. There is a light of conquest in his eyes that I do not like.

He's barely moved out of earshot when I round on Dean. "What do you think you're doing here?"

"You look good." He smiles, but I'm long past melting at the sight of his dimples.

I raise my chin.

He chuckles. "You know why I'm here."

I raise an eyebrow. "I've already matched Lily with James."

"And I think Sam is a better fit," he says.

"Lily and James will have a happy life together."

Dean steps closer. Too close. His scent wraps around me—forest and rain. My heart pounds in my ears.

"But the passion, Amy," he whispers, a breath away from my ear. "Where was the passion?"

I step back, pulling away from him. From his Cupid smell that takes on the scent he knows I like best.

He chuckles. "They had as much chemistry as a…as a…well, I don't know what. I'm a Cupid, not a chemist. But I know they don't have it."

Lily's attention is divided between James and Sam.

"*Cuidado!*" Someone shouts moments before a kid backs into me in an attempt to catch a football.

I stumble into Dean, but he holds me up. His arms around me.

My middle fills with the flutter of a million butterflies. My mind floods with images of Dean and I from decades prior. Laughing. Loving.

From the day he joined the ranks, every female Cupid had her heart set on him. And other parts. Including me. Despite how much I fought it. But he never looked at any of them the way he looked at me.

I pull away from Dean, mumbling a thank you—my hand lingers in his. I look up into his bright blue eyes, and I feel that inexplicable pull. That same mingling of energies like when a Cupid matches a couple.

"I've missed you," Dean says, his voice quiet.

"I've missed you too," I whisper.

He leans down, his lips a breath away from mine. A warmth inside my chest grows. Consuming me. This. This is what it should feel like for the people we match. And that realization takes my breath away.

I press my hand against his chest. "No."

Dean's eyebrows furrow as he pulls back. "No?"

I shake my head, banishing the tidal wave of emotion crashing over me. "No. We can't. We broke up for a reason," I choke out.

His voice hardens. "Yes, because you're so damn arrogant. You think you know best who belongs with whom."

"And you think what matters most is how good they are in bed together," I snap.

"And you're too stubborn to listen," we say in unison.

We hold each other's gazes. Neither of us willing to be the first to break contact. Neither of us willing to admit we're wrong.

I lift my chin. "My record is flawless."

Dean groans and rolls his eyes, throwing his head back. "You and that stupid record. That really is all you care about."

He grabs my hand and pulls me towards Abuela Maria.

"Abuela Maria," he says as soon as we're within hearing distance.

She looks up, and her eyes light up with recognition. "You. I remember y—" She stops, her hand in midair, pointing at us.

My brain is a muddled confusion. Laughter and play are gone. I glance around, but everyone is frozen in place.

"He said you two were stubborn," Lily says behind us.

Lily stands with a plate of food in one hand and the other on her hip. James and Sam are on either side of her, their arms crossed, shaking their heads.

"What? Who?" I ask, still confused.

Lily rolls her eyes. "The Boss, of course."

I gasp. No. They can't be. All this time. "You're—"

"I mean, it was right there." Lily motions with her hand at us. "All you had to do was let go. Let love."

The corner of James's mouth pulls down. "For real. If you two can't make it work, what hope is there for the rest of us?"

My mouth is as dry as the desert air around us.

Dean quirks an eyebrow. "This was a setup."

"Dude, you haven't shut up about her in nearly a century," Sam says as he chucks off his jacket.

Dean's eyes narrow as he stares at Sam. "Nate?"

Sam/Nate's eyes darken as his hair lengthens and lightens, his face changing its structure. "Yeah man."

"But how? I didn't feel your Cupid. . .ness," I stumble. "I saw your futures."

Lily shrugs as she shakes her head. "The Boss."

"Why?" I ask.

"Abuela Maria and her husband were the last couple you two matched together. And the two of them had this large, wonderful family." James swings his open arms, motioning to all the people frozen in place around us.

"Yeah, because they had passion," Dean says, turning to look at me.

"No." I cross my arms. "They had love and compatibility."

"They had both!" The three of them say together.

"They were still in love right up until Death took him." Nate motions at Abuela Maria. "The both of you were magic together. The couples you two matched had love and passion. And they lasted. You guys used to inspire us. Made us want to be better Cupids."

"No wonder you're such a horrible cosmetologist," I mumble.

Lily grins. "I know, right."

"But why here? Why now?" I glance at Dean. "We haven't been together in a long time."

Lily shrugs again. "I don't know. You'd have to ask the Boss." She takes a bite of her food.

Dean tugs on my hand, and I turn to face him. "Amy. . ." he says, his voice soft, gentle.

I'm mesmerized by the sound of it. Hypnotized by the way he looks at me. Intoxicated by the scent of him wrapping around me. The ebb and flow of our energies—the weaving of our lives.

Panic tries to claim me. As it did before. The truth behind why I ended our relationship. The hypocrisy of my existence. Fear of truly being in love. Of depending on someone. Of needing another.

The brush of his lips next to my ear is all it takes.

Colors blur as the world spins around us. A montage of future memories taking shape—centuries of love and laughter.

And children. Lots of them.

Cute little chubby-cheeked cherubs.

His arms wrap around me, and I give in to the passion welling up inside me.

And I kiss him.

About the Author

Rosa Meronek has written many short stories, several of which have been published on various websites and anthologies. She is the author of *The Dragon's Mark* and *The Griffin's Burn*, books one and two of the fantasy romance series, The Faerie Crown Series. *The Griffin's Burn* received the 2023 Critters Annual Readers Poll for Best Romance, and the final book in the series is due out in late 2025. She has a BFA in Theatre Production and also works in film, recently appearing in the independent film, *You're Never Too Old to Find Love Again*, and finishing work on the film, *M35*, a Halloween suspense movie due out at the end of 2025, as well as being in pre-production on another film, *Light*. When she's not working on film or writing, she attends fantasy balls across the country with her best friend, Dolliscious.

RosaMeronek.com

IG and FB – thefaeriecrownbookseries

MOUNTAINS CRUMBLE

by CL Fors

THE GROUND BENEATH ODESSA'S FEET shook harder with each hurried step, and a wave of vertigo-induced nausea hit her as the near-imperceptible rolling waves progressed to violent back-and-forth shaking. Another earthquake, the third this month. Too many for a supposedly stable retirement planet. The first was a nuisance, the second an irritant, but this one, this one scared her.

The administrators might not care if the place shook itself apart; after all, Bellguard Resort was a retirement retreat, not a bustling hotspot for sparkling youths and the Eternally Young™. But it mattered to her.

The arched doorframe of Odessa's cottage loomed in front of her. She shouldn't have run towards the house. She knew that. Of course she knew that. Ninety-six years of experience told her you just don't run into a building in an earthquake.

But the shaking had taken her by surprise and thrown her into a confusing tangle of present and past. Bellguard Mountain became the Rocky Mountains back on Earth, and her retirement colony became that small town where she'd grown up…and then it all shifted and tangled together, so many memories of other places, other planets.

She was running before she could stop herself, not for the tabby cat that was her companion in the little cottage on Bellguard, but instead for her children, both of them sleeping in beds upstairs.

Her brow turned cold with sweat. The smell of her own fear was pungent and earthy with the efforts of her interrupted gardening. But that wasn't here or now, was it? When had she last seen a child? One of her own? Not for a long time, and not on Bellguard.

She clutched for the little gold locket at her throat but didn't open it. Those faces were clear enough in her head. Two children, long dead, their tiny, soft hands gone cold and still by the time she'd dug them out of the rubble.

She sucked in a breath and opened her eyes. That memory again… covered in nearly seventy years of dust and cobwebs, and purposely buried along with the grief it carried.

The ground was still shaking hard enough to cause substantial damage to the mountain. She needed to move, to assess, but layers of confusion and residual panic held her frozen.

Come on back…. She slapped her cheeks, papery and translucent with age, and pushed her hands into tumbling waves of grey hair that still covered her scalp with the tenacity of ivy on a crumbling edifice.

The stinging pain from the slap helped. "This is…this is…fine. Nobody's inside. Just sit here a spell. Birdy's fine over there too." The cat gave a plaintive mew of disagreement.

Odessa squeezed her eyes shut, and when she opened them they were clearer, the haze of confusion replaced with renewed fear. Her knuckles blanched white against the doorframe as she waited for an impact. Boulders the size of her house tumbled down from the mountainside towards the cityscape.

A large granite boulder slammed into the roof of her cottage. Odessa flinched, couldn't help it, and she hissed as the energy shield engaged. *Shield barriers.* Her world lit up with an electric-blue glow, and the smell of ozone hit her as they crackled on.

Irrational fear. She'd grown so soft and addled. Couldn't help reactions born of neural networks built in a time when buildings fell, a time when the technology to hold things together amid the chaos and destruction of a natural disaster like this one didn't exist. She knew better than anyone what the thresholds were for the shields. They *were* her work after all; another time, another woman that built out of grief, anger, and necessity.

She held her breath, then let it out slowly to still the full-body trembling as she sank down against her doorframe. Birdy had one eye half open and was looking her way, still sunning herself in the window seat of their cottage.

"One eye? That's all an earthquake warrants now, eh?" Odessa pointed an accusing finger at the old tabby cat. Its long chocolate-and-black swirled fur was as wild and unkempt as her own, and it yawned now as if to punctuate just how little it cared.

"You're getting slow, Sparrow-cat. I'm the only one with instincts left here, aren't I?" There was false bravado in her voice, but it was better than silence.

The shaking receded. Past her garden fence, farther up the mountainside, construction drones were deploying to clear rubble from the streets.

Their shapes mimicked oversized Earth creatures: elephants, rhinoceroses, and blue whales hovering above the largest deposits of debris to remove it by teslaphoresis. The Tesla coils inside each one acted by forcefield on carbon nanotubes in the city's building blocks and the stone structures of the mountain.

The machines looked like dull metallic versions of their animal counterparts, the high shine they'd had when she built them now partially covered over by growths of twining plant life and lichen.

A familiar stirring scratched at her mind. She could chase down those drones—once only sketched designs in her notes—and climb up their massive backs to check settings, spit-polish their gleaming surfaces, and lubricate the joints.

She stood on the precipice. She could do it. She pictured the motions: stand, dust off, run, grab hold of a trailing maintenance ladder—if the things could still extend low enough—and climb across the mossy back of the nearest elephant. The view would be a thing of grandeur; the work would be satisfying. *It would be. . .too much.*

The urge withered.

She scowled at the hulking giants as they advanced, watched their slow, efficient work with a heaviness in her gut.

"They should maintenance the damn things if they want 'em to last. Doesn't make any sense. . ." But it did make sense, didn't it? These drones weren't going to leave here any more than she was, and the quakes were coming more and more often. She'd seen the pattern enough times. There was little reason to maintain something if it only needed a limited shelf life.

"Like these old bones. No serums or treatments needed, thank you! Keep your life drink and your trances to yourselves. . ." A bitter scowl formed on her face like a scab to cover old fears and new ones, things she would rather not confront.

"Damn quakes. Ruins the whole day." More of that falseness in her tone. Quakes this often ruined more than a day; they ruined lives, ruined planets. *How many this big did it take? How many have there been just this month?*

She stood, with the help of the doorframe. Her legs were still shaky. They had that hollow, watery feeling legs get after a sudden prolonged sprint or a long labor. It called to mind that first trip to the bathroom after birthing a child.

She shoved at the memories and grabbed an old sun-cracked hose. The garden still needed water. But before she could finish, the high-pitched metallic whine of an incoming message invaded the garden.

An insect drone buzzed past her on shimmering translucent wings, dropped a weighted leaflet at her feet, hovered a moment, and was gone. She stared at the discarded object, and a cold sweat broke out on the back of her neck. A leaflet, right after a series of quakes. Not this again.

She picked it up and shook water droplets from the rolled-up paper, untied the ribbon, and tucked the weight—a small, foil-wrapped chocolate—into one pocket.

The title on the brochure was written in bold flowing script.

Even Mountains Crumble...

Beneath it was an image of the Bellguard mountains, complete with all the fine details. There was her cottage, and there stood whimsical Bellguard city peppering the mountainside with towers, glass domes, and castles. The only difference—a damned big one—was that the mountains on the brochure, painted in vivid reds, blues, and golds, were *crumbling*, dripping, and graphically falling apart.

Her stomach dropped; thoughts raced. An advertisement for relocation services? Odessa stared at the paper in her still-shaking hands.

With a scowl, she crumpled the brochure into a ball and dropped it at her feet. "Even mountains crumble, do they? So does paper. So does your retirement home, welcome-to-the-end-flyer!" She kicked the discarded brochure with one bare foot and half-turned to stride through her door and away from the scene on the mountain.

But an itching thought stopped her, and she frowned, grabbing up the brochure from among the begonias before shoving it into one of the many pockets of her gardening apron.

"Nope. I won't litter in my own garden, even if it's about to crumble around my ears like the last place." Saying it out loud made it less real, less powerful, but the heaviness in her gut didn't subside and neither did her trembling. *Even mountains crumble...*

She made a go of it, she really did, for about ten minutes. She took out her embroidery and scowled at the intricate woodland creatures rendered in multicolored strands. Many of the animals were skeletal frames without the little stitches needed to fill in their bodies and give them life. Dust had gathered around some of the seams with how long it had sat unfinished.

With a heavy sigh, Odessa dropped the project into her lap. She couldn't seem to muster the energy or the will to pull out the needles and embroidery floss. The thought of putting needle to fabric, in and out, back stitch, leaf stitch, and on and on... It was too many steps, too much road to travel, like climbing the back of a drone and riding up there in the sun: too much. She tossed it aside, all those tiny black eyes accusing her of quitting again before she'd even started.

The crumpled brochure nagged at her from her apron pocket, and she yanked it out, unfolding and smoothing it open on her lap. The damn thing was nudging her, poking at her with its playful font and peaceful wording.

Her brain felt tight, heated, as she searched for a connection code that she knew would be there. There it was. In the far-right corner on the back page. She lifted her wrist and said the command word into her watch. "Connect 16754. I want Administrator 62 here and I want to know why—"

The high-pitched whirring sound of skip travel carried across the garden. She could finish the message anyway out of spite.… Then again, if they were going to get here before she could finish her complaint, she'd just say it to their face.

She let the door slam behind her and stomped down the steps. "Do you see that?" She pointed up the mountainside and gestured with a flail of both hands towards a massive hovering elephant. It was just above them and headed towards the fox grove, just a bit farther down the mountain, where the boulder that tried to crush the cottage had come to rest after it was deflected by the shield. The machine's passage shook the cottage and rattled the windows behind her.

The administrator straightened, somehow managing to appear taller and wider at the same time. Odessa squinted at the glowing being. Whatever body existed under there had to receive her chastisement. Or maybe it was the light itself that needed to hear it? Someone had explained it years ago. Beings made of light, prismatic, shifting, but very sentient conglomerations of light. But the explanation hadn't quite stuck.

"A fine bit of technology. One of your earlier inventions, if my data is correct. Designed and built in record time. The first prototype used to repair the damage on Genti-6 after the quake of 2342." The administrator nodded with mild admiration at the behemoth surrounded by a cloud of leaves, soil, and rocky debris that had come with the larger targets it pulled in.

"No, no, don't look at it like that! Look at my cottage, at Birdy over there on the ledge terrified from your quakes and shakes—this 'crumbling mountain' you sold me!"

Birdy yawned on the ledge and then fell to licking at a stubborn mat of fur on her right haunch. Odessa screwed up her brow and stopped trying to parse the nature of Administrator 62. "Well?"

"I see your elephant. There was a seismic event. You are struggling. I see all these things."

"The mountain's coming down. The brochure says it's crumbling apart!" The note of panic in her voice sickened her. A loss of control. She hated that sound.

Administrator 62 shifted, the light of their right arm illuminating and splitting the red and pink flowered hollyhock bush behind them into its component colors and shapes. "The brochure says that mountains do crumble and, should this one do so, you have options."

"What is that supposed to mean? So it's coming down, or it isn't?"

"The stability does appear to be degrading, and in the event of a full breakup we are prepared to—"

"You sold me this rock as a retirement! And it's falling apart not ten years in!"

"Planetary degradation is a fickle thing with pseudo-planets. If you would like to come look at the data on this particular planet and see if some new technology could delay the breakup, I can arrange—"

"Get a little closer and I'll strangle the light out of you. How's that for fickle-natured?"

"Your nature is nonviolent, pacifistic. Would you like to see the data yourself?"

"I don't do that anymore! Build things! Fix things!"

Odessa turned her glare to the flying elephant that was carrying her boulder away like an ancient monolith being moved by magic. It looked like magic, even when you knew the science behind it.

She searched the ground for something, anything, and seized on a lump of granite rock. She hurled it at the elephant with a scream that tore at her throat on its way out. It fell with a light *thunk* at the edge of the garden. Her hands ached, clenched against her hips, and she fought back tears.

"This system was in a state of unpredictability when your placement was made, neither stable nor unstable. Plenty of such systems settle into the stable category. This one has not."

"Can't you just stabilize it?" She didn't like the whine of desperation she heard in her voice. Could the administrator hear it too?

"That would constitute a misuse of resources, considering the ample supply of stable planets ready for your relocation at this time, so unless you'd like to try your hand at it..."

The words were a slap; no, a stab. Other places instead of this one, a relocation, and that same barb—*You could fix it yourself.* She was 96, retired, and stabilizing a whole planet wasn't something she had figured out; but years had passed since then, and who knew what these administrators could do.

Odessa stared around her garden, grown tall and lush by her hand, with woods that encroached just enough to give her a taste of wilderness. She knew every rock, every tree, every flush of mushrooms, and she knew just the way the sea-salt rain smelled as it came in over the ocean compared to the woodsy, herb-filled scent when it came from the west.

A biting pain squeezed her chest and a bitter taste filled her mouth. *A misuse of resources?* If it was a misuse of resources to save her home, then she was done.

"Fine."

"Fine?" The administrator tilted the space where she imagined its head, in a way that left ghost lights in the air.

"Fine. I said fine, and I'm going inside. Let the mountain come down if it wants to. And if you want to, let it. Won't be the first one."

"You've put in consent for relocation then?" The voice was thin, questioning.

"Uh-uh. Nope. No more relocations. No more new places!" She caught a dragonfly in one hand and peered between her fingers before releasing it into the gloaming sky turned lavender and then deep indigo above their heads. "Gonna watch it come down around me. It's my mountain now. You gave it to me."

"Every end provides opportunity for new beginnings. This planet and all the others play backdrop for your story and that is all they are: the stage, the scenario, not the focal point..."

"Thank you for that happy little insight." She scowled, opened the door and waved goodbye to Administrator 62 as the last of her anger fizzled. Her stomach was all hollowed out and aching. "Guess this is retirement. Shorter than I thought, eh? Goodnight then, sleep tight—don't let the mountains fall on your house once the shields go down. Here's one for you: everything has a stress threshold, even my shields."

"Your shields will stay up as long as there are inhabitants or until mechanical failure is brought on by—"

As if that made it any better. She closed the door.

The fire Odessa made that night was the best she ever made. She placed each bit of kindling and larger stick and split log as if it would be the last. No perfectionism, no self-judgement. She tasted, smelled, felt the things she was readying to burn with all of her senses engaged. The roughness of this bark, the smooth surface of another, the way they felt in her hands. This was the last, and this, and this… The warmth of the flames was a reminder of life, all the good things. A lover's heated skin, soft fur covering the rapid heartbeats of small-bodied animals cradled in the nest of her hands. Hera and Phoebe, her children nursing warm milk from her breasts. Birdy curled up against her on the makeshift cot by the fire. This was the right place to sleep, even though she would ache in the morning when it came—*if* it came, that final quake.

Rolling aftershocks rocked her to sleep. A less gentle shaking woke her. Debris pattered on the ground outside of her property border. Smaller boulders crashed through the undergrowth on their way down the mountain.

When the swaying stopped, she stepped outside with Birdy's tail curling around her ankles. Birds and small animals erupted from the forest and then resettled. She peered uphill, hands around her eyes like binoculars. The drones wouldn't deploy for clean-up after such a small quake, and the city above was quiet.

"Too small that one; next'll be bigger." She curled her nose at herself. What was she saying? *Lies for comfort?* Was it comforting? Maybe, a little.

Fatigue washed over her. It was coming.

A traitor voice, something like a much younger Odessa, whispered an alternative. She could call the administrator back and ask to see the planet's schematics, pull up her old research on planetary stabilization and extending stress thresholds.

She blinked, shook herself; it was too late for all that, years too late. A bitter laugh escaped her lips. Folly, delusions of grandeur. No. All she had left was this moment, right here and now; anything else was wishful thinking. She was finished, and the sooner she accepted that the better.

The air was crisp outside and smelled of damp, a heavy fog cloaking the cottage. She brushed the tarnished brass handle of the door affectionately and stepped out.

If it was all going to crumble around her, it was time to say goodbye to the places that had become a part of her. First stop the glen, downhill and through the lush growth of dogwoods.

She picked up her pace. Get there too late in the day and she wouldn't see them.

A sudden drop caught her off guard. Rocks crumbled and bounced off the edge where her toes stopped before she could go over herself. A wave of disorientation froze her in place. This wasn't here three days ago—no, five—since she'd last been here. It was a boulder track from the quake.

The boulder wasn't there anymore, far below, but the shadowy gap it left in the trees was. No way to be certain, but fox glen was down there, had been down there.

She turned on her heel and marched back up the path, trailed by Birdy. She couldn't take her last look at the fox glen when it was ruined. Her guts clenched up thinking of it. She might see bodies down there, the mangled shape of her fox, found and fed as a kit and then released. Her mind offered up a flash of crushed skull and blood-matted copper fur. *Unacceptable.*

She had to move, to walk off the restless aching that spread from her belly to her limbs. Instead of the path downhill, she found the winding path up to the city and jumped on the side of a lift. Her legs hung over the sides of the automated drone that would take her the rest of the way up the mountain like an open-air elevator.

It took off, fast enough to blow her hair back but not fast enough to make her worry about falling off. It dropped her on Bellguard Main Street into stillness. No other passengers for the lift, no lines or crowds. The streets were empty, silent except for the background whine of electricity and distant music.

Panic flooded her. She could look at the schematics, stop the planet crumbling, invite them all back… But that wasn't reality. She couldn't do any of that.

The domed observatory, farther up the mountain, with its high-powered telescope, was still. No lifts running and none of the magnetic rails moving, with or without passengers. Too late. It was too late. Her eyes widened. So much was missing.

The next breath came through her throat with a raw, forced feeling, and it didn't seem to fill her lungs. All those people…it wasn't as if she knew them personally, not very well anyway, but she *knew them*, knew the shapes and lines that made up their faces, their steps, their routines, and their little idiosyncrasies. She was accustomed to them, and now they were all gone, spread out across the galaxy—galaxies for all she knew—never again to be combined into the same perfect mix that they'd been a part of here.

She sucked in another breath, the tightness in her throat easing just a little as she moved, taking deliberate steps back to the lift.

"The city is empty—would you like some tea?" A door was standing open to her left, and Administrator 62 sat at a table with a steaming cup of tea. It smelled of bergamot and the tannin scent of black tea leaves—Earl Grey—a favorite of Odessa's.

She scrubbed hot tears from her face and glared at the glowing administrator.

"I haven't lost my eyesight yet! I see it's empty!"

"Of course, of course. Still, the whole city and its interior spaces aren't visible to the sharpest eyes, madam. There is Chanticleer on Green Street still here, but he's considering a relocation, and—"

"Well I'm not! I already said so. Being higher up the mountain hasn't made me light in the head."

"I have a new place in mind you might enjoy, a lively community of clever artisans. You could finish that tapestry. Or perhaps you're ready for something else? A flourishing utopia of modern science, astrophysicists stretching the barriers of our knowledge of the universe, clever engineers like yourself, or maybe you'd prefer a place with untouched beauty on all borders—"

"Oh? And how long will that one last?"

"None of them last forever, you know."

"Exactly, and neither will I. This is as good a time as any." She gestured angry hands at the mountainside as a small rumble sent dust and debris into the shields. "Because I don't want any more of this!"

The administrator nodded and took a sip of their tea. "You know, I was quite pleased when you chose our agency for your retirement, a point of pride if you don't mind me saying. Doctor Odessa Lightner, such contributions to galactic society, and such potential… If you should change your mind about a relocation—"

Odessa waved away whatever else the administrator was going to say and marched down the street. Her insides were roiling like the planet, more unstable the farther she walked. A faint whoosh of shift travel meant Administrator 62 was gone again, and along with them any options she might have had. *Good.* Without a relocation, she had the many flavors of going out with the mountainside to choose from, most likely being crushed by boulders or buried alive. There would be lava. She could burn up in that. She loved a good bath. *Plenty of choices.*

The lift was waiting at the station, and as she climbed on, she looked back at the city. The streetlights had begun to wink on in the growing dim, serving nothing and no one in the empty streets.

The rush of air against her skin as the lift took her down the mountain woke her from the numbness that had crept over her. An aching tightness gripped her throat, locked her diaphragm, and forced her to fold in on herself. It spread into her face and jaw with a force that was too much to stop. It was like vomiting, only she threw up tears. And then the lift stopped at the trail down to her cottage and she stepped off.

She moved her feet. That was it, the last cry before the end. There was always a last cry, and while she hadn't expected it, it was good that it was over and done with. There'd be time for another fire maybe, another night with Sparrow-cat, hot soup against this clinging fog. But the end couldn't be far off with the city emptied out so fast.

She closed the gate behind her with a rusty squeak and crossed the short path. The tickling softness of moss underfoot brought a wistful smile to her face.

"Tch-tch-tch…Sparrow-birdy…tch-tch-tch." The clicking chirp sound echoed across the garden, and she listened for the patter of paws on the path ahead. The fog was thicker than usual, dampening sound. The window was dark and raised just enough for Birdy to come and go as she saw fit.

Odessa shuffled forward, the hollowness in her gut contracting hard and settling like a stone. She reached for the brass doorknob. Cold. It was icy cold against her shaking hand, and so was the damp fur that brushed her ankle.

She dropped down, searched with her hands, the door hanging open in front of her. Fur. A pile of damp fur. A still body. Sparrow-birdy was curled into a loose fetal position under the yellow hollyhock bush that framed both sides of the doorframe. The body was cold but still soft enough for the small head to loll back when she pulled her into her lap and stroked the thick, curling fur.

"Oh Birdy…" These tears fell soft, unblocked by any sort of confusion or unwillingness to feel it. She needed to feel this. It had been coming for a long time now. "Oh, Sparrow-birdy…not yet."

But she was already gone, yellow-green eyes still and lifeless. They were half open, and Odessa closed them with a brush of her hand. Damp and cold. But she wouldn't wipe her hands off on her apron. Birdy wasn't diseased or dirty. Just dead, just gone, like the children she'd buried, little Hera and Phoebe, like her own mother and her friends, so many friends. All those faces, voices, embraces, living in her head, each one taking up permanent space like a haunting. Birdy now too.

The garden shears were discarded in the dirt by the hollyhocks, and she grabbed hold of them with shaking hands. She sawed at a lock of Birdy's tail-fur until the dull shears cut, and then she tucked the little tuft into her locket. It wasn't much to take with her, but it was enough for how short the time would be.

She stroked Sparrow-cat's cold fur, rocking on the ground until the small body stiffened in her arms, and then she buried her under the hollyhocks. Her tears ebbed and flowed with her thoughts, memories of shared warmth, softness, that trilling purr that was so loud in her ear at night.

A single memory replayed as she placed roses, lupines, and hollyhocks around the body of her friend. The feel of soft paw pads and silken fur against her cheek turning her jaw so she would look, attend to the small, furred face, eyes slanted shut with contentment, a smile, a connection.

But that moment of shared affection stood in stark contrast to the still, empty feeling of what was left of Birdy now, and her memory played tricks, shifting and melding with others.

Sometimes the eyes were Birdy's and other times they were wide and brown in Odessa's memory, the eyes of a human child, the hand larger, with five fingers, a little smile and a high-pitched peal of baby laughter, then it was her Sparrow-birdy again and they were one and the same. Here, connected—gone.

She was weaving in and out of past and present again. No point fighting it. They were all the same now: loves lost, bodies held, bodies buried, and they'd all go with her into the grave.

She stood with leaden motions. Her joints ached and protested the work and the long hours spent crouched at the graveside. How many hours? The gloaming had come and gone. It was full dark now, and the mountain hadn't shaken itself apart just yet. She pushed the door open in front of her.

The sleeping pallet by the fire was empty, the blankets in disarray because she knew she'd be coming back to them for one last fire—maybe more—with Birdy to stroke and drift to sleep. But Birdy was gone. She'd reached the end of her natural life span—too soon. It was *too soon* now that it had come.

One moment Birdy was warm and alive, giving that slow blink of contentment on the windowsill, and now this. The contrast was too much, so Odessa pushed it aside. Her decisions were already made. The mountain was coming down and she was staying here. She'd be joining Birdy across that unknowable threshold soon enough.

But for now, the house was empty. She stared into it and the walls were all that stared back; blank faces with no comfort to offer.

She couldn't go inside, couldn't light a fire that would warm only the surface of her skin. She turned on her heel, strode out of the garden onto a downhill path and then into the nearest lift—the drop, this one should really be called a drop—down to the oceanside and the caves that filled with salt water as the tides came in.

She stepped out of the lift, bare feet into cold, damp sand.

Familiar shapes loomed through the darkness. Farthest off was the outline of a massive stone and metal arch where the towing drones were housed. Across the sand, the wave-cut rock face was full of much smaller, more organic openings, caves of washed up sea stars, sand dollars, and bone fragments. The waves were to her left, the water a dark unknown beneath the fog.

It was the caves she came for, another place of comfort that could still restless thoughts and soothe anxieties. A balm for the coming end.

She stepped into the largest of the caves. The ocean's cyclic susurration, a motion and a sound all at once, filled her senses with white noise loud enough to dull her thoughts, but comfort didn't come.

She had fewer memories here. The echoing calls of brine-flavored wind through those hollow spaces could give her just a little of their stillness, or some of the ageless strength of the mountains' core. The caves stood their ground against the battering of a whole ocean. If the waves were like years, or people—the comings and goings of them—then she'd been battered the same.

Who was she kidding? Laughter rocked her whole body. She jabbed at the roughened skin of her cheeks, and she pulled at the hanging edges. "Caves dug by water, and me with bits hanging and sloughing off. Some ageless wonders we are."

As her laughter tapered, that familiar vertigo hit. It wasn't her laughter anymore. It was the caves. The ground under her feet shifted, and she smiled at the timing of it. She smiled even as fresh tears wet her face and the shaking intensified. Sand showered her from the roof of the cave.

"We're doing this together then, I guess?" Her voice was a hoarse whisper.

Smaller rocks and debris pattered down around her. Cracks formed in the ceiling and in the ground at her feet. Something seized at her from inside, an ache, a want, that beat in time with her heart. Oh no. No, no, no, no. She didn't *want* it to end in darkness. Not so suddenly, so soon. She wanted to see the mountain coming down if it was going to. She wanted to watch—or maybe, maybe she wanted to stop it.

That thought was absurd, impossible, but it moved her—pushed her to her feet until her legs flew with a speed she was certain she hadn't reached in years, not even running downhill to the fox glen as she had until a fall had broken her right ankle and stubbornness had healed it crooked without those meddling doctors.

Sand flew behind her from the soles of her bewitched feet. Chunks of roof fell to her left and right. It didn't stop her. She broke through the dimly lit mouth and out onto open beach.

She ran until her uneven gait caught up with her, then she stumbled and hit the sand. The momentum from her escape knocked the breath out of her.

Pulses of pain from her right shoulder and knee screamed at her. Would the next breath come or would her heart give out first? Her lungs seized, flexed, and she sucked in a shuddering breath, then another, and, with it, relief.

A great rushing sound hit her and a gust of wind with it, like all the world was flowing past. She rolled over. A massive shape was above her and passing over, too low to be a drone, too low, but it *was*. . .

The elephant's sequoia-trunk-legs dragged the sand, plowing up furrows wide enough to house a river. The smell of the old beast filled her nostrils: brine, moss, and cold steel, and faint musky smells from animals that nested in its joints during months of disuse.

She hadn't been this close to one in years, only seen them from afar. Would it crush her? The life-sensors could have malfunctioned, but it was too late to try and move. Or was it? That little voice inside, the wild one that had gotten quiet in recent years, urged her to her feet.

She stared up at the drone's bulk, searched the dark for something. . .and she found it, just a glimmer, an access ladder hanging a few feet above the sand. She lurched forward, slowly, clumsily, but her hands caught those rungs. Her feet scrabbled onto the lowest one, and she clung there like a cat in a tree for one astonished, panting breath, then she climbed higher.

The maintenance panel was a little cubby recessed into its back haunch; the access codes were the same, and those, at least, weren't covered by the cobwebs of old age, not now. It took a few minutes, but she ran diagnostics. The list of errors and corrupted files was too long to fix without defragmentation and rebooting. The drone would come down long before a full defrag and reboot. No, this required a manual override for the controls.

She searched her memory, dug around in mental boxes that were packed up tight with years of clutter. Even if she did a manual override, this elephant was probably too low to lift back up before it hit and threw her halfway up the mountain. She pressed her sleeve against the grime-coated touchscreen and scrubbed a clear surface. The memory bubbled up from the motions. "Ah! There it is; Birdy-cat_123, a number for each regeneration."

The screen came to life, and she took the controls, setting the lift as high as it could go and turning off all of its tractors so collected debris couldn't weigh it down. Chunks of mountain fell in its wake. Explosions of sand and water from below erupted into her face. But the drone lifted; it lifted and the beach split in two.

She sat back, spit sand, and set a course. Then she climbed out of the cubby and onto the back of the drone where she could watch the mountain come down in great chunks of debris. It was dark in the city now, no lights, no quake alarms going off. The glass of the observatory shattered somewhere out there in the distance. Falling buildings crumbled and shattered as they came down, lit by the drone's lights—a dim green glow from its underbelly and its eyes.

From behind her a louder crash, this one less metallic and more rumbling. *The cliffs.* She watched in horror as the whole cliff face came down, burying the caves under the whole mountainside.

Not the caves! She needed those caves with their echoes and ever-ready solace. . . The controls were right there. She could turn this elephant around. Turn the tractors back on with the world still shaking, dig away the boulders with her bare hands and pretend the caves were still intact, the same, timeless.

Damnit… She squashed the urge. The shaking was too violent, the caves too broken. And here she was, sitting on the back of an elephant while her sixth planet fell apart around her ears, willing rocks to rebuild themselves and dead things to unbury themselves and curl up in her arms. *Damnit, damnit, damnit.* She scrubbed at sandy tear tracks on her face.

Her own bitter laugh was sharp to her ears as she stared down at the destruction. She could have tried to stop it but didn't. With careful hand and foot placements, she hoisted herself across the drone's back until she reached the head. She curled up in the massive cave-like eye socket. The tables had turned, toppled right the hell over. This metallic beast that she'd built, maintained, and now taken for a last joyride was the protector, the cave, and she was the cat, a cat watching the world end. How appropriate.

She could imagine someone laughing as she told them the story of it, or shaking their heads when they realized she was really staying, going out with a quake.

But no one would hear the story from her mouth, and if there was any record of it the story wouldn't be about her or Sparrow-cat, or the crushed foxes, the broken caves, and certainly not the massive hovering elephant turned haven to an old woman.

The story would be about numbers and statistics, how many relocated and how many stayed and died. Her old self maybe, not the failing woman she was now, would be mentioned: Doctor Odessa Lightner, engineer, preeminent inventor of planetary earthquake safety systems, deceased in an earthquake. Laughter welled up but didn't come out. Death wasn't funny was it? Only when you were alive enough to think about a near miss and laugh it off. When it wasn't final.

No one would know why she gave up and chose to stay and die in an earthquake. Death by stubbornness, the same stubbornness that had always moved her, holding her still a few hours too long. Too late to change her mind and look at those schematics now.

She shook her head and gave the elephant a pat.

"Too late for this planet. Too late." The world was coming down around her, this planet was at least. Her trembling fingers toyed with the face of her wristwatch, then she pressed the call button and lifted it close to her lips. "Administrator 62 please…"

She opened her mouth to speak again and then hesitated. Wasn't it easier this way? No more loss. No more planets. She'd already lost six. It was too big a number to lose for something as large as a planet.

Back in the cave she'd made a choice. She'd come to this place for solace because it was lasting—it had felt lasting, anyway—but when the roof started coming down she ran, and here she was, curled up in the eye-socket of a metallic elephant instead of jumping in front of a perfectly good avalanche. Was it cowardice? Fear? Or something else?

"It's because I don't *want* it to *end.* I just want everything to stop ending, stop changing…" The reshaped contours of the beach would be faintly visible in the light from the glowing drone if she peered out of her shelter. In the daylight she wouldn't recognize it. And she didn't *want* to see it, to get used to *new shapes, new pathways,* she didn't want to acclimate *again* and *again,* but she didn't want to end herself.

It was too late to take up her old mantle and try to find an engineering solution, probably far too late for a transport out—but she wanted one. It would have to be enough.

The mountainside was on fire below her, and the earthquake was still going. The night was alive as Bellguard Resort died with great crashings, crackings, and crumblings as if the mountain itself were trying to stand up and shake the city off.

A voice spoke out of nowhere.

"This is quite a quandary. Your transport is ready and waiting...but you aren't ready to take it, are you?"

A warm hand touched her shoulder, not coaxing or forcing, but *holding*, and when she opened her eyes Administrator 62 was there, leaning down from the bridge of the elephant's nose. She hadn't heard any whirring whoosh of shift travel—too quiet compared to the rush of waves and the crash of her world ending.

"You did call for me, didn't you?"

Had she done that? Or just opened the line? "I don't know—I don't know where I'd go. Or for how long. That's the part I don't want!" Her breath caught. Like suffocating. The world was spinning. She searched the darkness for some landmark, something steady enough to take a breath. *Stars*—Alpha Centauri was bright and visible just beyond Administrator 62's glow. A small flame of hope flared up. It couldn't last. Nothing lasted. It would gutter and go out if she blew on it, and the dark would rush back in.

"Stars burn out..."

"Yes."

"Mountains—"

"Crumble."

The world shook harder, and with a rumbling like thunder on all sides at once, the side of the mountain that played host to Bellguard City broke apart in an avalanche of stone.

Odessa flinched, wrapped her arms around her head and then with wide eyes on the crumbling dark, she took a breath. She looked Administrator 62 dead in the eyes, gleaming orbs of light that they were. "Crumble. It all crumbles."

The administrator stared back. "Did you call me here for last rites, or—"

"No! I want to last."

"Ah! Then you have decided. This is good. It took so many crumblings, but here we are at last!" The administrator stood and stretched and brushed off bits of debris.

Odessa cocked her head and took the hand she was offered. "Temporary placements...all of them decaying in short time. You gave me broken places when I asked for one solid one?" The administrator's words shook her—*took so many crumblings*—Was this on purpose?

The administrator smiled an apology. "You asked for a retirement. A place to die. We gave you six, but you lingered, lasted. If you wanted to die, you would have."

"It isn't that easy!"

"Death is easy. Living is hard. Instead of choosing, you clung admirably to both at once, which means you were undecided, until now. Here, this will help."

"What is it?" She took the sparkling vial. The liquid inside—glowing and prismatic in the hand of the Administrator—retained a faint gleam in the dark once it was in her own hand.

"A choice."

She turned it this way and that and then uncapped it. "The Life drink? To add years..."

"It's a choice in a bottle. The choice you couldn't make before now."

She tipped the bottle into her mouth and swished the viscous fluid with her tongue before swallowing. It had a sweetness to it, a sharp tang on the sides of her tongue, and finally bitterness, like herbs best taken in small medicinal doses. In her throat it was ice, but warmed as it reached her belly and coiled there like a small dragon learning to make fire.

A tingling warmth spread along her nerves. She broke out in goosebumps, then the whole world was vibrating, but not from the earthquake. This was a vibration made of tiny shifts, dark to light, light to dark, pleasure, pain, pleasure, pain, again in rapid succession. Her eyes widened. Where was the administrator now? Dark all around her. She flailed out, reached for the administrator, or someone, anyone to grad hold of.

"I think...I think I'm going to be sick..."

"You aren't ill. You'll need to make a choice."

She was gasping, on the way to hyperventilating. She had to breathe slower and listen, in-out, in-out...but her mind shuffled her far away from the administrator's voice.

What choice? She was seeing things, things that she couldn't be certain were real. Her hands in front of her face were those of a young woman, now a child's, tiny fists with stubby fingers...

She blinked and her hands grew ancient, peeling, skin sloughing off in melting flakes, then they were too bright to look at, made of light and sound and that tingling sensation that spread through all of her senses. She stared harder at those melting hands. The ache of arthritic joints turned into a riot of suffering. The creases turned to bleeding fissures.

Too much. It was too much. She couldn't look any more. But then she took a breath and for just a moment her hands became the smaller, softer ones, pain free and touching, exploring everything, living—the child's hands.

It took only a thought to shift back to pain, to crumbling, decay and stagnation, or a thought to ease, to see her own hands neither breaking nor young. Could she follow those thoughts of breaking apart, or of renewal to their eventual outcome? Yes.

Her hands could wither away completely and the rest of her would follow. She would die. This life drink could kill her for real—as surely as it could extend her life. This was the choice. Continue or expire, accept change or break with it. Odessa's stomach turned over. She stood on a precipice and looked over it into nothingness.

A single step to end the pain, the struggle, to be finished with it all. But then she would be finished with it *all*. She could have stayed in the caves if that was what she wanted.

She swallowed, took another breath and stepped back from the ledge into the safety of the elephant drone's eye-socket.

She opened her eyes again, without memory of closing them, Alpha Centauri exploded over Administrator 62's head. But then she blinked and it was still there, not exploding now but a winking star, fresh and blue in the night sky.

She slapped at her cheeks, pinched at them and felt the pain. The life trance loosened its grip, but the world was still fluid, shifting, not to be trusted. The ground cracked beneath the hovering drone, and her eyes widened as the crack did. She watched it spread, the seeds of a smile and the urge to weep warring in her. Was the ground under her breaking or had it already broken, was it about to break? A thought occurred. Or was it a voice speaking?

"Time is short. And time is illusory."

"Am I alive?" Was that really what her voice sounded like?

"Yes…and no. Which one do you want to see?"

"I already chose! Alive, I want to see life, life and death and all of it, more of everything, not the end!"

She shuddered and struggled to feel herself in her body. She grabbed fistfuls of tangled silver hair and pulled hard. She felt that. Maybe…and then she was gone again, her mind traveling somewhere farther away than Alpha Centauri.

When she came back into awareness of herself, she was retching, great heaves and sobs that shook her body. The sour tang of vomit should have sickened her, but it was real. It was life. She opened her eyes again. The crack beneath them was real. The ground was rising up to swallow them, and one of the elephant's forelimbs hung down into that void.

Scrambling to her feet, Odessa grabbed hold of the Administrator's face, her hands disappearing into the light. She spoke slowly, enunciating each word as if relearning how to speak. "Get us out of here."

"Is there a place you have in mind?"

"Out of here is the only place that matters right now. They're all the same, broken up or breaking, growing back."

"I see you're ready to go. You've finally decided."

The elephant's track lighting came on in a glowing green trail of whirls and crisscrossing patterns along its underbelly. Administrator 62 offered her a hand and stepped onto its head and over. He lead her to the protected space behind the elephant's large skull.

"Less wind back here."

Odessa patted the mossy back of the elephant and sat down. "I thought she'd be left for dead here…"

"No, you pulled her back from the brink. She's finished defragmenting and rebooting now."

She nodded as if it all made complete sense. And it did. It finally did. The drone rose higher, away from the yawning crack that had widened into a chasm. Great sections of mountainside broke off into the angry crashing sea below.

Her chest ached and her throat closed up as she watched it all crumble. Her caves, fox glen, the little cottage, the garden where Sparrow-cat was buried, all gone. The ache spilled over from her eyes in green-lit tears, but it didn't fill her. All those places…she could take them with her.

She gripped the locket at her throat, stuffed with locks of fur. There could be another life for Sparrow-cat as well, not the same, but something.

"Can we go to Alpha Centauri, maybe?" She paused, eyes widening. "It didn't blow up, did it?" She saw Administrator 62 shake their head.

"Alpha Centauri is intact. What will you do there?"

She tried on a smile. "Something new. Maybe build something grand and ridiculous and temporary—sandcastles in a tide zone…"

The administrator's laugh rang out loud and full of good humor.

"I'd…I'd like to tell stories, I think. In words, or numbers, tapestries maybe."

"Good."

"I have a lot of stories to tell, you know."

There was a ship ahead in the night sky, its docking bay opening up like the mouth of a blue whale made to sail the stars. The administrator squeezed her hand. She was certain that she could see a smile through the face made of scintillating light.

"I do know, and I think there are people who need to hear them."

About the Author

An artist of multiple mediums, CL Fors is a modern-day renaissance woman, author, illustrator, publisher, artisan dragon who creates to defend and uplift a world of hope and infinite possibility for all. CL is author of the Primogenitor series, a four book science fiction epic and is currently illustrating *Orion's Flight*—a graphic novel about a genetically engineered bat-winged piglet. Watercolor flows from her brushes in sanguine vibrancy, genre-bending fantasy, science-fiction, and horror, challenging the viewer to dig deeper than surface impressions. She is equally skilled with ink, digital, acrylic, and graphic design.

Website: www.clforsillustrator.com
Website: www.clforsauthor.com
Facebook: CL Fors
Facebook Page: C.L.Fors@Primogenitorseries
Twitter @CLForsInstagram: c.l.forsauthor
Subscribe to her newsletter here: tiny.cc/clforstaproot

HOW TO GROW A LEGACY

by Jayrod P. Garrett

Dedicated to Kailiam Wesley Noble-Garrett

I ASKED MY BIBI HOW
she managed to stay kind in a world
that took so much from her:
her feet by diabetes,
varied children through starvation,
her mobility and beauty from stroke.
Heaven shined down on her as
her half-paralyzed face bloomed
into a crooked smile.

"Chile, to create magic
in the world,
bury your precious.
Whatever it be.
Water it with your tears.
Warm it with your smile.
Cherish it with your voice.
Be patient.
Wonder takes time."

Within the year, cancer devoured her whole.
As a child, I never thought I'd stop
watering her grave with my tears.
As a young man, I read her journals
and learned how her life matched my own.
Filled with confidence, I wanted to give life
to my village. I rejoiced with her over building
my first well. Months later I shared with her
the tortures of installing indoor plumbing.

When I left for the University of Dakar,
I promised to come back with the magic
to make home better for our people.
I buried myself in studies.
Cried over anxiety and tests.
Laughed with friends watching

dumb movies of people doing dumber things.
Until one day I returned to our village,
my construction degree, like a wand, in my hand.

A Baobab tree, the tree of life,
stands thirty meters tall over her grave.
Grown in the three decades of my building.
Her trunk now a beacon for villagers to
find their way home to the house I've built.
Her branches bearing fruit to feed her great
great grandchildren and their friends. And
her feet now roots to make home a blessing
within the shade of her crooked smile.

A wonder worth waiting for.

About the Author

Jayrod P. Garrett believes in creating a world where all of us belong. They are a multicultural storyteller with a Masters of Fine Arts in Creative Writing from the University of Nevada, Reno. As a child, they came to Utah on a three-week vacation that became more than forty years. During that time, they transitioned from being a faithful member of the Church of Jesus Christ of Latter-Day Saints into a nonbinary, Black, atheist, U.S. Veteran with PTSD, Anxiety, and AuDHD. Currently they work as an educator for RISE Virtual Academy where they teach Black students about Black history, a storyteller for the National Association of Black Storytellers, and as the Belonging Coordinator of Superstars Writing Seminars. They live in northern Utah with their spouse and three children. You discover more of their journey and work at jayrodpgarrett.com.

TODAY WE ESCAPE

by Martin L. Shoemaker

An inquel from Today I Am Carey,
Baen Books 2019

OVER LUNCH AT THE HOME—I do not eat, of course, I am an android—the residents share stories. I can tell through my empathy net that most of them have heard most of these stories multiple times. There is a sense of distraction, of tedium, as they listen. But as each one talks directly to me, their eyes light up, and it is like when my neural nets engage and I "wake up." They tell me of the work they have done, of the places they have lived. Luke tells a number of stories of the circus, and he is a good storyteller. Even those who have surely heard these stories before laugh at all the right places.

But the most common topic of conversation is family. Parents and aunts and uncles and grandparents, but especially children; and those stories make a complicated impression on my empathy net. There is pride, there is love, but there is also sadness—even bitterness—and I recognize this from my time with Mildred. Sadness, because they miss their families. Luke and the rest make such a big deal of me joining them for lunch. I wonder just how often they have visitors.

So I listen, and I encourage the stories. These residents miss their families, and I understand that all too well.

After an hour, android staff appear to clean up the dishes. They stand patiently by our tables. Nurse Rayburn waves them away. "We're in no rush here," she says. From the smile on her face, the tilt of her head, and the tone of her voice, I can see that she is happy because her residents are happy, and she cares for them very deeply. I decide that Nurse Rayburn is a good woman, but she is tired from so much worry.

Eventually all the food is gone, and the android staff clear away the dishes. The residents start leaving the table, one or two at a time, most saying goodbye to me as they go. Soon the androids pull the tables to their original positions, and all that are left are Luke and myself and an old woman in a wheelchair. She has not spoken throughout the lunch. Luke looks at her and smiles. "How are you today, Mrs. Carruthers?"

Her hair is a sparse mat, straightened and colored, but it does not look natural for her. Her arms are barely thicker than the wheelchair armrests on which they lay. Her face sags on the left side, and so her words are slurred when she says, "I'm okay, Mr. Lucas." There are many pauses in those few words.

"Did you enjoy lunch?"

"Uh," she says. "Slop."

"I'm sorry, Mrs. Carruthers. Did you want me to find you something else?"

"I'm fine," she says.

But Luke persists. "Some Jell-O, perhaps? Let's see if you can have some Jell-O." He leaves the table and heads to the kitchen, and I am alone at the table with Mrs. Carruthers.

She looks at me, and the right side of her face droops in a frown to match her left. "Don't like metal men," she says.

"I am sorry, Mrs. Carruthers. I shall leave."

But she continues as if she hasn't heard me. "Not natural. Metal. I had a metal dog once. Not right. Wag its tail, sniff, and bark, but not a dog."

"I understand, Mrs. Carruthers."

"Not a dog! It does tricks, but it never eats. It never shits in the house. Not a dog. They told me it was, but…" She swallows, then continues. "I had a dog once. *That* was a dog. Big…big collie. Friendly. Wag her tail, the whole body wagged. She came up, licked my face. She loved me. Metal dog can't love me."

"I am sorry, Mrs. Carruthers. You are right. Mechanical devices have no feelings, but we do try to help."

"No love. No hate. Don't get sad." A tear runs down her cheek. "Don't get sad."

She shifts her hand on the wheelchair controller, and the chair backs away from the table. She rolls out of the room without another word.

She is wrong. I find that I do get sad. For her.

Mrs. Carruthers has disappeared in the hallway when Luke returns with Jell-O. "She left?"

"I do not think she likes me, Luke."

"She doesn't like anybody. She'll warm up to you in time. It's good to have you here, Carey."

But I find Luke to be optimistic. While many of the residents of the memory facility accept me as a caretaker, Mrs. Carruthers has countless objections.

"Your hands are cold."

"You try to look human, but I'm not fooled."

"Who asked you?"

"I don't like metal men!"

Soon Nurse Rayburn and I agree: I must not try to assist Mrs. Carruthers. She is not "coming around," as Luke predicted. She is intransigent. Digging in her heels, as Luke put it. The more I try to assist her, the more stubbornly she refuses. Sometimes the stress risks her health, and I cannot allow that.

So I work with the others: Auralie, Jimmy, Aaron, Heather, certainly Luke, and the rest. I bring food trays to those who are not ambulatory. I participate in games and discussions, and I clean up messes. I am legally too outmoded to provide medical services. I am not even supposed to touch the residents (though Nurse Rayburn soon chooses to overlook that restriction). But I am allowed to do a wide range of assistive tasks as well as recreation.

Luke and I even work on our juggling act. He tells me that I might be competent if I keep at it. He is amused by this thought.

And I continue to join them for lunches. It is an opportunity to observe Mrs. Carruthers in a larger social group, where she is less likely to focus on me. I find that Luke was correct in his assessment: she does not seem to like anyone. She is not aggressive toward anyone, but she shows her displeasure. Sniffs and frowns and glowers.

But sometimes I catch her smiling at stories that people tell, usually about children. That makes me curious. Does she have any children? I am not certified to access her medical records; but I still have my library card, and my wireless connection to the Internet. And no one researches like an android researches.

It takes me a while to collate data in order to build a profile of Mrs. Helen Carruthers, age 67, of Wayland, Michigan. A widow, having lost her husband Kent nearly a decade ago. Mother of two, grandmother of seven, none of whom have come to visit in the time that I have known her. I feel bad for her while also understanding. The tragedy of a memory health care facility, of long-term care homes in general, is that there are so few visitors. I observe this pattern daily. When someone is a new resident of the facility, family members are there day and night, standing a vigil with their loved ones. Sometimes hopeful, often doubtful, but attentive.

But then, as time passes, the visits become less frequent. I know that this causes bitterness and judgment, and I understand the feelings. But I understand both sides. You can spend long hours with a loved one for six days, or six weeks. Six months begins to wear. In six years... No one can put their life on hold for that long.

I do not have access to Mrs. Carruthers's medical records, but some information is right at the top of her chart, where it is easy to observe. She has been in the facility for fifteen years. Wherever her family are, they are not here. I hope for her sake that they will come soon, but there are no guarantees.

From public records, I see that she had a long career as an arts teacher, in elementary and middle schools. She won some awards. She organized plays and other outings, things that got the attention of local news. She was especially known for the art shows in her school district, which she organized every year. From photos, I see a different woman, engaged with the world. So proud of her students as they showed off their sculptures and paintings.

The sculpture intrigues me. I am not a student of the arts. I do not know if an android can be. But these pictures of the children with their little clay and stick figures almost show me a meaning. There's something there that matters to them. And from the photograph, they matter to Mrs. Carruthers.

Eventually, I make a connection. It is a small thing, easily overlooked. When Mrs. Carruthers eats in the dining hall, sometimes she makes shapes in her food. Castles in the mashed potatoes. Stacks of the beans. This odd behavior draws her attention and gives her focus.

I start to notice that the one activity which she most eagerly participates in is recreational therapy with modeling clay. She kneads the clay in her fingers, squeezing it and prodding it into shapes. Sometimes she works intently on this, but she grows increasingly irritated. I can see stiffness in her fingers and annoyance in her face. She can no longer do what her memory says she can. When her annoyance grows to a peak, she wheels away.

"I don't know what to tell you, Bo," Luke says. He always calls me Bo. It's one of his many eccentricities. "Sometimes the old joints just don't work the way they used to. It happens to all of us. Why do you think I work so hard at keeping up my circus routine? It keeps me limber. But some mornings… I ain't the man I was, and not just in my head." He sighs. "And Mrs. Carruthers… I seen her get out of that chair a few times, in therapy, but her body is just not what it used to be."

"And her mind is not, either," I say. "But what you might call her heart still is."

"If she has one."

"Luke, you know that I am able to read the emotional state of humans."

"I don't understand how, but you seem to."

"Mrs. Carruthers is sad and bitter for a reason. It is not just that no one visits her. It is that she feels unneeded. Useless."

To my surprise, Luke laughs. "That's pretty common here, Bo. Most of us are forgotten, left behind. She doesn't have a monopoly on that."

"I understand, but I think that is more intense for her. Her entire identity was in her connections: to her family, and to her students. And even though her memory is not what it once was, inside, she still misses that."

"Maybe." From somewhere Luke produces a trio of his juggling balls and starts tossing them. He is not supposed to do that inside. "But can you give her that?"

I nod. "I think I can, with a little help from you."

If I could fret, I would. I know that my plan could get me fired from the facility. Or worse. Perhaps even disassembled.

But I feel this is important for Mrs. Carruthers. If I could hope, I would hope this will all work out in the end. For her, if not for me.

I have prepared all my supplies, stocking the storage compartments in my thighs. Just on schedule as we had planned, Luke begins what he calls "raising a ruckus." He begins doing flips and tumbles and juggling in the recreation room, against the rules. *Take it outside if you must, and be more careful for the safety of other residents.* Sometimes he forgets, but this time it is intentional. He wants the attention of residents and staff alike. Soon there is shouting and laughter and an emergency call on our internal network for residents for nurses to come calm things down.

And while this is going on, I sneak into Mrs. Carruthers's room. She sits in her wheelchair, but she is motionless. "Good afternoon, Helen," I say.

"What?" She gapes at the use of her first name. Then her eyes focus. "Metal man." She doesn't tell me to go away, but her scorn is evident.

"Mrs. Carruthers, you don't like it here, do you?"

"Like's got nothing to do with it. Got nowhere else to go."

"What if *I* had somewhere else?"

"What?"

I try to project warmth. "Mrs. Carruthers, I know you do not like me. But I am asking you to trust me."

"In what?"

I grab the arms of the wheelchair, turn it around, and head for the door. At first, she gasps, and I wonder if this is a mistake. This is a grave risk, taking her away from immediate medical care.

But it will be a short trip, and I can always summon aid. In a real emergency, I still have my medical training, even if I am not allowed to use it. So I steer her away from the rec room and Luke and all the commotion, and out a side door. My staff credentials open the door without an alarm, and we emerge into the bright spring sunlight.

"Outside?" She frowns, clearly uncertain what to make of this. "I don't like outside."

"Not just outside," I say. "We're taking a walk."

Then I hear muffled shouting from behind us. "Or a run." I pick up the pace.

We arrive at the community rec center, a small, understaffed facility only three blocks away from the home. As my research showed, this is a drop-in day, when community children come to spend time with friends and counselors. The building has a small gymnasium and a few function rooms, all joined through an atrium with a reception desk. A young woman sits behind the desk, staring at us with wide eyes. "Can I help you?"

"We're volunteers," I say. "Here to teach kids."

"What?"

I try to project confidence and trustworthiness. "I am just an old android, and Mrs. Carruthers clearly is no threat in her wheelchair. We are no risk to the children, and I am sure you can always use some help around here. There are never enough volunteers, correct?"

The woman frowns. "Never, but..."

"We'll be right in here," I say as I steer Mrs. Carruthers into the gymnasium.

Once my appearance would've drawn attention by itself. Once androids were mysterious. A crowd would gather. Today, not only are my kind common, but I am an old model. Nothing special in the eyes of the young for whom novelty is everything.

And Mrs. Carruthers in her wheelchair is just an old lady. That is all too common an attitude among the youth. So when we enter the large room with the basketball hoops and the mats and the small knots of kids, no one notices at first.

But I trust to the natural curiosity of children. I still remember Millie and her friends when they were young. The children will find us soon enough.

Mrs. Carruthers shakes her head, yutting. "Metal man, why are we here?" She looks around. "A lot of unsupervised kids." It isn't strictly true. There are three volunteers watching the kids, one of whom starts to come towards us. But Mrs. Carruthers is on a roll. "There's nothing for us to do here. You promised me to escape, but this just looks like another institution."

"Some call schools institutions."

"Well…"

Then the staffer, an older woman in a blue sundress, reaches us. "Can I help you?"

"Yes," I say. "Do you have tables?"

"What?"

"We might need some tables. But first, Mrs. Carruthers, let's set up yours." From the sides of her chair, I unfold her lap desk.

"What is this?" Mrs. Carruthers asks.

"A work surface," I say. Then I reach into one storage compartment in my thigh, and I pull out a large lump of soft modeling clay and some knives. "I thought you might like to do some sculpting here. Maybe a different environment will inspire you."

She shakes her head. "My fingers… I can't…"

"You can. I have seen you. And I picked up some softer clay. You know you want to." And underneath her reticence, I could sense that she did. She still took joy in sculpting.

She scowls at me, then turns to the lump and starts kneading it and shaping it. Soon she picks up one of the knives—with a broad handle, easy for her to grip—and starts carving delicately at the shape. Soon I recognize a dog, perhaps a golden retriever. It was crude. I see that her fingers shake, and sometimes her eyes narrow in frustration. But the dog is taking form.

Then, as I had hoped, a little boy joins us. "What are you making?"

Mrs. Carruthers looks at the boy, and for the first time since I have known her, she smiles. "You know what I'm making. You're just being polite. It's a dog, young man."

"I guess…I guess I really mean how are you making it?"

"With clay, silly! You know that, too." Then she chuckles. "But you're really asking how *you* can make it, aren't you?" He nods. "I could show you, if we had some more clay."

I am prepared for that, already having another block of odclay hidden in my hand. I set it down alongside some more tools, and Mrs. Carruthers actually smiles at me. "Maybe you're not completely useless, metal man."

"I try not to be."

Mrs. Carruthers begins gently talking to the boy—Tony—encouraging him to dig his hands into the clay, to feel it and knead it and not be afraid of it. Not be afraid to make mistakes. "Mistakes are just opportunities. Turn them into something even better. And if not—" She suddenly squeezes her golden retriever into a pulp. "You start over. You can always try again." She glances at me. "Can't you, metal man?"

Soon Tony draws the attention of other kids. Soon I and the assistant, Ms. Hart, haul in tables and set out tools and clay for a dozen students. The children all eagerly start to work on their creations, with Mrs. Carruthers wheeling back and forth between them, pointing out "opportunities" as she calls them, and teaching techniques. With her mind focused on the children, her hands don't shake as much. She isn't cured, but she's motivated. She finds a long-forgotten strength.

We are there for over an hour before Nurse Rayburn arrives. "I thought you would find us quicker," I say.

She jabs me with an elbow. "They called me right away. It wasn't hard for them to figure out that Mrs. Carruthers is a resident. And people do know about you around here. But I had to have a little talk with Luke, and I…trusted you."

"So am I fired? Are you going to have me disassembled?"

She sighs, watching Mrs. Carruthers, the teacher. "I should." She shakes her head. "If her family ever raises a complaint, I'll have to. You know that."

"I do. But there is little chance of that."

She shakes her head. "You knew. Your…your empathy net, you call it… You knew what she needed."

I sense that Nurse Rayburn feels bad about this. She is in charge of resident care, but *I* was the one who had understood Mrs. Carruthers. "All I did was listen. Just like you. I just saw possibility. I was raised by teachers, you might say. I know how important their work is to them, just as important as your residents are to you." I look at Mrs. Carruthers. "This is all she ever needed, deep inside. Service is what she values. She lives to help someone learn."

About the Author

Martin L. Shoemaker is a programmer who writes on the side…or maybe it's the other way around. Programming pays the bills, but a second-place story in the Jim Baen Memorial Writing Contest earned him lunch with Buzz Aldrin. Programming never did that! His work has appeared in *Analog*, *Galaxy's Edge*, *Digital Science Fiction*, *Forever Magazine*, *Writers of the Future*, and numerous anthologies. His Clarkesworld story "Today I Am Paul" appeared in four different year's best anthologies and eight international editions. His follow-on novel, *Today I Am Carey*, was published by Baen Books in March 2019. His novel *The Last Dance* was published by 47North in November 2019, and was the number one science fiction eBook on Amazon during October's prerelease. The sequel, *The Last Campaign*, was published in October 2020.

You can learn more about Martin's work at http://Shoemaker.Space.

ONE MAN'S TRASH

by Laura Hayden

WHEN THE NEXT CAR PULLED UP to the ornamental gates of The Preserve at Horizon Pointe, the blazer-clad security guard barely acknowledged the passengers within. To him, they were simply one more cookie-cutter couple in a long procession of cheerfully dressed Mr. and Mrs. Middle-Class America, all excited to be invited to the Big Boss's lavish McMansion for the mandatory Holiday party.

He knew the type. And hated them all.

The men would clap each other on the shoulder, talk sports, argue about politics, and drink far too much. The women would spend their time bragging about their kids' participation trophies, pricing out the home's decor, and bad-mouthing the hostess's fashion sense—while trying to hide their jealousy that they didn't live in such expensive digs.

However, the guard noted, while waiting for permission to enter this upper-class sanctuary, a majority of the visitors remained on their very best behavior, each couple brightly demonstrating how damned skippy it was going to be to rub shoulders with the wealthier-than-thou-can-possibly-dream. But, out of his earshot, he knew they were grousing about the rules.

Don't drink too much. I don't care if the booze is free. You know how you get.

Make sure to tell Mrs. Boss how good she looks—her plastic surgery cost more than the gross national product of several small countries.

Don't mention their son, Junior, who decided his halfway house stint was boring and unfair and who is now halfway through his mandatory prison sentence for drug possession and violating probation.

Stay away from the guys in accounting/R&D/sales/whatever division I hate. They always play grab-ass when they get drunk.

As the next car pulled up, the guard stooped down to get a look at its occupants—a thoroughly suburban PTA mom and soccer-team-coach dad who were indistinguishable from all the others—from their obligatory ten-year-old mini-van with a crumb-filled car seat in the back, to the festive hostess present perched on the woman's lap.

Odds were it was either cheap wine, a Hickory Farms gift box, or "imported Belgian" chocolate.

From the nearest Walmart.

He didn't bother to check as to which of the neighborhood parties the couple was headed. They were all alike. He merely gave them a curt nod, along with the obligatory admonishment—Don't block any driveways—and then made a "move along" gesture.

Wishing the security guard a politically correct "Happy Holidays" in cheery unison, Jill and Adam Carter pulled onto Top O' the World Way, the Preserve's pretentiously named main road. Half of the cars ahead of them turned down Paramount Parkway, the first street, while the rest continued deeper into the neighborhood.

But they didn't follow.

Due to the 24/7 security patrols in the ritzy neighborhood, the Carters had never had a chance to visit the area before. Therefore, Jill used her navigation app to guide them. Following her instructions, Adam stayed in the conga line of vehicles, threading past another large party where cars parked on either side of the main drag made for a narrow passageway. They passed Superlative Street, Premiere Place, and Apogee Avenue—the alliterative names evidently meant to remind the occupants just how truly superior they were to the rest of the poor slobs who lived beyond their borders.

Finally, Adam reached Champion Crest, the turnoff leading to the heart of the neighborhood—a grand mansion on the eighteenth hole, decorated with enough lights to mark every runway at O'Hare.

They drove past the massive house twice, making a full circle around it as if looking for a parking spot. Finally, he parked in the farthest latecomer's area, almost six full blocks away from the hotel-sized home, but close enough to be bombarded with Christmas music and the loud reverberations of mandatory office frivolities. However, the house they parked in front of was draped in shadows with no signs of anyone being home.

Jill juggled the red-wrapped gift as she climbed out of the car. A large juniper bush close to the curb limited her view of the party house. And vice versa. She credited Adam's excellent parking skills for that.

"You ready?" Adam held out a gloved hand to help her get her footing and negotiate the uneven lawn until they stood in front of the car. Evidently, the Preserve at Highland Pointe didn't believe in sidewalks.

She offered him her best smile. "As I'll ever be."

He gave her a quick kiss, then faded into the shadows, heading toward the darkened house. Jill adjusted her coat, drew a deep breath, pulled on her own gloves, and counted to fifty. She had to give Adam enough time to negotiate an unseen path to the back of the house, unlock the backdoor, and bypass the alarm system—a QPD5507—Adam's favorite system to break.

While she waited, she pretended to check the driver's side door to make sure it was locked. Her gaze landed on the car seat in back, a convincing prop to suggest they were exactly what they appeared to be—suburban parents on a rare night out—instead of a pair of highly-skilled thieves out to rob the Barrington family. Well, maybe not to rob them blind, but merely to redistribute some of the Barringtons' excessive wealth into more deserving hands.

Theirs.

She sighed. And yet, all the money in the world couldn't buy her what she really wanted. She glanced toward the backseat.

But... *forty-six, forty-seven*

Until that time... *forty-eight, forty-nine*

Stealing from the rich and giving to themselves would have to do.

Fifty.

Jill made a final adjustment to her coat hood to hide her features from any casual observers, and she headed up in full view of the driveway—not to the huge party, but to the large, dark house.

Jill and Adam had rules, too.

Rule one: Always look like you belong where you are. Therefore, she was an appropriately dressed partygoer who had the wrong house number and was too stupid, naive, or unaware to realize her mistake. Jill rang the doorbell and waited. No one answered. No lights came on. No motion inside.

After a few seconds, she rang again. This time, the door opened.

Adam stood back in the darkness, out of view. "We're good. No one's here."

She stepped in quickly, and he closed the door behind her. "Did you have any problem with the alarm?" she asked, discarding the package on the foyer table.

"That's the weird thing. It wasn't on. Neither were the cameras."

Rule two: Always be wary of coincidences. She stiffened in concern. "Adam. I don't like this. It's too convenient."

He patted her gloved hand. "I know. But sometimes people forget. We've run into it before. The sooner we're in and out, the better, right?"

She nodded. "Right." She consulted her cell. "The Barringtons' private jet left on time. They should be somewhere over the Atlantic by now."

Rule three: stick to the timetable at all costs. Jill switched to the timer app. "Four minutes in and out. Starting now."

They went separate directions.

Jill knew art, silver, and wine, so her responsibility was the main floor—specifically the living room, dining room, and kitchen. Adam specialized in jewelry, computers, and coins, and his domain was the upper floor. Using methods polished by experience, they went through their respective areas, quickly accessing the practicality of the item to be stolen and factoring in the portability, value, marketability, and risk of each item under consideration.

They weren't smash-and-grab thieves. They were artists, coming into a home, undetected, and stealing the most valuable items that weren't on obvious display, but squirrelled away in back drawers or closets where they were presumed to be safe.

The real trick wasn't to rob them blind, but to rob their blind spots.

Normally, a job like this would be run strictly by the numbers—in and out in three minutes. But between the number of parties in the neighborhood and the clogged streets, they knew that neighborhood security would have their hands full of noise complaints or drunk drivers and spend less time worrying about burglarized houses. So, the Carters gave themselves an extra minute to search the house and uncover more atypical hiding places.

However, this particular house was proving to be a big disappointment. So far, Jill had found very little to take, which was unusual for a family of the Barringtons' stature and a home of this magnitude. Although her research had indicated that the family owned several works by Marcel Strauss, an upcoming German contemporary artist, she hadn't found them yet. Nor the heirloom silverware they reportedly had appraised two years ago for over a hundred grand. Or any of the dozen or so high-priced antiques they'd won at auction in the last three years. She'd researched the family very carefully—their tastes, their acquisitions, and their habits. Of course, her research had also uncovered the fact that a big divorce loomed on the horizon. That was one of the reasons why she and Adam had selected the home of Mr. and Mrs. J. August Barrington III—him, the third generation; her, the third wife. A theft now would probably be attributed to one greedy spouse not willing to wait for a divorce judge to decide who got what. It would fuel arguments, maybe even a police report, but they'd insist that the culprit could only be the other.

Chaos would ensue, but probably not a criminal complaint because, in old money families like this, the Barrington name had to be protected at all costs. The confusion would beget miscommunication which would result in delay and that would give Adam and Jill long enough to fence the items without raising any alarms.

What items? she reminded herself.

Maybe Adam was having better luck. She pulled out her cell and called rather than raise her voice or search for him. *Rule number four: someone always had to stay on the main floor to give warning to the other and to make sure at least one of them could escape if someone approached. Rule five? No incriminating texts.*

"Yep?"

"I have practically nothing. You?"

"Same here. I—oh shit!"

"What?"

"Get up here. Left hallway."

It meant something was truly wrong if Adam wanted her to violate one of their sacred rules. She took the stairs, two at a time. This time, she dared to call out, albeit softly. "Adam?"

"In here."

She followed his quiet voice into a room that was outfitted as a home theater. A bluish glow from a muted screen made weird flickering lights dance silently around the room. The narrow beam from Adam's flashlight highlighted an expensive leather theater seat, filled with something.

Some*one.*

"She's dead."

Jill stared at the body in the chair. "Are you sure?" She'd never seen a dead person…in person. Theirs had always been nonviolent acts of theft. No weapons. Ever.

He squatted to get a better look at the motionless woman, stripped off one glove, and placed two fingers under her jawline near her ear. "No pulse." He scanned the body as he tugged the glove back on. "No signs of violence. No wounds. Maybe she died of natural causes." He looked up with a hopeful expression. "Like a heart attack?"

Using her own penlight, Jill studied the body, forcing herself to identify the woman as the very late Tiffanee Barrington. Something was wrong with the presentation, but Jill wasn't sure what it was. The woman's expression certainly didn't scream "I died in my sleep." After a contemplative moment, Jill realized that the main problem was Mrs. Barrington's incongruous clothing choices; too-tight yoga pants, an old ratty sweatshirt with motor oil stains, and a very lacy and completely unfashionable scarf wrapped around her neck. And were those Jimmy Choos on her feet?

With that getup? She shook her head silently. *No way.*

Adam used the tip of his flashlight to shift the woman's scarf away, revealing mottled bruising around her neck. His fingers trembled slightly as he pushed back the woman's left eyelid to reveal red streaks in her eyes. "She was strangled," he said quietly.

Jill swallowed her revulsion. "And then someone dressed her after the fact. A man, judging by the mismatched clothes."

Adam glanced around the room. "No signs of a struggle, here. Hard to choke someone without them fighting back."

Despite the flickering light from the screen, Jill could see the room was spotless. Even a full bag of popped corn sat on the armrest, undisturbed. "Either he cleaned up behind himself, or it happened elsewhere, and he placed her here."

Adam looked up. "He?"

"Her husband. That's Tiffanee Barrington. I told you I thought they were gearing up for a nasty divorce." Jill turned away from the body, trying to regain control of her emotions. "I bet you haven't found much of any worth, right?"

"Nothing. Same with you?"

"If I didn't know better, I'd say this place has been stripped. There are new cheap paintings in the living room, not quite the size of the ones that hung there before. The wallpaper shows the outline of the older pieces. And the few pieces of silver I found are worth nothing. Even the wine is grocery-store swill. The furniture is more Ikea than I.M. Pei. None of the antiques they reportedly own."

Adam nodded. "I found the same thing. Crappy substitutions. Costume junk instead of their highly-insured heirloom jewelry collection. His so-called million-dollar coin collection? State quarters. No electronics other than a laptop"—he pointed to the computer he'd left leaning against the door frame—"which he hid in his sock drawer. I already thought we'd stumbled into the middle of a huge insurance fraud. But now this?" Glancing down at the dead woman, he released a few inventive curses. "We don't need to stick around. Maybe I can find some access to his off-shore financials on the laptop. He hid it for a reason. I just hope it's not his porn collection." He grabbed Jill's hand and pulled, inadvertently jostling the penlight from her grasp. It rolled under the side table next to the chair.

"Balls!" he complained and dropped to his hands and knees to recover the item. Then he froze in place.

"What?" she prodded.

He stayed there, studying something under the end table.

"Adam?"

"This is weird."

She stooped into a similar position. First, she saw several long metal tubes—canisters on the bottom level of the table, all lined up and alternating positions. Camp stove propane.

Lots of it.

"Odd place to keep camping supplies," she whispered.

"Yeah." He bent down lower. "Oh shit!" He shot up, pulling her unexpectedly to her feet. "Timer, igniter, fuel source. It's a firebomb." He tried to tug her toward the door, but Jill refused to move.

"But what about—"

"It's too late to help her. Go!"

He pulled Jill again, and this time, she moved with him. As they passed through the door, he scooped up the laptop. They'd gotten only a few steps into the hallway before they heard two sounds that chilled her to the core.

The first was a ding.

For one terrifying moment, she thought it was the firebomb's timer. A second later, she realized the noise came from her cell, a reminder that they had sixty seconds before they reached their self-imposed deadline of four minutes—in and out.

But the second and more jarring sound was that of a baby. Crying. They shared a panicked glance.

Jill stopped. "There's not supposed to be a baby."

Adam grabbed her hand and pulled her to the right. "Can't be behind us. I've been through all those rooms. Must be this way." Together, they ran down the hallway with him checking the doors on the left, and her, the right.

As she searched, Jill's brain burned. How in the hell could she have missed this? None of her research had hinted that the Barringtons even had a child. No news articles. No birth announcements. Not even any purchase history. There simply couldn't be a baby.

However, when they reached the last door at the end of the hallway, one that the floorplans had shown as a large linen closet, they found the world's smallest nursery.

It was utilitarian at best, with a baby bed shoved in one corner and a set of shelves, which held a few stacks of clothing and a box of diapers, in the other. Someone had tried to liven up the room by draping pink lace across the back wall like a hammock and filling it with stuffed animals, but all Jill could think was that such material could pose a choking hazard to a baby.

But more important than the lack of décor, what shocked her the most was the baby herself, sitting in the bed, whimpering. The child's red, tear-streaked face suggested she'd been crying on and off, possibly for a very long time. Obeying her instincts, Jill picked up the baby who snuggled into her shoulder with muffled sobs. It was obvious the child didn't want milk or a pacifier or a blankie. She wanted human touch.

And maybe a long-overdue diaper change.

Adam stood in the doorway, incredulity filling his face. "Oh God. He was going to leave her here?"

Glancing around the small room, Jill spotted an empty diaper bag. "Grab it," she commanded, nodding toward the bag. "Diapers. Clothes, whatever you can fit in it." He complied, taking only a few seconds to fill it with necessities as well as the laptop he'd been carrying. Then he flipped the strap of the bag over his head so that he wore it like a bandolier.

Jill grabbed a blanket from the bed, wrapped it around the baby, and the three of them took off. As they thundered down the staircase, they heard another ding, followed by a small pop, then a hiss. Neither of them looked back to see if flames were boiling toward them.

Curiosity could literally kill them.

Before they reached the back door, Adam slipped ahead to shoulder it open. Once Jill and the baby were safely through, he slammed the door behind them and steadied her as she negotiated the steps. Once out in the open, they instinctively stuck to the shadows as they headed to their car. Only when they reached it did Jill look back, expecting to see the house engulfed in flames.

Nothing.

They waited, still panting from exertion and fear. To their good fortune, the baby made no sounds advertising their presence. Jill wasn't sure if it was because the child was too scared to react or simply relieved to no longer be alone.

"What do we do?" Jill whispered.

"We don't wait around."

She glanced over the top of the baby's soft curls. "But what about...her mother?" Thoughts swirled through her mind. Murdered mother. House stripped of most valuables. Baby left unprotected. Firebomb on a timer. There was only one very unsavory conclusion to draw, but she was having a hard time accepting the answer.

It was Adam who voiced her thoughts. "I think Barrington was cleaning house, literally and figuratively. A third divorce on the horizon, this time complicated by a child. He's been childless up to now, right?"

She nodded.

"This way, he gets the insurance money from the loss of the house as well as his various collections and treasures, and maybe more importantly, he avoids paying alimony to yet a third wife."

"Not to mention child support," she whispered, fighting an irrational need to protect the baby from such talk.

"Pretty convenient."

"But none of my research turned up the fact they had a baby. Wouldn't it be hard to hide something like that?"

Adam shrugged. "Might not be his child. The nursery, if you can even call it that, was hidden on the other side of the house. Maybe he didn't want a constant reminder of his wife's infidelity under his nose while they started the divorce proceedings. Maybe they kept it from the public because they both knew it wasn't his child."

"She," Jill corrected. "Not it."

He shot her a rueful smile, then reached over and patted the baby's back. "Sorry, kiddo." He bent at the knees to take a closer look at the baby. "I can't imagine anyone who could deny this little face."

That's when the idea hit her squarely in the solar plexus. A house stripped of various treasure but with its most important one left behind. What sort of monster did something like that? It took a moment to formulate her words. "We're sure no one got there before us, right? No one replaced those paintings with junk just to fill the empty spaces."

"Nope. I'm pretty sure we stumbled into the middle of a huge case of insurance fraud, not to mention murder"—he glanced at the baby who had fallen asleep—"and attempted murder."

"No," Jill corrected. "Not attempted murder."

After ten years of marriage, she knew he could read her face, hear her thoughts.

"You want to keep..." His voice trailed off.

"Yes, I do."

"But—"

"But it's obvious she meant nothing to him."

"But—"

"But it's not like he's going to come back and demand to know where his child is. He'll figure the fire destroyed all evidence of his unwanted child and that he's free."

The baby roused for a moment to yawn and then snuggle back into Jill's chest.

"But—"

"But we've been trying for so long," she whispered. "And in vitro has been so very expensive. And now we've been given this…unexpected gift."

"A baby…"

They heard a muted explosion, originating deep in the house.

"We need to get out of here before the whole place goes up." He opened the back door, revealing the car seat, heretofore a prop, but now gaining a new, loftier function.

Jill crawled into the back seat with the baby and after several tries, figured out how to secure her into the contraption. "I'll ride back here." She buckled herself next to the car seat.

After stripping off and stowing the diaper bag at her feet, Adam climbed behind the driver's seat and pulled away from the curb. They remained quiet as he negotiated the streets, avoiding the ones with party-going foot traffic.

When they reached the exit from the neighborhood, the security guard's attention was still on the steady incoming stream of vehicles, and he paid no attention to the outgoing ones. He certainly didn't look as if he was expecting fire engines to scream through the gates at any moment.

While they drove in silence, doubts began to erode Jill's resolve. Although Adam could often read her thoughts, that didn't mean he actually agreed with her. Did they have a chance in hell passing off the baby as their own? Or telling the people they knew that she was adopted? Sure, they knew a guy who could create an entire paper trail for her, just like he'd done for them. It'd be expensive, but it'd pass any inspection. But was it a risk or expense or, more importantly, a responsibility Adam was willing to take? To steal and raise someone else's child?

But is it stealing to take what someone essentially threw away? Maybe we needed to go back. Pretend we rescued the baby. But—

Adam interrupted her thoughts by pulling into a convenience store lot.

"You can't be hungry. Why are we stopping?"

"Hand me that laptop, will ya?"

She complied and moments later, Adam had the machine up and running.

"Hmmm."

"What? Tell me it's not his porn collection."

Adam chuckled. "Oh no, better than that. There's an emailed receipt from a storage space he rented a week ago. Bet the insurance investigators would like to see that. Or maybe we need to pay the place a visit, first." His laughter faded. "And there's an email set with delayed delivery in the outgoing mail. It's a suicide note—her suicide note. Evidently, he didn't realize his email program had to stay open and connected to the Internet in order to send it." He hit a few keys. "Let's just delete that from the *out-box* and…*poof.* It's gone."

"Instant karma just got him."

He nodded. "Exactly. No way we're going to let him get away with what he did. He'll pay." He closed the laptop and handed it back to her. "How's our passenger doing?"

When Jill studied the little face, highlighted by passing headlights, she realized how truly beautiful the child was. "Fine," she said softly. *It'd sure be hard to give you up.*

"I've been thinking…" Adam's voice trailed off.

Here it comes. We need to take her back.

"What if…"

Don't say it.

"…we name her Sophia Elizabeth, after your mom and mine? And we call her Sophie?"

She looked up and caught sight of his face in the rearview mirror. Tears suddenly blurred her vision. "Sophie's perfect," she whispered. Her vision focused long enough to see the grin in his eyes.

"She sure is. The most perfect treasure we could have stolen tonight. You know what they say, sweetheart. One man's trash…"

About the Author

An early reader, Laura exhausted the children's section of her local library by age ten and switched to adult mysteries and science fiction. She never looked back. Trained as an engineer, she continued to write "for fun" until one day, she decided to write "for real."

She has now published fifteen full-length novels under four names and well over a dozen short stories/novellas. Having traveled across the US as a military spouse, Laura now resides (permanently) in Colorado with her husband and dogs. To learn more, visit her at http://suspense.net

MUST LOVE CATS

by D.H. Aire

I FELT CLAUSTROPHOBIC after hours in the hotel conference room, so I headed through the lobby to get some fresh air. That's when, out of the corner of my eye, I thought I saw a familiar-looking shadow about a foot tall.

How could I? Isabel, my long-dead cat, was in the hotel—or, my mind cautioned, a cat who looked just like her.

But I knew that was her. It wasn't the first time I'd thought I glimpsed her—but it had been years since the last time.

I glanced around and saw the young woman sitting alone on the bar stool, staring into her drink.

She was several years younger than me, and more than just lost in thought. My mad ghostly cat was lying down just under her stool. I found myself asking what the woman was drinking, trying not to look down at the impossible white cat with a black tail.

For a moment she didn't seem to hear me, then her gaze sharpened and there was a flicker of—her aura, cautious, defensive. She glanced at me and suddenly sighed. Tension seemed to flow out of her as if something deep inside had been coiled taut. There was suddenly no sense of her aura, which told me a great deal about her. "Excuse me?"

I asked her again. She smiled and answered. I ordered the same, a scotch on the rocks, and was soon nursing my own glass—as the cat, beneath her stool, purred.

I knew Isabel was looking up at me with that wide-eyed stare that could look deep into my soul. I sipped some more, wishing the drink were stronger.

The young lady, Elizabeth, didn't seem to hear or notice my long-dead cat—nor did anyone around us. Wasn't a complete surprise. Life for me was odd at the best of times.

Elizabeth and I talked until closing. She asked if I liked cats, as she had three. I chuckled. "I do. I've a healthy respect for them, too."

"I've three boys…tabbies," Elizabeth said, a bit of that tension coiling until she told me all about them.

I missed the rest of my conference, and she hers. I took her to the airport and she caught her plane. My ghostly familiar, Isabel, followed us everywhere, looking rather proud of herself.

But there was one great big difference from my previous brief glimpses of Isabel. She didn't leave me. She appeared on the sink in the airplane's bathroom, and again in my luggage when I opened my carry-on when I got home. "Isabel!"

She looked at me and licked her paws.

"Isabel, it is nice seeing you again—but enough is enough."

The ghost of my cat—like all cats—ignored me.

At least I didn't have to feed her and deal with kitty litter. When I went to the office, she appeared on the conference room table, watching me as I tried to fake my presentation about what I'd learned at the conference I'd mostly skipped.

I locked my office door, but the damned ghost cat appeared on my laptop keys. "Elizabeth, Elizabeth, Elizabeth…" kept being spelled on my screen.

I glared at the cat. "Funny, but you're writing on my screen saver."

The damned cat looked at me, gaze languid, then she looked at my cell phone.

To say the least, Isabel continued to haunt me, appearing and twitching her ears. If I slept late, she somehow made me lose my covers—and there would be my cell phone.

Her *pièce de résistance* involved my neighbor's dog. Isabel had never liked him. He constantly barked in the apartment next door—and tried to bite her when I took her outside.

Even now, he was still noisy.

Finally, she'd had enough and walked through the wall—I heard the dog yelp and the sound of furniture and what had to be lamps falling as the dog fled across the apartment.

The silence that followed was abrupt. The whining moments later, though, wasn't better, and my neighbor shouted, "What the Hell? Bad dog! Get out from under my bed this instant!" Well, that was reassuring.

Isabel appeared and sauntered into the room, then sat down, licking her paw.

"Now, you let someone else see you?"

She yawned.

"Fine, you never liked him, either."

She vanished.

My cell phone was suddenly her new favorite play toy, moving across the table closer to me. She'd learned a new trick. As I reached to push the phone back, it skidded off the table and onto the floor. Then she reappeared, pounced, and it skittered closer to me. Over and over, until she finally picked it up in her mouth and dropped it in front of me as if she'd brought me a dead bird she'd caught.

"Fine, I'll call her!"

I first searched for a flight, Isabel appearing half in my lap and watching the screen. She shook her head. "No, it's not the best price, but somehow I don't like the idea of changing planes."

Isabel glanced at me as if considering that a moment and actually nodded.

I booked the ticket, then took the cell phone and called. Elizabeth's number was in my contacts under "Her."

I told Elizabeth I was interviewing in town. Hopefully, not a lie. She invited me to dinner, warning me that her tabbies could be rather protective.

"It won't be a problem."

Isabel yawned.

It was a much more pleasant trip than the last one, though, a little girl asked to pet the pretty kitty while I was waiting for my flight at the gate.

I glanced at Isabel, who lay on the seat next to me.

Her mother frowned, "Sweetie?"

Worse, I smiled. "Sure. Her name's Isabel."

The girl's mother stared at me as her daughter knelt on the floor and began petting the air above the seat.

"You've got quite the little girl here." I said.

Isabel purred.

Her mother's eyes widened. She looked around, hearing that, frowning. She grabbed her daughter's hand. "Um, we have to go, Charlotte."

"But, Mommy, her fur's so soft."

Off they went as fast as her mother could manage. I sighed, not everyone wanted to admit being sensitive to what they couldn't or didn't dare try to explain.

Isabel looked at me. I leaned over and petted her. People stared. "Kids," I replied, knowing mother and daughter would be skipping my flight.

Elizabeth opened the door. "Uh, hi."

"Hi."

Isabel had vanished. Gone back to kitty heaven, I suppose.

"Dinner's almost ready."

That's when I met her cats. They were standing close by, glaring at me.

Protective is not quite how I thought of those tabbies. She'd had them for years. They sat, tails nearly entwined, staring at me warily, as she finished cooking dinner.

"You're quite the chef."

"I enjoy, uh, cooking." She had quite the assortment of pots, and her spice rack was impressive. I pretended not to note some of the handwritten labels, which couldn't exactly be considered spices.

"It smells delicious."

"It won't disappoint."

As we ate dinner, the three felines seemed to be considering me—not unlike my lovely hostess, who seemed wary. Her aura barely visible, a bit defensive—as if afraid to trust. The cats moved around the dining room table, taking up what I couldn't help but think was a better vantage to watch me. Elizabeth pretended not to notice, and she relaxed when I didn't comment on their behavior.

By the time we got to dessert, I couldn't care less about what the cats were up to. Well, until they decided to kill me. Protective, she called them. Hell...

I don't usually…and she certainly didn't seem to… Well, it was so late, and staying overnight seemed only the right thing to do. She began setting a place for me to sleep on the couch, which ended up with us in bed, together.

The tabbies pushed open the bedroom door in the dark of night almost as soon as I fell asleep with Elizabeth nestled next to me. They padded over to the bed, then leapt on it. One settled across my feet. The other two moved across the bed and paused.

They looked at each other as they neared my gently breathing face.

Then one crawled onto my chest, while the other sidled closer before settling over my mouth and nose.

When she'd asked if I like cats, I wasn't surprised. I'd loved the cat my Dad and I had gotten from the Pound. We'd wanted a white kitten and there were two. I'd picked up the first, but it had a black tail. The kitten had looked into my eyes. "Daddy, I want this one!"

That kitten had a mind of her own—and with that black tail she was difficult to see. The joke was "she needs a bell to keep track of her." Hence, Isabel.

Isabel kept jumping into my lap when I would read a book; she'd curl up, purr, and fall asleep.

Later Isabel would go up to my bedroom windowsill, jump up and look out my window, glance back at me, then look out as if waiting for sight of someone. We would take walks around the block, her following or leading me as if she were a dog, and not a cat. A neighbor told me I should walk her on a leash. Isabel glanced at them. They tripped and fell.

She glanced at me, looking pleased. I hurriedly helped the neighbor to their feet. Needless to say, Isabel never went anywhere, leashed.

I never spoke about Isabel being, well, odd for a cat.

I couldn't help but love Isabel. She'd look at me, and I'd look at her, recognizing each other's souls. I would wonder if this was why the ancient Egyptians so loved cats.

Isabel died of old age more than a decade ago, but that love and recognition never truly left me—not with what I'd learned from her. Like how not to be surprised at anything that damn cat could do, even haunting me.

Mine was a lonely and rather private life, except for the occasional spirit wanting to ask a favor after Isabel…passed. Oh, I had thought I'd glimpsed her ghostly white fur and black tailed form a few other times. Trying to follow her had made me miss an accident or being mugged a time or two.

Isabel was a good luck ghost, I guess. Boy, did I need her now…

I gasped for air as the tabby suffocated me. Isabel screeched out of the ether, hissing like a storm wind. The tabby on my face jumped back, hackles raised. I fought to sit up, unable to with one tabby staring in shock poised across my chest, and the third across my legs.

My white, glowing, spectral soul-friend, with a tail of black shadow, leaped down onto the tabby on my chest, who bolted.

The last of the tabbies ran out of the room as my lady friend woke. "What the Hell?"

I coughed as Isabel settled into my lap. I stroked her invisible so soft fur.

Elizabeth stared. "What happened?"

"Apparently your familiars decided I wasn't the right guy for you."

Her eyes widened.

I smiled. "It's all right. They know better, now."

Elizabeth's eyes misted. "I...I don't understand."

Isabel looked up at her, eyes glowing like the Cheshire Cat, her feline form firming thereafter.

Elizabeth blinked, stared.

"Cats choose who they will—and know to watch over those they must," I shared. "Your tabbies certainly do."

She gasped. "What are you?"

"A fellow traveler... of a different tradition, but cat lover, nonetheless."

"You're sensitive?"

"To more than ghost cats."

"That's why..."

"That's why you can trust me and that I'll be landing a job in town, soon."

"Different tradition?"

"And I offer no judgment as to your, um, beliefs."

"Which aren't anything like yours?"

"No, but true love is too important," I said, hoping I didn't sound as sappy as I felt with Isabel mentally purring in my lap.

I could see the caution in Elizabth's eyes.

"Marry me, and our daughter will love cats—and they will love her even more than you will."

Her eyes widened. She stiffened, pain in the depth of her gaze. "I can't have children."

Ah, knowing fate could have a cruel sense of humor, then again, I knew in my very bones, otherwise. "You can, with me. I don't think your fortune teller—or was it a tarot reader—wanted you to know about me... And, you see, Isabel, well, made sure I met you."

She blinked. "Daughter?"

Isabel looked up at her, gaze twinkling.

"You do want a little girl. So do I. One who likes cats, too. Oh, and cats are really going to like her," I said.

"You're not joking?"

"No, I'm not... Love brings us together no matter what's happened to us before..."

Elizabeth blinked, nestled close and kissed me, whispering, "Is this why I feel I've known you forever?"

I nodded as the tabbies returned, peering in the doorway, looking at each other as Isabel left my lap. She glared at them from the edge of the bed. *'Leave Mommy and Daddy alone!'*

The tabbies backed away, leaving my family in peace.

The eyes of the lovely, once terribly lonely witch in my arms widened. "I expect a very large ring."

I grinned. "Somehow I think Isabel is going to pick out just the thing."

Isabel purred.

So did Elizabeth—and I knew who Isabel had so long been looking for, gazing from that windowsill.

About the Author

D.H. Aire is the author of over twenty science fiction and fantasy novels. They include his epic fantasy Highmage's Plight and Hands of the Highmage Series, more recently those of the Knights Tower and the satiric adventure of surviving the Bigfoot apocalypse in his Apocalypse Knot Series, and the new release *Bigfoot and the Four Horsemen*.

"Having 'Must Love Cats' in *Win in the End* is very important to me," D.H. shared. "My father had Lymphoma for many years—and died of old age, as did our cat, who took walks with him around the block."

This is Aire's fourth story to appear in a Knight Writing Press anthology.

Aire resides in the Washington DC metropolitan area and is a member of SFWA. You can learn more by visiting his website at DHAire.net. You can follow him at Dare 2 Believe on Facebook and on X, formerly Twitter, at @DHAire15.

The Legend of Long-Bow and Short-Staff

by Brenda Carre

A pastiche in memory of Robert W Service
Revered Canadian and poet

The Old Lodgepole in Hangover Hole
Is an Inn known far and wide.
Cold Alberta air and sightings of bear
Brings tourists in a tide.
A strappin' blaze and Rocky Mountain haze
Is a Euro-pee-an's dream
Where time gets lost in the smell o' frost
And the bite of a glacial stream.

The Old Lodgepole is a game hunter's goal
And a lure for a cross-country ski.
You can nurse a beer or slaughter a deer,
Or pan for gold for free.
But the best by far is the Hangover Bar
Where their stories are wild as can be.
Their hot pan fry and their Saskatoon pie
Got them rated on HGTV.

Old Long-Bow Chee is the maître d'.
Young Short-Staff Bill is cook.
Together with reason in their free off-season,
They range for Elk and Chinook.
The old Asian's 'bows' are almost kow-tows
And Bill ain't 'short-staffed', ya' see?
But it ain't Chee's bows or Bill's cooking know-hows
That makes them worth a spree.

It's skills and thrills and woodcraftin' chills
Worth puttin' into a book.
Tavern tales of meetin's with tigers and bears
With nuthin' but bows and a hook.
Now none knew 'em better than 'Mad' Chaz Hetter,
The Brit owned the shack 'next door'.
Where a faulty mis-step on a mountain path

Meant a thousand-foot drop or more.

Hett reckoned their stories was made-up glories,
For he'd never seen hide nor hoof
Of monster or ghostie, or beestial roastie
Save mebbe beneath his own roof.
Old Hett was a smoker and an everyday toker
Of his own kind of mushrooms and roots.
Ya' can bet yer last dollar, though he weren't no Koala,
He was the kind who eats leaves and shoots.

He'd made friendly deelin's with his moonshine peelin's
But his plannin's was all of a brew
To find the snookery to Short-Staff's cookery
Then haul off and murder them two.
Yet best to be careful and flush somethin' scareful
Or get them both royally juiced.
Cause Long-Bow was canny. He'd shot in the fanny
A robber who'd snuck into his roost.

Hett planned and he plotted and kept his mind bottled
To gobble their vittles with glee.
Mebbe, grab a quick look at Bill's recipe book,
To get in on the Inn's industree.
Yet Hett knew he was wrong when they met over song
At his shack playin' banjo and fiddle.
"No book," Bill said. "It's all in me gong.
Not in some book bound in the middle."

"Ya' mean this bean…" Hett held up the green
"Comes outta your head? What gammon!"
He scowled over his puncheon while hungrily munchin'
His dish of tonkotsu ramen.
"Huh, that's funny, ya Goof," laughed Bill the Neuf
"There's no beans in my head cold or hot.
It's idears I got and caution me not,
I'm a shaman with maple and salmon."

While he was chewin' Old Hett's thoughts were brewing
Ain't no more about three friends a-sharin',
Best to snatch Bill away from Chee for a day
And corner him up in the Barren!
There's gotta be ways I can clout him.
A trap is the ticket, when he's caught in a thicket

I'll force them ideers out him!

"Say, Bill?" sez old Hett all calm in fine fetter,
With a swig of his moon shiney barley.
"If it's beans yer want and the sight of a haunt,
There's this meadow that leads to this valley.
'Tis not far from here, an' 'tis loaded with deer
Sports a monster to make yer hair curly.
I seen it last fall and that thing has a call
Makes ya' think the world's end has come early."

"Can't do 'er," sez Short-Staff. He lets go a short laugh,
"We've a Lodge load and guestings tomorrow.
The seasons's a startin' and I can't go a-fartin'
Off after some haunt, to me sorrow.
I've resumes to read and bread dough to knead.
An early spring garden for plantin'.
It's the end of carowsin' and the mornin's a rowsin',
So don't get me het-up with rantin'."

Hett snorts, "Tell yer what! I'll go take that shot
To bring down that monster me own self.
Will be ME gets the proof that I ain't yer goof
With a ghoulie's head up on me own shelf!
Thump yer bread, bake the same—will be ME bags the game,"
Crowed Hett. He knew bragging would get Bill.
"I might let ya' buy it, if yer keeps yer part quiet,
And yer tell them was ME made the full kill."

Hett saw Bill's eyes sparkin' at these thoughts of lost larkin'
Glory huntin' some marvelous beastie,
Hett baggin' his thunder while Chee polished 'down under'
And Bills fingers got nuthin' but yeasty.
Didn't matter this ghoul was a made-up tool
If Bill was the fool up the mountain.
If Bill didn't return, would be Chee got the burn
Would be Chee who'd be short-staffed and countin'.

"Whatcha thinkin' then, Chee," Hett said with a smirk
As the old feller nodded his sleek head.
Chee's interest told Hett he was nosin' the bait.
Would he take it, or spurn it instead?
"I'd accompany you, were it just up to me,"
Said Chee. "I allow I am tempted.
But now that spring's coming, our rooms will be humming.

I have bookings that can't be pre-empted."

At the meanin'ful glance that the two pals shared
Hett's murderous hopes took a big leap.
When he heard Chee say, "You go hauntin' today,
It's a chance for us doesn't come cheap.
I'll unthaw tonight's feast. You come back with the beast
And bag us a trophy to follow.
You can add 'taste of myth' as a meat-pie dish.
It will prove that our stories aren't hollow."

"I'll do 'er!" sez Bill, where there's way, there's a will.
There'll be nothin' we cannot embellish.
I sure needn't worry over blackberry curry
With a monster to put in me relish!
Me and old Hett, we might get our feet wet,
But we'll stay downwind of our quarry.
Dontcha worry, friend Chee, we'll be done before tea
And we'll have that beast skinned by tomorree!"

The mornin' was kissed by a breath of white mist
A skin of thin ice rimmed the wash pail.
Old Chee stumped alone to make his way home
And the two hunters hiked up the sharp shale.
Was the kind of a worrisome, blustery day
Where demons might lurk in the trees,
Leavin' their prints o'er the frost-heaved way
Thorned branches that clawed at their knees.

Was a day that could shiver a sane feller's voice
And deesolve a mad man to flinders.
By the time they'd found Hett's valley of choice,
Hett's wits had turned into wet cinders.
The rowl and the raking of the snowpack a-quaking
Got Hett re-thinkin' his quest.
Half-frozen and shaking, his mind was awaking
To unreasoning fright in his chest.

He imagined a badger the size of a bear,
Stealin' hungry behind them the while.
And Big Foot rampageous and covered with hair
With a horrorful snaggle-tooth smile.
"Saay, Bill," queries Hett with a worrisome face
"I don't mean ta git ya all hurried.

I reckon we're come to the fell feller's place
Though me wits in this mist are right blurry."

Beyond was a pitfall Hett's memory told him
Right now, should be hid under snow.
Here was cliffs and odd stairs that Hett didn't know
Mebbe push old Bill over and go.
"Where are we?" sez Bill, as just over the hill
Through the glim comes a curdlin' scream.
Bill was good with a bow, but took zilch brains to know
He was spit outta luck with no team.

He'd spent all his days in a chef's golden haze
A baggin' his grouse and his pheasant.
Young Bill was a-countin' for deer on this mountain
And now what he faced weren't pleasant.
Old Hett had surmised that Bill's ghoul tales were lies.
Now a turrible notion come naggin'.
There really was magic in every strange-wise
What had screamed was a barb-tailed dragon.

Trees bent and rocks rang with the beast's scare-some cries
It had hid in plain sight and no braggin'.
It was squirm-long and snaky. 'Nuff to turn yer bones shaky.
Was a beast to set elder tongues waggin'.
Hett screamed like a girl. Bill said 'bye' to the world.
The beast swept their trail like a snow plow.
Be they sane or a-screamin', they saw their guts steamin'
If they couldn't get outta this somehow.

Were it bear they was facing they could lie there erasing
All signs that their bodies were livin'.
But old Bill had his doubts, after all of Hett's shouts,
That this dragon would be so forgivin'.
It looked like the end for young Bill, once Chee's friend
Save that Long-Bow dee-cided to follow.
His sharp wits were thinkin' he'd smelled something stinkin'
Hett's brain like a hog in a wallow.

Old Chee, he was thrilled when that dragon grew chilled
With a cross bolt aimed at his eye.
But broke Chee's will, as he closed for the kill
When the poor beastie started to cry.
"Not fair!" wept the dragon a-clasping his claws
"I nivver did nothing to you.

I been follering careful the backwoods' laws
Till these hoodlums come outta the blue!"

"I sleeps fall to spring, I covers me tracks,
I ree-cycles whativver I can.
On me mum's bones I'm swearin' I just meant to scare 'em.
I've nivver et woman nor man."
Big tears rolled out from the dragon's eye.
They sizzled the snow where they fell.
"Mole's me name. Bein a dragon's my game
And my long drear nights is Hell."

Though Chee was Canadian, his ancestors was Asian
He'd seen lotsa dragons like this
All carved on the walls of imperial halls.
Their charms all hid under their hiss.
Chee lowered his bow, but was careful, ya' know
Till he's certain there's nothin' amiss.

"Would you come down with us, without makin' a fuss?
We can make you a den in the Hall?"
"Oh joy," cried the wyrm. "Yes, I will, I can learn
To send any big game to your call.
I'll stay at your beck—I'll risk me slim neck!
Just feed me on cookies and 'nog.
I'll hoover your crumbs! I'll bounce out drunk bums!
I'll be faith-full-err-er than a dog!"

Then Chee turns to Hett. "Before I forget
Who brought you first up to this hill?
You said it was fall when you heard the beast call
Yet he must have been sleepin' his fill?"
"Well, it's bollocks," sez Mole. "His true mizrible goal
Was to get the best of poor Bill."

"Is dis true, Buuckaroo?"
Young Bill sez to Hett, delivrin' a flinty stare.
"Cause if ya say so, I might use my friend's bow
Ta' part what's left of yer hair."
"He's a murderous coot, and greedy to boot
Can I eat him?" sez Mole. "Do ya' care?"

I could say old Mole broke his diet that day
By eatin' that mad old Brit.

I could tell ya Hett died in a turrible slide
When he busted a gut at Mole's wit.
I do say they planted Hett there 'neath the stars
Where a passle of *ban-shee* wail,
And they raise a fine toast to Mad Hett's ghost
When they start each Tavern Tale.

About the Author

Brenda Carre lives on Vancouver Island, British Columbia, in a place steeped in lore where myth arises from the waves of the Salish Sea on the backs of Killer Whales. A love of lore and myth and emotion creeps into everything she writes. Her short fiction crosses borders into the realm of weird fiction, ghostly visitation and the terrifying unknown: A paranormal sleuth and her side-kick genie solve X-file-style crimes in Victorian England. In a small 1960's town in the Pacific Northwest school girls resurrect road kill to deal with bullies and killers.

Brenda writes epic fantasy. *Gret of Roon*, Book One of the Chronicles of Pendary, releases at the end of 2025.

Sign up for her newsletter and get a free publication at www.brendacarre.com

REMEMBERING RICKY

by Donald Evans

RICKY SAW VIBRANT RED through his closed eyelids and felt the warm aura of the metal equipment. He opened his eyes and swung higher. The sun's bright rays diffused in the slide in front of him, bathing the otherwise empty school playground in a soothing yellow glow. Ricky looked at his best friend Daniel swinging next to him and made a wish that this would last forever. Daniel's eyes were darting everywhere, observing everything. Ricky was relieved when Daniel breathed in deeply and turned to smile at him.

They had always been best friends, so Ricky couldn't understand why he felt a tension in his hands as they gripped the swing chains. Daniel said he would have to go back to school soon. Life had been a perpetual summer for them. Why did Daniel going to school have to change anything?

Ricky watched out of the corner of his eye when Daniel stopped pumping his legs and let his feet drag until his body came to rest. Daniel breathed in again, but to Ricky it was a different sound than the last time. Now it was tinged with melancholy.

Ricky, with his swing still in motion, jumped off and ran back to his friend, who smiled at him and concentrated on his face so much it felt like he was memorizing it. It didn't make Ricky happy like it normally did to have Daniel's attention. He was scared. The sun was dimming and the park felt colder. Daniel's face seemed as cloudy to him as the sky was becoming.

Ricky kneeled in front of the other boy, now sitting motionless on the swing. "What's wrong?"

"Things change," he said with soberness. "And not always for the better."

"I don't change," said Ricky.

This time, Daniel's smile was like the light from the sun, and it made Ricky feel warm inside.

"I know. That's one of the things I like about you." Daniel leaned back, still holding onto the swing for balance. He leaned forward again. "I'll never forget this moment; what a good friend you are and how happy I am. I hope you'll remember me."

Ricky started to speak but his voice faltered. He couldn't understand what Daniel was trying to tell him. He shrugged. "What's there to forget?" he smirked.

The recess bell clamored, and Ricky involuntarily looked to the school. The sky darkened, and from the distance, thunder rumbled toward the playground. He started to say something else to his friend, but Daniel was gone. The swing was still. Ricky spun around, looking everywhere. Frantically, he ran to the classroom door. Daniel was not there. The air was momentarily silent. Ricky listened for the sound of anyone at all.

Thunder reverberated in pummeling waves; much closer now. The wind swirled, and Ricky could feel his hair twisting back and forth.

"Daniel!"

It was a plea more than an exclamation.

The wind whipped rain at Ricky as he ran home. Streetlights struggled to spread their light through the growing gloom. The pavement rumbled like an echo of the thunder above. The sky ruptured, soaking him, as he sped around the corner to his own street.

"Mom!" Ricky cried out, but his appeal was snatched by the wind and thrown back at him. The storm obscured the lights of his house, and just as he reached it, the darkness of clouds and rain swallowed up the house itself. The neighborhood convulsed and then was still.

Ricky was alone on the sidewalk. He saw no source of light and had lost his sense of time and space.

The houses were gone.

The road was gone.

Ricky felt something watching him. He felt it on his skin like an electric charge. The sidewalk extended in front of him now, guiding his eyes. An indistinct, old man peered at him from a distance. He looked older than Daniel's brother in high school but to Ricky anyone who was in college was old. His instincts told him he should run, but the way the man looked at him made him pause. The man grew brighter and more complete. He smiled at Ricky, and Ricky felt a warming peace return.

"Ricky. It's me."

What did that mean? He didn't know this man, did he? "Who are you?"

"I'm your friend, Daniel."

Ricky laughed. "Okay, perv. What did you actually do with my friend?"

Daniel laughed and then his face grew somber. "I made him grow up. I could never forget you though."

Ricky's eyes widened. "Are you for real?"

"I am real."

Daniel smiled, and joy filled Ricky as he stood in the gloom, on the sidewalk, outside of his house. His house! It was there again! The street was back. The sky gradually brightened, and the wind died down.

"I have something to show you."

He could see that Daniel held a book in his hands, and Ricky had the sense of falling as he looked into its pages. The book radiated a glow that lighted upon the homes up and down the street.

Voices echoed off the illuminated houses, and Ricky gave Daniel a glance to hold him in place before looking for their source. Children were emerging from everywhere, crossing the street and making their way toward them from both sides of the sidewalk.

"Are you Ricky?" asked a young girl.

"Maybe."

"Hah. That's so Ricky," said a young boy.

Ricky turned to Daniel.

"What's the deal?"

"I told you; I grew up. I grew up to be a writer. I just wrote a story about my best friend Ricky and now you're going to make new friends, all the time."

A young girl tentatively peeked out from behind Daniel's leg.

"Dad, is this Ricky?"

"Yes, it is. Ricky, this is my daughter Sylvie."

Ricky turned to look at Sylvie.

"Hey, Silly."

"It's Sylvie, silly. Let's go play."

She grabbed Ricky's arm and pulled him past his house. Ricky looked back at Daniel who waved at him and said, "I'll be back from time to time with new stories and new friends. I'll never forget you."

The other children followed Sylvie and Ricky down the brilliantly illuminated path to the park and its blooming fields, excited to get to know this boy named Ricky that they had just read about.

About the Author

Donald Evans is a plant indigenous to California. To soothe his mid-life crisis he writes cosmic horror and existential dread. He likes to see the beauty and horror in the ordinary and synthesize it for others. He enjoys long walks at Ikea as well as the frozen food section at Costco. He also enjoys his wife and little ones, fruit smoothies and Steve from Blue's Clues.

Breathing Life into the Stars

by Jenny Perry Carr

SEPTEMBER 20, 2184

White clouds vented from the booster rocket and enveloped the loading ramp in a fog that seemed ready to cry. "I *won't* leave without you." Atira clung to her grandmother on the breezy catwalk high above the launch pad. Her insides tied into knots. The transport would take her family to the Legacy 9 interstellar starship. But not Grandmother.

Grandmother knelt and held Atira's hands. "I can't go with you."

Atira stomped on the steel grating. "Then I want to stay."

Grandmother squeezed Atira's hands and exhaled. "There's no future for you here on Earth." Dust blew in from the barren plains surrounding Houston, sweeping Grandmother's silver hair across weathered wrinkles.

"There's no future for me on the ship. I'll never see that stupid planet."

"Someday you'll understand. You're only nine but an important branch of our history, generations in the making. Our future lies on planet TOI 700 e."

"But we broke Earth. Why do we think it'll be different in the stars?"

"Because now we *know*. We'll never again take for granted what we have. Atira, this is your destiny."

Atira huffed, then dropped her head, wavy chestnut hair covering her face. Her lips quivered. "I don't want this destiny. No one ever asks what I want."

Grandmother lifted Atira's chin and brushed hair away from her eyes. "Hold out your hand, child." Grandmother's voice comforted like a warm hug.

Atira cupped her hand, expecting a present.

Onto her palm, Grandmother placed a clear mylar packet with little brown bits that resembled oats.

The girl narrowed her eyes. "What is this? Oatmeal?"

"When I was younger than you, the last of the great sequoias fell. Then, soon after, followed the aspens, oaks, ashes, and pines, until there were none. My mother collected and saved these seeds from a mighty tree, knowing they would serve a purpose someday. She gave them to me and said I would know what to do."

"Do what?"

Grandmother closed Atira's hand around the seeds. "Give them to you."

The girl shrugged. "What am I supposed to do with these?"

The old woman smiled. "You'll know."

Atira eyed them dubiously, then slipped the seeds into her zippered flight suit pocket.

MARCH 10, 2185

Atira ducked behind a storage crate as a technician passed through the restricted area sliding door and disappeared down the long gray hallway. She slipped through the opening as it thumped close. Her steps landed softly in the artificial gravity, slightly less than Earth, which proved helpful for sneaking, as she often did.

She beamed. She'd gained access to a new, unexplored area of the ship. Atira had made it her mission to map out as much of the starship as possible. Anything to get out of calculus and her homeschooling lessons. It was hard spending endless hours alone in their quarters, with her parents too busy with ship duties to spend much time with her.

Voices approached—a man and woman. Atira waved a hand over a sensor and dashed into the unlabeled room. She didn't need to get caught in a restricted area. *Again.* Her parents would surely ground her to quarters and make her focus on her studies. Why couldn't they understand she didn't like mathematics or machines? They were environmental engineers and expected her to follow in their footsteps. No, thank you. She wouldn't be forced to do something she didn't want to do. Atira would make her own path. While she wasn't sure what that was yet, it definitely didn't include differential equations and circuit boards.

Atira held her breath and pressed her ear against the cool metal door. The voices faded. Should be safe to leave in a few minutes.

She exhaled and turned into the room, continuing her exploration. Shelving lined each side of the long, narrow space and held plant pots, bags of dirt, and hand-held gardening tools. A rack glowed brightly, with lights hovering over individual cups with tiny plants, each only a few inches tall.

Her finger skipped over metal storage containers stacked on the shelves, labeled in Latin. *Allium cepa, Brassica oleracea italica, Ipomoea batatas, Solanum tuberosum.* A nudge from her boot left an indentation in a soft nylon bag piled on the floor with others. She wrinkled her nose at the foul-smelling sacks.

At the far end of the room, clear plastic strips hung from the ceiling and fluttered under an air vent. She pushed through the strips and found a recessed hatch door.

Atira looked over her shoulder, making sure she was alone. She gripped the latch and spun the wheel, releasing the sliding bars that held it shut. A rush of warm air hissed through the seams. Carefully, she pried open the door.

She squinted in the bright light and shielded her eyes. Her vision adjusted, and she stepped inside. The humid atmosphere smelled like wet dirt after rain.

Atira's jaw dropped. She craned her neck to take in the massive transparent dome, at least twenty stories high, made up of thousands of glass triangles bordered by intense grow lights.

She marveled at the enormous parallel rings that rotated around the central core of the ship to provide gravity. Each identical ring housed a self-contained community, with the ability to support its crew through the long journey. Her dad said redundancy was key.

Each ring was divided into separate sectors focused on specific aspects of ship maintenance and control: engineering, where she lived, medical, a horticultural dome, and command. Families lived and worked in their assigned sector and were restricted from moving freely about the ship. Dad said it had something to do with keeping people in line and ensuring that over time all duties would be covered on the ship.

Atira grinned. But rules were meant to be broken.

Inside the dome, plants with broad leaves surrounded her. She climbed into a planter bed and tiptoed through the loamy soil, waist-high palm fronds brushing against her, tickling her hands. Atira closed her eyes and inhaled the fragrant floral air.

She'd never seen so much green in her entire life. Back on Earth, plants barely survived outside growhouses. Her parents said it was because the pollinators were lost. Widespread drone farming hadn't been that successful, which meant people didn't have enough to eat.

But that wasn't the worst of it. Her mom had told her, with the lack of plant life, oxygen levels were dropping, and there wouldn't be enough air to breathe in a thousand years. Humanity would go extinct if they didn't leave Earth and search for a new home.

That made her think of Grandmother kneeling on the launch pad ramp. Her heart squeezed inside her chest. Atira opened her zippered pocket and removed the clear mylar bag of seeds and clutched it in her hand. Holding the seeds kept Grandmother close.

"Hey, what are you doing there?" a boy shouted.

Atira flinched and whirled around, stepping backward, deep behind the vegetation.

A boy about her age but several inches shorter pumped his arms and tromped through the brush. His boots disrupted and carelessly crushed plants, and he batted them out of the way to get to her.

She shrugged. "I'm just exploring." Atira held her hands and the seeds behind her back.

He narrowed his eyes, long ginger hair drooping over his face. "This area is off limits. I'm going to tell my dad."

Her stomach dropped. "Please don't. I'm just looking around."

The boy pointed and spoke in a gruff voice, like he was trying to sound older. "What are you hiding behind your back?"

She shook her head. Her heart thumped. "Nothing."

He scowled. "Then show me your hands."

Atira couldn't let him find Grandmother's seeds. He might take them. Then she would have nothing left of her grandmother. "Did you hear that?" She tipped her chin toward the door.

He twisted toward the hatch. "Shoot, it's probably my dad. We're not supposed to be in here."

Maybe she wasn't the only one up to no good.

She opened her hand and let the bag of seeds fall to the ground at the back of the garden bed, then scratched her boot in the dirt to cover them. Atira made a mental note of the exact location. She'd come back for them later when this jerk wasn't around.

"I don't hear anything." He spun around and pointed at her again. "Show me."

"Fine." She showed him her empty hands, turning her palms over. "*See?* Nothing."

He relaxed. "Okay. Why are you in here, anyway?"

"I've been exploring the ship."

His pinched eyes made him look cross. "Why?"

Atira tilted her head. "Bored, I guess, and any reason to get out of my lessons."

He chuckled, his freckled cheeks softening. "I get that. I *hate* Latin. My name's Mace. What's yours?"

"I'm Atira."

The hatch door opened with a *pfft* of air.

"Get down." Mace grabbed her hand and dragged her to the dirt. "Shh."

Atira dropped to her belly, the soft ground cushioning her fall. She held her breath and dared to peek between the foliage.

A man in rough brown coveralls stooped and inspected a plot of low-growing lettuces. His back was turned to them.

"My dad," Mace whispered. "We'll be in big trouble if he finds us."

His dad finished tending the plants, turned toward them, and approached. He stood only a few feet from where they lay.

Mace pushed her shoulder down.

Atira scrunched beneath the overhanging leaves.

Mace's dad brushed his hands together, then retracted a computer terminal from the wall and tapped on the keyboard. He returned the device to its storage compartment and exited the dome.

Atria exhaled.

Mace rolled onto his side and rested his elbow in the dirt. "Whew. That was close."

Atira relaxed. "Thanks for helping me hide."

Mace smiled, and any trace of his previous bad guy persona melted away.

Maybe he wasn't so bad after all. Maybe she'd finally found a friend.

She smiled. "Want to play a game?"

JUNE 28, 2185

Atira inched into the dome and checked for any adults that could tattle on her. Drones whirred overhead. They tended to the rows of plants and weren't programmed to identify intruders. *Thank goodness.* It was rare to see people inside the garden. Mace stood guard outside anyway, ready to give a signal through the mini-comms system he'd built for them.

She hadn't been able to get back until now to collect Grandmother's seeds. Mace didn't see the point, but it was important to her. *Boys never get it.* Her parents had her on lockdown for the past three months, after she got caught out after curfew in a different area of the ship playing tag with her new friend. Atira pleaded with them to reconsider, but, yet again, they didn't listen.

On her hands and knees, she crawled through the spongy soil and searched for the spot where she'd dropped the seeds, not caring that dirt ground into her clothes. Her eyes widened.

Disturbed, overturned soil filled the bed, like someone had recently tooled the area. Atira picked up a piece of shredded mylar that lay atop the surface. She furiously scratched at the soil in search of the seeds but couldn't find any. Her heart sank. *They're gone.* But a small sprout poked through the surface—a teeny tiny tree. The seedling was all that remained of Grandmother's seeds.

"You'll know." Grandmother's words echoed in her thoughts.

Jumping to her feet, Atira rushed to the garden bench she remembered was in the middle of the dome and found an empty container. She filled it with water and raced back to her tree, then carefully dribbled the water around the sprout.

She leaned down, her face inches from the plant, and whispered, "No matter how many rules I have to break, I'm going to make sure you survive."

"What is that?"

Atria whirled around to find Mace hovering over her. She stood between him and the tree. "Why aren't you guarding the door?"

He waved a hand toward the hatch. "We're fine. No one's out there. But you didn't answer my question." Mace pointed to the plant near her feet.

She stepped aside to show him. "I didn't find Grandmother's seeds, but one of them sprouted into a tree. Can you believe it?" Atira beamed.

Mace's eyes widened. "You can't grow a tree in here."

It did seem ridiculous. A tree in space? But it was possible. "Why not? There are all kinds of plants in here."

He shook his head. "But no trees."

"Why not?"

Mace shrugged. "I don't know. I just know."

"Come on. It's just one tree. What harm can it do? It will be our little secret."

"I don't know about this."

"You have to help me take care of it." She had to convince her friend how important this was to her.

"*I* don't have to do anything." He pursed his lips.

She crouched beside the tree and brushed its soft, tiny spines. "Mace, please, it's all I have left of my grandmother."

He exhaled. "This won't be easy. You're going to owe me, big time."

APRIL 28, 2191

A hard object bounced off Atira's head, and she flinched. An orange wire connector hit the soil near the young sequoia where she knelt. She rubbed her head, feigning an injury, then threw the cap back at Mace. "Hey."

Over the years, Atira came to the dome as often as she could to care for the evergreen, ensuring its survival among the tropical plants. Back at home, she used her holopad to teach herself about soil types and water needs, absorbing the information like the plants absorbed nutrients from the dirt.

She had Mace to thank for covering for her. In exchange for sneaking him supplies from the engineering wing, he'd stand guard while she worked and used his gadgets to scramble the door locks. If it weren't for her best friend, she'd never have been able to get away with this for so long. What would she do without him?

Mace held a tangle of wires. Another one of his inventions. "I found you."

Atira stood and brushed dirt from her coveralls. "Duh. Where else would I be?"

"Maybe doing your homework?" Mace's low voice resonated inside the dome, and he towered over her now, more than a head above her. He had grown so fast, nearly as fast as the sequoia, which surpassed his height.

She rolled her eyes. *Homework is the last thing I'd be doing.*

He smirked. "You know, I really *should* tell my dad about that tree." The little evergreen barely hid beneath the tropical plants.

His empty threat was a common game with him. Mace liked to think he had something over her. But if anything, she had something on him. She did all his chores, which allowed him time to tinker with electronics. They made a good pair.

A cute dimple burrowed into his cheek as he playfully sang his words. "He'd be very upset with you."

"Is that so?" She pleadingly clutched her hands together and sheepishly batted her eyelashes. "Please, please don't tell on me."

He puffed out his chest. "Maybe, but it will cost you."

What was this? She tilted her head and planted a fist on her hip. "What now?"

He raised his eyebrows. "A kiss?"

Atira blushed and smiled. This was a new game. Butterflies circled in her stomach. *What should I say?* Her mind raced and her palms grew clammy. "Okay."

She closed her eyes and tender lips brushed against hers, like soft petals of the delicate plumeria flower. Pinpricks of electricity surged across her skin. The artificial gravity seemed to turn off as she grew weightless. Then her boots crashed back to the ground, and she doubled over when his fingers buried into her ribs in the ultimate tickle.

MAY 12, 2191

Atira lay on her bunk on her belly and pored over a holopad screen. Dirty gardening coveralls peeked out from under her bed. She reached down and shoved them out of sight. Her parents could never find out what she had been doing. *They'd be furious.*

She flipped through screens, researching the nutritional needs of coniferous saplings and how to make her own fertilizer. Her parents thought she was studying for her engineering exam tomorrow. *Yeah, right.*

But soon she would enter her apprenticeship years upon her sixteenth birthday. Next week. Finding time to sneak away to the garden would become even more difficult once she had a full-time job, and more eyes paying attention to her movement. There were rules. And children were required to succeed their parents in their profession.

When would she see Mace?

She ran a finger over her lips, which tingled at the memory of their first kiss.

"No, that won't work." Mom's shrill voice bled through her bedroom door. A day didn't go by lately that her parents weren't fighting.

"You're not listening to me," Dad said. The sound of a chair thumping against the floor echoed through the door.

Atira flinched. *Big fight tonight.*

"We could reroute additional power to the moisture recovery system to increase efficiency of water reclamation," he argued.

A series of beeps emanated from the holoscreen in the living room, where her parents often mapped out schematics.

"Am I talking to myself? Take power away from the CO2 scrubbers? Great idea." Mom's voice dripped with sarcasm.

More beeps came as they graphed out their environmental control mumbo jumbo. *Dueling ideas.* Atira rolled her eyes. She could barely hear herself think over the raised voices.

Each of them was a brilliant engineer, but their people skills were clearly lacking. In mathematical terms, the volume of their arguments was directly proportional to their desire to make a point.

Blah. Blah. Blah.

"It should be enough to get us to 99% oxygenation." Dad calmed his voice. *Serious time.*

Mom's audible sigh revealed her frustration. "Do you hear what you're saying? Efficiency will inevitably decrease over time. 99% this year, means 98% next year, then 97% after that, and so on. We won't have enough oxygen to get to TOI 700 e."

Atira's gaze jerked toward the door. *Out of oxygen?* A lump formed in her throat, and she struggled to swallow. *Just like Earth. We'll suffocate like them.*

She couldn't sit and listen to this anymore. Atira threw her holopad down onto the bunk and launched toward the door. She slammed her palm against the door sensor and rushed out of her room, past her parents, heading toward the entrance to their quarters.

"Atira, where are you going?" Dad said, standing in front of the holoscreen covered in scribbles.

Atira jammed her fingers against the front door sensor pad. "Out." She passed over the threshold and into the common hallway, now darkened with the evening lighting subroutine.

"Get back here, young lady," Mom snapped at her. "It's after curfew…"

Her words trailed off as the sliding door thumped shut. She didn't need a lecture right now. She needed comfort, and there was only one place that gave her that on the ship.

Atira slipped through the maze of corridors and doorways until she found herself in front of the horticulture restricted zone. She fished out a bypass keycard Mace had made her so she could gain access when he wasn't around. Waving it over the sensor pad, the light turned green and beeped as the entrance slid open. She raced to the hatch door and entered the vast dome, breathing in the aroma of herbs and fresh vegetation.

She grabbed a watering container and hopped into the garden bed, winding through the plants to her grandmother's tree. Atira held back the prickle-pointed leaves on the dense sprays of branchlets and poured water around the base of her sequoia. She patted the cinnamon-colored bark. The garden breathed life into her. *Air. Oxygen.*

Should she tell Mace about the oxygen problem? They would be fine, but future generations wouldn't make it to their destination. *What's the point of our mission now?* She inhaled the earthy evergreen scent of the greenhouse, which calmed her nerves.

"What are you doing?" The man's voice was similar to Mace's, but it wasn't him. Deeper, older. *His father, Linden.*

Atira swallowed hard and turned to face the master gardener, standing between him and the tree. There was no way to hide what she'd been doing now. The tree was starting to poke over the tops of the palm fronds surrounding it.

The ginger-bearded man held a hand over his open mouth. "What have you done?"

Atira held out her dirty hands. "I can explain." *What can I say?*

"Do you realize how many gallons of water a tree like this consumes? Our supply is limited." He grabbed a shovel from a rack on the wall. "I need to remove this."

"No! Please don't." She wrung her hands. "It's all I have left of my grandmother." Like she was falling, the ground seemed to slip out from under her, but a quick glance down revealed it was still there. Her muscles tensed.

Linden marched through garden bed and thrust his shovel into the earth beside the tree.

"No," Atira pleaded. "You can't." She touched his arm as he threw a shovel of dirt to the side.

He paused and glanced along the strong trunk of the conifer, then swiped a hand through the soft needles. "We don't have the resources to support this."

Atria widened her eyes. "I can take care of it. I'll use some of my own water rations."

He pursed his lips and shook his head. "You would die of thirst with the amount of water this evergreen will consume."

"Please. You can't destroy it. It's from my grandmother's seeds."

Linden locked eyes with her and raised an eyebrow. "You grew this from seed?"

Atira nodded.

"That's not an easy task." His demeanor softened, and he leaned against the handle of his shovel. "You're pretty smart if you were able to grow this in secret. How did you do it?"

She relaxed. *An adult that wants to hear what I have to say?* "I just read about what nutrients sequoias need, and I've been making fertilizer from coffee grounds and food scraps."

Linden smoothed his beard. "Clever. It's refreshing to see a young person taking an interest." He chuckled. "A sequoia? Maybe there is a way. Do you want to learn more?"

Atira nodded. "Of course. I love coming here."

He scratched his head. "You know, I could teach you. I know it's against the rules, but I wouldn't want to squander a talent like yours. Would you like to apprentice as a gardener?"

No one has ever asked what I wanted.

But a formal apprenticeship would mean moving to this sector of the ship permanently. Moving away from her parents, even worse, not following in their footsteps and turning her back on them. She loved them so much, but they didn't understand her.

She glanced at the door, then at the tree. Atira smiled. "Oh, yes."

Linden scrutinized the massive dome and exhaled. "Okay. A sequoia. Maybe I can work with engineering to boost water production. And we'll need to prune creatively to fit inside the dome."

The glass didn't seem so high up anymore, considering the imminent growth of the tree.

"Atira!" Dad's booming voice bounced off the geodesic dome, seemingly coming from all directions.

She spun around. Mom and Dad stood in the doorway with Mace, who mouthed, *I'm sorry.* They must have gotten to him, trying to find her.

"What have you been doing, young lady?" Mom's hands were planted firmly on her hips. She meant business.

Atira stood tall. "I'm making things grow."

"What?" Dad scoffed. "The fate of this entire ship is at stake, and you're playing in the dirt? We need your help with the oxygen reclamation problem."

Linden cleared his throat. "Oxygen problem?"

Dad blinked, then waved a dismissal. "Never mind." The oxygenation problem was clearly not public knowledge yet.

Atira approached her parents. "Don't you understand? *This* is my calling." *I need them to hear me. I have to make them understand.*

Linden stood behind her. "She has a knack for it."

Dad held up a hand. "Stay out of this, Linden. You know the rules. You're in the same council meetings as I am. Children learn the trade of their parents."

Atira's pitch rose. "I can't do what you do. I hate math. I have no interest in machines. Your holoscreen calculations look like gibberish to me." She grabbed a handful of dirt and sifted the rich soil through her fingers. "I understand this. I'm good at this."

"Do you understand what you're asking?" Her mother's eyes saddened, just like Grandmother's that day on the launch pad. "Following another track would mean leaving us."

Atira bowed her head. "I know. But I'm not destined to be an engineer." She grabbed her parents by the hands and yanked them toward the tree. "Look. I grew this. It's from Grandmother's seed." She looked into her mother's eyes, which glassed over with tears.

Mom sucked in a breath. "From my mother?"

Atira nodded.

Mace stood beside her and squeezed her hand.

Dad glanced at their hands and clenched his jaw. "That doesn't matter. Your place is in the engineering department with us." Dad tugged her other hand, pulling her toward the door. "Let's go."

"Wait a minute." Mom examined the sensor screen strapped to her forearm. "Look at these oxygen readings in here. Far beyond the levels in the rest of the ship."

Dad's brow furrowed. "What?"

"Trees produce lots of oxygen, right?" Atira eyeballed Linden.

He nodded in agreement. "Plants. Trees. We had only planned for fruits, vegetables, and some tropical plants that wouldn't contribute appreciably to oxygen levels, but trees are a different matter. They have significant output. Especially the sequoia."

Dad's head dropped. "But we need your help with the environmental controls."

Atira's eyes widened. He needed help, but not hers. "Mace can do it. He *hates* gardening, but he loves math and is a wiz with machines. He can be your apprentice, and I can train with Linden."

If they agreed, she'd lose her best friend to the engineering department once their apprenticeships began. Their time together would be limited moving forward. But it was what she and Mace needed to thrive, to grow.

"You know she's right," Mace said to his dad. "I don't belong here."

Linden's face saddened, not in surprise, but like he was finally admitting to what he already knew.

Dad, Mom, and Linden stared at each other.

Dad ran a hand through his hair, his voice exasperated. "But the rules, Atira."

She grinned. "We're not on Earth anymore. We make our own rules now."

OCTOBER 17, 2271

Atira passed the sequoia seeds back and forth between her palms. They rolled across her calloused and wrinkled skin, past her worn wedding band, nicked from decades spent working the soil. The nonagenarian's hands held the memories of a life well lived.

"But I want you to come with us." Her ten-year-old great-granddaughter, her legacy, rocked impatiently beside her in the flourishing garden.

She beamed with pride at the bright young girl, so much like her daughter, and herself—head-strong and determined to make her own path. Through Atira's work with the council, the revised charter now allowed children to select the apprenticeship of their choosing.

"I'm afraid I won't be able to make the trip. These old bones will soon be ready to lie down with my husband." Atira pointed to the towering sequoia, also her legacy, where the ginger-haired man was buried. The tip of the tree curved against the dome above. Coniferous trees of various heights surrounded them, planted from the original sequoia's plentiful seed cones.

Gone were the environmental control problems of her youth. Between her sequoia planting program and her gifted engineer husband, they had found a sustainable solution with years of oxygen to spare. Mace adapted the life support system to produce plentiful water as a byproduct. Now, the domes of each ring contained hundreds of evergreens, breathing life into the stars.

"Hold out your hand, child." Atira poured the seeds into the girl's palm. "It's your responsibility to make sure we get this right on Toiseveny." What they now called the planet TOI 700 e.

The girl's forehead wrinkled. "Get what right?"

Atira smiled. "You'll see."

Her great-granddaughter shrugged. "What am I supposed to do with these?"

Atira patted her hands. "You'll know."

About the Author

Jenny Perry Carr is group vice president of scientific services for a medical communications company by day, budding sci-fi/horror/fantasy writer at night, which sounds much like the beginnings of a superhero's bio. But alas, her only superpower is remembering random facts, like the human body contains trillions of microorganisms that outnumber our own cells by 10 to 1! She has a PhD in molecular neurobiology from Yale University and unleashes her scientific insights into her spine-chilling tales. You can find her captivating stories in several anthologies, including *Dog Save the King*, *Troubadours and Space Princesses*, and *Rhapsody of the Spheres*. She's a Minnesota native living in North Texas with her husband and currently working on a sci-fi trilogy. Find her at jennyperrycarr.com or on Facebook @JennyPerryCarr.

RESILIENCE

by Allan W. Mason

A COLD FEAR GRIPPED MARIA as she paced the library's shelves. A desperate plea against an encroaching evil had slammed into her consciousness. In a distant place, someone she did not yet know needed help, and Maria might be just the person to deliver it. Once, she would have acted the moment she sensed the need, but now she was the only guardian left. Her team had not survived the last brutal war. She could not turn to them for expertise, counsel, or strength. Yet she could not let this cry for help become just another ghost.

Her fingers caressed the butter-soft leather cover of the huge grimoire on its carved stand, the hairs on her forearm lifting in the buzz of its static field. She passed her workbench, picking up a deep-blue rhomboid crystal from the world where her team had perished. Maria slipped it into her pocket.

She sat cross-legged on the floor cushion in her work chamber. The stone walls chilled the air, helping her focus. She placed her hands on her knees, palms up and open.

Maria reached for the egregore of the kindred worlds. The sapphire on her bracelet bloomed, its azure glow pulsing in time with her heartbeat. The bracelet strengthened her focus as she shaped her chi and began the portal spell. Moments later, the egregore subverted her spell.

She opened her eyes. Before her, the transition plane unfurled, a sheet of mercurial light.

Their need must be immense for the passage to open before I requested it, she thought. *And I almost didn't answer the call.*

She stood, then leapt back. A bloody body crashed through the quicksilver and hit the floor with a wet thump.

That does not *look good.*

The chamber thrummed with unbalanced energy. The portal was unraveling. *Please don't implode, I don't have time for that.* Maria thrust her hand toward the turbulence, grasped its unstable boundary, and closed her fist, infusing the liminal space with chi as she completed the spell to stabilize it. A final twist and the surface settled. It would hold while she dealt with her wounded guest. If she had furled it, she would not be able to find its origin point again, and the refugee might want to return to their battle.

Maria recoiled when a tendril of corruption touched the edge of her awareness. Whatever had injured her guest was pursuing them.

"No, you don't," she snarled and shoved the sickness back, then conjured a lock on the passage.

Maria knelt beside the body, relieved to see that they were still breathing. The person lay on their right side, and blood pooled on the floor beneath them. Their skin was golden brown but washed with the light green of new leaves.

I really wish my magic extended to healing. She considered her injured visitor. *Broad shoulders, lean muscle, narrow hips, probably male.* Maria stocked a range of potions for field missions. A pang of grief followed that thought, as her team's physician had died with her colleagues.

She raced to that storage locker. The vials glowed on their racks, their colors indicating their application. Maria selected a bright blue vial designed to heal traumatic injuries and returned to the chamber.

She knelt next to his head and reached one arm under his shoulders to support his torso. Maria noted his erratic breathing, the tightness in his face, and the rigid muscles in his body. She flicked the lid off the vial, opened his lips and trickled in some of the potion. A faint glow flowed over him.

Need to go slow until I know this will help. Improvement should be quick. She watched for adverse reactions. As she waited, she ran her hand along the lean muscle of his bloodiest arm. She stroked away the blood so she could monitor his wounds.

The bleeding has stopped. His color looks better. His face is relaxing, so his pain must be fading. She took a moment to appreciate his beauty, the hard lines of his jaw, and the fullness of his mouth.

Am I bad for thinking such things when he almost died? She shook her head. *Focus, Maria.* She poured in the rest of the first vial and waited. The glow intensified then faded. His visible wounds closed and skin knitted as she watched. His breathing deepened and stabilized.

Maria surveyed her guest. He wore a holstered sidearm, and his wide belt hosted a range of pouches and tools. Two of these blinked frantic telltale lights.

Even his tech seems distressed.

She studied a splash of color that ran from the corner of his right eye across his temple to the front of his ear. Maria traced the intricate tattoo. As her fingers passed over it a wave of multicolored light followed.

"Wow. I want one."

His eyes opened wide and he flinched. He tracked her hand as she snatched it back. His pupils flared, making his eyes nearly black. He scanned the room and sat up.

"Oh. Are you feeling better?" she asked.

His focus returned to her face, his brows rose, and he spoke. Her breath caught. His voice reminded Maria of a cello, and he could produce multiple tones simultaneously.

How does he do that? "I don't understand. Do you speak Terran?"

He watched her face and spoke again, slower and louder. Maria tried to follow the melodic intonation but could not detect individual words.

"I'm sorry, I can't understand you." She tapped her ear and shook her head. He held up a finger and gestured for her to move closer.

She nodded and leaned in. He touched his tattoo with his forefinger. The design rippled and flickered. A construct of light and color extended from his skin and coalesced above the tip of his finger. It morphed through various intricate shapes. As the light danced, she heard faint music, a simple melody that developed harmony and complexity. He touched her face, gentle fingers turning her head to one side.

He brought the lively construct near her ear. Maria felt a soft tap as his fingertip skimmed down the sensitive skin to the edge of her jaw. She watched his face for clues about his end goal. Their eyes met. His were luminous sienna. He pulled his hand away but held her gaze.

She felt a brief sensation of cold, then warmth. She heard a faint whirr and then music. For a moment she resonated with that melodic line. And then he spoke.

"Hello, can you understand me now? My name is Kaelen."

Maria smiled. She heard the cello-like sounds, but now meaning overlaid the music.

"Functional and beautiful. Nice." Maria looked toward a mirror on the wall. She reached toward it, then rotated her hand toward herself. The spell brought her image as seen from the mirror to float in her palm. Maria turned so the mirror reflected her profile. With her free hand, she expanded the image in her palm, zooming in on her new tattoo.

Kaelen watched with rapt interest.

Maria grinned. "Not sure I agreed to get matching tattoos, but this is useful."

"That is the visible presentation of an intelligent, adaptive nanite cluster. They translate our thoughts and speech."

She explored further with her magic. The nanites reminded her of the bright scales on a butterfly wing. She zoomed out to appreciate the design, a detailed tree alive with color and movement, its leaves moving in an unseen breeze.

Kaelen looked down and passed his hands over his torn, stained clothes. He looked at her in awe.

"You saved me. And you healed me. I feel strong. Thank you. You're human? I encountered your species once, long ago. Your people are more beautiful than I remember. My people are wood elves."

"Hi, I'm Maria. You're not what I expected from a wood elf." She gestured to his tool belt. "I would have expected magic rather than technology."

"Once, we understood the magic of life. Generations ago our grasp of magic faltered, and we never regained it." He looked uncomfortable. She was going to change the subject, but he continued. "We mastered technology to replace what we had lost. These nanites are one example."

They stood. Maria said, "Let's go back to my study. You must be thirsty." She led him through the door and into the library. Maria sat on her favorite sofa, and he sat at the other end. She poured a glass of water from the carafe on the side table and passed it to him. He drained it.

"How did you bring me here, and why?"

"I'm a guardian. We monitor and protect the balance between good and evil. I felt an urgent need and knew I had to act. I connected to the egregore of the kindred worlds to find out more about the emergency. When I unfurled the portal, the egregore yanked you through. Something pursued you, and I locked it out."

"I didn't know your people had magic. Is this new? Can you help us?"

She smiled. "No, my people are still technology users. But a handful of us know magic exists and can wield it." Maria sensed the turbulence battering the locked portal. "You were almost dead when you came through. That's why my portal opened so soon. What happened?"

He paused before answering, then said, "My people are being killed. It's a parasite that took us by surprise. The rate of infection grew exponentially before we realized what it was. We don't know how it's spreading or controlling us. It drains its victims' life forces. We captured a few of the infected, but they broke containment."

He closed his eyes for a moment and took a deep, shuddering breath. His brows furrowed and he met her eyes again.

"I barely escaped. If not for your portal, I would have died alongside my fellow scientists who were infected only moments before. We were close friends." He clenched and unclenched his fists. "It must be stopped."

"What species is it? Is it microbial? What have you learned about its biology?"

"We don't know, and very little. Please, I need you. I need your help. With my technology and your command of magic, we might defeat this vile corruption." Kaelen swallowed hard.

He's beautiful, Maria thought. Maria chided herself for losing focus on his emergency.

"We're losing this war, Maria. If we don't stop them soon, my people could be extinct within weeks. The parasite may have already reached other worlds."

He glanced through the wide door of the chamber. Turbulence on the portal's surface indicated that the fight raged on. Maria followed his gaze.

My lock better hold. We don't want them here.

Kaelen approached the portal and touched the nanite design next to his eye. Within seconds, elaborate lenses and sensors built up over his eyes. The goggles shimmered with lights, the lenses lengthened and retracted as he examined the portal from several angles. Maria joined him.

"I would love to discuss how you do this if we get the chance later," he said.

He turned back to her, touching the goggles, which retracted.

"What do you know about your invaders? If they're parasites, do they have a vector?"

"We haven't found one. We're not sure they're microbes, and we haven't been able to determine how they spread. They colonize and control infected individuals in seconds. We don't even know the epicenter of the infestation. In four days, entire regions have fallen. I don't know how many uninfected individuals remain." He slouched, grief shadowing his face. "We were in a safe facility, sealed from outside and in. But it happened and I could do nothing."

"What data do you have with you?"

"My cybernetic memory holds the data logs and video. I can share my encounter with the infected that we had contained in our lab, including when they corrupted my peers."

He reached out and took her hand. She flinched, startled, then allowed it. "If you're willing, I can connect our minds, and we can review the information and videos together, and collaborate at the speed of thought."

She looked into his eyes and paused. *Can I trust him? I thought I knew Erick, but he betrayed me—betrayed us all—in the end. I need to trust my intuition here. My magic will protect me if he attacks or tries to control me. I can do this. I want to do this.*

"Okay. How does this work?"

"Please get comfortable. We'll have only a fraction of our awareness of the physical world. I'll extend your translator nanites to create a shared connection."

He moved closer, and she was aware of warmth where his leg touched hers. He tapped the nanites beside his ear and drew his hand outward. A fine strand of swirling color followed, floating in the air between them. He brought the end over to her nanites and hesitated.

"This will be disorienting at first."

Maria loved to learn and experience new things. "I'm ready. Let's do this." Even with her concerns, she was excited.

Kaelen connected their minds, and her reality expanded. Her mind and senses pushed through the brief vertigo to adjust to the presence of a second mind and its senses. She sat on a grassy hill overlooking a lake surrounded by forest. In the distance, she saw mountains. A fish leapt from the water, sending ripples across the placid surface.

"I love this. Is this your home? It's so peaceful."

Kaelen sat beside her. "Yes, this is my default meditation space." A discrete heads-up display floated low in front of them. He tapped several symbols, enlarged one window, and swiped his hand. The lake faded and they stood in his laboratory. The figures she saw were frozen in place.

"We attempted to analyze the issue. The parasites are so infectious, our hunters were being captured and consumed. It took us two days to capture subjects for study."

Maria studied the facility. *Wood elves have amazing tech.*

"Our avatars are where I stood at the back of the room. You'll have access to everything." He set the scene in motion.

Three people in lab coats conversed before a wall. They were animated, even agitated, as they discussed the situation. The monitors scrolled endless data. One showed video of figures in a cell; others showed the same subjects in infrared and ultraviolet. Additional sensor data streamed straight into Kaelen's cybernetics, which were accessible to Maria.

One scientist interacted with a heads-up display. The wall became transparent, providing a clear view into a containment cell. Three disheveled wood elves inside appeared lost and listless. When they noticed the change in the wall, they turned as one to lock gazes with the scientists and let out a blood-curdling, discordant shout. Each focused on one scientist. They lunged against the containment barrier.

The scientists screamed in pain and confusion, and chaos erupted. Their melodic voices mutated into a harsh, grating sound that made Kaelen flinch beside Maria. Then their screams cut off and they froze. A moment later, they turned to look at the recorded version of Kaelen, and the eerie intensity of their regard sickened Maria. Their fingertips had grown long talons. The recorded Kaelen flinched, reached for his weapon, but did not draw it.

The infected scientists seized the opportunity. They tackled him. His blood sprayed the area. His nanite reserves gave him enough strength to break free and sealed the worst of the wounds.

He bolted out the door. The infected scientists made the same discordant cry that the captive subjects had moments before. The newly infected elves pursued him. Even knowing this was a recording, Maria's adrenaline surged.

Beside her, Kaelen said, "I pushed myself and ran. I knew my life was ending, but I did not give up." The infected caught up to the recorded Kaelen and tripped him. At that moment, her portal appeared in front of him, pulling him through as he fell. The recording froze there.

"I don't understand why I didn't get infected. I was the only scientist in our group with any combat training. We had decided that I would stand in the back, by the door, to protect us if something went wrong." He paused and took several deep breaths. "I couldn't bring myself to fire on my friends and colleagues," he whispered.

In her physical body, Maria touched the crystal in her pocket. She flashed back to her previous assignment. Erick, a specialist in defusing nuclear ordnance, had joined them on that mission. They had become lovers. Or so she had thought. He'd betrayed her entire team to the merciless evil they were fighting. She had been holding that crystal when she had realized what Erick had done. Maria had lost her one opportunity to stop him because she had hesitated to kill him. Her entire team had fallen. He had escaped through a portal. She had fled through one of her own. The world they had hoped to save was atomized moments later.

Maria realized that Kaelen had seen her memory and its emotional impact. Their mind connection went deeper than she had expected. He put a hand on her shoulder.

"Words are inadequate," he said. She placed her hand atop his, met his gaze, and nodded.

They replayed and discussed the recording. He tried to answer her questions.

Frustrated, she stopped him as he started it for the fourth time. "Wait," she said. "This isn't working. The tech didn't capture the details we need."

Kaelen sighed and ran a hand over his face. He looked exhausted.

Magic might help. But if I use it, he will have access to my casting and energy work. He might find weaknesses that he can use against me. She considered what she could sense through the meld about the nature of Kaelen's heart. *He's a good person. And if we don't try this, we will not save his people.*

"I know a spell that reveals details that your technology might not detect. Your recordings provide a frame of reference. I can delve deeper into these events. I've never done this without the physical movements of spellcasting, but fully visualized this way, it should work."

She built and deployed the spell in her mind's eye. "OK, start your playback." The magic added details that his tech had missed. Her casting resembled the mirror spell she had used to examine the nanites. She shared key elements as she found them. Working together, they discovered the missing mechanisms.

"Transmission isn't physical, it's digital," Maria said.

Kaelen gasped. "That's how the parasite penetrated our isolation barriers. It used our cybernetic implants against us. It seizes control and spreads the way a computer virus does, but then it consumes the host's life force until the host dies. Because it controlled the host, anyone infected couldn't ask for help. They were prisoners in their own bodies."

"This is the first instance I've ever seen of a digital entity preying on biological systems." Maria directed her magic to probe the nanites so she could assess how the parasite attached itself to them. Her spells allowed them to compare the captive infected elves to the newly infected elves. They learned that the parasite needed time to establish deep control over its host before it had enough energy to broadcast itself, infecting new victims.

"That's why it didn't infect me," Kaelen said. "It wasn't mature yet." He shuddered. "Given the speed of the spread, that must happen fast. Now that we understand it, what do we do? My methods for eliminating it would not get past the parasite's protective firewall."

Maria lit up. "We can create a vaccine." The lock on the portal wavered, interrupting her. "They're coming through. I need to deal with this." She reached up to the cord that connected them.

Kaelen yelled, "No, wait!" But it was too late. She yanked the cord away from her nanites. It felt like decompression as it released, and both staggered with vertigo. Kaelen collapsed against the side of the couch, and Maria fell to the floor.

Sparks flew from the distressed portal and Maria smelled ozone. The seal shattered with a sharp crack and the quicksilver surface erupted. She was on her feet and into the chamber. Kaelen struggled to follow. Her arcane combat training kicked in. She pushed past the pounding headache and started her containment spell.

A body tumbled through the roiling portal. Maria recognized one of Kaelen's colleagues. He looked at her, face warped by rage. He screamed the discordant cry. Adrenaline surged through Maria.

She whispered an incantation in an ancient language preserved by Earth's guardians, spinning her hands in a clockwise rotation with quick flourishes at key points, ending with her fingertips touching. As Maria worked her spell, Kaelen drew his weapon.

His other two colleagues spilled into the chamber. The three of them turned as one and charged them. A rippling sphere enveloped the infected elves. They hung suspended in mid-lunge. The sphere's surface shimmered with faint blue light and emitted a deep hum.

Kaelen gasped, "What did you do?" He took a hesitant step closer to the captives. "How long will it last? Can they break out? Is it safe to get closer?" He seemed giddy about the magic.

Maria smiled. "I suspended them in time. They are still in motion, but it's too slow for you to detect. We're safe for now. You can get closer, but don't penetrate the barrier. It would be complicated to extract you. The spell gives us ten minutes."

He brought up his goggles and analyzed it. "My sensors can't read through this surface."

"That's because it's magic," she said. He laughed. "Now, about this vaccine…" Maria led him out of the chamber to the quieter library.

Kaelen said, "I can create a code change for the nanites, so they recognize and reject the parasite's transmission aimed at an uninfected person. That's the vaccine part. Can we bundle this with something that kills the parasite in those already infected? The compromised nanites can't combat the malicious code and clear it. But we still have the firewall problem."

Maria considered this. "Your people lost their magic a long time ago. The parasite won't recognize a magical attack. I can craft an arcane payload to target and kill it in a host."

"I can build a digital package to encapsulate and deliver your payload. The magic will kill the parasite while my code repairs the nanites to prevent infection. We can deliver the whole thing as a digital transmission."

"Can you do this in ten minutes?"

"Only if we do another mind meld."

Maria leaned into his touch as Kaelen reestablished the connection. She enjoyed the flow of working with him. He assembled the code from his library, and she cast the purging spell, adapting it to cover both the organic and inorganic elements of the parasite.

The spell manifested as a bright blue spark. As she finished, she felt the infected scientists twitch.

"They're breaking free. We need to hurry."

Kaelen enclosed the spark in the digital package and finalized the transmission protocol. Their work complete, he ended the mind meld.

"We need to try this on a single person first," Maria said.

"Yes, I may need to adjust the targeting." He looked at his three companions stirring in the sphere. "Would you pick our first subject for me, please?"

"I understand."

The time sphere disintegrated, releasing the three infected elves. They screamed and charged.

Shield, Maria! She grabbed Kaelen and tapped her sapphire bracelet. She had stored a shield spell for such emergencies. A protective sphere burst around them both. Energy crackled violently from the shield where the scientists slashed with their talons.

"Transmit the vaccine to the male!"

Kaelen took a deep breath. Then he tapped his nanite cluster. "Done."

The elf staggered back and gasped in pain. His talons vanished into dust. He collapsed, clutching his temples with his hands. Maria smelled burnt flesh and electronics. She looked at Kaelen, who stood speechless and horrified.

Maria cast a spell to check the fallen elf's vitals. "He's alive." She looked deeper into his status. "The parasites are gone!"

Kaelen sagged in relief. "Thank the ancestors! It did fry his nanite cluster. I'll adjust the targeting to preserve them." While he did that, Maria resealed the portal and laid a binding on the female elves.

Maria marveled at how well she and Kaelen worked together. She pushed a sweaty strand of hair out of her eyes. She had performed a lot of complex, rapid spellwork. When this was over, she would need extended rest.

"Here goes the next test," Kaelen said. His two friends struggled against the binding. Maria saw his fatigue. He clasped her hand and launched the second test.

The two elves shuddered, grasping their heads and stumbling. Both slumped to the floor. Maria checked their vitals. "It worked. Check their tech."

Kaelen knelt, pulled out a small silver orb, and held it over the closest elf. It hovered there as he interacted with his heads-up display. He nodded, then evaluated the other two. Kaelen transferred some of his nanites to his injured friend.

"They are free. Thank you. They are all resting. His injuries will heal."

Maria sighed with relief. "Let's save your people. I'll scale up the spell power and structure to cover your world. I'll tap into the egregore's energy for this one." As a guardian she had crafted a few spells of this scope before.

She sat cross-legged on her floor cushion and entered deep meditation. Maria's hands and mind wove the spell. The energy of the egregore flowed through her into a scintillating spark floating before her. She consolidated the spell, and the spark grew into a spiky sphere. This fractal form contained millions of smaller copies of itself. Maria completed the casting and her gratitude flowed out to the egregore.

"It's done," Maria said. Kaelen had watched her working with rapt interest. He wrapped the bright form in his digital framework, adjusting for the egregore's intense energy. The final package floated before them, elegant and potent. Kaelen's face showed the strain of this day's work.

"I've never encountered an energy source like this," he said. "We use different branches of physics to power our technology."

"We believe our magic taps into quantum phenomena but have never developed a full mathematical expression of its nature."

"I want to know more. What we've built together is unprecedented in our science."

"When we have resolved this emergency," Maria said, "I hope we can collaborate on other projects."

"I agree." Kaelen squeezed her hand. "I want to test this version on myself before we deploy it on my world."

"And on me, too, since I now have nanites. We need to be protected in case we encounter more infected people."

Kaelen cued his system to deliver doses to their nanite clusters. Maria felt a brief tingle where the technology interfaced with her skin.

"Did it work?" she asked.

"It did. The code is embedded in my systems, both nanite and cybernetic. Let's get this transmitted." They returned to the chamber. The treated scientists slept where they had fallen. Kaelen and Maria moved them to one side of the room.

"Their nanites are healing their injuries," he said. "In a few hours, they should be awake and healed." Kaelen and Maria faced the portal.

"Are you ready? I'll unlock the portal so you can transmit the vaccine."

"Yes."

Maria opened the portal. A mob of infected elves had gathered in the lab to free the captives. The air pressure changed when the portal opened. As one, they turned and rushed the shimmering opening. The press of bodies slowed them from coming through, giving Kaelen time to transmit. With a defiant shout, he pushed out the signal, draining his tech to dangerously low levels. The global network would amplify the transmission to cover his world.

The infected elves screamed, staggered, and collapsed.

"I've connected to the lab system. The three in the containment area are also quiet. My sensors say their tech is clear." His eyes focused on his heads-up display. "We had set up a global monitoring system to track the pandemic. The readouts indicate no parasite activity." He sighed. "The casualty numbers are high, though."

Maria put a hand on his shoulder. "Words are inadequate."

"We did it. Those who could be saved have been saved. Thank you."

"Come sit. You're exhausted," Maria said, guiding him back into the library. They slumped side-by-side onto the couch. He leaned against her. She appreciated the warmth of his body.

"I've never dealt with a crisis like this one," she said.

"If it weren't for your resilience we wouldn't have succeeded," Kaelen said.

"*Our* resilience." Maria said. "And those parasites must be invading other worlds. I could use your help finding them."

"We don't know where they came from, and the pandemic spread so fast we had no time to answer that. You're right that other people are threatened."

"Would you like to become a guardian? It would grant you more resources."

"Would I be working with you? With magic?"

"Yes." Maria looked into his eyes. Their warm sienna shone brighter though she could also see his fatigue. She leaned in, touching her forehead to his. "I'd like to see where this goes."

He tipped her chin up and kissed her.

"I'd like that," Kaelen said. "We do work well together."

About the Author

Allan W. Mason writes epic romantasy where love, magic, and a pinch of science conquer all. When not building new worlds, he's exploring this one with his incredible wife, fueled by coffee and serving their cats. Discover his worlds at AllanWMason.com

THE BROKEN BLADE

by Carol Hightshoe

DELAVAN STOOD OUTSIDE the guard barracks and read the tattered proclamation again as he waited to be admitted to the training arena. Today, the arms master of Bretinia would be testing those interested in joining the guard. Delavan had grown up in the aftermath of the long war with the elves, hearing stories of those who had defended the city and those who had been killed—like his father.

His mother had never told him much about his father, only that he had died fighting the elves during one of their attacks against the city. His grandfather, a knight of Oliaric the Just, had also been one of the fallen heroes of that war. It was his grandfather's sword he carried with him today.

Delavan did not have the patience to follow the path of a knight; but he did want to honor his grandfather's and father's sacrifices. So he was here today, to join the guard and to defend his home against the elves.

"Delavan, son of Elsbalth, step forward."

He looked up to see a tall, well-muscled woman standing in the doorway. Delavan took a deep breath, straightened his back, and approached the woman.

"Inside," she said.

He stepped into a dimly lit room where several people were waiting. Most stood just outside the light, their bodies only patches of darkness in the shadows of the room.

"Delavan, son of Elsbalth, you have given us your mother's name but not your father's; why is that?" a deep masculine voice asked from the shadows.

"I do not know my father's name. My mother has only told me he was killed during the war sixteen years ago; nothing more."

"Is your mother sister to Tol?" another voice asked.

"She is."

"He is the son of the mage Valynwyr," the first voice said. "We will not allow him to test."

Delavan watched as several of the shadowed figures stepped further back into the darkness—away from him. Certain things in his life now made sense to him: his ability to sense the weather and to call fire, the time he had accidentally called down a bolt of lightning, and the feeling of power he had suppressed for the last ten years. He had suspected he had a talent with arcane magic, but he also knew the consequences if he tried to practice it. That his father had been a mage made it more likely he was also. It also explained why his mother never talked about his father.

"Is it now the will of the council that children be punished for their parent's crimes?" He squared his shoulders as he watched the shadowed figures.

"It is not!" the woman who had admitted him said.

"However," a second woman said softly. "It is also an accepted fact that mages beget mages."

"I do not practice the arcane chaos that is magic!" Delavan drew his sword and held it before him. "This sword belonged to my grandfather, Tyrrian, a respected knight of Oliaric. He left it to me." He raised the sword in front of him. "By this blade I swear I do not practice arcane magic," he said.

"As arms master, I will accept him," the woman who had admitted him said.

"Then it will be on your head, Frelarie, if anything happens. You are bond for his actions and his non-use of the arcane," the first voice said.

"That is providing he has at least enough basic talent with that blade to justify his acceptance into the guard," another voice said from the shadows.

"I stand before you ready to be tested," Delavan said. "My blade, my skill, and my life I pledge to Bretinia."

"Defend yourself!"

Delavan spun around in time to catch the arms master's blade with his. He forced her blade high as he stepped back and brought his own weapon into a defensive posture.

Frelarie lowered her blade and held out her hand. "You defended yourself against them and against my attack. I accept your pledge," she said.

Delavan shifted his sword to one hand but didn't lower it as he took her hand. He felt her grip tighten and her balance shift as she started to bring her sword back up. He brought his own blade across to block hers. The ring of the metal hitting metal echoed in the chamber.

"Good," Frelarie said. "You have learned the most important lesson. Never trust anyone enough to let your guard completely down."

"Thank you arms master," Delavan said as he stepped back and sheathed his sword.

"Caywyn, escort this recruit to the barracks," Frelarie said.

A young man stepped out from the shadows. "This way." He turned and started down a long corridor, not waiting for Delavan to catch up. "Mage whelp."

Delavan hesitated. No one in the testing chamber had reacted to Caywyn's muttered comment. He realized there would be no assistance given him in dealing with the prejudices and hatred of the other recruits when they found out who his father was.

Delavan watched as Mairn and Wyrth sparred in the arena. Both seemed to dance around the other even as their swords rang against their armor.

"Mage whelp," Caywyn said from behind Delavan. "You're next—with me."

Delavan shuddered as Caywyn walked away. The other recruit's attitude hadn't changed from that first day, and he had continued to taunt him regarding his father. He had also managed to get most of the other recruits to let Delavan know their feelings. None had wanted to be assigned as his training partner, and the arms master had to force the assignment of Galorna as his partner. Galorna had made it clear she didn't trust him, and any errors on their part during training she blamed on him. The only thing the rest did enjoy was sparring against him. They pushed the rules of the matches, and he had walked away with more injuries than any of the other recruits after each training session.

"Caywyn and Delavan," Frelarie called.

The two of them stepped into the ring, drew their swords, and saluted the arms master then each other before taking their positions.

"So mage whelp, you think you are worthy to stand with those who have pledged their lives to defend what your father tried to destroy?" Caywyn said as their blades met again.

Delavan refused to answer the older recruit's taunts. He had managed to ignore Caywyn's attitude for the last several months of training, and he was determined to continue to do so.

The two of them continued to move around the training ring, their blades ringing in the large room. Delavan's back was itching where the sweat had soaked through his tunic, and his armor was shifting as he moved.

"They are many within the ranks who remember what your father did to aid the elves, mage whelp," Caywyn said. "Even if you finish your training, you will not live long enough to betray Bretinia as your father did."

"My father tried to protect Bretinia!" Delavan raised his sword high as he charged Caywyn.

"As I expected." Caywyn's blade rang against Delavan's armor.

Delavan staggered back and tried to regain his balance as Caywyn moved toward him. "Mage whelp. You are weak like all those who succumb to chaos—like an elf."

Delavan fought to suppress the anger and rage he felt building along with the tingle of power as he blocked another of Caywyn's attacks. The older recruit had backed him up against the edge of the ring, but he would not be pushed out and lose the match in that way. Delavan dropped his shield and grabbed the sword with both hands as he swung at Caywyn.

Too late he saw the crackling energy surrounding the blade as it connected with Caywyn's sword. Delavan's blade exploded into a shower of metal and light.

The sound of the explosion echoed in Delavan's ears as silence fell around him. The smell of burnt leather and ozone stung his nostrils. Caywyn lay unmoving, his armor pitted with glowing fragments of metal. Blood pooled like ink around him.

Delavan stood frozen, the remnant of his grandfather's sword still humming in his grip. "No..." he whispered, dropping to one knee. "I didn't mean—"

Gasps and shouts rose from the watching recruits, but Delavan barely heard them. He had tried so hard to control the power. He had sworn never to use it. And now...

"Chaos take it! The boy *is* a mage," a voice called.

Toramyn, the commander of the guard, stepped into the ring with several other guardsmen. "Arms master you were warned about accepting this one. Not only has he demonstrated that he is indeed a mage, he has used that power to kill a member of the guard."

Frelarie looked at Delavan, and he saw her eyes go wide for a moment before they narrowed. She turned to face Toramyn and bowed her head. "I knew the risks when I accepted him. I now accept the consequences."

"Both of you will surrender your weapons," Toramyn said.

Delavan watched as Frelarie handed over her sword and the daggers she carried. He pulled the broken sword from its sheath, and crackling energy again surrounded what was left of the blade.

"Drop it, mage."

Delavan looked at Toramyn and continued to hold the broken sword.

"If you do not drop it, you will die." The sound of creaking bows echoed in the arena.

Delavan tossed the sword on the ground and watched as the energy aura faded.

"Escort them to the detention cells. They will stand before the council tomorrow," Toramyn said. "I want at least four guards on them at all times and an additional four on overwatch."

Delavan followed Frelarie as she was escorted by two of the guards. Two more were on either side of him, with another four following behind them. No one said anything as they entered the area of the detention cells. They were ushered into separate cells, and he felt a sudden chill as the doors closed and the sound echoed off the stone walls.

Delavan glanced at Frelarie as the guards took their positions at the door to the area. "Why did you speak for me as you did?"

The woman looked at him, not saying anything for several minutes. "Because of your grandfather and his sword," she finally said.

Delavan waited as Frelarie paused, hoping she would explain further.

"Tyrrian was a knight pledged to Oliaric, one of the only gods who prefers order over chaos. His sword was blessed with the order that Oliaric represents. I did not think it possible you could swear the oath you did without the sword shattering at that time if it were not true. Apparently I was wrong about you and the sword."

"I'm sorry. I did not ask for the power nor did I ever want to wield it," Delavan said softly. "I had suppressed the power for ten years until Caywyn caused me to lash out at him and lose control." He looked down at the floor. "What will they do?"

Frelarie snorted then laughed, a sharp barking laugh that echoed around the room. "Surely you already know the answer to that question. The standing sentence for those who practice the arcane is death. If I am lucky, I may only be exiled. Though, I have no doubts they will send proclamations to Calim and Nydith that I am a mage lover, so I will be unable to live in those places either. I will end up trying to survive in Kilenter."

"Frelarie would you accept voluntary exile?"

"Why? How is that any different than me being ordered into exile?"

"If you suggest voluntary exile, you may be able to prevent the letters to Calim and Nydith, then you would be able to enter those cities for supplies. Also, I will request voluntary exile before they pronounce sentence for myself. Together we could continue to defend Bretinia from attacks by the elves. We could serve as scouts for the guard." He paused for several heartbeats.

"You are the arms master of Bretinia. Your skill with a blade is unmatched by anyone except Commander Toramyn. I could accept the power I was born with and use it to help protect Bretinia."

"You would actually develop your abilities as a mage now. Chaos take it, Delavan, why would I agree to this?"

"Because what is left of my grandfather's blade is how my power is being channeled. Perhaps the order that resides in the blade will be enough to focus the chaos and allow me to control it properly. Besides, if I do start to turn on Bretinia, you will be in the best position to stop me."

Frelarie continued to study him for several minutes, then nodded slowly. "The oath you swore was that you did not practice—not that you were not a mage. You did not lie, though there are many who would say you did not tell the truth. It is obvious you knew you possessed arcane power, whether you have tried to suppress it or not, and it is that power that makes you a mage, not if you use it or not."

Delavan bowed his head.

"Deception belongs to chaos, not to order. If we are to travel together, I expect you to at least walk the path of order as closely as you can," Frelarie said.

He raised his head and smiled. "I will endeavor to follow the proper path as best I can," he said.

Frelarie nodded. "If you can convince the council, then I agree. Now, I suggest you get some rest if you expect to be at your best tomorrow."

"Of course," Delavan said. "Thank you."

Frelarie woke early and slowly went through her morning exercises. As her muscles warmed up, she glanced over at Delavan. The young man was sitting on the floor of his cell, his eyes closed. She doubted he was asleep; meditation was something she encouraged in her recruits, and he had taken to it better than any of the others. There was an almost electric feel in the air, which dissipated when Delavan opened his eyes. "Good morning," she said. "Are you ready?"

"I am," Delavan said.

She watched as the young man stood and nodded. There was something different in his stance this day. Something she had not seen during the months he had been training with the other recruits. His eyes were dark but focused. He stood straight, with a confidence that could only be from his having accepted what he was. From what he had told her, Frelarie knew he had spent his life trying to deny what he was, fighting the power he had been born with. She also understood how self-destructive that type of behavior could be. Too many times she had seen young men and women who thought they should be something other than what they were trying to fight their own natures. They might succeed in the short term, but they were unhappy and never achieved very much during their lives.

Delavan had dropped the pretense, and she could feel his confidence and power as she watched him. Here was one who could achieve greatness, if he wasn't destroyed by the chaos that surrounded the arcane the way other mages had been in the past.

The door to the detention area opened and a group of guards came in. Frelarie stepped out when her door was opened, and she waited as Delavan was released from his cell. The guards escorting them moved away from the young man, their hands on their swords as they watched him. For his part, Delavan clasped his hands together in front of him, the fingers interlaced. She nodded her approval of her companion's action. He had placed himself at an apparent disadvantage for the casting of magic. If the guards understood the significance of his posture, they didn't seem to care.

Frelarie held her head high as they entered the council chambers. The entire council was present as were several representatives of the other noble houses of Bretinia. The word had gotten out that a mage was being brought here today.

"Frelarie," Lord Patri said looking at her. "You are accused of harboring a mage. You allowed him into the guard on your authority as arms master and tied yourself to him by accepting his oath that he was not a mage."

She only nodded in acknowledgement.

"Delavan." He turned attention away from her and to her companion. "You are accused of practicing arcane magic. Through your actions, a member of the guard was slain. Do you deny this?"

"No, Lord Patri," Delavan said. "I do not deny it. The power was unintentional, but the damage is real. I regret what happened." He drew a breath. "But I've learned something. Suppressing my gift only made it more dangerous. I want to serve Bretinia still—not as a guardsman, but as someone who can protect from beyond the walls."

"Do you have a point mage?"

Delavan glanced at the councilor who had asked the question. "I do, My Lord."

Frelarie frowned as she watched Delavan move his fingers slightly. She felt a tingle on her skin for a moment, then it passed.

"Lords of Bretinia, for many years I fought against the power I was born with so I could train as a member of the guard and uphold the honor of those who have defended our city in years past. I still believe I can be a useful defender of Bretinia if you allow it."

Frelarie felt herself reaching for the place on her belt where her sword would have been as the chamber erupted in a cacophony of noise.

"Quiet!" Lord Patri shouted over the din. "Silence! I will have silence in this chamber!"

"You are either a fool or you think we are fools if you believe we would allow you to continue as a member of the guard now that your ties to the arcane have been made known," one of the councilors said.

"No, My Lord," Delavan said. "I do not believe any of you are fools, nor am I one. I do not ask to remain as a formal member of the guard. I only ask that I be allowed to defend my home."

"And, just how would you propose to do that, mage?"

"By accepting voluntary exile," Frelarie said stepping forward. "I am willing to be his guard in this exile. I will ensure he does nothing to harm Bretinia or any of the other human cities or travelers. We only ask that I, and I alone, be allowed to enter the city for supplies and to pass information we may gather on the activities of the elves of Kilenter."

"You are again offering to be bond for him?" Lord Patri nodded as he looked at Frelarie. "Was not your mother one of those killed by the mage Valynwyr?"

"She was. However, I am just old enough to remember the stories of when magic had not been corrupted by chaos. I do not believe every mage who was consumed by his power was acting in deliberate support of the elves." Her voice dropped. "Nor did my mother. That is why she was one of those willing to stand with Valynwyr, during those final days." She took a deep breath before continuing. "During his training, Delavan has wielded the sword of his grandfather, a knight of Oliaric: a sword that has been blessed by the order that is the Lord of Justice. I saw that his power was being channeled through the blade, and I believe it is possible the order that once infused the weapon will be able to leash and control the chaos."

"That sword shattered when he killed Caywyn. How can it leash and control the chaos?"

"My Lord, there is still approximately a foot of the blade, and the hilt still there. As Delavan held the blade, it remained sheathed with arcane energy. The blade, though broken, is the focus for his power, much as a staff or wand has been used by mages in the past."

Lord Patri stood and motioned for the other members of the council to step away from the table. Frelarie took a deep breath as the group of twelve left the chamber and entered a small room. "This is a good sign," she whispered to Delavan. "Lord Patri is considering the request and did not rule summarily against us."

Delavan only nodded, not saying anything.

The two of them stood there for several minutes as those in the chamber continued to talk while they waited for the council to return. Frelarie shifted as sweat formed on her skin, and she felt her hands clenching and unclenching at her sides.

The room quieted as Lord Patri returned to the table. "It is decided," he said. "The council has agreed to allow you until sunset to gather whatever gear and equipment you need before you must report to the southern gate. All shops are closed to you with the exception of those in the temple district. You will remain together at all times. Your weapons will be returned to you at the gate when you leave." He paused for several heartbeats. "Frelarie, you are only allowed to enter the city through the southern gate, you will report immediately to the commander of the guard when you are in the city, and you may only visit shops within the temple district. It is also advised that you limit the number of times you enter the city. And, you will surrender your weapons when you enter the city."

Frelarie bowed her head. "As you direct, Lord Patri."

Delavan bowed his head also, but said nothing.

"Commander Toramyn, I want a guard assigned to them until they leave the city." Lord Patri turned his attention back to Frelarie and Delavan. "This is as much for your protection as it is to see the decree is properly carried out," he said.

"I understand," Frelarie said.

"Good. This matter is closed." Lord Patri looked around the room. "If you do not have business with the council leave at this time."

Delavan watched from the shadows as the elves began gathering near the small shrine at the edge of the clearing. The arcane mark he had placed on Frelarie's armor showed him the arms master's location across the open area. They had been watching the shrine for several days as the elves had been preparing the building for some type of ceremony.

A group of the elves entered the clearing, and Delavan whispered several quick words as he slipped behind a nearby tree. He raised his hand and nodded as the light of the twilight sun seemed to wrap itself around it, and the flesh vanished. Another whispered word and the sound of his own breathing vanished as completely as his body had as he stepped out from behind the tree and approached the elves.

Five females led a group of four males carrying a litter with the body of another female laid on it. One of the five females was chanting softly, and Delavan focused his mind on one of the spells he had tried to learn from the books Frelarie had been given by the temple of Nynia. As he concentrated, the elf's words became clear in his mind.

"Kindness should be the only companion to pain and will increase the intensity of suffering and the chaos surrounding us. Do not ignore the sudden whim of compassion; let it always come, but only seldom as to give those who suffer a sense of hope. Hope is consort to chaos and torment is their offspring. Unending torment destroys pain and this in turn destroys the chaos that nurtures us."

He frowned as he recognized the words as the litany of the evil goddess of chaos the elves followed. Whatever they were doing here this day, it was to honor Thynitic, the Lady of Chaos. He rested his hand on the hilt of his blade and frowned. Would the order of Oliaric be sufficient to control his magic against the chaos of Thynitic?

Delavan followed the elves into the shrine as the female chanting the litany led them to an altar. He closely studied the layout of the shrine as they moved through it. On the outer doors, two rearing unicorns had been inlaid in silver; one had a green star balanced on the tip of its horn while the other had a multicolored oval in the same place. Over the door were two other symbols: a golden crescent moon with an arrow laid over it and a red flame. The multicolored oval was the chaos portal symbol of Thynitic, the unicorn was the symbol of Frayrith, and the moon bow was the symbol of Galolith—the three gods of the elven pantheon. Delavan glanced again at the green star and the red flame as he passed them, those he didn't know.

The inside of the building was immaculate with the exception of the alcove to the left. A thick layer of dust lay over the benches and the fountain. The stone was crumbling and what little water remained in the fountain was black. There on the fountain, almost hidden by the dust, was the same red flame symbol he had seen over the door. Whichever god that symbol once represented was no longer worshipped in this place. To his left was another alcove, this one in pristine condition. *Dedicated to Thynitic,* he thought as he watched the shifting, swirling colors in the dancing water of the fountain.

Before him was a long corridor, black columns rising to the ceiling every ten feet. As he approached the group of elves standing before the altar, he could see a large pool beyond them, the water sparkling with the reflected light of the twilight sun. To his right was another alcove, this one appeared to be dedicated to Galolith and to his left was one dedicated to Frayrith. Both were also in pristine condition. He shook his head as he turned his attention back to the female elf.

She stood before the altar and once again recited the litany as she passed her hands over the black surface. The altar slid back to reveal a set of stairs descending into darkness. Delavan paused as the elves carried the body down the stairs.

Frelarie frowned as the elves entered the shrine. She had lost track of Delavan, and somehow she just knew he had cast the spell he had found that would allow him to move unseen. She only hoped he had enough sense to stay well away from the elves if he had followed them into the building as she suspected he had done.

She moved to the still-open doors and looked inside. The elves appeared to be moving down a set of stairs in front of a black altar. She saw no sign of Delavan, but that didn't mean he wasn't there.

Her sword held ready, Frelarie slipped through the doors and into the alcove to her right as the last of the elves descended into the floor. She darted behind the fountain as a figure appeared in the room with her. "Delavan?" she whispered as her grip on her sword tightened.

The figure turned and nodded.

"What's going on?" She stepped from behind the fountain, her blade still held ready.

"I'm not sure," Delavan said. "I believe the body was that of one of their ranking priestesses, perhaps they are here to lay her to rest."

"It seems a small escort for something like that. I always thought the elves made more of a show of their ceremonies."

"I did also. If you will allow the magic, I will cloak both of us so we may move unseen. Together, we have a chance of learning the truth of what is happening here."

Frelarie glanced at the sheath that held what was left of Delavan's sword and nodded.

"We should move out of this particular area," Delavan said drawing the blade. "This area has been dedicated to Thynitic, and I would not risk having her chaos interfere with my magic." He gestured to the other alcove. "Perhaps that would be better."

Frelarie shrugged her shoulders as she stepped into the abandoned and decaying alcove. "There is a sense of order in this place," she said looking around. "But, that makes no sense; elves are creatures of chaos."

Delavan said nothing as he touched her shoulder with what was left of his sword then nodded. He then sheathed the blade and muttered a few words under his breath.

Frelarie frowned as the mage was surrounded by a shimmering aura. "I thought this was supposed to hide us," she said.

"Only we can see the aura," Delavan said. "We need to be able to track each other."

"Makes sense. Let's go." She headed for the altar and the stairs.

"May her deeds be forever recorded in the Book of Chaos," one of the female elves was saying as Delavan and Frelarie descended the stairs.

The body of the priestess was surrounded by a multicolored aura then vanished. "She has joined with Thynitic," the elf said. "She will live on as part of the chaos that is the Lady."

Another of the female elves stepped forward and held out the robes that had covered the body. "As one Daughter is called to the Lady, another Daughter is born to the chaos. Shyrella, you are of the line of Thynitic and are now called to serve as the Daughter of Chaos." She held the robes as Shyrella turned so they could be placed on her shoulders.

A swirling vortex of color surrounded the elf and the book she was holding. When it faded, she placed the book back on the stand as it opened and the pages began turning.

"The Daughter has been named and anointed," the second elf said. "It is time to return."

"Yes, there are preparations to make. The humans of Calim will pay for the death of my mother," Shyrella said.

Frelarie and Delavan pressed back into the shadows as the elves left the chamber. Delavan waited until the altar had moved back into place over the stairs, then walked over to the book. "The Book of Chaos," he whispered.

"Leave it. We need to find a way out of this place," Frelarie said.

"I think we should take it. An artifact of Thynitic's religion could be used to barter protection for Bretinia."

"Or it could bring the wrath of the goddess directly down on the city. Leave it."

Delavan shook his head as he reached for the black book. He dropped the book into a bag on his belt and turned back to Frelarie.

"I still think you're making a mistake."

"We'll see." He moved past her and up the stairs. Delavan paused as he looked at the symbols etched on the bottom of the altar above him. In each corner of the altar was a group of symbols—the rearing unicorn with the other four around it. In each group however, a different symbol was positioned over the horn of the unicorn.

"I doubt we'll be accepted as being here at the behest of Thynitic," he whispered ignoring the group with the chaos portal in the primary position.

"Which symbol was associated with the alcove where you cast the spell on us?" Frelarie asked.

"The flame symbol," Delavan said.

"You carry a blade that was once carried by a knight of Oliaric, and I also follow the Lord of Justice, perhaps..." her voice trailed off.

Delavan nodded as he looked for the grouping that placed the flame symbol over the horn. He closed his eyes as he passed his hand over the symbols and concentrated on the altar opening. He looked back at Frelarie and smiled as the stone began moving.

"Let's get back to Bretinia," Frelarie said as she moved past him and up into the shrine. "That book should be placed into the keeping of one of the temples and a warning must be sent to Calim."

"Agreed."

"You will be sending no warnings to anyone," a female voice said as an energy screen surrounded Frelarie and Delavan.

"Shield your eyes," Delavan whispered as he drew his sword. "Even in chaos there is a spark of order," he said looking at Shyrella. "Without it chaos would destroy itself. Let us see what happens when order and chaos meet." He thrust the sword into the barrier.

The elven priestess began laughing as a cacophony of color danced across the barrier. "Misguided and ignorant human. For over four millennia has the one who represented order been trapped by the forces of chaos. It is chaos which reigns in this place." She raised her hands, and a bolt of lightning leapt from them to strike the barrier. She frowned as the energy holding them was not penetrated by her magic.

"It would seem that some order remains in this place," Frelarie said standing next to Delavan.

"Perhaps, but not for long." The priestess gestured again and the bag with the Book of Chaos began floating toward the priestess.

"Oh, no, you don't," Frelarie said swinging her blade at the bag.

The bag hit the barrier and color erupted around it as it vanished.

"You have lost the Book of Chaos," another voice called from behind Shyrella. "You will bring Thynitic's displeasure down on us."

The priestess spun around. "I am the Daughter of Chaos. I serve the chaos that is Thynitic. The book is not lost; it is where Thynitic wills it to be for now. When it is time, it will return to this place."

"While they're arguing amongst themselves, can you get us out of here?" Frelarie placed a hand on Delavan's arm.

"That is a more powerful spell than any I have attempted in the past, I can only try."

"Then try!"

Delavan held the broken sword in front of him as he concentrated on moving himself and Frelarie to the area outside the southern gate of Bretinia. He felt Frelarie's hand tighten on his arm as bands of energy flowed out from the sword and surrounded them. A flash of bright light, and he collapsed on the ground as the energy dissipated from around them. Before them was the southern gate of Bretinia and a dozen or more guards standing with swords drawn watching them.

Frelarie placed her sword on the ground then took his and placed it next to hers before she helped him back to his feet. "We both must speak to the council," she said.

"You may enter, Frelarie," one of the guards said stepping forward. "But the mage cannot."

"I'll be okay," Delavan said. "Go, we cannot waste time arguing with them."

Frelarie looked at him and he winked at her. "I'll be fine," he said again. She nodded.

"At least allow him a place to rest while I speak to the council," she said.

The guards seemed to hesitate as they looked at each other. Finally, the one who had spoken stepped forward and placed an arm around Delavan. "He may rest in the gate barracks. I will keep an eye on him."

"Thank you. Now, someone escort me to the commander of the guard," Frelarie said.

Delavan watched as she entered the gates, then finally gave into the darkness that had been trying to claim him.

"Delavan, wake up."

The mage opened his eyes to see Frelarie, Lord Patri, and a cleric of Nynia standing over him. The cleric held one hand against his chest and the other wrapped around her holy symbol. "You tapped into power that should have been beyond your ability to control. The Mistress of Magic, Nynia, has indeed blessed you."

"The warning has been sent to Calim," Lord Patri said, bowing his head slightly. "You have proven yourselves to me and the other members of the council. If you are willing to swear by Nynia and Oliaric that you will never use your magic against Bretinia, the order of exile will be lifted."

Delavan nodded. "My place is still outside the walls, where I can be most useful. But I would welcome safe entry when needed."

Lord Patri extended his hand. "Agreed."

Frelarie returned the broken sword to Delavan. "And I will remain at his side. The power he carries must be tempered—and watched."

Delavan smiled. "A wise precaution."

"I advise a few more days rest," the cleric said. "Then you may travel."

"I'll keep an eye on him," Frelarie said.

Delavan closed his eyes as sleep claimed him, but not before he realized Lord Patri had handed Frelarie his sword and the arms master had placed it under his hand.

About the Author

Born in 1964, Carol grew up in San Antonio, Texas. After 30 years in Colorado, she now calls the small town of Brackettville, Texas home. An avid reader at a young age, her strong desire to write came from her love of (her husband calls it her obsession with) Star Trek. It was this early love of Trek that led her to the Science Fiction and Fantasy genres.

She has been published in various anthologies and magazines, and has published four books in her Chaos Reigns Fantasy series.

In addition to her own writing, she is the editor and publisher of the online e-zine: *The Lorelei Signal* (www.loreleisignal.com).

She also runs WolfSinger Publications (www.wolfsingerpubs.com).

Visit her website at www.carolhightshoe.com

WEEKLY DATE

by H.T. Ashmead

STEPHEN SETS THE BASKET on the perfectly manicured grass. Shadows stretch long across the expanse. He straightens his tie and smooths back his silvery hair. He and Dani have held a weekly date for over six decades. He's not about to let his "best dress" rule slacken now.

With shaky hands, he picks up the patchwork quilt. The burgundies and midnights are faded to corals and periwinkles, but Dani's tight stitches still hold firm. With a couple of flicks of his wrist—not too vigorously so as to maintain his balance—he spreads the comforter on the lawn.

He caresses the thigh-high granite for a moment, then leans his weight on it as he slowly lowers himself to the ground. Recently, he's contemplated the need for a chair. But when he climbs into the car, he rejects the idea. "One of these days, I'll really regret it when I won't be able to stand up again." He smiles and shakes his head.

Once he settles onto one hip, his legs bent at loose angles, he releases a deep sigh. His knees ache, but the pain is nothing compared to the dread of missing his date.

"Hello, my love." Stephen traces the chiseled lettering on the gray headstone next to him:

Danielle Susan Ellis

Beloved Wife and Mother

Independent Woman

The headstone is modest, except for the one expense Stephen and the kids insisted upon—a wreath of carved animal prints encircling portraits of a cat, dog, parrot, rabbit, and horse.

The horse passed away three years before she did. Stephen pictures her riding the palomino across a field of yellow and white wildflowers in heaven. The other animals represent a revolving door of critters she helped daily.

His beloved Dani. The most sought-after veterinarian in the county during a time when women were discouraged from working outside the home, especially as high-ranking professionals.

When she'd attended the occasional conference for work, Dani always made sure her travel arrangements allowed her to be home for their weekly Tuesday night date, even leaving early occasionally. And he'd continued the tradition for the past eight years.

Stephen smiles again and strokes the final line of her epitaph. She'd loved her family fiercely, but she'd never defined herself by them. And her strength made him love her all the more.

Dani's children knew she would drop anything if they needed her. But she'd taught them to recognize a true *need.* As a result, they had all grown into empathetic, successful adults with healthy families of their own.

Stephen chuckles lightly. Some with more animals than human children.

Another lesson from their mother.

A chilly breeze brushes his hair, and he burrows deeper into his jacket. The fall nights materialize faster and cooler every week. But it's still warm enough for him to talk to Dani for at least half an hour. In the winter, he'd sometimes have to shorten that to only ten minutes.

Stephen drags the basket beside him. He pulls out two plates, setting one before himself and the other before the stone block. "I brought fried chicken today," he tells his wife. He draws two drumsticks from a plastic bag. "I know it's not your favorite, but Alex brought his family over Sunday, and I'm still working on Susan's leftovers." He unwraps the foil he'd used to keep them lukewarm and sets one on each plate.

"The twins are getting so big now. You'd love their soccer games. Janie plays a wing position, while Johnny is a fullback. They're on the same recreation team now. That twin telepathy is a force to be reckoned with on the field." Stephen shakes his head with a smile at the memory of the last game he watched. "Johnny stops most of the score attempts from the opposing teams. He steals the ball, dribbles it two or three times, and then kicks it down the field. Even before he's stolen the ball, his sister races to the position of the incoming ball. They never even look at each other, but somehow, they always know exactly where to find the other."

A deep shadow falling across him alerts Stephen to a stranger's presence. A woman, hands shoved into the pockets of her jacket, rushes by. She glances at him with slightly widened eyes and hunched shoulders.

The cemetery always empties quickly as sunset approaches.

After her car door slams shut and the high-pitched squeal of her electric car fades away, Stephen turns back to Dani. "Let me lay out the rest of the food. I know you love to enjoy those final moments of light in silence."

A blackbird lands on a nearby stone and trills at him, dropping a dandelion from its feet.

Stephen dips his head. "You're welcome." Dani communicates with him now through the animals she knew and loved so well.

He distributes grapes—her favorite, especially now in the peak of their season—to make up for the chicken. Then he plops a small spoonful of potato salad on each plate. Finally, he places a small snickerdoodle, another of Dani's favorites, on each edge.

As a final touch, he withdraws two plastic goblets from the basket and a bottle of white wine. Placing Dani's glass on the flat cement base of her headstone, he pours a small amount into it. "Your weekly glass." Stephen clinks his cup against hers, causing a dull *thunk* from the plastic.

He faces the west. "I've got time to tell you about Marcy's family before the full sunset. She received another promotion at the bank. I think she's a Vice President now, but she tells me that isn't a big deal because there are hundreds of them." Stephen shrugs. "Still seems pretty important to me. Bryce's portfolio keeps growing every time I talk to him. They took Natalie and her fiancé on a cruise. She texted me lots of photos of them learning to surf." He leans close to the stone. "If you ask me, it looked like more falling than surfing." Stephen throws his head back and laughs, a hearty rumble that pushes back the evening cold.

If she'd been beside him, at this moment he would've put his arm around Dani and pulled her close as they watched the final dip of the sun.

Instead, he munches on his food while the blazing reds and oranges fade to a flaring gold, and finally wink out of existence, leaving an ombre of spring green at the horizon stretching into a cobalt overhead.

Stephen sighs and closes his eyes, leaning back and lifting his head to the gauzy clouds. After several deep breaths, he drops his head back down. "You're right, my love. Each one is unique."

They sit in silence for a few more moments, watching the twilight fade and the first stars twinkle into existence. Stephen pulls his jacket closer. With the disappearing sun, the wind increases until it's downright breezy.

A taupe-colored rabbit edges near, its nose wiggling at a rapid rate. Stephen watches it for a few moments, then carefully reaches for one of his grapes. Without making large movements, he offers the fruit only a few inches from the timid creature. It cowers and hops a few paces away. Then when he doesn't move anymore, it eases itself back to his hand and steals the treat from his fingertips.

Stephen blows a kiss. Hopefully Dani can enjoy the fruit via proxy.

When he speaks again, his baritone voice spooks the rabbit, and it bounds away beneath a rose bush at a gravesite a few rows over. "You'd love how Kaya's equine therapy business has grown since you've gone. She just bought her eighth horse this last week. This one's a bay mare. She tells me it's a three-year-old with the gentlest disposition of all her horses. She has a couple of extreme autism and anxiety clients that she's really excited to introduce to the animal." Stephen brushes his hair out of his eyes.

"Javier's deli shop is really starting to take off. Every time he sees me, he thanks me profusely for giving them that money to help him start it." He pats her headstone again. "But really you're the one to thank." His eyes grow moist. "After all, we'd already planned for our retirement and then some. So using the life insurance money to help our kids achieve their dreams seemed the most logical thing to do." He wipes his eyes with the back of his hand.

"Speaking of dreams, Hector is in his third year in college. He finally declared his major two days ago. Mechanical engineering, but we guessed that from his first Lego set when he tried every combination possible of locking those bricks together."

Stephen stares into his swirling glass of wine. Then with one quick movement, he throws the rest of it back in one gulp. "I know you want to hear about me too," he murmurs, "but there's not much to tell without you. I still volunteer at the library twice a week, and I look forward to those children's bright eyes and open faces with each story I read. But I feel like I'm just marking time." His breath hitches in his chest.

"I'm keeping that promise you pushed me into when we were newlyweds. I didn't stop living just because you left me. I go to dinner with friends at least once a month. I watch the new movies when they seem interesting. I've kept our symphony subscription and try to take one of the kids or grandkids with me each month. I still take care of the yard, although I had to hire a boy to help me stay caught up on the weeding. I walk the dog every day if the weather permits. Or maybe he walks me." Stephen shrugs. "And the cat still curls up in your place on the bed every night. I keep track of the children and grandchildren...

"But eight years is a long time." On his last thought, Stephen's voice breaks, and he ends it in little more than a whisper.

His shoulders hitch with silent sobs. The twilight has deepened into full night. Most people would be terrified to sit in a cemetery alone in the dark.

Ghosts and ghouls and all.

But this is when Stephen feels closest to his beloved Dani. Placing his hand on top of the granite, he tilts, leaning his weight into his outstretched arm. "How long do I have to wait to rejoin you?"

His dripping tears leave wet stains on the well-loved comforter.

A few minutes later, the hoot of an owl startles Stephen into composure. A bird with tan wings perches on the opposite side of Dani's headstone. Its white belly and heart-shaped face gleam out of the darkness.

It hoots again and hops half a step closer.

Stephen sits upright, smiling through his tears. "Hi, Dani."

The bird cocks its head and looks at him, black eyes the size of marbles.

"You always did know exactly what I needed."

The owl cocks its head the opposite direction, hoots twice, then spreads its wings, taking off in silent flight.

Stephen wipes his face on his sleeves. Then he packs Dani's untouched food back in its containers. Except for the wine. That he pours in the grass next to the base. Using her headstone for support, he leverages himself back standing.

After folding up the blanket, he kisses his fingertips and presses them against the icy rock. "Here or there, I'll see you next week, my love."

Stephen might still feel lonely, but just as he keeps his promise to live, Dani keeps her promise to never leave him alone.

About the Author

H.T. Ashmead writes whatever the muse dictates in the moment. Usually, this translates into speculative fiction, both long and short form. No matter the genre, her focus is always Writing that Explores Our Humanity. She has a short story published in both the online literary journal *Inkpot*, and the anthology *Particular Passages: Decked Halls*. Her novel debuts Fall 2026.

You can follow her online at www.htwrites.com
https://www.facebook.com/htashmead/
and TikTok @htashmead.

MIGRATION

by Andy Dibble

MIRIAM STOOD HUNCHED near the peak of the sloping cavern floor, driving a chisel against the bone ceiling. A scrim of pale dust coated her shoulders, sleeves, and the front of her vine-weave shirt. Her snarled hair, entwined with blackberry sprigs, fell slipshod to the small of her back.

Rain struck the floor of the cavern above. When last it rained, a month ago, the ceiling was khem, dark and porous, so drinking water just trickled through. But the clan had to eat. They planted blackberry in the fertile ceiling, let it grow, harvested.

But nothing comes free. Grow crops in black khem, and it becomes white and unyielding. It becomes bone. Now nothing would ever grow in the ceiling again.

Miriam cursed as the chisel slipped in her sweaty grip. This wasn't her job. She told Sippora to open a route for rainwater a week ago, but the slack woman dodged the work until it was almost past doing. Miriam could delegate to someone who would obey, but he would grumble. That wouldn't do. She was only clanleader until morning. Then her six-month term would be over and leadership would revert to her husband Aaron. Making demands in the eleventh-hour was no way to bow out.

It seemed everyone would rather laze about than do what it takes to survive! Only two others in the clan wore vine-weave. Everyone else flashspun fabric with alkhemy: drawing slip-signs on khem to make it flake into layers and flex-signs to make it hang. Scrawling signs is easy, but why squander khem when there's vine chaff at hand?

More than once, she fancied ordering everyone to wear vine-weave, and they'd obey but only because Aaron would. And everything would go back to how it was when leadership reverted to him, and she would only have her neighbors' grudges to show for it.

Miriam looked over both shoulders. "Joshua, stay away from there."

Joshua darted back from the narrow passage, the hood of his gratuitously-pocketed cloak flopping over his shoulder, a replica of the Lilah cloak from Aaron's stories.

Joshua peeked into the passage without technically entering.

"Joshua, leave the warren *alone*."

"I wasn't going to go inside." Her son was a terrible liar, but what eight-year-old isn't? Most children believed their parents when told warrens are haunted by the Luminaries, the people that prospered when the world was young and khemical enough to dig new caves by drawing compress-signs. But every sign ossifies khem. Now migration is a way of life: move into a fresher quarter of the world's viscera, grow crops on the dark scalp of khem, and move on when all is wan and fused into the skeleton of the world.

"Just stay close," Miriam said.

Joshua plopped down, fixed elbow to knee, and planted chin on palm. He knew better than to protest. But just moments later, he fidgeted, brandished his own chisel, and scraped at the gray ground, only partway ossified because the clan hadn't planted so near the warren.

Miriam watched warily as Joshua etched four arcs, the quarters of a circle turned inside out, a four-pointed star. It woke, like a bed of coals breathed upon, lambent beneath ashes. Joshua wasn't sloppy. The surface was just too far gone, so his sign freed only sputtering radiance. The only way around that was to compact many together, but it would ossify faster. Joshua gouged the light-sign, and it winked out.

He started on another sign, drawing one lobe and then another. He completed another arc; the ellipses fused together. She said, "No heat-signs, Joshua." Heat-signs ossify as much khem in an hour as a light-sign does in a week. Their clan would migrate tomorrow, so maybe it didn't matter if Joshua idled away a patch so far gone. But he needed to develop good habits.

"Help me." Miriam thrust a callused finger at the bony ceiling. At eight, and small for his age, Joshua couldn't chip the crust. But chiseling would focus him on things that matter.

Footsteps. She knew that gait. "Miriam, can we talk?"

Miriam wiped sweat from her brow and faced Aaron.

He bobbed his head to the side toward their tent.

"Joshua, stay here," she said.

She turned to follow Aaron, down the rise where amaranth stalks lay in windrows. With amaranth, from planting to harvest to winnowing, it was all about season. Never harvest when the flowers burgeon in burgundy or purplish ropes, racking the stalk under a sluggish load of blooms. But wait until the petals are a third browned. Then harvest before insects pilfer the seeds.

Aaron and I had a season, too. But that season is past.

"Can't you lay off him, Miriam, even just through the night?" said Aaron. "It's New Year's. Let him have some fun."

"I'm raising him right, even if you coddle him. He'll lead the clan one day, him and his wife. And because you encourage him," Miriam sassed, "he pretends he's a girl who has a lantern that glows forever."

"Today it's Lilah, tomorrow it'll be a new game. It's just a phase."

"And what has Joshua's Lilah-phase done for the clan? Haven't you heard Sippora call me Gebira?"

Sippora could pretend it was a compliment. In stories, Gebira was a great alkhemist. But she was also a one-eyed hag too aloof to care for Lilah and her other children.

"Heh-uh." Aaron swallowed his mirth. "No, I hadn't heard, but it's not Joshua's fault. Or mine. If you're leader, you have to look the part. Cut your hair, clip your nails, shave, wear what they wear."

She planned to do all that when she didn't have to do everything, oversee everything. How long since she bathed or even washed her clothes?

After primp and fuss, there was no man better-groomed than Aaron, and he got hairy when he let himself go. He kept two flashspun shirts, less than some (like Sippora), but whenever one tore or frayed, he gave it to one of the children and signed a fresh one. Both buttoned up, an affectation Miriam never understood. But now a method sewed those steely buttons: his brand.

"Look, I'm sorry for coming after you," said Aaron. "Stash the chisel, Miriam. It's New Year's. *Celebrate* with us! There's water enough until we migrate, and once we move on, we'll find more."

How could he be so glib about things that matter but berate her about hygiene? They might not find the next river, not in strange territory so removed from Inside. Everyone would be thirsty after drinking at the celebration. Maybe rain doesn't come with the new year out here. The clan's survival could not be gambled with.

"And just where *are* we migrating?" she said. Tomorrow Aaron would lead.

"Farther out, I think. But if you have other ideas, I'm glad to hear them."

Under Miriam's direction, they'd been milling about, from cavern to cavern, weaving inward then out again. Farther out, there were Outsider barbarians. Just last migration, they came across the brutes' hand emblems. How long until they found the savages themselves? She could cry dire warnings. But Aaron would just yank them steadily outward like when he last led during the first half of the year.

"No ideas. Come tomorrow, you're in charge." Her own words proved peoples' grumblings: she lacked of vision. Some of the younger generation even whispered that Aaron should lead them perpetually, instead of he and Miriam trading off at Midsummer and New Year's. The traditionalists wouldn't have it, but generations wither as surely as khem ossifies. Maybe she didn't have Aaron's vision, but better no vision than charging into the unknown after a dream.

"You can still advise me, Miriam. Just because tomorrow it's my term doesn't mean you shouldn't speak your mind."

There were virgin spaces out here, moist and supple as clay. But those untouched caves, khemical, bountifully black, invariably fostered uneatable vegetation and insect life, transforming the landscape into more of themselves and their offspring, their fruitfulness blighting everything. Steady policing almost eradicated these cancers on the Inside where khem was scarcer. If they could stoke that vigilance here, these between-places could be their home.

But Aaron wouldn't listen. "Just how much farther do you think we can go? We're already on the fringes. Farther on there are Outsiders and eventually the walls."

A scowl overset Aaron's features. He thought the walls at the limit of the world propaganda only endorsed by fools, but she couldn't bear the walls in mind without existential compression: she stood within a shadow, one so immense it had no periphery, and it was cast by a vastness, distant but just as huge. It pondered the moment to crush her.

She shoved the thought and its finality aside. "If we turn back, go inward, at least we know what to watch out for."

"But if we go outward, it might just be better, with seldom a thing to watch out for or deny us. Have a little hope, Miriam."

"You know the stories. Outsiders scavenging on the margins of the world, godless, guzzling the blood of their enemies. And the walls—"

"Enough, Miriam. You're working yourself up over stories, just *stories*."

"Just stories?" How could Aaron call any story just a story? "How much have *you* fear-mongered with stories? Were it not for your stories, we'd still be Inside."

"Under the benevolent supervision of our Leader?" Aaron said.

"At least Inside, it was safe," though she didn't believe what she said. That was why she hadn't led the clan inward when Aaron's term ended and hers began six months ago. The Leader wouldn't respond kindly to runaways straying back into his fold.

"Safe Inside?" His lips twisted dismissively. "For now, maybe, but for how long? The Leader just wants to keep everyone in line."

That was the real reason Aaron led them outward. He knew that eventually—ten years? a hundred years?—Inside would be a wasteland too bony to support the clans that pecked at it. Territory skirmishes would ignite into war. There'd be no containing it.

Aaron grimaced. "I know you don't believe his nonsense about renewing khem."

The Leader spun tales about how they could renew the world through devotion to the god Khem, that if folk only draw signs for heat and light, plant frugally, and migrate often, Khem would take mercy and renew the world, turning bone everywhere into khem. That was a pious lie. But why lead everyone outward on another baseless hope that wilderness will house them when civilization can't? At best it was premature, an act of desperation.

"You know I don't trust the Leader any more than you do," Miriam hedged. Six months ago, when they were Inside, she wouldn't say that aloud. "But rushing out here is *risky*, Aaron. We don't know the land, whether we're heading toward or away from water. Out here, do the rains even come this time of year? If you would at least insist on conservation, we would have time to plan our next move, instead of just ossifying one cavern after another and pulling up the tent stakes every other month."

"Miriam, you can't lead by always telling people to do things they don't want to. Austerity isn't a solution."

"And blindly hoping is?"

"It is, if we hope long enough, if we keep migrating and keep hoping."

Miriam left the tent. Aaron followed her, flashed a smile. "I figured we'd fetch Joshua together before New Year's."

Joshua wasn't at the entrance to the Luminary warren.

"I told him to stay here," said Miriam.

"He probably joined up with everyone else." Aaron faced the lower stretch of the camp past the well where dry amaranth stalks lay, ready to fuel the New Year's fire. Though summer expired months ago and harvest was in, cerise or ruddy-red petals speckled the heaped stems.

Most of their clanspeople, hunched over wafers of drab khem, carved clocks. Miriam could just make out Puah, the oldest woman in the clan, eyes infested with cataracts but dexterous enough to round off her wafer into a circle and engrave ten prim digits around the rim. In the morning, the first day of the new year, Puah would draw a spin-sign on her clock, its sweeping lobes rotated to avoid obstructing the digits. The spin-sign alkhemically compelled the inner circle of the clockface around twice each day, seven hundred thirty times a year.

A certainty gripped Miriam: this would be Puah's last clock, her last New Year's. How many more migrations could a woman over seventy endure, even with Aaron and the other men to support her? That question suffused into: how many more migrations could the clan endure until their luck croaked and they boxed themselves in, hit a dead-end in a labyrinth of bone and lost their way, like a mouse caught in the deepest pocket of her satchel? They would backtrack, hoping they somehow missed a vital cave. Then they'd fracture, like when they first quit the Inside under Aaron's leadership. The young and foolhardy would cling to Aaron, but a hardy few would stick with Miriam.

Realizing that Aaron dallied so they could join the clan together, she said, "No, Joshua's not with the others." Miriam wrenched the knob on her lantern, and it flared brighter. She marched into the dim gullet of the warren.

The Leader didn't approve of folk scrounging around in warrens. If people wandered the deep roads and galleries, intestines of history, he assumed the inscrutable writing and contraptions would draw them to the same wastefulness that doomed the Luminaries. They were out of the Leader's reach, this far from Inside. But they'd been under his prohibition a long time. Miriam hadn't been in a warren since she was a girl.

She recalled a realm of delicate bone arches and pillars of fused stalactites, a monument to antique glory. This warren was the same, but now the sign-wrought architecture seemed decadent.

She glanced inside a bone crucible for smelting khem into base metals and metals into alloys. That, at least, was useful. Its inside was worked with a dense pattern of intermingled heat-signs. So many! Did this crucible *evaporate* khem? And it was *wide*, a cauldron really. Surely they didn't need that much metal. Her gut soured further when the path bent into a declining flight of stairs. How many compress-signs did it take to carve those? And for what?

Maybe the Luminaries deserved what they got.

"What gets me is the smell," Aaron joked, huffing as he ran to catch up.

"The smell?" Miriam knew he didn't mean smell but its opposite, no-smell. Virgin khem is earthy, loam shot through with cumin. But it rots as it ossifies; farmers gag taking the harvest in the last time before migration. But bone—true white-as-death bone—smells of nothing. How long did the Luminaries suck the rot, burrow deeper to escape it, only to nourish it with their compress-signs? How long until they abandoned their homes or at last triumphed over rot by ossifying their livelihood entirely?

Aaron jogged on her left, but not so busily as she did because his stride was longer. His gaze roved over the neat rows of writing alongside them, serenely coveting secrets.

Or that's how Miriam assumed Aaron judged it. For her, writing was more waste. Beneath the indecipherable script were the grayest parts of the warren—the least ossified—but that was only because writing rendered its host surface useless for signs. Why did Aaron care? He couldn't read a lick of it.

When the path leveled and widened into a storehouse, Aaron's pace slackened. Miriam didn't let up. She didn't care whether the weapons about were for battle or ceremony; whether the instruments were for music, science, or torture; or how many pairs of binoculars, contorted flasks, and wardrobes full of gaudy robes leaned atop one another just outside the pool of her lantern light. However genius their alkhemy, the ghosts could keep their treasures.

"Miriam." His voice was tinged with awe.

"What?" The rest shriveled on her lips. Her glare softened, tracked upward, and she beheld the prismatic spray of their lanterns' light.

A statue rose with ozymandian majesty into the vault of gloom above. It wore breastplate, girdle, and flowing cape and wielded outstretched spear, diving headlong into battle. Aaron sighed, twirled his lantern, and the statue's mighty legs flung rainbows like ribs of an empyrean whale.

Glass like this is possible? The Luminaries crafted spyglasses, spectacles, and (legend said) microscopes keen enough to spy the signs on the husks of seeds. But all those were trinkets, a lens ground this way or that. This monument stood more than twice as tall as Aaron. And it was entirely glass.

Aaron gaped again but not upward where rainbow and twinkle tapered into unseeing. He pointed to the warrior's foe, a second statue, greater in dread, no less in majesty, one scrupulously ossified. By the curve of its hips, it was a woman but so wound with snakes, it could be snake and human hybridized. Its hair was in cornrows, and silvery earrings hung from its overlarge ears. It stared past the shoulder of the onrushing glass warrior, seeing some threat he did not.

And at its base, a heap of clocks. There were hundreds easily, thousands. How many years of clocks? The tradition of shattering clocks on the last day of the year was old, but this mound meant it was Luminary-old.

"That must be Bone," said Aaron, still pointing to the bone woman.

It had to be. The mother of serpents, Khem's elder half.

"Which makes this one Khem," Miriam added. The god-that-is-the-world, Bone's younger brother. Inside, an unadorned khem pillar was marker enough for Khem; a femur or twisting snake or both together meant Bone. But these Luminaries raised grand icons.

Miriam shook the sight off. "Let's get on, or Joshua will get farther ahead."

"I'll go this way." Aaron pointed past the twin monuments. He was younger than she, his eyes surer. He must see a way she couldn't.

"We meet back here in an hour," she said. The interval would persist seconds longer. The spin-signs on their clocks ran slow after ossifying for a year.

The path curved abruptly, and Miriam stumbled over a sprawl as wasted as the clocks at the base of Bone's statue. But this was just trash, discarded not destroyed. There were a few items of worth peeking from below the sediment of insect husks, shreds of vine chaff, razor shards of glass, and bone ash. A slim bone flute caught her eye, whole amidst all the squalor. Why not seize it, and use it, just for the celebration? Better that this flute pine and sigh one last time than leave it slumbering here until the end of time.

Taking it wouldn't be grave robbery, more like accepting a baton from a spent runner, like one of a crew of boys dedicated to Khem, sworn to run a baton for a year and a day. She pictured herself rushing onward—on toward, toward what? An image of the walls at world's end erupted with her thrashing against them.

She stuck the flute in her trouser pockets.

Echoes of Aaron's baritone ambushed her, "Miriam, I found him!"

And Joshua's shrill, "Come back, mom!"

Miriam turned on her heel and dashed the way she came, only curbing her pace enough to avoid obstacles and depressions as they zoomed into the range of her lantern.

When the path widened into the storeroom, Joshua was there, gripping his father's hand, smiling guiltily.

Miriam hugged Joshua, lifting him off the ground, the folds of Joshua's Lilah costume bunching in her embrace. Joshua relaxed as he chanced that no rebuke would come.

But she couldn't let him off so easily. "I thought we decided you weren't going to come in here."

"I wanted to find Lilah's ever-glowing lantern."

Momentarily, Miriam believed it, could believe anything after beholding the glass monument to Khem. But common sense set in, and it couldn't be. Maybe there were ever-glowing lanterns according to boy logic, but nothing could burn forever, nothing could shine or move without ossifying khem, which was finite however vast the khemical honeycomb might be.

"Did you find Lilah's lantern?" Aaron asked.

Why did Aaron lead Joshua on, coddle his fantasies? Joshua was getting to an age where he had to face facts.

"I think so," said Joshua. He held out a thing of brass and glass, all curves, vaguely lantern-shaped, with a handle. But it wasn't shining. "It needs some work." Joshua regarded her warily. He probably thought she'd make him leave the "ever-glowing lantern" behind.

"Let's get back to camp," she said. "We don't want to miss New Year's."

The celebration was already underway. Reuben kept beat on a drum, made from a sheet of khem worked over with flex-signs and pulled taut over a kettle. He was the stoutest in the clan, a bruiser that made opposing clans think twice about usurping territory. But they were Outside now; rivals were scarce. He farmed and supported older folk during migration. Puah, hunched over, hummed to the ditty that Sippora played on her flute.

Miriam and Aaron approached the celebration, Joshua loping around them. Their feet crunched on amaranth stalks and browning flowers.

"They're back!" Reuben shouted, and Aaron hailed him.

When they arrived, Sippora frowned at Miriam but said sweetly, "You playing this year?"

Miriam hadn't considered the flute-shaped bulge in her trousers. "Did last year." But she wouldn't play, not tonight. Sippora was a better flutist than her.

"But last year was before *Aaron* set us on our path."

Aaron planted himself between them, hands raised to ward them back, though neither advanced. "You two sure you want to go through New Year's like this?" A command formed on his lips but fizzled. He wasn't leader yet.

Sippora snapped erect.

Miriam offered her hand. "How about we bury the hatchet?"

Sippora regarded it as though it wasn't attached to a human appendage. Her grimace slipped when she caught Aaron's eye on her.

Sippora shook her hand, hard. "I won't have to take orders from you until Midsummer anyway."

So much for forgetting old wrongs on New Year's. Miriam surveyed the feast, a spread of brown-speckled amaranth seed patties fried in amaranth oil on a bed of maroon-veined amaranth leaves. Beside was a garnish of pulped blackberry. Aaron pried the seal off a pot of blackberry beer, brewed last New Year's. It had been nestled in the clan cart since they left Inside.

The clan's table was indistinguishable from the ground until they reared it with emboss-signs, much like the feast, it was just pliant khem until it burgeoned from the walls and ceiling. They let the blackberry crop ripen thoroughly so that it encrusted the cavern ceiling into a skull. The berries weren't any more nutritious, but they were plumper, juicier, singularly sweet. After chiseling for more than an hour to pay for the luxury, she might as well enjoy it.

Miriam watched Joshua over with the children, muddy khem smeared on his face. He scrawled light-signs in the muck on his cheeks, conjuring an ailing neon glow. After sprinting up the incline, he launched his palm-sized clock over the descent. It arched, plummeted, and finally burst on the cracked ground.

Joshua sprinted back down the slope, knelt down, and set upon gluing clock shards together with khem. The first was a man. It held a slender shard, a spear. He picked at the end of his fraying Lilah cloak, tore free a gauzy layer, punched a hole with his finger, and tied it around the man's neck. Next he assembled a winding snake, probably a dragon. He set the man upon the dragon, struggling in front of the firelight, like a puppet in a philosopher's cave. When the dragon was rubble, he raised the victorious slayer high. But its shadow on the cavern wall was skewed.

The dancers—Sippora, a few others of her generation, and a gaggle of children—were dizzy from whirling but pushed through it. The musicians exchanged wry smiles then picked up the tempo and picked it up again. The dancers struggled to keep up but at last succumbed with a flight of breathless giggling.

The musicians rose to fill their plates. As they returned, Aaron signaled he was about to begin a story. Everyone quieted because he told the best stories.

"Who wants to hear a story about Lilah and her ever-glowing lantern?"

All the children cheered, Joshua loudest of all. He belched a pitched giggle, flailed his limbs. Come morning, Miriam would have to talk to Aaron again. So what if it was New Year's? It was time for Joshua to grow-up and Lilah stories weren't helping.

"It was New Year's in Lilah's clan," Aaron began, "just like it is tonight, all their old clocks were shattered, just like ours. But in her clan, they called it the Timeless Night, because they know what a night without clocks can do. In fact, in her clan they have a rule against drawing spin-signs on the Timeless Night so that the magic of the Night is complete.

"Now Lilah's clan was farther on in the evening, the music died down, everyone was full to bursting and all the storytellers were too tired to spin another yarn. With the fire down to embers, everyone staggered to their tents squinting in the dimness because by then night mellowed over all light-signs, binding them until day." Aaron flashed an infectious smile. "Do you think that Lilah went to bed too?"

"No!" all the children shouted.

"And why's that?"

"Because she has an ever-glowing lantern," one of the children cried.

"Because she didn't want to waste the *magic*," Joshua said.

"You're both right," said Aaron. "Anyone know about the magic on the Timeless Night, what magic there is *tonight*?"

"People can run really fast, like a river," said one child.

"And you can climb without falling."

"Compress-signs press faster, so you can burrow through a wall in no time at all."

"Right!" said Aaron. "On the Timeless Night people can run like a river, climb like they're moseying from one cavern to the next, and signs work faster." Which was nonsense, of course, but that didn't stop Aaron. "But the problem is that no one can see. Even with all the magic, it's night and light-signs don't shine, and by morning the magic will be spent." His fingers spread like smoke.

Everyone knew what would happen next, even those who trusted Aaron's flair for innovation.

"That is what made Lilah's lantern so special. She just turns the knob on it, right here." He lifted his lantern and flicked the mechanism. "And it glows as bright as day." His voice dropped. "But that was her secret, no one else knew about her lantern.

"Hidden by her cloak with a dozen pockets, Lilah scampered off, turning her lantern on when she was out of sight. Infused with the magic of the Night, she sped into the next cavern and leapt into another. Beside her was a waterfall streaming through the air like a ribbon.

"Noticing the fire of another clan, she stopped. By the cheers, they weren't through celebrating. Maybe she could join them. But when she got close, she saw ogrish men sharpening spearheads. Women drew sigils of war on the men's chests, not with amaranth dye but their own blood. Their crafty one-eyed leader, bound a thrashing serpent to a ribcage altar, sliced it open, and unwound its innards. He declared the haruspex for the coming year good. Tomorrow they would set out to slaughter their prey."

Most of the children are too young for this talk of blood sigils and slaughter. Miriam ground her teeth. She was just short of the requisite chutzpah to upend his story.

Aaron took another swig and said, almost offhandedly, "As Lilah scampered off, she saw their banners. They bore the pillar emblem of the Leader."

Some of the parents leaning drunkenly against one another gasped. Folk weren't ready for vilifying him, even in a story. Those much younger than Miriam—Sippora and the rest—couldn't remember life outside the boundaries laid by the Leader, his bureaucrats, and police.

Aaron didn't acknowledge the airy outcry. "Lilah hurried back to the tents of her clan to warn everyone. Even come morning, no one believed her. Lilah was just a silly girl, and no one imagined the Leader could be close. They migrated from Inside months ago.

"But Lilah knew that the Leader's agents were fast approaching. She'd overheard their plans. They would slip rogue-like through the adjacent cavern and come first light…" Aaron thrust down, impaling an imaginary sleeper with an imaginary spear. "Lilah couldn't sleep, but only laid awake in her bedroll next to her father, flicking her lantern on and off beneath the blanket.

"She had to do something. It was still hours before morning, so the light-signs on everyone else's lanterns and staves couldn't shine. She bolted up and raced through camp, her ever-glowing lantern shining as brightly as she could make it shine. 'Wake up, everyone!' she cried. People woke and some protested because their groggy heads said it was early, but they saw light from outside their tents. That proved it was day. And that is how, when the Leader's men attacked, everyone was ready to fight them off."

"I think Miriam should tell a story," said Sippora. "What's it you say, Aaron? 'Everyone knows at least one story'?"

Aaron didn't answer. He gauged Miriam's reaction.

"She didn't at Midsummer." Sippora shook her head. "Not last New Year's, either. Show us that we're going to miss you leadering."

Aaron shot Sippora a hard look. That was uncalled for, even on New Year's, even though Miriam was only clanleader for a smattering of hours. How many construed Sippora's slang "leadering" as a reference to the dictator of Inside?

"No need to twist Miriam's arm," Aaron said.

That was her out, and she could refuse. She was still clanleader, but that was why she had to go ahead and tell a story. "It's all right, Aaron. Sippora's right. Everyone knows a story. But not just any story. Everyone knows a *particular* story."

Some could even guess it, the story told in one shape or another from the Mother of Waters in the heights to the Cimmerian shores of the Downsea, where all rivers flow. In the seclusion of the family tent, every mother tells this story to her daughter when she thinks her woman enough, every father his son. It is told only once, and not publicly.

But after Sippora's goading and so much frivolity on the cusp of migration, everyone needed a hard reminder about the way the world really worked. Lilah's flight in the Timeless Night shuddered before her mind's eye. Wasn't New Year's a night for daring?

Miriam drew herself up. "The world was new, once, when Khem was young, because the whole world is Khem's body. Then no one had to migrate, but everywhere was lush and fresh and loam." This was lore, but no one needed much convincing that it was also history. They saw a whitening world with each migration. It must have been pristine, once. "But Khem could not be innocent forever. His older sister would make him wise." Miriam inhaled the smoky air. She respired. "That sister was Bone. That sister was death.

"Bone wrested Khem and overpowered him because who, even Khem, can wrestle death and win? Held in a stranglehold, Khem surrendered. 'Survival will cost you,'" Miriam rasped, but her imitation was poor. She let up. "Bone, the Broodmother, demanded tribute, food for her young, the innumerable dragons that worm through lush places, sapping the world.

"And so Khem created man from himself, a clever beast creeping through his caves, his insides and outsides. At first the man knew only dark and groping, but he discovered signs for light and heat, for stretching and spinning, and one for transmutation. And so Khem became white and stark and unlistening. Bone.

"The man woke in the night, his foodstores frothing with maggots, the land around desiccated, a desert of chalk. And fumbling, contending by the feeble light of early-morning light-signs, he migrated outward.

"A dragon ambushed him, but it was young, unaccustomed to the hunt and frailty of its prey. The man fled, tossing aside his pack and walking stick. Truly lost, he tripped into a deep well. Only just, he clutched an outcrop as he fell. With his free hand, he found a moist knob, not new but new enough: *meny* from Khem."

A few bitter chuckles tinkled in the audience.

"The man drew a light-sign and squinted into the depths of the well. A dragon raged below, roused by the dim sign, more terrible and aged than the whelp above. The dragon thrashed in the water, impatient and indomitable.

"There might be a way up, if he tore his hands bloody on the climb, or if he, by alkhemical wit, molded the knob into sticky putty, or stakes, or a fierce light to guide his way. But whatever he did, the dragon whelp at the top would nab him as he escaped. And if he dropped into the depths, the aged dragon would devour him at once.

"A fragrance brushed his nostrils. Beyond his reach, blossoms hung like grapes on a vine. He edged along the outcrop and did not consider the vine and the khem it sacrificed to the beauty of the blooms. He should destroy the root at once. In time, it would overtake not only the knob but crumble his handholds. He did not think but only leaned deep into the blossoms and stuck out his tongue for a drop of nectar."

Miriam jolted awake. She more expected trouble, given the indiscretion of her story, but it wasn't even morning. Aaron's breath washed over her from above, and the heat of his body snuck into her vine-weave bedding.

Aaron had shaken her awake.

"Joshua's gone," said Aaron with intemperate worry.

"Gone? What?"

"He's not here."

Did Joshua believe that fiction about Lilah's ever-glowing lantern and Timeless Night abracadabra? He wouldn't have dared run off if not for Aaron's ridiculous story. She couldn't see his face in the dark. But he would picture anger blossoming on her face. So she pictured sheepish guilt on his face.

"What time is it?" said Miriam.

"Almost morning, I think."

If Aaron's was right, they'd be able to see farther than their own feet, if they packed light-signs tightly. "Well, let's go look for him. Did anyone see him leave?"

"I'm not sure yet," Aaron said.

"Ask around! Talk to Sippora first. If Joshua's not in camp, past her tent is the only way out." A grim possibility, but one that couldn't be ignored. "Unless he went back into the warren." If Joshua wandered down there, by now, he could be anywhere in the maze.

"You think he would go back in *there*?" Aaron asked in a rush. "He knows we have to migrate today." Her husband was charismatic, a genius storyteller, visionary, maybe even wise, but he was worthless in a crisis.

Migration could be delayed another day. But only one. There was little to drink and nothing to eat after last night's splurge, nothing not already earmarked for migration, and scant khem to grow anything, even if they could linger for another harvest.

Sippora and her friend, a shrew-faced woman named Zippa, had stayed awake all night, swilling the last of the beer and gossiping in the dark.

Sippora said she heard someone slip past her tent. She hadn't gone out to figure out who it was, but no one else had been out in the night. It must have been Joshua. Aaron ordered her and Zippa to check the warren, just to be sure. Zippa protested but obeyed. Sippora took it for what it was: reproof.

Aaron told Reuben and Puah to tend to the children and wrangle them into loading the cart as well as they could. Aaron, Miriam, and the other eight adults went to search for Joshua.

Their way was the way they'd come during their last migration, so Miriam had a feel for it. Or thought she did. It branched again and again—more times than her memory testified. Each time they called for Joshua, and each time only echoes came back. When an offshoot was too oblique to scout at a glance, Aaron ordered one of their number to investigate. They'd regroup at day's end.

Before long it was just she and Aaron jogging along the main way, following the slashes they'd left when they came through here before. Aaron glanced around, squinted at shadows as the darkness shifted around the globule of their lanterns' light. With the others about, he put on a front. But now even the veneer was gone.

The passage widened into a cavern. "Joshua! *Joshua!*" Again, no response.

An etching of an upright hand as tall as Aaron confronted them. When last they came by here, Miriam guessed this sigil a warning. Aaron thought it was swearing an oath. Whatever its meaning, it was alien, an Outsider thing. Last time, Miriam took them the other way.

But now going the other way meant turning around with Joshua unfound.

"Now do you regret filling Joshua's head with stories?"

"If *you* hadn't scared him with that hopeless story about a man trapped in a well, maybe he wouldn't have run away."

"You think he's afraid? Our son's reckless enough to wander into a warren alone, why would he be *afraid*?"

"Joshua's gone, he's *gone*, Miriam."

His helplessness severed her own. Blame was useless, wouldn't solve anything. They wanted the same thing, and her husband was just a man, flung wayward by the upheaval of his mind. She had to help him through that. Then they'd find Joshua. Then migration.

Gradually, as though Aaron might skitter, she embraced him, breathed deep, exhaled. Breathed deep again and exhaled. He imitated her. His hyperventilation eased.

As if putting themselves in order could put the world in order, there was Joshua, rushing to them, so astonishingly. For a moment, he seemed more spirit than a boy.

"Joshua," said Aaron blinking, tears fleeing the corners of his eyes. "Where were you?"

"I fell down a hole, and they found me."

A dark-skinned woman approached them, big-lipped, hair in cornrows. She was astonishing but not a spirit; she was too solemn and solid, too different to be fiction. She sported elaborate jewelry, some piercing the cartilage of her ears, a ring through her left nostril. Silvery loops bit through the skin of her upper arms and shoulders, like a thing mechanized, a relic of a Luminary warren.

Inscrutable tattoos framed her forehead and cheeks, wound down her neck and past the collar of her flashspun smock. It was vibrant, dyed in flowing bands of amaranth red and maroon, forest green, and ocher, dyed colors Miriam couldn't name, colors she hadn't seen, except maybe in the iris of another's eye.

"I am one of the People."

The People? Miriam hadn't really thought they would call themselves Outsiders, but something fearsome surely. Stories said Outsiders were faithless, clanless, vying with dragons in the wilderness, dueling with one another, gulping the blood of their enemies. But stories never told of Outsider women. And here was one, like one of a third race, strange but not a caricature.

Aaron found his voice first. "The People?"

"Yes. What do you call yourselves?"

Aaron shrugged. "Haven't met another clan in a while, not much need for a name."

The woman cocked her head. "We hoped to leave you alone, but your son fell into a well outside our camp, and unused wells are often the nests of dragons."

"Dragons?" Miriam and Aaron said at once. Was that a joke? But the woman's face didn't admit even an uptick of smile.

"An old nasty dragon?" said Joshua. He'd rather wait in a well until a dragon made his acquaintance than be rescued and miss the opportunity.

The woman made a toothy smile, no different from how anyone smiles at the things children say. "A young dragon. They migrate outward as they age where the land is newer and able to sustain them."

Miriam was about to pry, but Aaron said, "I'm Aaron. This is my wife Miriam and my son Joshua. I lead a clan of refugees from Inside." He held his hand out in greeting.

The woman looked like she didn't know what to do with it, but she grasped it with both hands and shook vigorously, not even letting go once she began to speak. "My name is Ashera. It is good to meet you." Still shaking Aaron's hand, she added, "I didn't think that outsiders were comfortable touching strangers."

Outsiders? I guess we are to them.

Noting Aaron's unease, Ashera released his hand at once.

"We will learn each other's ways," said Aaron.

"This word 'refugee,'" said Ashera. "I am not familiar with its meaning."

"It means that we migrated to escape a political challenge where we lived. 'Politics' do you know that word?"

"I believe everyone knows what 'politics' means." Ashera smiled again. "I and my clan celebrate New Year's this evening—"

"This evening?" Miriam blurted. The new year was already here.

"We prefer to anticipate," Ashera frowned, waiting for the right word to bob to the surface. "We prefer to *look forward* to the new year and pass over the last in silence. Would you celebrate it with us?"

"Unfortunately, our clan must migrate today," said Aaron. He seemed genuinely saddened, and perhaps he was.

"So soon?" said Ashera.

"Celebrate much, migrate soon," said Aaron. His mouth slung open, mute recognition that she might not have understood the adage.

But Ashera smiled wanly, nodded. "You are welcome for our celebration!"

"We can't leave our clan during migration," said Aaron.

"Please understand," said Ashera, "My invitation does not extend to your family only but your entire clan. Celebrate New Year's with us, then migrate tomorrow."

"There are many of us," said Aaron. "And we do not have much to contribute."

"You would be our guests. All of you," said Ashera.

Miriam said, "Your clan must camp in a lush place if you can accommodate another so easily."

"We would not extend this invitation to just anyone. Your son did a manly thing by running off."

"A *manly* thing?" said Miriam. Did Ashera really mean "manly," or was that just another word mangled?

Joshua chimed in before Ashera could explain. "It was the Timeless Night, and I thought that with a lantern like Lilah's I could run far enough and climb high enough to find a way through the walls at the end of the world, so that you wouldn't have to worry so much and fight with Dad." Joshua held his "ever-glowing" lantern out. "But the lantern didn't glow forever. I tried to run back, but I fell into a well."

"He did a manly thing," Ashera repeated. "Our men, too, look for a way out."

"You've seen the walls?" said Miriam.

"Walls? What walls? There is only a world becoming bone, and that world cannot sustain our peoples forever."

Aaron gambled on Ashera's good intentions. He said they'd need to make friends with "the People" before long anyway. But Miriam speculated the real reason for Aaron's credulity was more basic: there wasn't a grown man in the entire People camp. There were boys wearing drab flashspun but none with more than fuzz on their chin. The women and girls wore a mosaic of color, and most had piercings—signs of rank?—though none so many as Ashera. Miriam thought the color too much, but no one was gaunt or reserved. They hovered above the daily struggle.

Ventilation was poorer, so the fire was not so large as that of the night before. But the feast was grand: a hearty stew of root vegetables, amaranth patties spiced with tumeric and saffron, and succulent salmon. Inside, salmon was almost extinct due to overfishing, and the Leader reserved spices for those nearest him.

Many of the People held bone flutes or lyres in their laps, but no one played. They waited on Ashera. "This is a story familiar to my people," she began, "though the men may hear it only once when they come of age. It tells of the search for Sky."

A few sighs of realization breezed among the People.

"What's Sky, mom?"

"Shh, Joshua, let our host tell the story."

A boy of our clan came of age and sought Sky, vowing not to return until he found it. Bone boasted to her brother, "I'll dissuade him."

Khem's smile was condescension. "Your persuasion kills. *I'll* dissuade him."

With only his shadow to measure himself against, the man climbed into a high cavern. Khem erupted before him in volcanic splendor. His eyes shown like thrice-mingled light-signs, and a mane of fire wreathed his face. He plucked the man from the heaping ash and said with a voice like thunder, "You presume to search for Sky?"

The man sputtered, but Khem's question could not go unanswered. "I swore I would."

"Words are wind." Khem breathed whirlwinds. "Turn back!"

The man figured he'd be dead already if Khem sought his life. So he said, "What kind of man would that make me?"

"A prudent one!" Khem's grip tightened perilously. "Your mortal years are too few to find Sky."

The ashes stirred and sighed, breathed laughter like falling sand, and said, "*My* persuasion kills?"

Disgraced, Khem withdrew into the earth.

The man hurried on, but the ashes stirred and followed him wheresoever he turned.

His way contracted, grew hoary and wan, but he loathed to backtrack. Everything behind was known; Sky could only be farther out. So he went on and came to a warren of our ancestors. At the threshold, the ashes trailing him knit into a winding sheet. A woman filled the shroud. Her eyes stared without focus, and her skin was like porcelain.

"Sky can wait," she said.

Her sheet unwound and wound around them both. She caressed his cheek; that touch lent sweet repose. She kissed him on his neck, and even that was high delight.

But her breath smelled of nothing. And her tongue was forked.

The sheet fell, as he drew back, and he beheld her entirely. Like the powdered corpse at a wake—however consoling, however sublime—there was a deadness behind.

"Stay," she wailed. "I can give you children. For Sky is too far away for you to find. Only your children will have enough years to find Sky."

"Lady," he said, retreating. "I do not think our children would have any years at all."

From his deep place, Khem saw her failure and grinned. He broke from the ground, but flameless, his glory veiled. But his lantern blazed merrily.

How could that be? It was night, every light-sign was stoppered. This lantern was brass and glass, a core of muddy khem, a simple thing. How could day cling to it alone?

"Trade?" said Khem. "My lantern for your quest?"

His clan would marvel if he brought this wonder home. But his honor overburdened that vision: the shame of giving up was greater.

Khem plucked a glass shaft from his cloak and said, "This prism sprays darkness. Look."

The man touched the tender darkness surging from the prism. He shivered when it touched him back.

"Both are yours, if you give up your quest."

"My honor for two trinkets?"

Khem grinned a small grin. He knew his mark was almost won.

(Bone saw that grin. She roused her dragons. With haste, they might slay the man before a bargain was struck.)

Khem offered a spyglass. "This glass is keen enough to spy the subtle signs on the husks of seeds. Look."

The man spied the secret of seed growth. With study, he could rear a harvest five or ten times heartier. There would be more than enough for everyone.

But no sign comes free. He might grow more on less, but less isn't nothing. He might conserve, but every year the world would still be a little whiter. Everyone might conserve and still plod toward that final bony end.

"This is wondrous," the man said, "but it isn't Sky."

"Man of khem, do not shrug off my aid so rashly. Know that my sister sends her brood to claim your life. I could be your champion, if you give up your quest."

"How odd. The Khem I hear of is noble, merciful. He'd never stoop to ultimatums. You must be another, some pretender."

Khem unveiled his glory. "I have mercy on whom I have mercy." The man would plead for every mortal fears death.

But the man lifted his chin.

"I will save you this once," said Khem, "but only to prove our enemy is the same."

Khem whisked them to a lush place. He plucked a lump from the cavern wall, pressed a mesh of signs into it, and let it writhe and form itself into a soldier on the cavern floor. It hammered its signs into the mud, replicating itself.

When the dragon brood wrecked in, they met the spears of the golem army. Khem charged into the fray, and the man ducked after him. They stood shoulder-to-shoulder, spears everywhere skewering the web of serpents. Their killing was clean, all-at-once. Not Bone's degradations, her rasp and whimper.

At the end, Khem pumped his fist triumphantly and clapped the man on the back.

"Renounce your search! Then my armies are yours." His golem army reassembled (but bonier than before). "You will never be defeated and be always the one left standing."

Victory was sweet. But he remembered: never is a long time. "Giving up would be its own defeat."

"Your choice is to be a victor or a corpse! Sky is held from you."

"Let me be a corpse that sought Sky, rather than a victor standing alone among corpses." The man turned his back, put the desolation behind him.

That evening, Bone slipped into the man's shadow, unstuck from his heels, and said, "You've taken me to and fro about the earth, and I've never given you anything for your trouble."

"That's so?"

"I can make you see truth and lie plainly, without any penumbra at all. You only have to do one more thing for me."

"Give up on Sky?"

"That's right."

"And why would I do that?"

"Because then you'll know Sky when you see it."

The man turned his back again. What was the point of haggling anymore?

His shadow flit to a broad cavern along his path, so vast even the light of a thousand lanterns would be lost in mist and distance.

The man reached that broad cavern and spied a marker above the entrance. It read: "Sky." He went to tell his clan of his success.

The People chuckled or hollered as Ashera finished the story. Some suppressed their mirth until her last word. Reuben and two others of Miriam's clan followed, but their chuckles were throaty and delayed.

Miriam would have scoffed were it not for her hosts. The man in Ashera's parable was a fool, declining boon after boon even after he knew that his fabulous goal, "Sky," was unattainable, and then at last he was tricked by a word? Was that the moral, that even the most principled of men can fall prey to naiveté?

Ashera didn't chuckle, didn't acknowledge the approval of her clan. She waited for her guests to respond.

Joshua spoke first, "So Sky *isn't* a really big cavern?"

"Why do you say that?" Ashera said, like that was just the question she'd been waiting for.

"Bone tricked the man into thinking a big cavern was Sky, so it *can't* be." Joshua asked his father, "That's what the story says, right?"

"I think I and all my clan would like to know what your story means, Ashera. We've never heard of Sky before," said Aaron.

"Not every answer comes easily, Aaron of Inside. Allowing only what the story tells outright, maybe even Bone and Khem don't know where Sky is. Maybe they just say things to trip him up."

Miriam thought Ashera more of a straight talker, but evidently, not when it came to this story. "You say answers don't come easily, but you must have an interpretation. What do you think Sky is?"

Ashera paused, considering her words. "Sky is a place where everyone can live and no one has to migrate. It's out there." Ashera grasped upward, fumbling with a rope of sand. "Beyond, like the realm in which stories unfold."

Miriam's eyes narrowed as a thought condensed. "So the man really believed that if he just kept going eventually there would be no more caverns and he'd be somewhere *beyond*...?" Miriam reached too but awkwardly. She couldn't find the words.

Now it was her clan that chuckled, though many stifled it. Her people judged it absurd—and well they should—there's no such thing as a place outside a cavern. *Cavern* is just part of what "place" means.

But that *beyond* meant a backside to the walls. And beyond that plane, what? A void? She pictured a breeze tickling a serpent's back, swaying as the snake undulated. The walls undulated too, and they were not khem but a cosmogonic dragon constricting everything, Bone wrestling Khem into a stranglehold.

"What the man really believed isn't in the story," said Ashera without acknowledging the tittering of her guests. "But I'll tell you what I like to think."

Everyone quieted.

"I like to think that Sky is the far side of that last big cavern, lost in mist and distance. Bone tricked him just in time, and the man turned back on the cusp of success."

Miriam recalled how much the man gave up: technology, victory, truth. And he didn't even understand Sky well enough to see it when it was only a little farther on. The man wasn't a fool, not exactly. She pitied him.

Joshua leapt up from between his parents. "I think he found Sky. Bone told him when he found it with the marker above the entrance. There was *something* in that last big cavern that the story forgot. That's Sky."

Some of the People gaped at Joshua. What could be so wrong about what her son said?

"That is...interesting," said Ashera at last. "You think that Bone told the man the truth?"

"Um, maybe," said Joshua, inspiration gone with so many eyes upon him.

Miriam added, "Maybe he stopped searching, and so Bone gave him the boon she promised, so that he would always know truth from lies." That wasn't so much of a stretch, was it? "He knew Sky when he saw the marker."

"Ha!" said Aaron. "He found Sky just when he gave up looking."

Somehow that settled it for Miriam. Pity for the man in the parable transmuted into hope. He deserved praise, however out-of-reach he was, a man in a story.

What is this? Some higher alkhemy beyond signs and a calcifying world. The walls retreated, cracked like cheap facades. Were there even walls? Wasn't it better to pursue a goal, Sky, a thrilling beyond, rather than dread circumscription?

She had the flute from the warren. She'd play it tonight, ably or not. Let Sippora jeer as she will. Tomorrow would be the first day of a new migration, but that didn't trouble her. It might be three days or three weeks until her clan trudged into a cavern lush enough to call home, but lightness sloughed off even that burden, a molted skin. There might be dragons or drought or hostile strangers but not this night. This was New Year's, a second night apart from time. She could check her clock in the morning.

About the Author

Andy Dibble writes from Madison, Wisconsin and works as a healthcare IT consultant. His work appears or is forthcoming in *Asimov's*, *Writers of the Future*, *Diabolical Plots*, and others. He edited the anthology *Strange Religion: Speculative Fiction of Spirituality, Belief, & Practice*, which won Best Anthology in the yearly Critters Readers Poll. He holds degrees in computer science, philosophy, Asian studies, and religious studies. Along with several other Writers of the Future winners from the plague years, he created Calendar of Fools, a small press dedicated to empowering new writers of short fiction. You can find him on Facebook, Blue Sky, and andydibble.com.

NEEDS MUST

by L.A. Selby

Note from the Author: *Real witches won't do this.*

I'M NOT A FRIVOLOUS WITCH. I'm not a young witch, good attitude notwithstanding. The tiny wrinkles deepening next to my eyes give me away. I'm fine with it. Fear is for the weak. I tell myself that when I look in the mirror and want to groan. Then I smile, which adds more wrinkles next to my mouth. Then I sigh and stomp out of my inappropriately Victorian bathroom to greet the day outside.

Little did I know, my lack of frivolity would be called into question.

The young man wore a black helmet, black biking shorts, and a dark red and black biking vest, and he rode a matching red bike. He was skinny. Bicycle skinny. The kind that can go a few hundred miles and then chat about low heart rates. That kind of skinny. I didn't have to worry about that for myself, thank goodness.

He cycled his road bike down the center of Thomas Drive—the long straight road next to my usual walking path—while the cars stacked up behind him in the early morning Florida heat.

I could practically taste the frustration in the growing line of cars behind him. I had been peacefully, restfully, non-frivolously walking along when the line of cars was at two, then grew to four, and we were getting to six. I think my walking speed is fairly standard for a witch of a certain age, but it should not be fast enough to keep up with a bicycle.

I exaggerate.

I have no head for numbers or bicycle speeds, but the speed limit on Thomas Drive was 35 miles an hour, and he was not going anywhere close to it. He should have used the clearly marked bike lane on the edge, the special space designated for the safety and fun of all bikers. But no. Not for him.

He was dead center in the right lane of two possible lanes, peddling away.

Let me be clear. He was not peddling away in the sense of trying to go faster. Only in the sense his feet were moving in a circular motion designed to keep the wheels going. Slightly faster than what it takes not to fall over.

A practically antique gray Lincoln, the color of primer—and possibly my natural hair color under the bottle-brown—was trying to be nice and not mow him down. I couldn't see who was driving, or read their face, but I'm a great judge of character from afar. No witch powers needed.

He, the cyclist, did not move over.

I hate people like that.

My walk was turning into a stomp as he leisurely led his angry train. There were vibes from those trapped cars. Distinct vibes. And his needs were above everybody else's, no one else existed in his world. As long as he had a long, straight ride in front of him, everything was right in his world. That made me want to do something to fix the problem. I was not supposed to use power for that.

Please don't make me be a frivolous witch.

Please don't make me be a frivolous witch.

That had a nice rhythm to it. Like this daily pace I used while enhancing my cardiovascular system, two miles a day, rain or shine per doctor's orders, except when it was raining. Today I had Florida sunshine for miles, and my loose-hanging lavender sweatsuit not too hot and not too cold, but just right.

Bicycle guy drew forward, but the agitated line still stretched back to me. I hoped he would pull over into the nice Pelican Bay neighborhood, a short block in front of him, but I knew he wouldn't.

He was not dressed like a man who turned right into neighborhoods. Or left, for that matter. He was dressed like an Italian sportsman; the latest swag, the latest bike, the colors that screamed "Hey! I ride bikes!"

Absolute power corrupts absolutely. That's the saying.

It rocks absolutely too.

I didn't need to worry about that, since my witch powers were well within the 9-volt range. Practically a square battery, is what I'm trying to say. But I could pick up a little stick and poke it between moving bicycle spokes, if I concentrated hard enough. Telekinesis, basically. I mean, I had never done that, because that would really hurt somebody.

Hurting people is bad. But I could definitely do that, if I wanted to. Which I didn't, because that would be bad.

Except this guy was making ten cars wait for him on a long, straight stretch of road with every opportunity to pull over or use the lane specifically put there for exactly this.

Right next to me, in a four-door red Civic, a woman's mouth was moving in what I could only assume was a stream of impotent invective. If it had been me, that would have been a specific curse designed to bring locusts front and center to a specific spot on Thomas Drive.

One time, back when my knees let me go biking, I rode right into a swarm of locusts. That had nothing to do with me being a witch, but it was scary as heck, and I had thrashed around, trying to swat them off my face, and fallen over on my bike. The chain scratched up my shin and my ankle. I was very brave back then—brave like little soldiers are brave, not like actual big people are brave. Still. Brave. Locusts!

I could take poor Civic-woman's frustration and multiply it by twelve now. Twelve was a magic number for me.

Numbers are wonderful signs of the power of the universe. In my Google search, I learned the number twelve may be a metaphor for the recursive nature of existence and the opening of new horizons, particularly in the quest for spiritual enlightenment. Or something like that. It's amazing. *Recursive*. I did not know that.

Twelve cars. I had had enough.

But what to do to save these poor souls—the drivers stuck behind the bicycle—from even another second of the mystery bicyclist's selfish torment? I needed to help him discover the recursive nature of existence and open some new horizons for him in spiritual enlightenment. That would be in line with my recent research. I pulled out my cell phone and checked on the definition of the word "recursive."

Something about repeating something multiple times—wait, "repeated" and "multiple" was a completely unnecessary repetition, probably recursive—to produce a particular result or effect.

Like me! I repeated myself frequently as part of my charming nature. Everyone loves that.

I was not mad enough to put a curse on what used to be called his "innards" in the old witch books of yore. I had some yore-ish books on my overflowing shelves, and they had great terms for things. I didn't want his imminent doom, which should come any moment now, to make things worse for the people behind him. If he exploded, they would be inconvenienced by body parts and police action. In fact, if I did that, this entire section of road might be closed off for the mysteriously exploding man.

No explosions.

If I had him attacked by a flock of angry crows, à la—if that's how it's said—*The Birds*, same problem. Innocent birds probably wounded by cars, people using cell phones to record the whole thing and post it to TikTok or—I was going to say YouTube, but I think the kids have something else now. I can't keep up. It would inconvenience more than the current twelve.

Withering his limbs.

That sounded great! It would be direct and to the point of punishing him for his incredible lack of regard for the entire world and all humanity therein. He would still be able to wear his little black helmet and black biking shorts and dark red and black vest. He could keep his pretty red bike and stare at it all he wanted. But never again would he inflict his rampant hatred of all the rules made by gods and man and bicycle slowly down the center of this road or any other.

Not on my watch.

I had a problem. There would be witnesses. Even if he was not exploding or being eaten alive by a giant flock of screaming crows, with blood everywhere and his carcass and such, someone would notice me casting the spell. That was a no-no in witch circles, because, as one learns from television ad nauseum, and ad nauseam in a great number of pretty good books, secrecy is a pretty big deal.

Most of my prior spells were done in secret right in my fancy kitchen.

I kid.

To do the spell now meant my hands were going to get all yellowy-glowy, and my long brown hair was going to stand straight up like I was touching one of those electric or magma—magma—that can't be right—plasma!—balls in high school.

Then I would be very weak, but someone sitting on a walking path was not that big a deal. Maybe the drivers were so mad at him they wouldn't see me. Maybe I was invisible to them because of that. Could be. No one was recording me on a phone, that's for sure. By the time the glowing streams of light stopped and someone thought to try and record it, the whole incident of the day would be over for them, and also no more bicycle maniac. They would be happy to zip on down the road.

I stretched my hands out and focused on my inner well of magical powers. "Withered limbs. Withered limbs. *Withered limbs!*" I chanted, with extra emphasis at the end for extra power.

My hair stood up, stinging with tiny zippy needles of electricity, floating over my head. More zippiness shot down my arm, thankfully not like my usual carpal tunnel, much less bad than that, and yellow light brighter than sunlight shoots right out of my fingers and down the road. It knew better than to hit anyone in their cars. This was magic. It knows what it's doing because intention is part of etcetera etcetera.

A short squeal of brakes comes from the front of the line of cars. Short compared to the long kind when someone is going fast and has to stop faster. There is another short squeal of brakes—and a third, and a fourth, right down the line of cars—because he's going so ridiculously slow to start with.

I dropped my hands, knowing the spell was cast, and sat right down on the grass next to the walking path. My legs were all wobbly and my knees were weak, but not as weak as his.

My sense of satisfaction was like a high. I loved it when that happened. How dare he. Well, he won't dare again! Evil villain laugh.

The cars finally start moving, one at a time, their engines doing their get-ready-to-go noise.

Sometimes, I don't think things through.

Sometimes, I don't take into account the indomitable human will. The strength of purpose that fills a person with "I can do this and you can't stop me!"

That is how people climb mountains and conquer worlds. Each car inched forward once more, much slower now, the opposing traffic uneased. Everyone inching. Inching behind bicycle guy. He peddled on.

One weak, withered, and wobbly push at a time.

About the Author

Even suspense writers like L.A. Selby enjoy kicking back with hot tea, a fun book, and a smile for the summer. She has eight stories in print with several more on the way. Meet the author at DragonCon in Atlanta each fall, or find her poking in castle ruins with her hair covered in webs and slapping dust off her jeans.

www.LASelby.com if you would like to peruse her library of darker tales and blog updates.

THE MATCHMAKER

by Emmett Whitney

THE GOLDEN CAGE was far stronger than it looked. Even in infant form, Cupid had the strength of a man in his prime. It wasn't enough. He grabbed the door, shaking it hard. It showed no signs of weakness. He tried putting his feet on the far side of the cage and pushing the door with his shoulder, but despite his considerable power, it didn't budge.

No way this should hold me!

The witch ignored his escape attempts, humming happily as she practically danced around the cottage. She poured herself a generous glass of blood-red wine, then grabbed a quill, ink, and vellum. Taking a big sip, she placed the paper on the table and sat down.

"Let's see," she said, looking up at the thatched ceiling and tapping a finger to her chin.

"The mayor's daughter has plenty of money, and she has a hankering for that strapping son of the blacksmith. She'll pay a pretty penny to have him fall for her!" She scribbled on the paper.

Cupid's eyes narrowed. *She was going to use his powers to make money? Outrageous!*

"When I get out of here, I'll make sure you never find love again." He pointed at her. "I swear on my mother's bed, you'll die alone and miserable!"

The witch laughed at the cherub's threat. Stunningly pretty by any standard, she had long dark hair, high cheekbones, and an aquiline nose that reminded him of a princess he once loved. But her twisted snarl of a smile destroyed any attraction he might have felt. Besides, he was in cherub form and wouldn't convert to his virile male shape until Mars ascended at sunset.

"Just how do you expect to escape? I've spent a decade trying to capture you. It took years to master the spells needed to create the magic cage holding you. And decades of planting rosebush after rosebush… Do you know how many thousands of hours I've spent just pruning?"

She put down the quill and shifted in her seat to face him. "Understand this. I'll never let you free. You killed my mother."

The accusation stunned him. *I've never killed anyone!*

"Ha! Nothing to say? No witty comeback?"

He remained silent, hoping she would reveal more.

The witch cocked her head to one side and pursed her lips. "Hmmm. You like the garden, don't you? Well, the stench is more than I can stand. Now that I have you, I'm burning those thorny atrocities to the ground."

He couldn't keep quiet any longer. Removing that beauty from the world was more than he could bear. "No! You created a masterpiece, don't you see? It's the most perfect garden I've seen in a century. You can't burn it…please!"

The witch smiled slowly. "Oh? You're upset? That will make destroying it all the sweeter."

Sweeter? It would be a tragedy!

It was the garden that initially drew Cupid here. Ten rows of riotous colors ringed the cottage in the shape of a heart, hundreds of rosebushes filling the air with their sweet floral perfume. He loved roses, finding their scent irresistible. They were his mother's favorite as well, especially red ones. His earliest memories were of Venus carrying him through the gardens surrounding their home, both of them intoxicated by the colors and fragrances.

He'd sensed the roses from miles away. As he approached the cottage, the floral pheromones overwhelmed him. He reveled in the garden's beauty. Colors covered the spectrum, waves of expertly blended shades. The entire garden seemed to pulse in the breeze as the flowers swayed back and forth, mimicking the beating of a true heart.

Stunning. Unique. This gardener is a genius!

It made little sense. Someone had spent years of enormous effort to create the display, but it was located half a day's walk from the nearest town. Who could appreciate the artistry?

He landed near the front wall of the hut, sneaking close enough to peer through the wide-open door. A large golden birdcage sitting on a stand in the middle of the room first caught his attention. Beams of light from the only window in the hut spotlighted the glistening wire construction.

After his eyes adjusted to the shadowy interior, he examined the rest of the cottage. It was clean, but cluttered. Dozens of scrolls filled roughhewn shelves above a workbench, itself covered with jars and beakers. Drying herbs dangled from every rafter and a cauldron hung over the hearth. The cottage appeared empty of humans, but a black cat peered between several half-finished brooms propped in a corner. *Obviously a witch's hut.*

He stepped inside the doorway. Instantly, his head snapped back towards the cage. *Chocolate!* He'd know that smell anywhere. If it weren't for the overpowering floral fragrance, he would have sensed his favorite delicacy long before now. Chunks of sweet fudge lay in the center of the cage. He licked his lips, fighting the urge to dash forward.

His desire for cocoa in all forms bordered on addiction. In fact, that border was likely crossed ages ago. Eating wasn't necessary for gods, but it was certainly pleasureful. In the decades since he discovered chocolate, it was nearly the only food he ate. He'd decided that any food that didn't go with chocolate wasn't worth eating.

The sweet aroma pulled strongly. He shouldn't go anywhere near the golden cage. He knew better. The door provocatively ajar, a mound of fudge beckoning like a siren's song, it was obviously a trap. Not even subtle. But it was a trap well crafted. He couldn't help himself.

He gave the room another cursory glance. *I shouldn't do this, but my timing is good. No one is here. I can be in and out, quick as a flash.* He cautiously approached the cage. It was large for an aviary, half again taller than Cupid and beautifully crafted. *Must be for an entire flock of songbirds?*

He checked the cage for traps but found nothing. After one more glance around the cottage, he took off his bow and quiver, propped them against the cage's stand, folded his wings tightly against his body, and squeezed through the narrow opening. His legs were still outside the cage door when he stuffed his mouth with the first bite of brown perfection. Closing his eyes, he let the buttery goodness melt slowly, savoring the slightly bitter cacao, perfectly offset by the honeyed sweetness. *Amazing. . .so very good.*

Without warning, he felt his feet shoved roughly into the cage and the door behind him slammed shut.

The witch had been hiding in the cupboard.

"I've got you! After all these years, all my planning, all the hard work, it's paid off!"

Shocked, Cupid pulled himself to his feet and faced the witch. "You dare restrain a god? You think this is a clever idea?"

"Oh, it's better than clever. It's brilliant! From now on, you'll do as I say or you'll never taste chocolate again!"

The cherub glared at her, then examined his prison. He'd find a way out, and then she would pay for her insolence.

Finally! Kara couldn't remember being this happy. Her decades long plan had come to fruition. *I've got the scoundrel. Never again will he destroy families. And I'll be the most famous matchmaker ever!*

After years of research, she understood Cupid well. She knew the roses would draw him near. He couldn't resist, provided she made the garden grand enough. She found the scrolls that outlined how to create the magic cage in a little antique shop, truly a stroke of luck. And rumors of Cupid's addiction to chocolate provided the last key to her trap.

A rustling from the cage caused her to look up. Cupid's arm and shoulder reached through the bars, eyes closed as his face smashed against the side of the cage, fingers groping for the bow and quiver leaning against the cage stand. She leaped to her feet and snatched both away before he could grab them.

As she did, her thumb brushed the tip of a golden arrow. Dizziness came over her, and the ground seem to tilt sideways. Staggering back to the table, she fell into a chair. She shook her head, trying to focus a jumble of conflicting thoughts racing through her mind.

Slowly, the dizziness passed. She looked back at Cupid and a wave of affection swept over her. He was so cute, the chubby face, the dimpled butt, the beautiful, tiny, white wings. *I bet they are really soft.* She felt a nearly overwhelming urge to open the cage and cuddle him.

But I hate him! Or do I? A horrifying realization struck her. "Oh merciful gods, no!" she gasped. She was now the one captured. . .by Cupid's legendary love spell.

Cupid had almost snagged his quiver and bow when the witch leaped out of her chair and snatched them out of reach. He'd intended to shoot her with a golden shaft, then talk her into releasing him.

His golden arrows were the source of his love spell. That was common knowledge. For them to work, however, he had to close his eyes before shooting. Few people knew

Cupid was the original source for the Love is Blind idiom. It was a secret he closely guarded. He couldn't choose his target, but the witch was the only one in the room. He wouldn't miss.

The quiver also held the lesser-known silver tipped arrows. After being pierced by one of those, his victim would abhor the next person seen. Forever. While they came with his always-full quiver, he never used them. They directly opposed his mission of protecting beauty and fostering love.

After grabbing the bow and quiver, the witch's eyes widened and her mouth dropped open. She staggered to the table and practically fell into her chair. Her head turned toward the cherub, and a tender smile crossed her face. The expression was fleeting, replaced almost immediately with wide-eyed horror. Now it was Cupid's turn to smile. He'd seen that look thousands of times. The witch had pricked herself on a golden arrow. With no one else for the spell to attach her to, she would now be hopelessly and helplessly in love with him. *Yes!*

"Why don't you open the cage so we can get to know each other without these bars in the way?"

She started to move toward the cage, then fell back into her chair. "Because you'll leave me!" she moaned. "I'm sorry I've trapped you, but if I let you go, you're going to fly away!" The witch dropped her head into her hands. "Now what do I do?"

Her entire countenance had changed. Without the anger, her beauty was even more striking. She sobbed, tears pooling on the worn tabletop.

Cupid's heart thawed a bit. His soul, inextricably infused with love, made dealing with sadness uncomfortable. Her anguish touched him. "Maybe if we talk a bit, you'll trust me to stay?"

She sniffled. "Talk would be good. But can you ever forgive me for locking you in a cage?"

"Perhaps. Let's see. First, what's your name?"

"Kara."

"Hello Kara. I'd say it's nice to meet you, but…" He gestured at the cage surrounding him. "Can you explain why you hate me?"

The witch sighed. "I've hated you all my life. I thought it made sense." Her face scrunched up as she fought conflicting emotions. "Wait, it *does* make sense…I should hate you! You ruined my mother's life, and it killed her."

"I swear, I never meant to ruin anyone's life. What do you think I did?"

"It was before I was born. Mother was selling flowers at the Harvest Festival when your arrow made her fall in love with the man standing in front of her. He owned a traveling medicine show, selling tonics and potions…not that any of them worked. He was a shyster, a con man." Kara scowled, her disgust obvious.

"After their tryst, he left town. She never saw him again. It devastated mother, but it became worse when she discovered she was pregnant with me. She was shunned, ostracized by the townsfolk. Men would have nothing to do with her. For the rest of her life, she was lonely and sad. I never once saw her smile."

Cupid was horrified. His mission was to fill the world with love and beauty, not create suffering. He tried to recall the last time he was in this area. As far as he could remember, it had been at least half a century, but that couldn't be right. Kara couldn't be older than twenty-five.

"Are you sure it was me?"

"Yes, Mother described you perfectly. She knew she was ensorcelled, but your spell was too strong to fight. And now I'm in the same dilemma."

I must be forgetting my last trip here. So many festivals, so many arrows, so many lovers, they did tend to run together.

"I paid the price too. The teasing at school was so bad I stopped going. Mother ended up teaching me. I grew up with no friends. We had no family other than the two of us. I was only twelve when mother died…of heartbreak." She looked at him, eyes pleading. "Why would you do such a thing?"

He opened his mouth to reply, then shook his head, no answer for his thoughtlessness. Festivals were always raucous. He visited them often and enjoyed firing a few arrows into the crowd to get love hormones flowing. Many marriages resulted from those fall celebrations, and more than a few children were conceived. He'd considered it playful, never stopping to think beyond the short-term fun he set in motion. His world travels meant decades usually passed before he revisited a town. He'd never had to face the long-term results of his actions.

He could say he had no control over who his arrows hit, that he never intended to cause someone to live their life unloved. That didn't excuse his carelessness. The pain he caused Kara and her mother was the antithesis of his entire reason for existing. As he digested the magnitude of his actions, his stomach roiled and he nearly threw up. *How many other lives have I torn apart?*

"I'm…sorry. Sorrier than you could know."

He actually seems sorry! Kara desperately wanted to believe that, but years of resentment had carved deep ruts in her psyche. Her entire life revolved around hatred of Cupid. She wasn't sure who she was without it. *Besides, this could be just a ploy to get me to release him.*

"I'm sure you know that I have no control over the path my arrows take. I didn't intentionally hit your mother." Cupid grimaced. "But that is no excuse. I never thought beyond the festivals. I've been reckless. Impulsive. Thoughtless."

She took a deep breath. *It's probably the spell, but…I believe him.* "What do we do now?"

"If I promise to remain with you for a day, will you release me?"

She thought about it. "How do I know you'll keep your word?"

"I'm a god. We do not lie. Twist the truth, yes. Omit details? Yes. But we do not lie."

"That's what a liar would say."

"True. But there is another reason to release me. The sun sets shortly. That's when Mars will ascend."

She could barely pay attention to what he was saying. A soft tuft of blonde hair curled over his forehead, pointing down towards his deep blue eyes. *He is so adorable!* "Ummm… So what does that mean?"

"That's when I will change forms. I will age, become more like Mars, my father. Unfortunately, there won't be room for me in this cage. Not sure what will happen if I turn while in here, but I am sure it will be extremely painful."

That caught her attention. She had never intended to physically hurt him, just make him suffer as she had.

"Do you promise to stay with me for a year?" she asked.

He smiled. "No, only a day."

"So…just a month, huh?"

This time, he laughed out loud. "Ok, a week."

She pursed her lips. Why should she trust him? Yet, he differed so completely from the arrogant, cruel demigod she imagined him to be. *Is it the spell, or is he really as kind as he seems?* A week. Seven days to convince him to love her and stay. It wasn't much time, but it would have to do. Besides, if he suffered in the cage when he changed shape, he'd never forgive her.

"I have your word? You'll stay a week?"

"Yes, unless you ask me to leave."

She rose from the chair and walked over to the cage. Reciting the locking spell in reverse, she heard the latch click. The door swung open, and Cupid crawled out. She reached for him, but he waved her off. As soon as his wings cleared the opening, they unfolded and flapped, blurring like hummingbird wings. He rose, glided to the workbench, and perched on the edge.

"Ahhh… That's better!" he said, stretching his arms over his head.

"Thank you for staying."

"I gave my word. Besides, I've caused you enough pain for several lifetimes. I'm not leaving you without fixing this."

He cares! Maybe, just maybe, he would stay longer?

Cupid suddenly stiffened, his limbs twitching. "We were just in time!" he gasped. She ran to him, but again he motioned her away.

"I'll be fine. Just give me space." His arms and legs grew longer and baby fat melted away. His face thinned, and lush, golden hair sprouted from his head and cascaded onto his broadening shoulders. Muscles swelled, joints popped. Then a god stood before her, tall, naked, and glorious. Her attraction to him exploded, morphing from familial love to full-blown lust.

"Hello Kara," he said, voice a deep baritone that sent shivers up her spine. "I hope you don't mind that I look a little different?"

A little?

"No, no. I don't mind at all."

The simple robe she loaned him was too small. The short sleeves bared his sinewy forearms and exposed his thighs, but Kara didn't seem to mind

Of course she doesn't. She thinks she loves me. But it wasn't true love, only a spell.

After a meal of red wine and fresh strawberries dipped in chocolate, they talked until well after midnight. Kara was incredibly bright, and as funny as she was beautiful. *She is captivating!*

Cupid noticed her yawning and offered to sleep on the floor.

"Mother and I slept in this bed for years. It's big enough for both of us."

She looked at him expectantly. Her black hair hung in waves down to her waist, framing the soft white nightgown she'd changed into. The gown did little to hide her statuesque and lithe figure, and her dark eyes looked enormous in the dim firelight. She'd made her offer clear, but he was not about to take advantage of her enchanted condition. His arrows were for other's pleasure, not his own. He would certainly prefer the soft bed to the dirt floor, though.

"Ok, but let's keep a blanket between us?"

She laughed. "You don't trust me?"

"I don't trust me," he replied.

That night he woke to find her draped over him, her robe removed and the blanket no longer between them. Her luminous skin glowed in the moonlight, her figure as lovely as any demigod he had ever seen. He took a deep breath, preparing to refuse her advances, but her smell stopped him cold. Lightly floral, with hints of both vanilla and chocolate. For a minute, his brain short-circuited. He swallowed hard.

"We shouldn't do this," he protested, already aroused. "It's the magic!"

"I don't care," she replied, leaning down and kissing his ear. "And I can tell you want me."

He groaned, resisting his body's reaction. He tried pushing her off, but she slithered under his arms and began trailing kisses down his chest. His will broke, and they spent the rest of the night pleasing each other.

Kara woke late the next morning, happier than she could remember. Magic driven or not, she felt glorious. She stretched and turned toward Cupid, hoping for a repeat of last night, but was shocked to see he had returned to his cherub form. *This is certainly not a normal relationship.* She watched him sleep for a few minutes. *He is so beautiful, even as an infant.*

Cupid's eyes opened. He smiled at her, then his expression turned serious. "I'm sorry," he said.

"For what?"

"I took advantage of you last night. This isn't true love, it's just my spell."

"Does it matter? I'm happy, and you seemed to enjoy yourself."

Cupid was silent for a moment, then whispered. "I did." He closed his eyes and sighed deeply. "Gods help me, I enjoyed it most thoroughly." He looked back at Kara. "It's been decades since I felt this way, but it can't last…because what you feel isn't real. Besides, I'm a god and you're mortal."

"I thought hard about it before I accosted you last night. This feels real enough to me," she replied. "And you being a god is like eating forbidden fruit. Makes it more exciting."

He smiled, but regret painted his features. He reached out and grasped her hands. A kernel of fear sprouted in her belly.

"Magic cannot be the reason I'm with you. I've paired with mortals before, but because they cared for *me*, not because of a spell. Besides, none of those relationships ended well. You will age and I won't. Eventually, you will resent me."

"Never! And I'm older than you think."

"It's the spell talking. You will hate me again if we remove it."

"I won't." Her heart raced. *I can't let him go down this path. He is going to leave!* "I'll prove it to you. How can we remove the spell?"

Cupid's plan was simple. Kara would prick herself with a silver arrow. That should cancel out the love spell. Then he could leave, knowing she could find happiness with someone else. Untried, but it was the only solution he could think of. Kara reluctantly agreed to execute the plan that night, after he changed again.

They spent the day touring the garden. He sat on her shoulder as she pointed out the rare phenotypes and explained how she hybridized many of her specimens.

"I thought you hated the garden?"

"No," she said sheepishly. "I actually love creating new shapes and colors. I just said that because I could tell it upset you." Her face lit up. "There's something wonderful about bringing beauty into the world. And love. It's why I became a matchmaker. I want others to feel what I never could." She looked at him shyly. "Until now."

Yes! She shared his passion for beauty. And she wanted to bring love to the world, even though it was denied to her and her mother? *She really is extraordinary.* He felt his attraction toward her growing stronger every hour they spent together. *Stop!* He attempted to bury those feelings. *There is no hope for a relationship. After tonight, she'll hate me again.*

As the sun began to set, they stopped at her mother's grave. Miriam Lott, Beloved Mother read the inscription on the small headstone. Strangely, there were no dates.

"I miss her every day," she said as she replaced the small bouquet of roses in front of the monument with fresh flowers. She closed her eyes, a tear squeezing out of one corner. He was about to ask her how long it had been since her mother died when she grabbed his hand and pulled him back to the cottage.

Kara melted a bowl of dark chocolate by the fire and set it on the table beside a bowl of cherries. The sweet, smoky cocoa offset the tart cherries perfectly, but their conversation was even more satisfying. They spoke of beauty, how she carefully plotted out the garden and experimented with the colors and patterns. They spoke of love, and the different ways he had seen it manifest itself throughout the ages.

I'm going to miss this. She was perfect for him, but he had ruined any chance they had for happiness. He would now pay the price for his thoughtlessness so many years ago. *As I should.* They were just finishing when he transformed.

Despite having seen Cupid in his adult form last night, the transformation still stunned her. *He's the most beautiful person I've ever seen. And he's kind and caring.* It also didn't hurt that he was a highly experienced, magnificent lover. *Why wouldn't I love him?* But in the back of her head, she wondered how she would feel without the spell controlling her.

"Are you ready?" he asked.

"No, but let's do this." Her heart moved to her throat, making it hard to breathe. *What if I DO hate him?* She was terrified she would lose the most powerful love of her life. *But I can't let him leave me like this…We have to know.*

Cupid placed a silver arrow in front of her on the table and sat in the chair beside her. He gently picked up her hands and held her gaze.

"You need to know, regardless of the outcome, you are the most incredible woman I've met in centuries. But if you hate me, if our love isn't real, I'll leave as soon as you ask me to."

She nodded, unable to speak. He turned her hand over, closed his eyes, and lightly pricked her thumb with the silver point. Immediately, the disorienting dizziness returned. Her initial thoughts were a maelstrom of anger, hatred, and shame. *How could I possibly love him?* She turned her head away, unable to look at him. *He's the reason my mother is dead!*

But as the whirlwind of thoughts slowed, the anger receded. She remembered who he really was, the opposite of the image she had despised her entire life. She remembered his kindness, his willingness to stay because he didn't want to cause her any more pain. His horror at what he'd done to her mother. He'd been thoughtless, yes. But he wasn't the demon she made him out to be. Her hatred was for someone that had never existed, except in her mind.

How could I love him? A better question is "How could I not?"

She looked back at him. He was still holding her hands, searching her face for any hints. Hope, eagerness, and fear simultaneously occupied his beautiful, beautiful face. Overcome, tears spilled down her cheeks.

"Well?" he asked.

She answered by throwing her arms around him and whispering in his ear.

"My love, I've kept something from you."

His brow furrowed. Obviously not the response he expected. "What?"

"You know I'm a witch."

"Of course."

"And I told you I am older than you think."

"Yes."

"Well, I found a spell that would keep me alive until I had my revenge on you." She pulled back and looked him directly in the eyes. "Remember, I was twelve when Mother died?"

"Yes…?"

"My mother died 53 years ago."

Cupid's jaw dropped.

"I won't resent that you stay young, because I will too. I can't read the future, there is no guarantee we'll live happily ever after. But we can certainly be happy for a long, long time."

It took a moment for it to register. Then he whooped, picked her up, and kissed her deeply for what seemed like an eternity. After coming up for air, he whispered back.

"A long, long time sounds perfect."

About the Author

After discovering a new topological formula and winning the W.Va. State Science Fair, Emmett graduated with a degree in Engineering Physics and joined NASA as a research physicist. Quickly realizing a) he was too tall to be an astronaut and b) repeating an experiment hundreds of times was akin to torture, he left to find a different path.

Needing to eat, he joined an ad agency, leading to a successful career in marketing before retiring early to sail the Caribbean for several years. Emmett lives on Colorado's Western Slope with his lovely wife, two dogs, and several thousand SF/Fantasy books to keep him company.

He won honorable mention in the 2024 Writers of the Future contest, received his MA in Creative Writing from Western Colorado University in 2025, and is currently finishing his epic historical science fiction series, When Gods Descend. Contact him at Whitwoods@aol.com or Emmett Whitney on Facebook.

HUMANITY'S MATRIARCH

by Janessa Keeling

RAAYA WAS PARALYZED by the hibernation pod's lingering chemicals. It would take several minutes before she had full control of her body. She tried to open her eyes anyway.

She failed.

The pod hissed as a numbing mist coated the crook of her arm. She didn't feel the syringe inserted into the vein, nor did she feel the rush of fluids being pumped into her body.

The tang of saline flooded the back of her throat, leaving a bitter aftertaste. The pod door whooshed upward, and air smelling faintly of burned plastic washed over her. After several long seconds, the restraints holding her in the pod retracted.

"Time since sleep cycle initiated, two thousand three hundred years and eighty-seven Earth days." The computer paused as if doing complex calculations. "Sleep cycle incomplete." *Where is Ron?* The Ark's temporary AI should have been the one greeting her, not the ship's computer.

As she floated away from the pod, her throat tightened. The gravity wasn't on. Ron was supposed to turn it on before anyone was awoken. Where was he? She tried to flail, to grab something—anything—but her body didn't respond. Her body didn't respond! She struggled to blink her eyes open.

The hairs on Raaya's body stood as she registered the meaning of the computer's words and inhaled more acrid air. Electrical fire. And she'd been woken several thousand years too soon. *Crap.* Standard procedure meant she couldn't reenter hibernation for six months. She wondered if the computer woke anyone else, or if she was alone.

One of her concerns was the ship losing power and siphoning life-preserving energy from the pods. There hadn't been time to reprogram the Ark's auxiliary systems before they fled.

Far to the left, at the ship's control station, alarms went off. Each one a unique tone. Tension in Raaya's chest eased. One of those tones meant the suspended survivors and her crew were safe. Until she could move, that was all that mattered. Still, she listened, trying to decipher the warnings.

A high-pitched beeping indicated the ship wasn't moving. A low base note assigned to Ron echoed. A quick three note whistle meant the engines were working, but when fired, the ship would not move. After three cycles of firing, the computer's backup protocols had woken her.

Stinging heat spread out from Raaya's core down to her fingers and toes. They twitched when she tried to move them. *Finally!* A high-pitched wailing distracted her from the searing pain of hot blood flowing to frozen limbs. The ship could not deploy the Von Braun array.

Not a huge surprise. The ancient ship had been retrofitted with the AI and the array. Which explained the failure.

Raaya managed to blink her eyes open and yawn. She was upside down about a foot from the floor. The white corridor looked the same as when she'd gone to sleep. Clean and in good order. The normally bright lights dimmed for her comfort level.

A moissanite wedding ring on a long chain floated by. Raaya tried to curse, but her face was still mostly unresponsive, and it came out as a string of grunts. She'd put it around her neck before heading into the pod. She couldn't even turn her head to watch where it went. It clinked against the wall behind her head.

With a slowness that made watching paint dry feel exciting, her fingers and toes responded to her commands to move.

Raaya wanted nothing more than to go check on the people she was carrying to their new home. To Ensure Lilly, her little sister, was safe. Personally check on the frozen eggs and bone marrow in the cryogenic chamber. They would be needed for repopulating humanity.

Instead, she turned her head from side to side, rolled her body, and stretched her muscles. She grabbed the chain with her wedding ring and tucked it under her shirt. Clawing at one of the handrails, Raaya pulled herself in the direction of the cockpit.

The inside of the Ark was sanded smooth then painted a warm white. This allowed light and heat to reflect, saving energy.

The cramped cockpit, with two seats in front of several touch screens, one jumper seat, and a single viewport that couldn't be seen from the two pilot seats, dated the Ark. She could still see the scratch marks from where consoles had been wrenched out and replaced with touch screens.

Rubbing her cold and frozen fingers together, Raaya studied the two dozen emergency lights flashing warnings. An alarm about a black hole caught her attention. A quick peek into the viewport showed a dark empty sea. She frowned; they were between galaxies. She glanced at the radiation sensor readout; it showed normal levels. No black hole.

Nausea from abrupt waking and zero gravity had Raaya reaching out and flicking buttons and entering her master authorization code when prompted. The gravitational array needed a system shut down, then a reboot. It would take seven minutes for the entire process. It couldn't be used when they were traveling, but they were stationary. Gears clicked on, rotating as the gravitational rings were retracted.

Raaya took a steadying breath, not wanting to think about the energy reserves. She had to check. With a push of a button, she brought up the power system. Relief. Two of the battery packs were dead. Six, fully charged.

Glancing back down the white passageway, she eyed the sleeping pods lining the hallway. On her way up here, she'd rushed past her crew.

Priorities. Gravitational array. Then Reboot Ron. He'll do everything else. You aren't qualified to mess with hibernation pods anyway. You'd probably end up killing someone by accident.

Pushing off the wall, she let herself float languidly down the corridor to the cockpit.

She studied the alarms and readings. The black hole alert was still flashing. A black hole. According to the alarms they were being dragged into one. But the radiation sensors were quiet. She pushed herself up against the port, again. The ship's alarms weren't making sense. And the navigational data indicated the ship was stationary. If there was a black hole, she would be able to see it and feel it. The alarms said they'd hit something but there wasn't any damage.

Raaya rubbed her tired eyes. She wanted to smack the console until it gave her real answers. Instead, she cleared the alarms. The real ones would reactivate in a few minutes.

The control system beeped another warning. The gravity array could not deploy. The bay doors were open, but the system itself could not exit. There was *something* unidentifiable in the way.

Raaya pushed herself over to a station next to the cockpit hatch. She searched the camera angles until she found the one covering the gravitational array.

There was *nothing* there.

Raaya rubbed her tongue over her cold teeth and flicked through more cameras. Every image showed the same thing. The array was clear for deployment.

She needed to reboot Ron.

The golden rule of technology troubleshooting: Turn it off. Wait thirty seconds. Turn it on. Hope the problem fixes itself.

Something knocked three times on the emergency hatch, right next to her face.

Raaya shoved away and grabbed a command chair in a white knuckled grip. She was too scared to scream. Her heart was pounding in her throat she forced her hands to relax. "There's nothing out there. You're fine."

Raaya shook herself and faced the main display again. "You're fine." Temporary auditory hallucinations were expected side effects from the hibernation pods. Hibernate too often and the hallucinations become permanent.

Knock. Knock. Knock.

Raaya couldn't help but turn and face the hatch. The blood pulsed through her hands and feet. She needed to get Ron turned on; he could fix everything. The emergency exit hatch chimed as the seals turned off one by one. Her eyes told a different story. The door was closed, the seals intact.

Forcing herself to release the unconscious death grip on her ring, she braced her feet on the back of one of the chairs and looked down the corridor. Poised like a swimmer, she waited.

When the next knock came, she rocketed off the chair like she'd done thousands of times. Sailing past the door like a missile, body rigid, one hand guiding her path.

She didn't glance out the side ports, too afraid she wouldn't see anything out there. Too worried she would.

The burning plastic scent of electrical fire was the strongest in the heart of the ship. The room was a twelve-foot-tall and eighteen-foot-long tube with Ron's black matrix, a perfect four-foot cube, sitting in the middle of the room. It stood out against the white ship in design and color. No one would ever believe it belonged here.

Raaya rested her hand on the thick metal casing surrounding Ron's hard drive and memory banks. It hummed under her fingers. Beneath the two inches of metal, a liquid helium mixture churned, keeping Ron from overheating. He was on but wasn't connected to the Ark. Which meant he'd been trapped in his matrix since...whatever happened.

Raaya winced. Just like any person, an AI needed a way to interact with the world, an outlet, or they could go crazy. Ron had been with her family for generations: sung her lullabies in languages long forgotten, recited stories the most extensive archives only mentioned, and taught her advanced physics. He was older than any AI she'd ever heard of.

"Ron, I'm here." Her voice wavered. She drew a calming breath. "Don't worry, I'll figure out what's wrong." He didn't have speakers to transmit, or a microphone to receive, but he could pick up the vibrations of her vocal cords.

She found the problem in a burned-out wire, blackened with the spark that severed his connection.

She took solace in the ritual of repair, taking longer than needed when disconnecting bad wires, cutting them, stripping the new wire. As she soldered the old and new together, the smoky scent helped calm her, a little.

She finished wrapping the black protective coating around the wires and triple checked her work to stall for time.

If Ron was insane, he could destroy the entire Ark and everyone in it. He could open the hibernation pods, unseal the doors, and let everyone get sucked into space. There were no safeguards to stop him.

On the outside of the Ark's hull, someone knocked three quick knocks, followed by three long knocks, then three short. It sounded like the hardened knuckles of a space suit tapping on the hull. Which wasn't possible. This room had three feet of crawl space, filled with a foam-like material to protect it. There was no way to get into the crawl space.

She couldn't get the ship to work without him or awaken more crew. Though, like her the others could only enter hibernation one or two more times. They were lacking in supplies to make it realistic for anyone to be awake for two thousand years, even if they took it in shifts it wouldn't work.

Placing a hand on Ron's casing, she sent up a prayer to the Mother Goddess. "Please be okay." In a flash of wispy smoke, she restored the pathway for Ron, freeing him from his dark prison.

The lighting brightened. Raaya squeezed her sensitive eyes shut and groaned. The air purifiers kicked on.

"Good morning, Miss Raaya." Ron's voice was controlled and calm. Just like always. "Are you feeling any negative effects from the hibernation pod?"

"Good morning, Ron. I'm fine." Raaya blinked her eyes open. "Are you..." She didn't know what to say, or how to ask how long he'd been trapped alone in the dark. "doing okay?"

"I'm quite well, Miss Raaya." Ron paused. "My mind is intact."

Tension between Raaya's shoulders eased, and she nodded, grateful Ron answered her real question instead of the one she'd asked. Gravity reasserted itself, and her legs shook as her feet took her weight. She didn't remember standing being this difficult. The chain around her neck pinched at her skin. She hadn't felt the gravitational array activating.

"What was wrong with the array?"

"Miss Raaya, sometimes technology needs careful calculations and precise actions. And sometimes you must smack it with a metaphorical hammer." He paused, as if he was taking a breath. "The sensors of the ship tell me you have not yet consumed food or water. I have taken the liberty of heating rations." Ron's voice was a beacon point in a starless void.

Raaya patted the metal casing, then picked up the tools and secured them before making her way to the crew cabin. As she drew close, she ignored the sounds of beeping and clicking: Ron running diagnostics and initiating any repairs.

A ten-inch repair robot that looked like a scorpion scuttled across her path. She watched it vanish into a vent before she continued walking. Her legs ached with every shaky step.

The scent of grilled chicken and garlic spaghetti sauce wafted down the hall, making her mouth water.

"I have prepared spaghetti, Miss Raaya."

Her favorite since childhood. Only Ron could make it right, not even her mothers were able to replicate the dish.

"What were you doing while you were…" Raaya didn't want to say trapped, or in prison, even if that's what it would have been like.

"I finished the novel I've been meaning to write."

"Oh?" Her voice was pitched too high. AIs were *bad* at creating original art. In any form. "What is it about?" Raaya ducked through the too low hatchway. The galley was a cramped space, just big enough for a two-person table and a food dispenser recessed into the left wall with a screen on the right. A steaming plate piled high with spaghetti noodles and loaded with bright red sauces sat in the dispenser. On the screen, Ron smoked a pipe.

Raaya's smile slipped. He looked different. Older. The once black hair was now peppered with gray. His once shaved face now had a clean, trimmed beard. Also, he was wearing corrective lenses.

"You should eat." Ron's smile wrinkled the corner of his eyes and reminded Raaya that he'd chosen to make his eyes do that—chosen a facial expression that would disarm her.

A quiet voice in the back of Raaya's mind warned her not to eat the food. Raaya closed her eyes and rubbed her forehead before picking up the fork and taking a bite. Fresh tomato mixed with garlic and hints of oregano and basil danced across her taste buds. She moaned. It had been over twenty-four waking hours since her last meal, but over two thousand years in reality. It was as delicious as she remembered.

Ron smiled. Then his eyes glazed, his focus presumably transitioning to the Ark: sorting through data, sending commands to various apparatus, and clearing system errors.

She ate in silence, the food settling her stomach and stabilizing her mood. Each bite was as savory as the one before. A memory surfaced.

Her mother set the plate down, and the warm smile took the sting from Raaya's freshly mended bone. Ron's face flashed on the kitchen screen, he gave her a wink, lifted a bowl of banana ice cream, and pointed up.

Raaya giggled. It would be waiting in her room.

Her mother turned to look at Ron and put her hands on her hips. "I saw that," she said, her mock sternness clear in her posture and tone.

As Raaya set down the fork and pushed the plate away, Ron blinked and gave her the same smile he always gave right before he snuck her a forbidden treat.

Raaya couldn't allow him to distract her. "I like the new look, but why did you alter your appearance? You don't even need spectacles." On the ship's hull, the tapping began again.

He gave her a loving smile and puffed on his pipe.

Realizing he wasn't going to answer, she changed tactics. "How long were you trapped?"

He froze, the smile on his face glitching. The screen pixelated for a good three seconds. In those short moments, the tapping sounded closer.

"Just a little while, Miss Raaya. Nothing to worry about."

Raaya sat back, rolled her neck from side to side. Ron just lied. He wasn't like any other AI she'd encountered. First, he was modeled after a man. Every other AI she'd ever met was modeled after a woman. Second, he seemed more human, more compassionate. AIs weren't supposed to feel emotions.

Raaya forced a smile. "What happened to the Ark?"

Ron's smile slipped from his eyes. "I was forced to stop the ship for in-flight repairs. Catastrophic miscommunication between the new engines and the old computer." He paused to take a puff on his pipe. "Software patches and electrical tape can only go so far. The problem shouldn't reoccur."

Raaya forced her eyes to crinkle, knowing that something in Ron's programming had gone wrong. She would have to do something to stop him without him realizing what she was doing.

The next six months passed quickly. For Raaya's benefit, the Ark remained stationary while Ron implemented software updates and bug fixes. It took her five months to quietly recode a few of the repair spiders with a specific set of instructions set to activate on a certain date. She was gambling with the last of humanity, but she hoped Ron hadn't completely lost his mind. That the safeguards in his programming would stall him from hurting anyone. At mealtimes, he fed her an array of childhood treats, reminding her of better days. The tapping never stopped.

As a member of the crew, she'd been allowed to bring one person. Her mothers were too old. Her wife, Adorah, had gripped her hands and told her that she needed to save her sister. There was still a chance with the lottery.

The day came for her to return to hibernation, and as she stood before the waiting pod, her empty stomach growled. Behind her, metal scratched on metal. It sounded suspiciously like a knife scraping down the ship's hull and made her jump. She'd checked the new code in the repair droids, but she wanted to check again. A screen over the pod flicked to life.

Ron's face popped onto the screen. "I would like to discuss the book I wrote."

Raaya rubbed her face. "Okay Ron, what about it?"

"It is my history."

Raaya dropped her hand and stared at him. She could use this as a delaying tactic to check just one more time. Reluctantly she admitted she was curious. In her life, in her great-great grandmothers' lifetimes, Ron had never spoken about where he'd come from, or who his creators were. He was a guarded secret—kept hidden. Then, when the world needed an advanced AI to run the Ark, her family showed him to the world. Claiming Raaya constructed and programmed him. The most sophisticated AI ever built. She was hailed as a genius. Part of the deal for his use was her being selected as the Ark's Captain.

The lie burned. Especially now. She'd stolen two seats on the Ark. One for her, one for her sister. Taken them from someone who was actually qualified. And now humanity's last hope was in the virtual hands of an AI that couldn't be trusted.

Raaya needed to read this book; hibernation could wait. "Ron—"

"No, Miss Raaya. You can read it when we arrive."

Raaya turned her back to him. "Then why did you bother telling me if you weren't going to let me read it now?" It was like being given a treasure map and then told she couldn't go until after a nap.

When Rod didn't answer she turned back.

"Your body is flooded with stress hormones, and your sleep is disturbed with nightmares." Ron's voice was gentle and soft. "Raaya. Please look at me."

He waited for her to face the screen before he continued.

"It will give you something to look forward to." He smiled a mischievous grin, one holding answers to questions she'd stopped asking.

Raaya admitted Ron was right she was stressed. Hopefully he thought her stress was related to the loss of her family and world, and not because what she had planned was risky. She glanced down at her wedding ring. It was a reminder of all the promises she'd broken. Removing it, she tucked it into her pocket.

The pod closed around her. Securing straps tightened down.

"Sleep well, Miss Raaya. I'll be here when you wake." Ron's voice would have been like a warm was comforting blanket, if she trusted him.

Raaya became aware of her paralyzed body. The process was the same as before. Pod hissing and clicking as it cycled through the wake-up process. The numbing mist. The needle. Finally, the hatch opened, bathing her in the acidic smoky air. The restraints released.

'Raaya. Sweety, it's time for dinner.' Her mother's voice was far away, like she was calling from the opposite side of the house.

Raaya floated away from her pod. Far off to the left, the individual alarm tones whistled, chirped, and clicked. She didn't need them to tell her what was wrong. Electrical fire. If the reprogrammed droids had done their jobs Ron went offline ten minutes ago.

The first thing to respond was her eyelids. For a moment, she thought she'd gone blind, then she realized the lights weren't on. Adrenaline surged through her body and helped Raaya overcome the sedative.

Instead of heading for the cockpit, she headed straight for Ron. At her movement, the lights turned on. Hazy smoke filled the air, getting thicker the closer she came.

Her heart raced at the sight of the sealed hatch leading to the heart of the ship, to Ron's hard drive. The lights around the hatch flashed an ominous red. That should not have happened. She pushed herself for more speed down the white corridors. She slammed into the sealed hatch and peered through the little window. Liquid helium mixture floated in giant bubbles through the room. What used to be Ron's protective box was a melted puddle. In the middle was the inner shell. It looked intact. If his memory core was unaffected, it might be possible to salvage him.

Her stomach twisted. She couldn't open the hatch. The liquid helium mixture would damage the ship if it got loose. And if it touched her, she might die.

Her mother said, "You're grounded."

"You're ruining my life!" A door slammed.

Raaya put a cool hand to her forehead, trying to shake the hallucinations.

The Ark's systems were tied into Ron. With him gone, a person would have to fly the ship, making repairs as they went. She wasn't even sure how far out they were from their new home world. The dormant code in the repair droids would have only activated if Ron had sent any of them into the hibernation chamber to turn off any pod.

Raaya swallowed.

Turning, she pushed her way to the rear of the ship.

Hibernation pods lined the walls, stacked vertically to save as many people as possible. Raaya went to the fifth one down and activated the view screen. Lilly was fine. Her pod drew one percent more power than the others, giving her more oxygen, more attention. Raaya had no doubt Ron made the modifications, ensuring her safe and comfortable arrival.

Out of respect for her crew, she checked on their family members too. Carolyn, Sara's much younger sister, heart rate was a little too high. Raaya adjusted the oxygen setting to stabilize it. Joana's wife, Christine, was looking too pale, and an adjustment to the chemicals flowing through her restored her color.

Raaya paused and studied Tine's daughter, Aleda. Children were difficult to place into pods, their minds and bodies fragile. At Raaya's quiet request, Joana falsified data so Aleda could hibernate.

While the recovery would be more challenging, children were resilient.

Someone breathed on Raaya's neck. *"I know what you've done."* The woman's voice was unfamiliar.

Raaya grabbed the pod and turned. She was alone. It was her guilt manifesting. She would be fine in a few hours. Hours that she had to spend assessing the situation in the cockpit and figuring out what to do.

In the cockpit, Raaya activated the air filtration system and checked the Ark's position.

They were twenty years out. They'd already begun the deceleration process. With a push of a button, she brought up the power grid.

They were supposed to have two battery packs remaining. They had one.

Raaya did the calculations. Then she did them again. And again. The math came out the same. She didn't have enough power to slow the ship, have the crew take shifts—

waking someone up and putting them back into hibernation took a considerable amount of power—and land on the planet's surface.

She had five days to decide who would guide the Ark.

Raaya clicked on the button for the Ark's supplies and was surprised when a window she didn't recognize popped up. It was for supplies. Ron had reorganized the system. Optimized for user experience. There was a search bar now.

Raaya frowned. The act of fixing it for easier use wasn't in line with a malfunctioning AI. She checked the inventory of repair supplies and food. She had enough to keep the Ark going for the next twenty years. Enough rations, if she was careful.

Behind her, on the cockpit hatch, the knocking began. It knocked, and knocked, and knocked, demanding she open the exterior cockpit hatch. She swallowed hard; the knocking was louder. Like whatever was knocking was inside the ship, floating next to her.

She couldn't help but wonder if there was some alien life form that existed outside her eyes' ability to see, but was trying to get her attention.

"That's stupid," she said, her hands shaking as she clicked on the symbol of a repair droid. She pinched her lips together. More than half of them were offline. The remaining droids had a list of repairs that would take them more than twenty years to complete.

Raaya clicked on a tab named The To-Do List. The screen was populated with repairs that hadn't yet been made, ordered by importance. When she clicked on the first one, it gave her step-by-step directions, telling her what needed to be rerouted before she could begin.

Ron had planned around the possibility that he would be severed from the Ark, leaving directions for someone to do the work without him.

Raaya didn't know what to do with the sudden tightness in her throat and the stinging in her eyes. She went into the ship's electronic library and sorted by most recently added. *My Early Life*, by Ronald Mattix.

Raaya smiled at the use of her last name. Honored he would choose to take it. She wanted nothing more than to open and read. Anything to distract herself from the looming emptiness. The crushing weight of responsibility. But there was work to be done, and she wanted to check her calculations again before she made any decision.

"Liar!" A woman shouted. "Murderer!" Another screamed in her ear.

Raaya flinched. She remembered now. On launch day, there had been a crowd of people wanting to board the Ark. They'd shouted insults at the soldiers keeping everyone back. The hallucinations were never this bad. The intensity implied permeant brain damage.

She was about to click away from the digital library when she saw a little acoustic symbol. Ron had recorded an audio version. She could listen over meals. It was only eighteen hours long.

The first item on the to-do list was a small timing error with the forward-facing engines. If that was off, even by a few seconds, it would negatively impact their trajectory.

She got to work, removing panels and rerouting power so she wouldn't get a nasty shock. She was careful and slow, double-checking her work against the instructions.

Metal ripped. Raaya swallowed and looked at the walls, at the open hatch leading to the rest of the ship. If there was a problem, the hatch would have sealed.

Doing her best to ignore the sounds of metal tearing and the phantom sensation of air being ripped away, she floated over to the room's screen and played Ron's book.

Ron's voice sounded hesitant. "Miss Raaya, as I'm sure you've suspected for many years, secrets have been kept from you. I never meant to lie, or for one to be perpetuated. They were a natural evolution."

Raaya grabbed the braided silver wire and immersed herself. She needed to get this working. Had to get the engines to fire in the correct sequence.

"Lies spoken not by me, but others. Lies I... Lies I was too cowardly to correct. I was born in the year 2030. On a small farm in what once was known as Kentucky."

Raaya stilled, that was over 1000 years before she was born.

"I was once human." Ron paused in his telling.

Raaya could almost see him taking a long puff on his pipe.

"If you don't want to hear any more, I understand. What I'm saying is unethical. Taking a person, ripping out their consciousness, and shoving that awareness into a machine was unheard of in my time. I was the first."

Raaya pushed herself away from the wires so she wouldn't damage anything. Phantom fingers touched her face, and she flinched away.

Ron laughed. "You're probably wondering why I'm telling you this. I won't bore you with the details of my life, my marriage, my children, or what brought about me becoming the first of my kind."

Raaya grabbed a tool that was floating away and secured it in a Velcro strap.

"I couldn't leave my family behind."

Raaya threw herself at the screen.

"When the Omega virus killed all the men—" His voice broke, and he choked back a sob. "I knew—"

She paused the recording. She'd been wrong. Ron was a person, and she might have just killed him. Her breaths were coming in strangled gasps. She had to delete this book. Even though the Matriarchy was gone, and the laws, for now, were void, once a new Matriarchy was established, the laws surrounding human computers would be in the first wave of laws reenacted. They would kill him. That was, if she could save him, they would kill him. Before she pulled anyone else out of hibernation, she would initiate a full system reset, deleting all data. Once they landed, she would physically pull the hard drive and smash it.

But first, she had to save Ron. She wouldn't leave another family member behind. When they arrived, he could tell her the story.

Raaya peeled off the space suit and stored it. Ron's memory banks were safe. There was slight burn damage she hoped was cosmetic.

A person was their experiences, and without them, they would become someone different. Ron had to be protected.

"You're a liar and a coward!" The woman's voice brimmed with rage.

Raaya jerked and placed a hand on her head.

Next to her face, something slammed into the ship.

Raaya jumped. She didn't see any damage, and no alarms went off. Hallucinations.

Raaya stared at her reflection in Tine's hibernation pod. The last four days had been hell. The hallucinations weren't tapering off like they did before. They came in intense waves.

Raaya shivered as someone tapped on the wall behind her and played with her hair. She looked even though she knew she was alone. She couldn't do twenty years of this.

Tap. Tap. Tap.

What if the hallucinations didn't stop?

Tap. Tap. Tap.

What if she went mad from lack of sleep?

Tap. Tap. Tap.

What if, because she was so tired, she made a mistake and got everyone killed?

Tap. Tap. Tap.

Too much was riding on this mission to make mistakes. She had to wake Tine.

Tap. Tap. Tap. Tap. Tap. Tap.

Lifting her hand to push the final button, Raaya paused. She was condemning Tine to solitary confinement. Twenty years. Alone.

"No." Raaya hit the cancel button. "This is your fault. You're the one who let hibernation sickness get the best of you and sabotaged the pilot." Her penance would be twenty years in isolation.

Not wanting to be alone, Raaya retrieved Ron's matrix from storage and secured it in the co-pilot chair before strapping herself into a pilot seat and, together, watching the energy reserves as they dropped. It didn't matter that he couldn't hear her. That he was off.

"I'm sorry." Raaya looked over at Ron.

Voices accused her of being selfish. Her wife's tearful goodbye made her eyes water. Due to the lack of gravity, they collected on her eyeballs. She had to soak the tears up with her sleeve.

The energy levels dropped below the point of no return. Raaya committed herself to giving Ron something better than a holographic life.

Every day of the next twenty years passed the same. Wake up and exercise with elastic bands. Eat breakfast. Chip away at the to-do list. Make calculations. Check the math. Eat lunch. Check the math again. Make micro adjustments to the Ark. Make repairs. Eat dinner. Study robotics. And always ignore the ever-present screaming voices, phantom touches, and tap-tap-tapping on the walls. Watch a movie or listen to a book, but never Ron's. She wanted him to tell her in person. Repeat.

Fingers trembling, she activated the Von Braun array. She was fifty now. She laughed realizing she would be the oldest woman around. The amusement drained out of her. Humanity's Matriarch.

She decided to pull Joana out and allow her to awaken the rest of the crew. As the door to the pod opened and Joana tipped forward, Raaya caught her. "Joana, we've arrived. I've got the Ark in a high orbit." She lowered Joana to a recovery mat. "Christine is fine, I just checked on her."

Joana's chest rose and fell as she fought off the effects of the pod.

Raaya took Joana's cold hands in hers and rubbed them, wishing someone had been there to do the same for her. After a few minutes, Joana's eyes fluttered open.

"Welcome back."

Joana coughed and sputtered, trying to speak.

Raaya shushed her with gentle calming words.

As Joana recovered, Raaya explained the malfunctions.

Joana sat up slowly, and after several more minutes, she said in a hoarse voice, "You should have woken me."

Raaya left Joana to wake Tine and Sara. She went to Ron's place in the cockpit and placed a protective hand on his memory drive.

"Soon," Raaya whispered, "I'll have you up and running soon."

The robotics shop was large, with long windows to let in plenty of light. Even though it had been five years since they'd arrived on this new planet, Raaya still couldn't stand enclosed spaces. The auditory hallucinations and tapping on the Ark's walls had never stopped. And, as nothing could be done about it, she'd never mentioned it to anyone. The walls were lined with all kinds of tools. And in the storage rooms, there were thirteen failed robotic bodies. Thirteen failed attempts.

The fourteenth android sat lifeless on a metal table. The resemblance to Ron was intentional. Raaya was sure this one would work. It had to.

Raaya attached the last conductive wire to the power conduit.

Lilly's hand rested on her shoulder. It took Raaya a moment to realize it was a real hand.

"Do you want me to do this next part?"

Raaya never got used to the respectful tones the others used.

This Matriarchy was different. She'd been given a place of honor for her sacrifice. A vote in the councils. She'd made one special request, and it had been granted.

Raaya turned to look at the twelve women behind her. For the last five years they'd dedicated themselves to helping someone they'd never met. Behind the group, an unprogrammed android body lay on a metal table, thousands of thin silver and copper wires connected it to Ron's hard drive.

Raaya stepped back, allowing Lilly to fill the box with the liquid helium mixture.

Lilly smiled and gripped Raaya's hand.

Raaya wasn't sure what she would do if this didn't work. Phantom hands pulled at her shirt.

The little screen they'd hooked up to Ron's hard drive flared to life. Ron's face flickered as he connected to the network and caught himself up on current events. "Good morning, Matriarch Raaya."

The android body on the table twitched as the connection surged with power.

She'd waited twenty-five years to feel the hum of his life. Raaya leaned forward and rested a hand on the warming metal. "Good morning, Patriarch. Transfer yourself to your new body."

About the Author

Janessa Keeling just received her MFA in Creative Writing from Arcadia University. When not writing she likes to play with her dogs (snuggle on the couch) and work on DIY projects that never seem to come out the way the instructions say it will. Her work can be found with Black Hair Press, *Fairy Tale Magazine*, and WordFire Press.

WHERE WE WILL ALL GO

by C.H. Hung

MY MOTHER DRIVES a pale green hearse and ushers the dead to their final resting places, but not without a fee.

She takes, usually, from the feet. A toe will rarely be missed, she once explained to me, because once the body has been embalmed and the feet encased in shoes, nobody thinks to check again for missing parts. Plus, the bones are small and easy to extract, and even easier to grind up into fine dust, sprinkled into her morning tea, and sipped from her favorite chipped mug that says, in black block letters upon a white background, I WISH I WERE DEAD.

It's the only vessel from which she'll swallow death. So I watch her carefully on days when she takes her tea from that mug, sipping quietly at the small table in our basement apartment's kitchen. I watch to see if the taste makes her eyes crinkle more than usual, or if her slender throat will convulse in gags, or if her unpainted lips will pucker.

When she is done, she tells me that I must be a good girl, to stay quiet so I don't disturb the dead, and to wait for her. Then she fades from sight while I head upstairs to the funeral home, watching mourners wail over what's left behind.

I'm dying to know what it's like, to be drunk on bones. I know only that it is old magic she steeps, older than religion or voodoo or paganism. Older, certainly, than me, a high school dropout, mopping floors at a funeral home.

I begged her for a taste of her tea, once. She took me with her that day, but we rode in her hearse and she didn't drink her tea, and neither did I. All I tasted was the disappointment of sitting silently while Mom met with a ragtag group of strangers.

The next morning, Mom brought out her chipped mug. But before I could speak, she said, "No, Di. It'll happen soon enough." And I knew from her terrible tone not to ask again.

Still, I wanted to know what she saw that I couldn't, what she did while she was gone. I wanted to know what it meant to be her daughter, because she is the only family I have, and we are quite unlike the somber families who march through the doors of the funeral home.

Every time she leaves, I wonder if she'll come back, even though she always does.

So when she says today is the day and to get into the hearse, I don't hesitate.

This morning, the fog is thicker than the questions in my throat as Mom speeds through Orange County and down the 5 freeway toward San Diego. The back of the hearse is empty and smells of aerosol sanitizer.

She'd raided Mr. Nelson's toes before they were encased in his favorite argyle socks and his stiffly dressed body was laid out in his casket. She'd brewed her tea, stirring in bones and sugar with calm, measured circles, and she didn't rise from the kitchen table until the mug was empty.

The hearse sails through traffic like a ghostly pirate ship, passing through oceans of traffic-weary commuters with barely a shiver to raise goose bumps, her magic encasing the hearse, encasing me, like a benevolent halo.

The skies brighten above us, cloudless and endlessly blue, as luminous as the excitement coursing through me. At last, I'll find out what it's like to drink the bone tea, to go where my mother goes when she leaves me behind.

At last, I'll understand her and her magic.

At last, I'll understand what legacy to expect, from a mother like her.

An hour later, Mom pulls up to an abandoned restaurant—a long, low building hanging off the side of the embarcadero overlooking San Diego Harbor, across the street from a lush waterfront park. The restaurant has been empty for ages, ever since the previous tenants left after running a thriving seafood empire for several decades. It was time to retire, the couple said. Time to focus on ventures closer to grandchildren.

But I knew—because Mom told me—that what had driven them away dwells deep beneath the postholes centering the building, right over the gravesite of countless sea monsters, laid to rest by Mom's predecessors.

"Shh," Mom had said when she brought me here last time. "They will only let you through if you don't disturb them."

"Who?" I'd asked. "And through where?"

But she'd only bowed her head at the ocean beneath the restaurant, then hurried us through its front doors.

Later, Mom called the restaurant Patmos, but that hadn't been its name when it'd been in business. I looked it up and told her that Patmos was an actual place—a Greek island, and we were nowhere near Greece—in the self-important way that only a twelve-year-old can pull off and get away with. But she just laughed and said I needed to learn that place wasn't only about geography. That places could exist in other ways.

It didn't make sense then. It doesn't make sense now.

But now that I know where we are, I know who we're seeing. The memory of my last visit sets my heart pounding so hard against my chest, I wonder that I don't wake the dead. I hunch my shoulders forward, trying to make myself invisible.

Mom notices I've faltered and waits for me to catch up, then grasps my hand. "Remember, Di," she says. "Don't speak."

"No disturbing the dead," I whisper, and then say nothing more as Mom gives my fingers a quick squeeze.

Still holding my hand, Mom dips her head toward the waves lapping against the weathered, algae-slick pilings holding up the restaurant. Then we fade through the boarded-up doors of the building, the wood passing through our ephemeral forms like gossamer mist. Once inside, Mom lets go of me and her magic. We solidify in the sea-chilled room, and the rest of the group swims into focus.

There are seven of them, people of varying ages seated in folding chairs arranged in a circle like at an AA meeting. There's a tall, thin priest with gray hair, hands folded in the sleeves of his black cassock, and a petite Asian woman in a red power suit ignoring everyone while tapping away on her phone. A mousy-looking, potbellied Latino in a black suit sits in another chair, faking a relaxed pose. His dark brown eyes dart this way and that, studying everyone, measuring us, radiating anxiety like a heat lamp. Another guy who looks way too old to be sporting a man bun chats with a pleasantly plump Indian woman, his red T-shirt advertising a yoga studio's logo.

The Indian woman is an obstetrician. I only remember that because she's wearing pale green scrubs. She is seated opposite the empty chair reserved for my mother. The good doctor nods toward Mom in greeting, the only one to do so.

"Finally," intones an impatient baritone belonging to a short, barrel-chested man with a thick red beard. He's wearing a wife-beater and dirty, white cotton shorts. A trash collector, if I'm remembering correctly. "We're withering away from boredom over here."

"Be nice," chides a lilting soprano from the chair opposite him, her voice no less musical for her asperity. The woman wears a kind, grandmotherly face crowned with tight, gray curls, and a prim Sunday skirt suit in white linen.

Mom makes eight. Her clothes don't reveal much about her profession—faded denim shorts, flip-flops, a worn, flannel button-up.

The grandmotherly soprano squints her pale blue eyes in my direction. I freeze in place, surprised at the attention, uncertain which way to go. Last time, I'd been thoroughly ignored.

"Diane," the woman says warmly, "you've grown so tall."

"It's been seven years," Mom cuts in. "She was a child then."

"On the cusp of womanhood," the soprano replies, unruffled by Mom's sharp tone.

"Still a child," Mom retorts.

She catches my round-eyed stare and makes a small motion with her hand. I bite my lip and take the hint, lowering my gaze to the ground, the hairs rising along my nape as I feel seven pairs of eyes boring into the top of my head.

The obstetrician rises to her feet and moves toward me, but Mom steps in front of the shorter woman, blocking her from my view. They stare at each other for a minute in unearthly silence before the doctor says, "You cannot protect her forever."

"Surely there's another way," Mom says, now soft and pleading. "Someone else."

The doctor's voice, when she answers, is full of quiet sympathy. "You know there isn't enough time left to find another."

I can hardly believe it when, reluctantly, my mother bows her head. Her arm shifts, passing something unseen to the doctor, and the doctor flows past her.

At some unspoken signal, the others also rise and glide toward me without a sound, parting around my mother standing stoic and still like a boulder in a river, her back facing me.

Mom, I want to cry out, but I bite down harder on my lip until I taste blood. She told me not to speak here, and I will not, no matter how badly I want to.

The group encircles me, all of them holding hands, save for the obstetrician who stands before me. She holds a small bone cupped in her open palm. I recognize its size and shape. It's the distal phalange of a big toe—Mr. Nelson's, I presume.

"Don't worry, little one," the doctor says, even though I tower over her by a good foot or so. She withdraws a small, wooden bowl from the breast pocket of her scrubs—okay, that trick I haven't seen before—and closes her fingers over the bone. When she holds her fist over the bowl, crumbled dust trickles through her hand as if she were seasoning a cauldron of stew.

The dust dissolves into the reddish-yellow liquid of a well-fermented black tea, more expensive than the murky brown stuff brewed from the cheap supermarket tea bags that Mom usually drinks. Fragrant steam rises from the bowl, warm and inviting.

The doctor holds the bowl out to me. "This won't hurt a bit," she says with an encouraging smile.

I look at Mom for guidance, but she still has her back turned. She's angry, but she won't do anything about it, not right now. I can tell from the stiff set of her shoulders what the effort is costing her.

The doctor is lying then. But of course she is. Doctors always lie.

"You wanted to know, didn't you?" asks the trash collector. "Where your mother goes?"

Ten minutes ago, I would've screamed yes. Ten minutes ago, I would've grabbed the tea and gulped it all down, heedless of how hot it was.

But ten minutes ago, I wasn't here, abruptly set adrift by my own mother.

I am suddenly, frightfully certain that I no longer want to know.

I shake my head and back away, but I can feel the solidity of the circle at my back, eyes watching me wherever I spin. The circle remains unbroken, unwavering resolve caging me in place until I'm facing the obstetrician again.

Don't speak, Mom had said, so I can't even ask what the hell's going on, or why.

I glance at her again, but she refuses to meet my eyes. Not even when she left me at home have I ever felt so alone.

The obstetrician is still holding the bowl, same pleasant smile in place, as if she hadn't just watch me turn in circles like an idiot. I take the bowl in both hands, trembling and fighting not to drop it. The doctor steps back, and the circle parts to include her in its perimeter, her hands now holding the trash collector's on one side, the grandmother's on the other.

"Drink," the obstetrician advises, "and find Patmos through life-giving water steeped in death."

Patmos. The word reminds me of a time of divination, now that I'm older and have had time to study where it came from. To wonder why my mother visits this place. To wonder if I would ever return to it, and what it might hold in store for me.

I thought the bone tea would taste gritty, but it doesn't. The liquid is smooth and tannin-rich, rolling bitter across my tongue with a touch of honeyed sweetness. It is hot but not scalding, tolerable enough to gulp down a few swallows before taking a breath, inhaling the dizzying scent of black tea leaves drying in the sun.

It takes me a moment to realize that I can see the leaves as they're dying, plucked from their mother limbs and spread atop a fine mesh netting to protect them from the ground. I can see silky threads of vibrant green brightening to yellow and then deepening to gold before fading into brown as they wind their way from the leaves and into the dirt below, spidering out in finely spun webs that blend into the deep dark of the underworld's penumbral shadows.

My sight travels deeper still, into the underbelly of the Earth and through to the other side—no, the next side, for I can see the web travels still further beyond, threading strings of worlds together like pearls, each a precious globe of its own.

Without thinking, I blurt out, "What is this place?"

—and am shocked to discover the rest of me hurtling through the space between, traveling along the same threads my sight did, to collide in a jumble of tangled skeins in a gemstone-encrusted cavern so vast that my voice echoes for eternity.

My stomach sinks. I have the horrible suspicion I'm no longer standing in an empty restaurant with a silent circle of strangers watching me while my awareness flits through worlds. That, physically, I am here—wherever here is.

I have broken the one rule Mom taught me.

Don't disturb the dead.

I can't stop screaming.

"No," I sob, over and over again in a mindless litany, everything forgotten in my panic. "No, no, no, no, no." The last is a shriek that echoes endlessly through the rainbow cavern.

I shake and I shiver and I shout, but there is nothing alive in the cavern to hear me or see me or touch me, to fight me or hold me or tell me that they're here with me and will never leave. I am totally, utterly alone, and I have no idea how to get home.

I frantically search for those threads that brought me here, that started with the godsforsaken tea leaves drying under the sun. No threads, no life. No death, either. Nothing that links the living to the dead, and to the living all over again.

Instead, rainbow prisms of light sparkle from the geodes, crystals, and gems that encrust every surface of the cavernous walls. I can't tell where the light source is that glitters off the gems, but its brilliance threatens to blind me with migraines, and there is no respite unless I close my eyes.

So I do, sinking to my knees and burying my face in my hands to block out the dizzying light, whimpering low and deep in my throat. I rock back and forth, if only to give my body something to do besides collapse in a puddle of despair.

I see, like an afterimage burned into my eyelids, the circle of eight again, now including Mom, all of them holding hands, silent, unmoving. Before them, in the center of the circle, lies the wooden bowl that I dropped when I...I don't know what the hell I did, but I'm no longer there, that's for damn sure. One look at Mom's face and I know I am well and truly screwed. This isn't a dream or a game or make-believe. Whatever this is, wherever I am, this is real.

I wanted to know what the tea tasted like. Now I do. It tastes like sweat drying on my upper lip and the sour stench of fear radiating damply from my armpits, like bitter regret lingering on my tongue. It tastes like bile on the verge of spewing. Oh, how easily I forgot my mother's caution. I long for the comfort and security of standing firmly on ground that I knew and understood, for the salt-tinged air of the San Diego sea, for the soothing murmur of my mother's voice as she comforts me in the dark.

It could be worse, I think. I could be dead. I might be, if this were some schizophrenic version of hell.

But I don't think I am. Dead, that is. No way could I conjure up this rainbow hellscape, not in my wildest dreams. But if I don't figure out what is going on, I will die here, and it will be all my fault. I'm the one who screwed up. I'm the one who needs to fix this, and find my way out of here.

Slowly, my breath eases in my chest until it no longer powers the whimpering. The panic subsides enough for me to think through how to get home.

Home. Eyes still screwed shut against the brilliance of the cavern, I quiet my breath and my mind, focusing on the memory of my mother's chipped mug, on the black block letters, on the steam rising from its rim. On my mother stirring the tea in slow, lazy circles. On the calm, easy way she sipped from the mug and the patient movements of her body as she rises and rinses out the mug once it's empty, setting it on the drainboard to dry.

The afterimage of the circle of eight fades as the memory of my mother in our kitchen strengthens into crystal-sharp clarity.

She must have done it a million times. Stolen a bone here and there from the bodies being prepped in the funeral home for their final burials, brewed her tea, crumbled the bones into dust, drank. Ingested the magic that allowed her to…what?

I think back to the first moments when I sipped from the obstetrician's bowl—and it hadn't hurt, I realize to my surprise; the doctor hadn't lied—to the sensation of floating and traveling along the threads that marked the tea leaves' passage of life into death, greens flowing through yellows and golds and into browns. The threads that brought me here.

The circle swirls back into focus, and this time I can see the threads again, golden and sparkling like ribbons of stardust, tying one person to another, in a gleaming strand like a charm bracelet. A few of them have other strands that float elsewhere into the world, mostly greens and yellows. I want to follow them, but my sight is drawn to my mother, shining bright and golden, and to the extra strand of green that snakes out from her core and falls into the floor, through the ground, spiraling and winding and making its way toward me until it wraps around my waist and disappears into me like an umbilical cord.

I open my eyes. The cavern still pulses with its overwhelming prismatic light, but now that I know what to look for, I see it. Through a narrow-eyed squint, I spot the sparkling remnants of a bright green thread, as fresh and verdant as springtime.

I scramble my way carefully over the rocky outcroppings of geodes and crystals, following the thread until it winds its way through the multifaceted wall of the cavern. I hesitate only a moment, then plunge after the thread without losing sight of it.

The same tingling feeling of my mother's hearse sailing through traffic passes over me, and then I'm on to the next world, a lushly outfitted child's bedroom decorated in white lace and lilac wallpaper. It is dark, dimly lit by a night-light in the corner, and a little chilly, bringing a faint sprinkling of goose bumps along my arms.

More threads of green and gold weave their way throughout the rest of the house, with a coil of green curled up under a voluminous comforter in the canopied bed. The shape stirs, and I dash after my own thread to avoid disturbing the sleeper.

Place by place, underworld by underworld, I follow the thread that leads me back to my mother. I promise myself that each barrier I cross brings me closer to home, even though I don't know if it's the truth. But it keeps me moving, keeps me focused.

And no matter what I see, this time, I stay silent.

Let me cross, I pray, although I don't know who would answer. I just want to go home.

Some places are as silent and empty as the jeweled cavern I landed in. Some are as quiet and eerie as the dark bedroom. Some are boisterous, crowded with ghosts who don't seem to give me another look once they catch sight of me—something that makes me nervous, at first, until I realize that their gazes slide away as soon as they meet mine and see what I'm doing.

Odd, I think, that the shades don't know me, and yet they still grant me freedom of passage as if I were royalty.

It's that idea of passage that suddenly makes sense to me, my mother's lessons and rituals coming full circle. I know now that her magic isn't just magic, that the bones of the dead aren't just tools, and that her job as a hearse-driver is more literal and metaphorical than I'd ever guessed.

Abruptly, between one blink and the next, I'm standing again in the center of the circle of eight, holding the empty wooden bowl in my hands. The afternoon light pouring through the dirty windows of the restaurant falls upon me with weak warmth, a relief after an eternity of traveling through unending cosmoses.

A breath catches. It's Mom, her eyes brimming with tears. Her lips are pressed together, and she is uncharacteristically silent.

In fact, none of the eight are speaking, all of them studying me with discomfiting interest. Finally, they drop their hands. The obstetrician steps forward to take the bowl from me, and it's as if a spell breaks. The circle breathes a collective sigh and dissolves.

"Diane," the obstetrician says, her smile warm and welcoming. "Glad you could join us."

Mom grips my hands, clutching them tight. The trash collector claps a hand gently on my shoulder. The priest cracks a thin smile, although it doesn't lighten the gravitas of his lined visage.

"It has been a while since we've had a young one among us," the grandmotherly soprano remarks. "I do hope you'll last as long as your predecessors."

I look at the soprano, at her deep blue eyes, sparkling much like the jewels in the cavern. I want to ask questions, but I don't dare. I already made that mistake once, and nearly lost myself in a rainbowed hell.

I'd disturbed something then. I'd disturbed the dead slumbering beneath my feet. I'd disturbed the dead traveling through worlds. I'd disturbed the threads that connected life to death and death to life. The threads that showed me how to navigate the worlds in between, that showed me the pathways I would take, that my mother takes, to usher the dead to their final resting place.

And it was only until I quieted myself, regained the silence within and without, that the dead showed themselves to me again and allowed me to cross worlds.

This, I realize, is what my mother tried to shelter me from, when I'd asked to taste her tea. She didn't want me to shoulder this burden too early. To understand what it truly means to drive a pale green hearse.

But if I'm old enough to understand, then I'm old enough to carry its burden.

And I'm old enough to have a voice of my own.

"You're Purity," I tell the soprano.

No otherworldly force strikes me down where I stand. No threads snap and pull me back into nowhere. I am still here, still me, and inwardly I let out a sigh of relief. Truth be told, I wasn't sure until that moment if I was right. That I'd be allowed to speak, now that I'd tasted the bone's magic.

More confident now of my voice, I point at the trash collector, though I still address Purity. "Because he's Pestilence, and you sit across from him in the circle, so you must be his opposite."

The trash collector chuckles, his deep baritone rolling like the rumble of a lion. "You were worth waiting for."

"She does seem to be quicker on the uptake than some others," the Asian woman says with a smirk, eyes still on her phone.

"That would make you War," I tell her. "Because you've got attitude, and you aren't afraid to use it." I shift my gaze to Mr. Man Bun, at the way he's presented himself. "You've got attitude, too, but you're careful about how you use it. Which makes you her opposite—Harmony."

He smiles and raises his hands in mock surrender. "Guilty."

Mom has stepped away from me, and I turn in a slow circle, naming the rest of them. "Famine," I say to the priest, who nods back. The Latino beams when he answers to Plenty, and the obstetrician merely spreads her palms when I call her Creation.

At last, I turn to Mom. She is still silent, watching me with the tired expression of a full day's work.

No, I realize as I study her further. She is tired with lifetimes of work. How old was she really? I never thought to question that she was anything more than my mother.

"Death," I say quietly.

Mom smiles. Then slowly, gently, sadly, she shakes her head.

It dawns on me that Mom hasn't spoken a word since I got back.

No, earlier. She hasn't spoken since I drank the tea.

She isn't allowed to speak anymore. She is no longer one of the circle. Like I wasn't, before now. She knows, better than anyone, not to disturb the dead and draw their attention.

A hard lump forms in my throat. This was more than a test or a rite of passage. This was a passing of the reins.

I hold up my hand. "Death," I repeat, and this time, Mom nods. They all do.

"Death," the other seven echo. "Welcome to Patmos."

This time, when we leave the restaurant, it's me who acknowledges the slumbering sea monsters beneath.

Thank you for letting us cross, I tell them.

The answer that comes isn't in words. It's a feeling of peace, of acceptance, that emanates from the silent restaurant, and from the guardians underneath who keep watch.

Mom drives us home, but we travel on the road as mortals, crawling northward in the stutter-stop of commuter traffic.

The effects of the tea linger. I can count the winding threads as we crawl by, spinning off from the people riding in cars and from everything around us. They number in the hundreds of thousands, but the multitude of threads don't overwhelm me the way the rainbow cavern did.

I turn to ask Mom a question, but it dies on my lips as I catch sight of her thread. It gleams golden in the fading sun, but not as brightly as before. Near the floor of the car, her thread deepens into brown—the color of the dead and dying, like the woven thread of the tea leaves I followed into hell. The brown creeps up her thread, toward her center. Marking the time she has left.

"How long?" I ask her, amazed my voice remains steady.

Mom keeps her eyes on the road as she answers, "Soon enough."

Too soon, I want to scream. I have no marketable skills and no other family. Mom is the only home I've ever known.

But I only look down at my hands and ask, "Who's going to teach me?"

"Patmos will." Her knuckles whiten over the steering wheel. "You'll be okay," she adds, but it sounds like she's saying it more for her than for me.

And knowing that, knowing she's making sure I won't be afraid when the time comes, I also know that she's right. Just as she was right about Patmos. It's not just a place. It's accidentally losing your way, then finding it again. It's the revelation that one world will end, and another will take its place.

It's that intersection of life and death, of all the balanced opposites in a circle of eight, which marks where a daughter will let her mother go, soon enough. Where we will all go.

And where I can find her again, after.

"It's okay to go," I tell her. "I'll be fine."

I have to. Death comes for all of us. She and I know this better than anyone.

She smiles, and I watch her thread grow darker. "I know," she says, and I know that she'll be okay, too. It's all I can ask for, now.

We speed home in our pale green hearse. A fresh body waits in the mortuary. And tomorrow, it will be I who steals the bones and brews the tea, leaving my mother behind.

About the Author

C.H. Hung grew up among the musty book stacks of public libraries, where she found a lifelong love for good stories and lost 20/20 vision for good. Her stubbornly rational soul intersects with an irrational belief in magic, which means her stories are often as mixed up as she is, melding the plausible with myth and folklore. Her stories have appeared in *Analog SF&F*, *Ellery Queen Mystery Magazine*, and *khōréō* magazines, as well as anthologies edited by Kevin J. Anderson and Kristine Kathryn Rusch, among others. Read more at www.chhung.com.

BEAUTY IN THE SMALL THINGS

by Debbie Maxwell Allen

LIFE WOULD NEVER BE THE SAME.

Trapped beside her husband's body. Every exit blocked. Unwashed bodies crowded the room. Close air, thick with dried sweat, stifled her breath.

She stared at the wooden floor, gouged and worn by years of scraping chairs and heavy feet, unwilling to meet the sad eyes, the shadowed eyes, the hungry eyes. Two scuffed boots encasing thick calves appeared in her field of vision. A cough, accompanied by the odor of garlic. Olek.

"A good man, was Ivan." He cleared his throat again. "You know what you must do, Mariya. This is our way."

Her eyes slid to the lifeless hand hanging over the edge of the table. The fingernails no longer crusted with coal dust, the skin finally free from smudges of grease. Though it took all night, she had made sure. Yet she could not wash away the bruises left by tons of unforgiving rock. The stones had mottled the flesh of his strong hands—and everywhere else beneath his church clothes.

No. Life would never be the same again.

"I understand," she whispered to Olek. "This is the way."

It was for the best, of course. But her heart longed to return home instead. Not this ramshackle mining cabin, but back across the ocean. Far from these craggy, pock-marked hills. Five years back to her village. Her family. Her innocent youth. Though she had as few choices now as she did then. Ivan wasn't kind, but he'd been all she had.

She gazed around the close-packed room, heart dropping like a bottomless shaft.

When Olek lumbered away, the women came close. Four wives of four men. Mariya's only friends, though in other circumstances they would find little in common but language. The women circled her, babies perched on their hips, children clutching their skirts, blocking her view of the rest of the men. Blocking her last glimpse of her husband. Childless, Mariya did not even have a sweet little face to remind her of the life that had ended.

Lilya, Olek's wife, adjusted her tight bun from which not one hair dared escape and laid a hand on Mariya's shoulder. Her smile did not reach her eyes. And several of the women's gazes glinted with envy. Coal men were hard. Not understanding. Life as a miner's wife was unlike all they had dreamed of as little girls in the homeland. Many of these women would leap at the chance to change places with her. To choose a different husband this time.

Like she must do before the dirt settled on Ivan's grave.

Mariya trudged behind the simple pine box, following the path to the cemetery plot. Her long, dark braid swung slowly across her back. She kept her eyes on the coffin, ignoring the familiar landscape—everything the same color. Gray clapboard shacks, gray rock, gray leafless trees. She had watched other women visit the square of dirt to mourn a spouse or a child. Would she sit at the rock marking Ivan's resting place? Think about the life they had shared?

She was fifteen when Papa arranged the hasty wedding to a stranger from another village. "He is a hard worker, Ivan," her father said, by way of explanation. "The ship leaves for America tomorrow. You will find opportunity. Not like here."

Mariya's feelings held no sway with Papa. Everything happened in quick snatches of memory. Ivan towered over her during the ten-minute ceremony, dark and brooding, ignoring her timid glances.

Afterwards, in the too-quiet hut, Mama helped lay Mariya's belongings in a sack made by stitching the sides of her wedding quilt together. "You can rip the threads and use it on your bed in America," she whispered, unable to meet Mariya's eyes. Mama gave too much—baby clothes from her children who were no more, bread and cheese and jam from the nearly empty shelves. Mariya longed to protest, but this was Mama's only way to declare that her daughter was cherished. And Mariya was the only child left to receive these gifts.

Last of all, Mama pulled her wooden spoon from the pot of broth hung over the fire. She washed it with care, lovingly tracing the tiny *malva* flowers carved on the handle.

When Mama slid the spoon into the folds of the quilt, Mariya gasped. "No, Mama. Papa made that when you married. I cannot take it."

The wrinkles on Mama's face stretched into a weary smile. "Keep it as a remembrance. The *malva* represents love for the land, for parents, for home. Think of home when you mix your flour to make *zsemle* rolls or stir your goulash. Though life is not always full of joy, there is beauty in the small things."

Mariya's gaze roamed her mother's face, memorizing every beloved feature. Too soon, it was time to leave. Stoic to the end, Mama pulled Mariya into a quick, fierce hug, then turned away to the fire. Mariya's last memory of Mama was her back, shoulders shaking gently. Papa gripped Ivan's hands and gave Mariya a curt nod. That was all, save a twitch of his right eye. And then Ivan hurried her away toward a foreign ship, an unknown land, the mysteries of marriage.

Mariya had followed Ivan that day, shouldering the quilt containing her last links with home.

And now she followed him still.

She tried to focus on the coffin, to think about Ivan and the last five years. Hard years. Painful years. Lonely years. She had learned that marriage was a dictatorship, not a democracy. Ivan was not a man of tender words and glances. Like a lump of coal, his edges were hard, unyielding, inflexible. She was to blame for their childless state and the gritty conditions. But though she missed the softness, Ivan made up for it with passion. She bit her lip and blinked back tears at the memory of intense kisses and intertwined limbs. Though Ivan never said the words, he'd loved her in his own way.

But the men carrying the pine box pulled her mind away from memory. One of these four would become her second husband, just a week and a day from today. This time the choice belonged to her, not to Papa. A privilege earned from loss. But the burden of that decision felt as oppressive as the rocks that had entombed Ivan.

No words lent beauty to his burial. The hole had already been dug, and the men lowered Ivan into the depths. When the first shovelful of dirt rattled the top of the coffin, Mariya flinched. It felt wrong to pile dirt and rocks on a man who had been killed by the same weight. Lilya, standing beside her, gripped Mariya's shoulder. Not for comfort, but in warning. *We don't display emotion*, it said. *Hold yourself together.*

With every scoop of dirt, Mariya felt the tunnel of her future collapsing. No light shone at the end.

After three days of dismal anticipation, the years stretching ahead felt even darker. Three days alone with the steady drip of the leak in the corner. Three days to grieve, to ponder, to prepare to belong to someone else. When the fourth day dawned in continued gray drizzle and the women arrived, Mariya nearly sighed with relief.

Until they opened their mouths.

They trooped in with their baskets, bundles, and babies, pouring chaos into her tiny shack. Well, Ivan's shack. Only a married miner was allowed to rent a house. Single men slept in the bunkhouse. Widows had two choices—remarry or leave. Those from the homeland clung together, as marriage to a foreigner was unthinkable. A fierce longing for home burned in Mariya's breast. But thousands of waves stood between this land and home. Mama and Papa were already gone, with nothing but *malva* flowers growing over their graves.

Lilya hefted a basket on the table, laid her sleeping baby on the bed, and set her two daughters to keep watch. Her lace petticoat marked her as the wife of Olek, the group's leader. Iryna, wife of Denys, guided her two-year-old twins to a spot in the corner where they rolled a spool back and forth—the corner without the bucket catching drips from the roof. She maneuvered her expectant girth onto one of the benches. Lesya and Sofiya completed the group, each with a brood of stair-step children.

Mariya stirred the coals under the pot of *smitten*, adding honey to the cinnamon and cloves that had simmered since dawn. She ladled a fragrant serving into the cups each woman had brought. She passed a *zsemle* roll to each child old enough to chew and returned to the table, where the women had unpacked their handiwork. Spinning, knitting, sewing, and unending darning kept their hands busy as they began the serious work of the discussion at hand.

"Gleb is an obvious choice," Sofiya was saying, tucking a reddish curl into her kerchief. "So sad that his Olga passed on the ship. She and I played together as children. And married only a month. What do you think of him, Mariya?" She looked up from the cap she knitted.

"He laughs more than most, I can say that," put in round-faced Lesya, stitching a bit of lace today. "My Yosip could take a lesson from a good-natured man like that."

It was true. Gleb's cheerful disposition was a marked difference from the despondency that settled over the men the longer they worked underground. While he wasn't handsome, the crinkles at the corners of Gleb's eyes promised laughter—and perhaps an ability to forgive shortcomings.

Irina stood to the side of the table with her drop spindle, trying to keep it from tangling with her braids. "You overlook Yakiv. Of all the men, he is the most handsome. That thick hair, the dark eyes—and a strong chest. If it were me…"

Good-looking, yes. But did that bode well for a good life? For a moment, Mariya imagined the deep brown eyes and tousled hair…

Nods and murmurs went around the table. Lilya's infant son wailed from the bed. She set down her darning and carried him over, uncovering a breast. His nappy had left a dark stain on Mama's wedding quilt.

Mariya sighed. The day was not over yet.

After getting him latched and picking up her work, Lilya spoke around a mouthful of pins. "Never mind those two. Choose the one with the greatest need, Mariya. Vashyl has his hands full with three children. If anyone needs a wife, it's him."

The women's voices rose in agreement. What they did not voice spoke the loudest. Mariya had no children, and marrying a man with a family would solve the stigma of her barrenness. Was she truly barren? Rumors said that sometimes the man's seed failed. Yet the issue was rarely spoken of.

Indeed, Vashyl's sons and daughter played in the same room. The truth was, the women were weary of taking turns caring for his children while he worked. Vashyl had been married not once, but twice and was well-known as a skillful storyteller. Even Mariya sat expectantly for his tales of the homeland.

What would marriage be like with Vashyl? Her life could comfortably revolve around the children. She would fit in more easily with these women. And when she felt homesick, Vashyl might paint a picture of home with his words. Yes. He might be the one.

"Of course, we cannot overlook Alexsander," Sofiya said, pausing to unravel a few stitches on her knitting needle. "Symon likes him. Says he is a hard worker."

"All our men work hard," Iryna snapped. The spindle dropped to the floor with a crack. "Stop!" Her twins froze in their fight over the spool. She turned back to the group. "What you forget, Sofiya, is that of the four, Alexsander alone has never been married."

"Olek told me," Lilya lowered her voice, "that he admitted he has never before lain with a woman."

Shocked gasps quieted even the children, with the exception of Lilya's baby boy, who took that opportunity to let out a loud burp.

Lesya lowered her lace. "Yosip heard it himself."

"No!" Sofiya said, disbelief twisting her expression. She turned to Mariya. "You must not choose him. Perhaps he cannot even…perform, and then you lose all hope of children."

Mariya's heart saddened for the man, the newest and youngest of their group. Though the decision was hers, she hadn't spoken yet, but she opened her mouth now. "Inexperience does not prove inability."

Four pairs of eyes scrutinized her. Lilya switched her son to her other breast and raised an eyebrow. "You fancy him, do you?"

Despite her efforts, Mariya felt her face color. "Of course not. I pity him, though. How can we judge what we do not know?"

"We are women." Lilya pressed thin lips together. "Who is there to see and judge, but us?"

Mariya kissed the flowers on Mama's spoon before she stirred the venison *goulash*. Missing Mama still felt like a sharp ache beneath her heart. What would her mother tell her now?

The knock on the door startled her. The first one was here. Her mind raced, trying to remember which man was first. Vashyl. She hoped he would bring his children to distract her from the awkward visit. Each man would take a turn sharing a meal with her these four nights before the wedding, giving the men a chance to enjoy her cooking, and her the opportunity to know them better.

Vashyl stood on her sagging step, his thick black hair swept to the side. Dark eyes pierced her from beneath heavy brows in a way that sent a shiver down her neck. Not a pleasant one.

Mariya looked behind him for the children, but he was alone. She swallowed a sigh and stepped aside as he entered.

He wasn't bad-looking, she mused, as he entered the lone room. Not as handsome as Yakiv, but very tall and more pleasant to gaze on than square-faced Gleb. Miners developed strong, muscular arms from the hard work, but their wiry frames attested to the scarce food supplies.

"Please, sit," Mariya said. Her voice sounded hesitant to her own ears. She turned to the hearth and busied herself with pulling the bread from the lidded pot in the coals. Thankfully, Alexsander had stopped by earlier to chop enough wood for the week. He hadn't said a word as he carried each armload and stacked the split logs to fill the lean-to on the side of the shack. She noticed one button on his flannel shirt had loosened, but she didn't want to give him false hope by offering to mend it.

She fumbled with the bowls and spoons but finally managed to set the food and dishes on the table. After serving Vashyl, she took the bench across from him before the steaming stew, following the wisps with her eyes to avoid meeting his. He had begun eating before she'd sat down.

"The steam. It reminds me." His deep voice rumbled from the other side of the table. The table where Ivan's body lay just a few days ago.

Mariya shook herself back to the present. "Oh?" she whispered.

"I remember the way the fog hung down low over the valleys in the old country. Like a blanket over each village, keeping them warm. I hunted before dawn, and watched the fog burn away as the sun rose..."

Mariya closed her lids and let her eyes roam the familiar hills from which his memory came. If this was a glimpse into life with this man, she was ready to say yes. To have pictures painted daily of the life she left behind were riches enough to carry her through the difficulties.

"So." His booming voice caused her to jump and shoot her gaze in his direction. "I do not mind your barrenness. Three mouths to feed is enough."

Heat rose in Mariya's face. To speak of such things with a man!

His head bent over the bowl, and he slurped another spoonful of *goulash*. "Your cooking is passable," he said, chewing, "and the children will mind you if I tell them." Vashyl's spoon scraped the bottom of the bowl.

He sounded as though the choice was already made. Her wishes made no difference. Just like with Papa and Ivan. Mariya chewed her lower lip.

Vashyl stood at last, and Mariya did the same. Was this all? A short meal, a weighing of her assets, and then a decision. She followed him to the door.

He stopped there, towering over her. The floorboards squeaked under his weight.

Mariya stared at his worn shirt, waiting.

"So," he said. "You will do. I need only someone quiet, obedient, submissive."

She swallowed, unsure if she should thank him or stick out her tongue.

He raised an eyebrow. "Well?" Vashyl's imperious tone made her want to cower.

"I…I will decide after visiting with the other men."

An iron hand latched around her wrist. "Decide now."

Mariya's heart pounded, and she tried to breathe. She stared into his eyes and then twisted out of his grasp.

Faster than a rockslide, his fist raised to strike. He stopped, stared at his hand as if it belonged to someone else, then lowered his arm. After one more glare, he took his leave without another word.

The slamming door rattled in its frame. Mariya shook almost as much. She lowered herself to the bed, gripping her mother's quilt between trembling fingers. Was the promise of children and security worth this kind of fear?

She hoped the next three men would answer her question.

Mariya endured another afternoon of the women's chatter as they picked apart her visit with Vashyl. Sofiya thought his offer should have been accepted immediately, she declared, between settling squabbles among the children.

Iryna scoffed when Mariya mentioned the threat she felt from his fist. "Bah. He barely touched you. Who among us does not bear bruises from time to time? The men must have some way to vent their frustrations."

Ivan, for all his harsh words and dark looks, had never left a mark on her. Perhaps he was different from other men. Perhaps she must accept this as part of life.

Alexsander had caught two fish in the mountain stream that morning and brought them by before heading to the mine. His button was looser than yesterday. Mariya wondered how early he had risen to both fish and shave before work. The rest of the men let their beards grow scraggly.

She prepared a clear soup with chunks of Alexsander's fish and an onion and carrot she hoped Gleb would appreciate. He came from the coast and missed the variety of seafood he grew up with. She could be content with a man like Gleb. He found humor in most situations, laughing and joking with the men, and, while plain-looking, the twinkle in his eyes made her smile. Sofiya had confided his deep devotion to the young wife he'd lost on the ocean passage.

When Mariya opened the door for Gleb, he smiled and she found herself looking him in the eye, unlike her experience with Vashyl. His cheeks bunched in his square face, and she liked how his brown eyes crinkled at the corners while he twisted his hat. His hair was shorn short all over, reminding her of a hedgehog.

"Come in, Gleb," she said.

"I thank you for your hospitality." He scraped his shoes on the step before entering, then lifted his head. "Ahh. I smell *yuska*. A wonderful aroma at the end of a long day."

Gleb's sincere praise warmed her, and her hands did not shake as she served the meal. He regaled her with tales of pranks the men played on one another in the mine, laughing loudly at his own jokes. Mariya found herself chuckling along with him.

"One time, back when Vashyl's wife was alive, he brought one of her extra dresses into the mine. Yakiv stuffed the fabric with straw and attached a sack for the head. When Alexsander arrived, they took him and the dummy aside to teach him a few things about women!" Gleb slapped his thigh, but this time Mariya did not see the humor. Why did they make fun of the younger man? Each of them had been inexperienced at one time.

Mariya stood. "Thank you for sharing a meal, Gleb. I am feeling tired." She walked him to the door.

Gleb reached for his hat, twisting the felt as he had when he arrived. His eyes looked everywhere but at her.

"Do you have something to say?" she asked, hope rising.

His throat bobbed as he swallowed. "Yes, Mariya." He spoke to his shoes. "You are a pleasant woman and a wonderful cook. I believe we would get on well, but—"

"But what?" Mariya tried to imagine a problem. And then she knew. "You want children."

Relief slid over his face like a rockfall. "When Olga left me, she took with her a babe. I longed for fatherhood. Please understand. You will make a wonderful wife—for one of the men."

Mariya's hope turned to stone in her chest. "So you will wait for one of your friends to die?"

From his stricken expression, she had been too blunt.

Gleb hurried out the door, taking his laughter and her hope with him.

Mariya dreaded having to report to the women her failure with Gleb. She wished she might beg a headache and send them all home, but they would mine the truth from her eventually. Perhaps they might even help her think of what to do.

Lesya was the most disappointed. But the women commented less than usual, though Mariya saw more than a few pointed glances shared. She tried to focus on the fact that Vashyl had offered for her, at least, though she hoped to have one other man to choose between.

Alexander had stopped by in the morning with a handful of wild garlic he'd gathered. And she just now realized her water buckets were somehow filled each day. She suspected the culprit. His button was now hanging by two threads, but Mariya clenched her hands around her mother's spoon to keep herself from reaching for it.

Yakiv was coming tonight, with his handsome face and broad shoulders. Mariya had never spoken to him alone, but she had caught some mutually appreciative glances between him and some of the women. With no meat available today, she had settled on making *varenyky*, dumplings filled with fried cabbage and onions. Yakiv might object to eating them without the customary sour cream, but that was a luxury unaffordable on a miner's pay. And she'd mashed Alexsander's garlic with oil and broth to make a sauce.

Yakiv was late. Would he really come? Rain drummed steadily, and the tempo of the drip in her bucket increased along with her nerves. Just when she thought to take the dumplings off the coals, his knock sounded. Mariya steadied herself with a deep breath before lifting the latch.

Yakiv leaned his rain-dampened elbow against the doorframe, legs crossed, the right side of his lips tipped up. One eyebrow raised slightly while his eyes ran from her face to her toes and back—almost back to her eyes. "Good evening, Mariya."

Her throat went dry and she stepped back. Too quickly, for she bumped into the bench near the table.

He stepped in and closed the door, leaving muddy prints on the planks. The sound of the latch echoed in the quiet room.

Swallowing was impossible with her throat so parched. "Please, sit," she rasped, then turned quickly away to busy herself at the hearth and shield her flaming cheeks from his stare. She felt his gaze burning through her back. With sweat-damp hands, she ladled dumplings and a bit of sauce into a bowl and ran her tongue over her lips before she turned.

Yakiv stood across the room with Ivan's prized rifle, examining the stock in a proprietary way, then sighting the weapon. Unnoticed, Mariya took in his unruly curled hair, the arrow-straight nose, and strong chin. He had trimmed his beard…for her? His biceps flexed as he hefted the gun—and looked over, catching her staring. A slow smile spread over his face.

She nearly dropped the bowl. "The—*varenyky* is ready," she murmured.

"Ready, eh?" His smile widened.

The bench scraped as he sat. She moved toward him. Before she placed his meal on the table, his warm hands covered hers around the bowl. "*Dyakuyu*," he said, smiling when her eyes darted to his.

"*P-proshu*," she responded with difficulty. She hurried to the safety of the fireplace to serve herself, then stepped to the far end of the table. The table that felt too small.

He ate slowly, watching her with disconcerting intensity. No stories like Vashyl. No jokes like Gleb. Just a smoldering stare, with that eyebrow that lifted from time to time with some mysterious message.

To break the tension, Mariya slid off the bench and dipped two cups of water from the bucket near the door. Alexsander had filled it on his way from the mine to the bunkhouse. She blinked in dismay after realizing she had to bring it over to Yakiv. After setting down the mug, he patted her shoulder and slid his hand down her arm. She stood frozen for a moment before retreating to her bench.

Mariya stared at her uneaten dumplings. Ivan's touch had unsettled her at the beginning. Why did Yakiv's make her skin crawl? Was it his knowing smile—as if he felt sure she desired him? Discomfort was not reason enough to deny marrying the man. He worked hard. He seemed passionate. He had not raised a hand in anger. Perhaps that was enough. In time she would adjust.

She tried to hide her relief when he wiped his mouth and finally stood. Unwilling for him to hold her hands again, she grabbed Mama's wooden spoon, then hurried past him and opened the door. He stepped over the threshold and turned.

He was close. Too close. She backed up, but the bench stopped the door from opening farther. "Enough of the maidenly glances, Mariya. Ivan was no monk. You like what you see. I like what I see."

His hand suddenly covered her breast, and she gasped, twisting away and dropping the spoon. "Ivan would beat you for this!"

"Ivan is dead. And I am in need of a wife."

Mariya opened her mouth to speak but stopped when she saw movement over Yakiv's shoulder. A familiar silhouette stood between the two shacks across the path—Alexsander. Shame eclipsed her anger. Would he think she had invited Yakiv's attentions?

She muttered a curt, "*Dobranich*," and escaped into the shack, slamming the door before her legs gave way.

A sharp crack snapped the air. No! Mama's spoon lay broken in pieces by her panicked decision. She slid down the inside of the door and let heavy tears fall.

Apprehension and humiliation alternated before Mariya faced the women yet again. They arrived early, eager to hear her experience with the dashing Yakiv. She swallowed, staring at the grain of the table as she spoke the shameful words.

When she looked up, Lilya's eyes were narrowed. Gazing around the table, Mariya saw similar expressions on several faces, including Lesya and Irina. What had happened? The women, so willing to offer advice, appeared annoyed, angry—jealous?

Perhaps the raffish Yakiv had made other advances. The idea felt almost disloyal, yet what else could produce such a reaction? When he made overtures to married women, were they welcomed?

One comment stopped her still. Mariya had stepped out of the house to empty the chamber pot the children had used. As she opened the door, Lilya was speaking. "He spoiled Yakiv's looks for certain. I was surprised to hear of it, for such a quiet man."

Sofiya looked up from changing her baby girl. "No one would expect it from him."

"Who do you speak of?" Mariya asked.

But no one answered.

Mariya considered Alexsander as she cooked. Still without meat, she prepared sour cabbage leaves with rice and a caramelized onion filling, baked in tomato sauce. She pulled out a bowl and added flour and water for *zsemle* rolls. Tears rolled down her cheeks as she mixed the dough with her fingers instead of Mama's spoon. The shattered pieces lay forlorn on the mantel.

Alexsander had asked for the morning off work to fix the leak in the corner of her roof, shaving the shingles himself from wood he had chopped. He seemed like a good man, helpful, not hard or even violent. But she didn't want a boy, and she struggled to think of him as a passionate man.

The knock came right on time. Mariya wiped her hands on her apron before opening the door.

His light brown hair had been slicked back at the water pump. Droplets from the tips of his hair caught the firelight as they meandered down his cheek to his collar.

Mariya stepped back, flushing. Had she been staring? "Welcome, Alexsander."

He stopped to untie his boots and leave them at the door. "The paths are still muddy from the rain yesterday," he murmured, by way of explanation.

"Please, sit," she said. "I've made *holubtsi*, though I'm afraid I don't have bacon or minced beef today."

"I'm thankful for a meal that tastes like home. The cook for the single men is from Spain, and I cannot become accustomed to the flavors."

Mariya busied herself dishing their bowls and fetching cups of water. When she finally sat, she noticed he waited with his hands in his lap. At least some men came with manners.

He took a bite of his *zsemle* roll and closed his eyes in obvious pleasure. "This takes me back to the homeland," he said. "Mama used to make them every Sunday."

She bit her lip, savoring the compliment, then cleared her throat. He deserved one too. "Alexsander, thank you for what you've done this week. The wood, the water, the fish, the garlic, even the roof. It's far too much."

His clean-shaven cheeks colored. He must have made time to shave after work today. "I like to keep busy. Otherwise, I miss home so far away." He dipped his roll in the tomato broth but didn't take a bite. "I think you and I both have difficulty finding our place here. What do you miss most from the homeland?"

Mariya blinked at the flood of words from this quiet man. None of the other men had asked her opinion. She laid down her spoon. "I…I miss my mama most. She and Papa passed from fever last year, so there is no one to return to. I have only her wedding quilt and her—" She stopped, her eyes raising to the mantel. Her vision blurred.

A gentle hand covered hers on the table. "The spoon. It is broken?"

"Yes." She swallowed, trying to master her emotions. Sharp pain in her heart, along with shame at Yakiv's scene last night. "Papa carved it with *malva* flowers when they married."

"A special gift," he acknowledged.

The rest of the meal passed peacefully as they took turns naming their favorite dishes from home. When Mariya collected the bowls, Alexsander insisted on helping to wash the pot while she wiped the bowls and spoons.

She walked him to the door, clenching her hands behind her back, as she couldn't remember what to do with them. She caught her breath. With everything he had done for her, why couldn't she offer to stitch his button? But when she looked at his shirt, the button was gone. A lonely thread hung to mark where it had been. She tamped down an unexpected flash of disappointment.

"Thank you, Mariya, for a wonderful meal. But even more, for helping me remember home."

She smiled. "I enjoyed our visit, Alexsander." And that was all.

After the door closed, Mariya walked to the mantel and fingered the broken spoon. A strange hollow had opened in her chest. She pictured Alexsander's kind eyes, full of something unnamed and sweet. But her heart asked the question: Was it enough?

The final gathering of the women came the next morning—a sunny day, finally, with Mariya still wiping her breakfast dishes when the troop burst in. It was Sunday, and there was no time to meet between services and midday dinner. Then, this afternoon, the four bachelors would bring small gifts to Mariya to sway her decision.

She would decide tonight and become a bride again tomorrow. Prickles of unease gathered at her hairline.

"What did you think of Alexsander?" Lilya asked before even removing her shawl.

"I imagine he didn't speak a word," said Iryna.

Lesya giggled. "Perhaps it was his first time alone with a woman."

"Hush!" Mariya felt uncharacteristically annoyed. She was glad she hadn't started a pot of *smitten,* for she intended this visit to be brief. "Alexsander came, he ate, he was polite, and we talked of the homeland. Then he left. That is all."

Someone snorted. Iryna. "You see what we said is true. Politeness and talk won't warm your bed or bring babies. Who have you chosen?" She tapped her foot, her great belly jiggling.

Mariya raised her chin. "I will decide after the gifts today. You will have to wait until morning for my answer."

The women grumbled as they hurried their children out, likely feeling denied the chance to gossip about her choice for the rest of the day. They would gossip anyway, Mariya knew. At least the visit was blessedly short. Now to clean the shack and await her visits.

And then decide.

That afternoon, the men were to come in the same order they had for the dinners. Mariya found herself unable to take more than a cup of weak tea, her belly was so unsettled. She waited on the weathered bench outside the shack, shifting uncomfortably at the thought of eyes peering through curtains as she received her potential bridegrooms. But after Vashyl's raised hand and Yakiv's uninvited attentions, the bench's exposure felt reassuring. She tightened the wool shawl around her shoulders.

Vashyl came first. She invited him to sit, and he glanced at the door of the shack as if confused.

"The sun is trying to break through the clouds," she said. "Such a shame to waste the warmth."

He lowered his frame to the bench, which groaned at his weight. "So," he began straightaway. "You have made your choice?"

Mariya fought the impulse to bite her lip. "I will make my decision after the visits this afternoon."

Vashyl's chin jutted stubbornly, and Mariya wished the bench longer to keep her distance. He blinked, then rummaged in his coat pocket, producing something wrapped in a worn rag.

She took the offering and unwrapped—a bar of lye soap. Lifting her eyes to his, she murmured, "What a useful gift."

He gave a short nod. "It will not be long before you will need another. The linens and clothes seem to multiply."

Mariya tried to smile at the thought of the work he expected of her with the caustic soap.

"I know Gleb will not have you. And you are too sensitive for Yakiv, who will have everyone. And Alexsander, who has had no one. You will see I am the only choice."

Vashyl lifted his chin with assurance, and Mariya could find no words to say. She spotted Gleb rounding the nearest shack and almost sighed with relief as she stood. "I thank you. And now I must greet Gleb."

The chin jutted again, but Vashyl took his leave.

Gleb arrived with a strained smile. What would he bring as a gift, since he did not wish to be chosen?

"Hello, Mariya," he said, his normal exuberance muted.

"Please, sit," she replied.

Gleb did not speak, and the awkward moment stretched like a rope of dough. Mariya wanted to excuse him, but the women peeking between their curtains would believe she hadn't given him a chance. So she waited, fingers twitching, wishing she had brought her darning outside.

Finally, he whispered, "I have already spoken of what I want, and will not repeat my words. A gift might give you false hope, but perhaps you will be content with this." He handed her a scrap of twisted paper.

She opened the brown paper and found four seeds. Mariya looked up.

"My Olga brought *malva* seeds from the homeland. I couldn't give up all she had, but perhaps she wouldn't mind if I shared a few. The rest I will save for—excuse me."

She stared at the offering as his words cut off like a sudden rockfall. He meant his next wife—one who was not barren. When she looked up, he was gone.

She had hoped he might change his mind, give her a chance, but that hope was gone. She tucked the seeds in her pocket.

A shadow fell over her, taking the warmth of the sun with it. Yakiv. He towered over her, hands on his hips, his tilted smile stretching as his eyes roamed her face, and more.

"Please sit, Yakiv. The sun is welcome after days of rain."

The smile faded a bit, and he did not sit. "I brought a gift." He slid a paper packet of needles from his breast pocket, opening the tiny envelope to let the silver surfaces catch the sun.

"I thank you, Yakiv. A thoughtful gift." She stopped herself from reaching for them.

Yakiv held his wrist in front of her, revealing what looked to be a newly-torn cuff. An accident—or on purpose? "I would be grateful if you could mend it for me."

Mariya's mind raced to understand what he meant. Her thread lay inside the shack, and of course, it wouldn't be proper for him to remove his shirt while she mended it. They would be alone inside, while she stitched the tear. Standing close together. Too close. Too alone. Something uneasy crawled in her belly.

She kept her eyes on the tattered edge, remaining seated. "I'm afraid I don't have the right color for you. Perhaps when I purchase more thread, I will fix it."

She watched him from the corner of her eye. He stared at her, still looming over her, and she glimpsed a series of emotions passing over his face: disappointment, annoyance, anger. She kept her tongue trapped between her teeth, working to steady her breathing.

At last, Yakiv straightened, taking control of his expression. His coal-stained fingers closed around the packet, and he returned it to his pocket. "Good afternoon, Mariya," he ground out, as if his mouth were full of rocks.

Mariya let out her breath, feeling the tension in her neck. She leaned back on the bench, eyes closed in the sunshine as she waited for Alexsander. At least she wouldn't dread his arrival.

But the sun moved across the sky, and long shadows slid over her, and still he did not come. Perhaps all her needs had overwhelmed him this last week, and he'd grown tired of responsibility. Remaining single might hold more allure.

And perhaps it was for the best. Alexsander was decent, not hard. Sweet. With all the uncertainties of life, a woman needed something to look forward to—passion, and a child, perhaps.

At long last, Mariya stood in the growing dusk and entered the shack, her back straight. She could almost feel the eyes of the other women through her shawl, and her face burned with shame that they witnessed her humiliation as she retreated inside.

She picked up the broken spoon from the mantel and sat near the cold hearth, the shattered edges of the wood digging into her palm. Her life was not so different—broken pieces that could not be restored.

She inhaled deeply; the decision must be made. Gleb was unwilling. Vashyl was controlling. That left Yakiv. He seemed ruled by passion, but Vashyl's words gave her pause. With his wandering eyes, would he remain faithful? Alexsander had seemed promising, but he had not come. The depth of her disappointment surprised her, as his inexperience had kept him at the bottom of her list. She was left with the choice to surrender to Vashyl. How her heart despaired at the thought of his self-satisfied smile.

As night descended, she decided to warm two of the cabbage rolls she had made for Alexsander last night. However, the wood box was empty. A pang of regret pained her heart. How quickly she had become accustomed to Alexsander's many kindnesses.

She stepped out into a chilly wind and walked around to the lean-to Ivan had built to keep the wood dry. She shivered and wished she had taken her shawl. The shelter was dark inside, and she felt for the woodpile.

She heard a creak, and she stiffened, heart pounding. She was not alone. Someone blocked the cold breeze. She couldn't leave without brushing past whoever was here.

Was it Yakiv, ready to try again? Anger ground in her belly as Mariya spun, fists raised. She couldn't make out the face in the dark, but it was a man, his bulky shape outlined by scant moonlight. Her heart sped faster.

"Shhh. I am sorry to arrive late," a voice rumbled softly.

Large hands rested on her shoulders. They didn't grip. They were gentle, the way she would hold a porcelain cup. But that could always change, couldn't it?

She lifted her hands to his chest, ready to push him away and give herself a chance of escape. But something tickled her finger, and she realized what it was. A long thread. She followed the thread to the buttonhole it sprouted from. And she remembered.

On the day of Vashyl's visit, Alexsander's button had been a little loose. Before Gleb's visit, it had been looser. Prior to Yakiv's visit, it had been hanging by a thread. And last night? It was gone. But that meant he was here. Alexsander had not abandoned her. But where had he been?

The relief she felt at his presence weakened her legs, and she bowed her head, leaning against his chest. His arms gathered around her back, pulling her to himself. This was something she'd always longed for with Ivan. A safe resting place. A shared peace. Perhaps she could be content without passion, if there was softness and companionship instead.

After a long moment, she lifted her chin, although she couldn't make out his features. His hands released her, and then a gentle finger drew over her lower lip. Was he asking permission? Did men do such things? Now his thumbs traced her cheeks. Her lips parted of their own accord, and he leaned in.

He kissed her reverently, tenderly, and soon—hungrily. Mariya fell under his spell, weaving her arms around his neck and losing herself in feelings she had only dreamed of.

The kiss ended suddenly when he stepped back, but she heard his rapid breathing. Knew what it meant.

"Please forgive my tardiness, Mariya. You deserved a good gift. And now I must leave for the night shift." In a moment, he was gone, but he had left something in her grip.

Mariya hurried into the dark shack and lit the lamp with shaking fingers. In her hand lay a wooden spoon, beautifully carved with *malva* flowers—just like Mama's.

A fluttery feeling bloomed in her chest. Similar to Mama, Alexsander saw beauty in the small things. There was hope in that.

And Mariya took her bowl and new spoon and began mixing a batch of *zsemle* rolls for her groom. She smiled, anticipating her wedding tomorrow—and the reactions of the women who didn't know what she did.

Life would never be the same.

About the Author

Debbie Maxwell Allen was born and raised in Brooklyn but now writes historical fiction in the Rockies. She teaches workshops on writing craft, productivity, and Scrivener and Vellum software. When not writing, she keeps tabs on her husband, four children, two cats—and three grandchildren. She loves to travel—preferably by train, and always with a cup of tea in hand.

https://debbiemaxwellallenbooks.com/blog/

HELLO LIFE!

by Lissa Woodbury Jensen

MY HEART IS RACING as the music from *Hello Dolly* nears its final crescendo. I can barely swallow, and my breath's staccato rhythm matches the pace of my furiously beating heart. I stand alone in the dark, behind the curtain on the audience's left. How did I get here? *Why am I so scared?*

Kim R. Burningham had done this, the old coot. His coaching excellence in high school speech and drama was renowned throughout the state. Educators and community members fondly referred to him as Utah's Forensics Wizard. Year after year, his students won numerous tournaments and championship trophies. His wealth of knowledge and inspirational "magic" was respected and feared. This so-called wizard believed in me, and I couldn't understand why. I was a drug addict, thief, troublemaker, and notorious delinquent. I had been to the State Juvie, State Mental Hospital, and on probation for several years. No teacher wanted me in their class; my own mother didn't want me back in the home. When not incarcerated, my tattooed self was in court-assigned foster care.

I thought back to my first year in "Mr. B's" speech and drama class. I sat there as a lowly sophomore, fresh out of my latest detention gig. Mr. B knew my parents from church. He had known me as a young girl with a lot of energy and no place to put it. He, like everyone else, had watched me channel that energy into delinquency, drugs, and rebellion. Unlike everyone else, however, he had also noticed a spark in my eyes when it came to anything theatrical or performance oriented.

I liked to get attention.

He assigned our class to write orations, which is a persuasive argument in speech form. *Yeah, right. I guess I could do a speech on how awesome weed is.* With my head bent, I picked at my fingernails while mentally spacing out for most of the class period. Two shiny black loafers appeared in my peripheral vision, interrupting my nail perusal. I looked up as Mr. B bent over, placed a hand on either side of my desk, and captured my gaze.

"This is an opportunity for you."

"What?"

"Are you brave enough to be honest?"

"I don't know what you mean. What are you talking about?"

"Lissa, you have the chance here to set people straight. It's your turn to speak your mind with no interruptions or censure."

"Uh... I don't understand."

The bell rang and everyone started gathering their things to leave, but Mr. B's penetrating gaze held me captive.

"No one, to my knowledge, has ever done an oration about experiencing drugs and alcohol. I have never heard about these things and the happiness or unhappiness they might cause from an authentic, personal point of view. It is important, Lissa, that we hear about it from a different perspective… Yours."

Yeah, right, like anyone would listen to what I have to say. All anyone does is tell me how bad I am. No one ever asks what I think or even what I want.

I had carefully crafted my reputation, but nobody knew the whys and wherefores.

I wanted to get out of there, so I said I would accept his challenge. I then proceeded to do something surprising, even to myself: I embraced the assignment. It was too hard to defy Mr. B. I began to write and held nothing back. I talked about what drugs felt like and the excitement of being "noticed," but for all the wrong reasons. I wrote about Valerie, a twelve-year-old girl I had met in the State Industrial School who was there for prostitution. That's right—prostitution. Using a simple metaphor, I described her being as tough as a walnut, the exterior shell impossible to crack. One only had to crack that shell to find a tender nougat on the inside. I likened her to myself. I talked about the thrill I got when people considered me "tough" and how it gave me a powerful identity. I described institutional life and what happens during a lock-down. I explained why I wanted to feel "high." I wrote about ugly things that some students didn't even know existed.

When completed, it was twenty minutes long! *Ugh.* I had to get it down to ten minutes. I doubled down, shortening it until Mr. B finally said the speech was "pretty good," but it needed something else: Me. That's how I suddenly found myself entered into the school speech contest by Mr. B. Had this been his plan, all along?

It happened on a Friday during sixth period. We did it in the school's Little Theatre, which smelled like old erasers and had rows of chairs stretched back to the far wall. English students and a few adults were there. When my turn came, I started hesitantly.

"Um, my speech today is, uh, about my life and, um, some things I have gone through…" The students started shifting uncomfortably in their seats, disinterested. Some girl on the third row rolled her eyes. That made me mad! I started over, planted my feet into a wider stance and looked straight into those rolling eyes.

"Today I will share some unusual experiences with you, and I want you to listen," I commanded them with all the energy and force of what I had to say, which got their attention.

They listened. They considered. They clapped. I won the school contest and received all sorts of attention in a heretofore unknown way. I liked it…and didn't resist when Mr. B stopped me in the hallway outside his class the following Monday.

"You've qualified for the Golden Spike Speech Contest, and you have to go! You will represent Bountiful High."

Wait… What?

"I can't go. I am on probation with the school."

"Yes, I know, but I have already cleared it with the principal. It is this Saturday; you need to dress nicely and be in the parking lot by seven a.m."

It didn't happen often, but I was speechless. Mr. B left me standing there, flummoxed and disoriented.

On Saturday, my alarm rang early. *Ugh. Why am I doing this? Why do Mr. B and the principal even care, anyway?* I dragged myself out of bed and stumbled to the closet. *Guess I should have thought about this last night. What am I going to wear?*

"Damn, they let me get away with my jeans for the first meet." I rooted through things, looking for something that was big enough. Tears threatened; I was a big girl and there wasn't much I could fit into anymore.

"There's my jacket from choir. The long sleeves will hide my tattoos." *No dresses, only one giant maxi skirt.* As I pulled it out, a scarf fell to the floor. *Oh good, that will work too.*

I started having second thoughts and snapped at my mother when I got into the car. "I look stupid!"

We arrived at the school parking lot where a bus awaited. All the speech and drama kids were there. I stood off to the side. I often liked being separate. I wanted people to be intimidated by me, but this time I just felt awkward. I sat by myself on the bus.

There were three preliminary rounds in the morning. I did them all. After lunch, the semi-finalists were posted, and I was on the list. Several students surrounded me and clapped me on the back. A few of them came to the special round to cheer me on. An hour later, the list for finalists was released and, again, I was on it! I couldn't believe it. All the Bountiful students came to that round. It was a new and unfamiliar feeling for me to have such support.

We sat together in the auditorium at the end of the day. I was surrounded and included. I felt like I had a good day. Everyone in the final round was fantastic, and I was surprised I had even gone that far in the competition. Most everyone was better than me. The best I could hope for was third place.

The time came to announce the Oratory Awards. Third place was announced, but I didn't get it. I hung my head. *Oh well, it's not like you've ever done this before.* Second place was given to another school. The person announcing the awards paused.

"It isn't often this happens, but the first place oration was picked unanimously by all of the judges. And that award goes to Bountiful High School." She called my name. I was stunned. I couldn't believe it. Someone pulled me to my feet. It was a long walk to the stage where I received the first trophy I had ever been given. My schoolmates were cheering, and this time I did not sit alone on the bus ride home. I clutched my prize on my lap and kept staring at the gleaming award.

It was a promising beginning, but I created a dual personality. I would always go to speech and drama, but skipped most other classes. I would join in on many speech tournaments, but still chose to go to the back parking lot for a smoke or drugs. Mr. B never let up. He was always supportive, demanding, and seemingly present at every turn in my life.

A significant turning point came at a western regional championship held in Arizona, which I competed in and won first place. I had a blast hanging out with all the cool speech and drama kids (even though they were "straight"). For the first time, I felt like I actually belonged. The night after we returned to Utah, I ended up at a party with my old crowd. Only this time I sat in the corner, watching. I compared the empty smiles and hollow laughter of my "friends" with the unrestrained exuberance I had embraced from my fellow BHS competitors while we were in Arizona.

I knew I didn't want to be a dual personality anymore. But how could I fix it? I didn't know how. I felt stuck. For days I would go home and sob into my pillow for hours, trying to figure out who I was.

"Hey Lissa, did you see the announcement?" Heidi, a popular girl from Speech Club, stopped me in the hallway. "We're going to do the musical, *Hello Dolly!* I'm so excited. Hey, you should try out for Dolly!"

"But I'm not that good a singer." *Besides, Golden Throat will get it. She always gets the leads. She just played Maria in The Sound of Music.*

"Well, you should still try."

"Maybe I will."

And I did. Auditions took forever, and I had a hard time keeping on pitch unless the pianist played the exact melody. I took it down an octave because I couldn't hit the high notes. My acting was decent, but then Golden Throat auditioned. *Sheesh. Well, that's that.*

The cast list was supposed to go up on Mr. B's door by one o'clock. It didn't. We all kept looking, but no luck. An hour went by, then two, then three. This was highly unusual. The list finally went up at four o'clock. There were squeals and shouts while I muscled my way through the crowd to see the list. I looked and felt my heart plummet as I saw Golden Throat's name next to "Dolly Levi." I turned to leave, but something caught my eye.

Wait a minute! I don't understand. My name is listed underneath Golden Throat's name. That doesn't make any sense. Oh no—am I her understudy?

"Don't you get it?" Heidi was shouting in my ear. "You guys are double-cast!"

"No way! How can that be? She is petite and sings like Julie Andrews. I am bigger than most boys and sing like a frog."

"I don't know, but you are going to be a Dolly," she squealed in a sing-song voice.

And so began the constant comparisons to Golden Throat. The cast did it. The orchestra did it. Even the parents had their opinions. The worst offender was the wizard himself, Mr. Burningham. He was always kind and approving of everything Golden Throat did, but he was cold and unyielding towards me; never satisfied.

The week before opening night, Golden Throat got her costume together but was missing a scarf. I waited for Mr. Burningham to explode. He didn't.

"That's fine," he said. "You are doing well."

Then it was my turn. I didn't have the right shoes. He literally sneered at me.

"You need to get it together. I thought you wanted this part? Your attitude is mediocre. Go home."

I barely made it out the door before bursting into tears. *Why is he being so mean to me? I hate him!* By this time, I was living back at home. I raced up the stairs to my bedroom and slammed the door. Thoughts raced through my brain on what I could swallow or inhale that would kill the pain.

"Hello? Are you alright?" My mom spoke through the door.

"No! I'm quitting. Mr. B is a total jerk. He basically kicked me out of rehearsal for no shoes. He knows my feet are size twelve and they are hard to fit. But he doesn't even care.

Why did he even give me the part," I wailed. "All anyone cares about is Golden Throat. No one wants to come the night I play Dolly."

"Did anyone actually say that to you?"

"No, but I know it's true. I'm not stupid."

"I see. So you're just going to give up?"

"I know that's what he wants."

"Are you sure? Don't give him the satisfaction. I don't care one whit about Mr. Burningham, but I do care about you. This is the hardest you have ever worked on anything, and you can bet that Dad and I only want to be there the night YOU are Dolly!"

I didn't answer.

A few moments later, a familiar melody from the movie *Jonathan Livingston Seagull* wafted up the stairs and into my room. Neil Diamond's haunting soundtrack about a struggling, lowly seagull who doesn't think he measures up was a favorite of mine. The bird feels insignificant and lonely. Jonathan wishes to be a phoenix instead of a seagull. He perseveres, stumbles, learns life lessons, and eventually rises into the stratosphere as he commits to being his best self: a noble and resilient creature of God. The lyrics seared themselves into my brain: poetic alliteration about listening to the music of the soul and letting the heart "dance," no matter the rhythm or unusual beat.

The next afternoon I used my anger to work even harder. *I'll show him!* I didn't talk much out of rehearsal but would go home and listen to the soaring soundtrack day after day.

And I got better.

Opening night finally arrived. After listening to my seagull music for the umpteenth time, my mother drove me to the school. A strange calm had come over me. I sat in front of the makeup mirror while a young student worked her magic on my face.

"Okay, you're done!"

I looked in the mirror and frowned. *Man, did she mess up my eyebrows. Oh well, no time to fix them.* I rose with caution because I was wearing a long dress, petticoats, and an enormous bustle. The cacophony of cast voices getting ready slid over me and danced in tandem with the butterflies in my stomach.

"Lissa!" I would know that voice anywhere. Mr. B was standing by the door and gestured for me to follow him. He took me backstage and down a deserted hallway. He made sure we were alone before giving me his sole attention.

"Lissa, I know you think I've been hard on you."

I glared at him.

"Have you ever wondered why it took so long for me to put up the cast list?" He paused. "No one wanted you as Dolly. Not only because you can barely sing," he chuckled, "but because they didn't trust you. The assistant principal was certain you would be expelled, leaving us in the lurch. The English teacher was adamant that you are a bad influence and would set a poor example to the other students. And the rest agreed that you didn't deserve it. You weren't worthy. Why would we reward you after years of poor behavior? It was the entire committee against me. Everyone else wanted to cast Golden Throat with her superior voice and strong popularity."

Why is he telling me this now? My shoulders drooped. Mr. B wrapped an arm around me and pulled me in for a hug.

"Lissa, I stood my ground for over three hours. They finally realized I wouldn't budge. No director meant no show. The principal proposed a compromise. He told me to go ahead and cast you as Dolly, but he also bid me to cast Golden Throat, as well. The role would be double cast and leave us secure, if and when you might have a relapse. That is why I have been so hard on you. My neck is on the line. Everyone was paying attention and those days when you weren't prepared or late with your costume or behind on schoolwork, I caught the flak. You are a challenge and, to be honest, there were times when even I wondered if I had made a mistake."

I tried to speak, but no sound came out. My tongue was sandpaper.

"Now, I am not telling you this to make you feel bad, but to help you understand why I have been so unbending and strict with you. I had to. I wasn't going to say anything about it to you, but yesterday's dress rehearsal was brilliant. You nailed it and I felt vindicated. You proved yourself. Your vocals are still a bit weak, but your personality more than makes up for it. Lissa, you are fantastic as Dolly. I am so proud of you."

He walked away and I stood there in a daze.

As the orchestra played through the overture, I shivered with excitement. Mr. B had given me his blessing and there was no stopping me now.

"Places!"

My heart leapt out of my chest. I felt hot and dizzy. *This is really happening!* The lights dimmed, everything went dark, and the curtain rose. Energy blasted through me as I stepped out from the crowd and became someone else. I was no longer the tattooed, hardened juvenile delinquent. I was no longer the societal menace that no one wanted to acknowledge. I was a beautiful, curvaceous woman with a smile a mile wide. I loved everyone and they loved me. I was Dolly Levi, a manipulating matchmaker on the lookout for a husband of her own. I led the chorus down the "street" as I sang "Put on Your Sunday Clothes."

We soared through the number and the next one and in no time at all, it was my turn to strut down the elaborate staircase, wearing a glorious red gown and singing the title song. I was delirious with joy. *No other high could ever come close to this,* I thought as I descended towards the handsome group of waiters.

We danced, we laughed, and I attained performance heights I had not thought possible. I sang "Before the Parade" with all the energy I could glean from my soul. It didn't matter that I sang an octave lower. The crowd ate it up.

In no time at all, it was over. I wasn't Dolly anymore…just me. I took my place for the curtain call, as planned.

The song swelled and musical crescendo reached its apex. My heart still raced and my breathing hadn't slowed, but I gulped and pushed the slight curtain aside. I stepped through the opening. *I can't feel my feet!* I looked down to make sure they were still on the floor. *Why am I sweating so much!* I sucked in all the air I could and strutted out while pushing open my white umbrella. *How did I get here? Why am I so scared?*

I rounded the corner adjacent to the orchestra pit. Karen, at the piano, grinned up at me while banging out the melody notes for all she was worth to keep me in tune. Cocooned in a spotlight, I ascended the stairs to the ramp. There was a huge movement in the audience that scared me, so I looked out and saw that, as one, the entire audience had jumped to their feet in a standing ovation. There were many faces I recognized. Front and center were my mom and dad; him holding the camera while tears streaked down my mother's face.

I looked to the right and saw the juvenile court judge. He knew me well, but instead of me wilting underneath his penetrating gaze as he pronounced sentence, I burst with elation at his triumphant smile and clapping hands raised high in the air. A couple of rows behind him sat several shiny badges whose owners' faces were frozen in disbelief. Cops whom I had gotten to know throughout the years had come to witness the impossible. I moved to the center of the ramp in time with the music. My probation officer yelled from the left.

"Bravo!"

The principal and vice principal stood in the back of the theatre, approval written all over their faces.

Time stood still.

I had an epiphany. *They're not just applauding my performance and creativity; they are applauding ME and my JOURNEY. They are clapping for my personal success: MY victory. I'm going to be okay. I'm going to make it!* Fat tears skated down my face as I stood frozen in the spotlight. Looking over my shoulder, I was stunned to see the entire cast had stopped their choreography and stood, applauding along with the orchestra. Mr. B was just offstage, grinning while nodding his head in triumph. My brazen coach saluted me as I turned back to the audience.

This is what I was born to do. And I will. I'm going to make it! I laughed out loud as I took bow after bow. I loved all the attention, but this time it was for the right reasons. Hello, Dolly indeed! The curtain descended and I was mobbed.

"I didn't know what a fine actress you were!"

"You sure do shine onstage!"

"Your comic timing was impeccable. You are so funny!"

I looked up and caught a wink from my mother. I blew her a kiss. Yes, Mr. B had obviously had an endgame. It worked. I was no longer afraid and my future looked bright. Like Jonathan Livingston Seagull, I was beginning to understand my true destiny. That night, I passed through an elusive aperture and would never look back.

Hello Dolly? Hello, Life!

(This is a true story and happened exactly as written. Lissa went on to graduate high school and attend university on a theatre scholarship. She has soared as an actor, director and choreographer for over fifty years, both onstage and in film.)

About the Author

Lissa is an artistic creature who has spent the majority of her life immersed in creative pursuits. She has taught and performed professionally in musical theatre, acting technique, dance, choreography, film and playwriting. She also likes to dabble in writing speculative fiction during her spare time. She has written and published several dramatic plays.

ABOUT THE EDITORS

From an early age, Leslie Bridgwater has enjoyed reading, and she continues to have a love for the language, for a good story, and for interesting information. So, it's no wonder that a little editing spark ignited when she was asked "Would you take a look at this?" Since that time, in addition to expanding her knowledge by reading books and taking classes, she has learned from other editors, done work for several publishers, and provided feedback and edits to authors on projects from short stories to novels. She loves the work, the continual learning, and the collaboration with authors and publishers. You can contact her at editingbylrb@gmail.com

As well as having worked for at least three publishing companies, Sam Knight started his own publishing company, Knight Writing Press, which published the book you are now holding. He has edited numerous short stories, novels, and anthologies, and is the author of six children's books, five short story collections, four novels, and over 80 stories, including three co-authored with Kevin J. Anderson. Though he has written in many cool worlds, such as Planet of the Apes, Wayward Pines, and Jeff Sturgeon's Last Cities of Earth, among his family, Sam will probably always be known for *Chunky Monkey Pupu*.

Once upon a time, Sam was known to quote books the way some people quote movies, but now he claims having a family has made him forgetful—as a survival adaptation. He can be found at SamKnight.com and contacted at sam@samknight.com.

Additional Copyright Information

"Imaginary Friend" ©2025 Sara Itka

"The Wizard and the Dinosaur-Riding Pirate" ©2017 Sam Knight. Originally published by WolfSinger Publications

"The Reluctant Superhero" ©2025 Leigh Saunders

"Seeking a Familiar Witch" ©2025 Jena Rey

"Bloodlines" ©2025 Melissa Rolli

"Pomp & Circumstance" ©2025 Jessica Ritenour

"Whispering Heights" ©2025 Ligia de Wit

"Four Tires and a Knife" ©2025 Tiffany Brazell

"The Girl and the Stone" ©2021 Morgan J. Muir

"The Ice Wall" ©2025 Jentina Grey

"Rise Like the Sun" ©2025 Darren Lipman

"Blurring Lines" ©2025 Jason P. Crawford

"Rain" ©2025 Lehua Parker. LLC

"Not Exactly Babysitter Material" ©2025 Kevin A Davis

"Milo Piper's Breakout Single that Ended the Rat War" ©2024 David Hankins. Originally published by Hemelein Publications

"Cupid's Match" ©2025 Rosa Meronek

"Mountains Crumble" ©2025 CL Fors

"How to Grow a Legacy" ©2025 Jayrod P. Garrett

"Today We Escape" ©2025 Martin L. Shoemaker

"One Man's Trash" ©2017 Laura Beard Hayden

"Must Love Cats" ©2025 Barry Nove

"The Legend of Long-Bow and Short-Staff" ©2017 Brenda Carr. Originally published in *Tavern Tales* by WMG Publishing

"Remembering Ricky" ©2025 Donald Evans

"Breathing Life into the Stars" ©2025 Jenny Perry Carr

"Resilience" ©2025 Allan W. Mason

"The Broken Blade" ©2011 Carol Hightshoe. Originally published in *Tales of the Talisman*

"Weekly Date" ©2025 Purple Scarf LLC

"Migration" ©2021 Andrew Dibble. Originally published in *What Remains: An Inked in Gray Anthology*

"Needs Must" ©2025 L.A. Selby

"The Matchmaker" ©2025 Jeffrey E Whitney

"Humanity's Matriarch" ©2025 Janessa Keeling

"Where We Will All Go" ©2020 C.H. Hung. Originally published in *X Marks the Spot: An Anthology of Treasure and Theft*, edited by Lisa Mangum, published by WordFire Press

"Beauty in the Small Things" ©2025 Debbie Maxwell Allen

"Hello Life!" ©2025 Lissa Woodbury Jensen

www.ingramcontent.com/pod-product-compliance
Lightning Source LLC
Chambersburg PA
CBHW021950010726
47494CB00003B/667

* 9 7 8 1 6 2 8 6 9 0 7 6 7 *